Benetan opened the door dow, pulled the curtains back,
force it open. Daylight and fre

And from behind the doc
years from him and propelled his memory back into child
hood, said, "Benet."

Benetan swore an oath never used in the castle, and spun
round.

He'd changed. Gods, how he'd *changed!* But there could
be no doubts. The awkward, rangy frame was just the same,
albeit gaunter; the mouth still had that familiar lopsided quirk
which made him look as though he were laughing and disapproving at the same time. And the hair, red as a sunset, instantly recognizable—

Benetan said, "*Kaldar Alvaray!*"

Kaldar was sweating despite the room's chill. He threw a
rapid glance over his shoulder, then pushed the door shut.
"You remember me?" His voice was tense, clipped. "I'm flattered, Benet. I'd have thought that after all this time you might
have forgotten!"

Benetan stood helpless in the middle of the room, stunned
beyond the ability to say anything. Kaldar, here, in the magi's
stronghold? This was *insanity*. He was dreaming. He *must* be.

Benetan had heard Kaldar's name bandied in the castle several years ago, when he'd caused a brief but intense furor at
the castle. It was widely known—or rather, widely *believed*—
that Kaldar had died three years ago, when a creature of
Chaos, conjured by the magi he'd defied, had separated his
soul from his body before consigning both to oblivion.

As though reading Benetan's churning thoughts, Kaldar
flashed a searing and humorless grin. "Surprised, old friend?
You shouldn't be. Your masters failed to eradicate me. They
may not know the truth or they may not want to broadcast it to
likes of you, I don't know which. But they failed. I'm no
ghost. I'm alive."

STAR
ASCENDANT

LOUISE
COOPER

A TOM DOHERTY ASSOCIATES BOOK
NEW YORK

TOR®

This is a work of fiction. All the characters and events portrayed in this book are either products of the author's imagination or are used fictitiously.

STAR ASCENDANT

Copyright © 1995 by Louise Cooper

Cover art by Gary Ruddell

A Tor Book
Published by Tom Doherty Associates, Inc.
175 Fifth Avenue
New York, NY 10010

Tor Books on the World Wide Web:
http://www.tor.com

Tor® is a registered trademark of Tom Doherty Associates, Inc.

ISBN: 0-812-55175-3
Library of Congress Card Catalog Number 95-30302

First edition: October 1995
First mass market edition: October 1996

Printed in the United States of America

0 9 8 7 6 5 4 3 2 1

This trilogy is warmly and appreciatively dedicated to June Hall, who, with her guidance, insight, and acumen, showed a directionless ditherer that she should stick to her guns . . . and by so doing brought Tarod and Yandros unequivocally back to life!

Star Peninsula

Uncharted

Northern Mountains

Tamure Bay

Forest

Western Sound

Forest

Forest

Plains
(Arabe

Forest

Prospect
Estuary

Sea

Kennet
Head

Whiteshoals Sound

Forest

Key

Desert
Roads
Rivers
Plains
Forests
Mountains

Summer Isle Straits

Summer
Isle

Bay of Illusions

WHITE ISLE

JMitchell 1985

STAR
ASCENDANT

PROLOGUE

In a dimension far beyond our Earth — though not beyond our imagination — there is a world of mortal men and women whose history is one of turmoil. In this world with its crimson sun and two moons, the forces of manifest duality, which we might call the forces of Nature, are in eternal conflict. Those twin, mutually dependent yet inimical and ever-warring powers take the names of Order and Chaos. And over the centuries their battle for supremacy has made this mortal world into an arena in which the gods themselves are the gladiators. Time and again the balance has swung. Time and again it will continue to swing; for the great lords of Order and Chaos are what their essences dictate; no more and no less. And from the strongholds of their separate supernatural realms, they vie constantly for control of the hearts and souls of humankind.

In the era chronicled in this story, the powers of Chaos hold sway. The ancient enemy, Order, is nothing more than a shadowy ghost consigned to the corridors of mythology; and Chaos's seven great lords, under the aegis of the mercurial Yandros, have for centuries been worshiped as the only true gods. Yandros's rule is a far cry from that which would be imposed by his counterpart of Order, Aeoris. For Chaos's watchword — or so its lords claim — is freedom. True Chaos acknowledges no fetters; true Chaos predicts and assumes nothing. Humankind may find salvation or damnation as it pleases, and it amuses the gods to watch their human followers make what sense they can of their existence and solve life's conundrums — or not — as they are able.

But where humanity enters the equation, a new catalyst comes into play. The purity of the gods' natures is tempered by factors beyond the control of either force. There is a maxim that power corrupts, and absolute power corrupts absolutely. This, as many mortals in the world of this tale have learned, is an enduring truth. And when Yandros gave free rein to the highly powerful sorcerers, known as magi, who form the ruling caste in this world, he also gave free rein to that capacity for corruption which is, perhaps, unique to the human race.

The magi rule in the name of Chaos. They speak with the gods; they command the powers of the gods' own realm. And from the stronghold of their black, sorcerously created castle on the bleak northern promontory known as the Star Peninsula, they reign with an authority that has never been seriously challenged.

For all their powers, however, the magi are still human. And the society over which they preside owes far more to human needs and desires than it does to those of their Chaotic masters. Their word is law; law must be upheld. So from the rarefied heights of the magi's rulership there descends a hierarchy of souls who, each in turn, serve their greater masters, and rule those below them with either the compassion or the ferocity that their natures — or merely their whims — dictate. And if the peace cannot be kept by force, there is always another weapon to fall back on: that of superstition and fear. For every man, woman, and child knows that the powers of Chaos are very real. And obedience to even the cruelest overlord is a less dire prospect than that of suffering retribution at the hands of a demon.

Life for the ordinary people of this world is not gentle. Yet though they may suffer injustice, tyranny, and hardship under the sway of their mortal lords, still the great majority are loyal to the great powers of Chaos. They fear their gods but they also love them, for catechism and history alike have taught them that Chaos is the only truth and all else is heresy. They know no other way: there is no other way. And, like an uneasy, half-alluring and half-ominous light gleaming on a dark road, there is always the possibility that they might be chosen to serve the gods more directly, within the black walls of the castle itself. For the castle is always in need of new blood. Strong young men to join the feared warrior elite who are said to ride upon demons. Girls, chosen for their beauty or wit, to become concubines and live a life of endless pleasure. Scholars, musicians, artisans, even menial servants. Many are taken through the black gates; the choice is random and there is no leave of appeal. Some go in dread and terror, and find only madness and death. But those who go willingly, and have the courage to withstand what will be demanded of them, can look forward to a life in which their deepest hungers, their wildest dreams, will be fulfilled. The promise of glory, or the peril of damnation — that is the chance, and the challenge, which Chaos offers to every human soul. And for centuries none have thought — or dared — to question the rightness of that way.

But, at long last, cracks are beginning to appear in the walls of certainty that have maintained the status quo for so long. The human factor, and the corrupting influence of power, has seeped like a cancer through every echelon, and the old, ferocious but exalted ideals are crumbling before a more venal philosophy. The aristocratic bloodlines of the castle are growing stale; boredom, fueled by the careless sense of invincibility, has led to decadent indulgence and the pursuit of pleasure as an end in itself. And the web of that influence is spreading to the greater world beyond the castle, where overlords, unchecked by their increasingly capricious and uninterested masters, feel free to seek their own gratification in any way they choose.

And in this climate of increasing negligence, the first seeds of dissent are showing signs of growth. Those who suffer the privations of their overlords' greed are beginning to whisper of another way of living: an old way, excised from the annals of history but still alive — if only just — in folk memory. It may be, they murmur, that Yandros of Chaos hears the prayers and supplications of his worshipers, but he does not choose to answer them. Is this, they ask, the justice in which their catechisms exhort them to trust? Or are Yandros and his brother gods as careless of their subjects' fate as the great sorcerers at the Star Peninsula? Might there not be greater justice, and thus hope of a better life, under the kindlier light of other powers? Other powers: other gods. The whisper is heresy; but it is growing. And once, so legend goes, there *were* other gods in the world. Chaos's most ancient and implacable of enemies, reviled now as demons and banished to the outer dark.

Until and unless a mortal can be found with the power, and the courage, to summon them back . . .

CHAPTER I

Benetan Liss."
    The flat, toneless voice speaking his name penetrated through the layers of a bizarre dream, and he turned in his bed, instinctively pulling the heavy covering up over his ears.

"Benetan. Stir yourself; wake up."

This time it wasn't a whisper but a command, and urgent. The two-mouthed thing that had been crawling across Benetan's dream landscape shivered and faded, and he awoke to blackness broken only by a small, unsteady pinpoint of light. Above the light two eyes gleamed in the darkness; then as his own pupils dilated he made out the indistinct shape behind the eyes; a ghost of a human figure.

"Wh . . ." Benetan swallowed the question unasked as his mind began to function. A hand loomed out of the dark to cup the candle; the flame reflected on thin fingers, then his visitor blew gently on the flame and it burned brighter, illuminating a narrow face etched in black-and-silver shadow.

"Savrinor . . ." The last traces of sleep fell away and Benetan Liss was suddenly wide awake. "What is it? What's the hour?"

"Second moonrise." Savrinor, whose official title was historian but whose functions ranged much further afield, moved toward the window and drew back the curtain. Cold light slanted in, turning the strands of his long, fair hair to gray and sharply defining the hawkish profile with its narrow, handsome nose, and he touched the candle to the small lamp at Benetan's bedside. "You'd better get dressed, my friend. There'll be no more sleep for any of us tonight." His eyes, pale blue and feline, met Benetan's in the gloom that the lamplight and moonlight did little to relieve. "He's dying."

Benetan sat up. "Tonight? How can you be sure?"

Savrinor shrugged, the gesture spare but eloquent. "I have ears, and I use them. There's movement below; the castle's bones are shifting, and there are already rumors of the Chaos Gate being opened from the far side. Something's coming through uninvited, and you know as well as I do that that can only mean one thing."

"An emissary?"

"To take his soul." Savrinor smiled a small, unemotional smile that didn't extend as far as his eyes. "Before dawn, I'd hazard. So you'll please our masters by preempting their order and being ready when they send for you."

Benetan started to say, "If you're right — " then thought better of it. Savrinor was never wrong; on the narrow path he trod between one faction and another, he couldn't afford to be. He swung his legs over the side of the bed and stood up. "I owe you a debt."

"No, no." Savrinor watched with something approaching detached admiration faintly tinged with envy as Benetan reached for his clothes. "I'm still indebted to you for that little dark girl you found for me on your last sortie."

Benetan's head turned sharply, eyes narrowed, looking for sarcasm. "You tired of her in four days."

"Maybe so; but it was a pleasant diversion while it lasted. So this is a favor for a favor, so to speak." The smile again. "To even the slate."

Savrinor maintained a tally of favors granted and favors received and, by his devious and often unfathomable code of ethics, could always be relied on to give or exact payment in kind to a scrupulous degree. Benetan nodded curtly. "Very well. The slate's evened." He began to dress, grimacing with distaste at the clammy touch of his clothing against bare skin. Savrinor continued to watch him, the pale eyes now hooded. As Benetan thrust his feet into his boots, the historian looked at the rumpled but empty bed and said:

"No company tonight?"

A curt shake of the head was his only answer. Benetan didn't care to discuss the intimate details of his personal life, and he certainly didn't want to let Savrinor, of all people, know about the quarrel — only the latest of many — which had provoked Andraia, his lover of two years' duration, to storm out of his room several hours ago. Guessing a fair proportion of what the other man refused to say, Savrinor hid a flicker of amusement, stored the information away in his mind for future reference, and changed the subject.

"Better stint nothing." He gestured toward the ceremonial accoutrements slung carelessly on a chair, which Benetan had apparently been ready to ignore. Benetan stared at him for a moment, then nodded acknowledgment. He clipped the heavy silver flashes with their seven quartz pendants to the shoulders of his tunic, then cinched the tunic with a wide black leather belt on which seven more gems of differing colors glowed like bizarre eyes in the dark. As he secured the complex buckle he caught a momentary glimpse of himself in the looking glass which was one of his few concessions to vanity, and repressed a faintly cynical smile. In the ambience created by gloom and shadows he looked every inch the perfect Chaos rider. Above average height, strong shoulders, lean but well-muscled body, and his face, though still youthful, had just a touch of hardness that lent authority. Even his hair, black as the castle stonework and uncut since the day he came to the castle, seemed to have been deliberately designed to give the right finishing touch. Highly impressive; a figure to strike fear into the minds of lesser mortals. Just as such figures had once struck fear into him. . . .

With a sharp movement born of exasperation and a modicum of sudden discomfort he turned away from the glass to collect the last piece of his apparel, a silver circlet. As he did so, Savrinor said, "Our masters will want an extra tally tonight, I think."

Benetan paused and looked up, but Savrinor's face gave nothing away beyond that small, sly smile, which was beginning to irritate him.

"Extra?" His voice was terse. "Why?"

Savrinor shrugged. "You know who the chosen successor is?"

"No, I don't. I'm not privy to the inner dealings of the magi."

"None of us are. But some of us pick up a snippet here and a snippet there, and when we're alone in our solitary chambers we amuse ourselves by making a pattern of those snippets, and the pattern sometimes forms a picture." The smile became a leer. "Your greatest defect, my dear Benetan, is that you have no curiosity beyond the demands of your duties."

"Twelve years in this place have taught me that it's safer to keep matters that way," Benetan retorted sharply.

"Safer, maybe. But far less interesting." Savrinor picked his way delicately across the cluttered room toward the door as though about to leave, then stopped and looked back. "So: your admirable prudence precludes you from wanting to know the name of the man who will step into the shoes of our First Magus. A pity." He reached for the door latch.

Benetan sighed. Games were a favorite pastime with Savrinor; if one wanted more than the most cursory information, one had to learn to become a player and abide by his rules.

"All right," he said wearily. "Tell me."

"Tush!" Savrinor raised a long finger as he looked over his shoulder. The weak lamplight barely touched him, and his face looked cadaverous and not quite human. "I wouldn't dream of compromising you against your will."

Not for the first time in their long acquaintance Benetan felt an urge to strike Savrinor. It would have been the work of less than a minute to extort the information he wanted; he was twelve years younger and several inches taller, and the historian was, besides, a notorious physical coward. But whatever Benetan's personal view of the value of Savrinor's friendship, he would make a very dangerous enemy.

He forced his shoulders to relax. "Please, Savrinor. I haven't the time or the skill to fence with you. Tell me."

Savrinor inclined his head with a graciousness that suggested a victor conceding the worth of an inferior opponent. Then he met Benetan's gaze and said: "Vordegh."

A cold worm moved in Benetan's gut. He mouthed the syllables of the name, though no sound emerged from his throat, then swallowed. "You're certain?"

"As certain as it's ever possible to be without official confirmation."

"But he's — "

Savrinor held up a warning hand, forestalling him. "Don't say it, my friend. Not in jest, not in heat; not under any circumstances." Suddenly all trace of banter was gone from his voice. "You'd be well advised not to even think it again, if you've any concern for your own future."

He was right. Benetan knew Vordegh's skills and temperament, although, to his eternal relief, he had never been a target for the magus's displeasure.

Yet, said a formless voice within him, and, hardly realizing that he did so, Benetan touched the small, star-shaped amulet that hung on an iron chain about his neck.

"So," Savrinor continued, quite softly, "you'll appreciate, I think, my anxiety that all should go smoothly tonight."

"Yes. And I'm doubly grateful to you for forewarning me."

"Ah!" Again the warning gesture, but now the sly humor was back. "Be careful, Benetan. I may take you at your word and alter the slate of our mutual indebtedness in my favor."

Benetan stared at him. It wasn't always possible to tell when Savrinor was joking and when he was serious. After a moment, learning nothing from the historian's expression, he shrugged, smiled thinly, and followed Savrinor out of the room.

In darkness relieved only by the faint eye of Savrinor's candle the two men made their way via the castle's confounding maze of passages and stairways toward the stables. A small door admitted them to the courtyard, and Benetan paused for a moment to breathe the chilly night air and take in his surroundings. Even after a dozen years he still wasn't inured to the effect the castle always had on him when seen in anything like its entirety; and at night the atmosphere that seemed to ooze from the very stones was doubly and unsettlingly enhanced. Grim black walls, their angularity a perverse joke on the part of the architects and their unhuman inspirers, rose foursquare to each side of him, reflecting no light, absorbing the gaze like dark vortices. At the quarters stood four titanic black spires, spearing savagely into a cloud-wracked sky and lit by fitful shafts of moonlight. Fighting the drag of vertigo to look toward their summits, Benetan saw that a high window in each spire was lit by a dim, uneasy glow, a sign that someone there watched and waited. He looked away again, quickly.

"You see?" Savrinor, at his elbow, spoke softly. "They're preparing. And if you stop still and concentrate, you can feel what moves toward us."

Reluctantly Benetan stilled his breathing, muscles tense. For a moment he could hear only the faint, ominous murmur of the sea far below, pounding the towering stack on which the castle was built; but then beneath his feet, far down in the foundations, he sensed a steady, pulsing vibration. Not a sound: it was pitched far too low to be audible to the human ear. But a movement, a shifting, something that stirred the marrow in his bones and made the cold sweat break out anew.

He glanced at his companion, his face taut and angry. "I haven't time to waste on esoterica, Savrinor. I must rouse my men."

"Of course." The historian fell into step beside him again as he set off across the deserted courtyard. The clouds broke, and though the second moon wasn't yet high enough to be visible, the first and larger hung like a disembodied face in the sky, blotting out the remote glitter of all but the brightest stars. Cold light showered down on the courtyard and the two men's shadows flowed before them over the flagstones. Benetan tried not to shiver: summer waned fast in this northern latitude and he could smell the change in the season on the sharp sea air.

Something flickered across the sky, a brief-lived shimmer like distant lightning. Involuntarily Benetan glanced up, in time to see a hissing charge of energy crackle between two of the spires' summits in answer to the celestial signal. His heart stabbed nervously and, unaware of the gesture, he made a quick, reflexive sign with his right hand. Savrinor, whose eyes missed nothing, smiled drily.

"You're right; there's a Warp coming." He glanced heavenward, speculatively. "More powerful than usual, I'd imagine. It should be an impressive spectacle."

There was a faint glow now in the northern sky; a sickly and unnatural radiance that hinted at something alien lurking over the horizon. Trapped lightning sang between the spires again. Unconsciously Benetan quickened his pace, until Savrinor was forced to jog to keep up with him. The stable block loomed in the moonlight ahead; he let out a pent breath as they moved into the shadow of the arched doorway, his tension easing as he heard the muffled stamp of horses in their straw bedding and smelled the warm, mammalian scent of them. Eyes gleamed in the glow of a single lantern, and at the sound of footsteps a shape shook itself from among a stack of hay bales in the far corner, rising to its feet with undignified and fearful haste.

"Captain Liss . . ." Relief colored the voice, and Benetan looked hard at the young sentry, who was hurriedly brushing hay from his clothing.

"Sleeping, Colas?"

"A moment's rest only, sir; I — " The lie tailed off and the youth swallowed. "I'm sorry, sir."

Aware that Savrinor was watching with lazy interest, Benetan said, "Don't let it happen again, Colas. Another time, you may be interrupted by someone considerably less tolerant than I am."

"Especially once tonight is over," Savrinor put in, stepping forward into the reach of the lamplight.

Colas's face lost all its color as he saw the historian for the first time, and he made an obeisance. "Master Savrinor! I — "

"Save your excuses for your commander, boy; I'm not interested in reporting such minor breaches of discipline to higher powers." Disdainfully Savrinor turned on his heel, and Benetan nodded to Colas. "It's all right. There's nothing to fear." He felt on firmer ground now, in an element that was familiar to him, and his sapped confidence was returning. "Get the grooms and weaponsmen out of their beds, Colas."

"Yes, sir." Colas had potential, Benetan thought: he was learning, albeit slowly, never to question an order. The youth headed for the inner door that led to the cramped dormitory where the stable servants were housed, then hesitated and looked back. "Beg your pardon, sir. Should I tell the grooms how many horses you're to need?"

Benetan made to reply, but before he could speak Savrinor laid a light hand on his arm. "I think not," the historian said quietly.

Benetan hesitated, then looked toward the far end of the stable, where an iron door, heavily barred but otherwise unremarkable, gleamed dimly in the shadows. He understood Savrinor's meaning. It was some time since the Chaos riders had been required to make use of their other mounts; but this was no ordinary occasion.

Repressing a shudder, he turned again to Colas, who was watching and awaiting a reply.

"We won't be using the horses tonight, Colas. We'll have other requirements."

"Yes, sir." The boy frowned faintly, but the full implications were lost on him: he was, Benetan reminded himself, a very new recruit to the elite ranks.

"Promising." Savrinor spoke mildly as the door closed behind Colas's back. "But not castle bred, I suspect."

"Colas came from a village in the east two years ago. He's learning."

"As you learned, of course."

"Yes." Their gazes met briefly, and Savrinor saw what he had anticipated in Benetan's eyes: distaste, and a growing tinge of fear. Lightly, he let his hand close on the captain's arm.

"Take advice from your good friend Savrinor, and don't expend needless energy on thoughts of what has yet to happen." His thin fingers squeezed, a little too familiarly for Benetan's liking, and he withdrew his hand with a final pat. "Dawn will come."

"I don't need — " Benetan began angrily, but before he could say any more a sound from somewhere within the castle silenced his tongue. Slow, sonorous, echoing, it was the voice of a single, deep-throated bell.

Savrinor's eyes narrowed with quick tension and Benetan saw his lips move, silently counting as the bell tolled. After seven strokes the deep, metallic voice fell silent, and the historian nodded.

"As I thought. We'd best go outside."

They moved into the courtyard. The quiet in the wake of the bell was eerie, and for several minutes the night's stillness remained unbroken. Then a door opened somewhere near the main gate, the sound of the latch carrying loudly and making Benetan start, and three men came hurrying across the courtyard. Others followed, and more doors were opening, dark figures emerging from the castle to converge on the stables. Metal glinted under the moon and Benetan heard the jingle of spurs and belt buckles.

"I should be elsewhere," Savrinor murmured.

"Yes . . ." With an effort Benetan gathered his wits. "Thank you, Savrinor. You've done me a service tonight."

The historian's answering smile was skull-like in the chilly light. "Good hunting," he said, and moved away as silently as a shadow.

"Captain Liss." The first group of men had reached him, and each touched a hand to the emblem of the Seven-Rayed Star at his breast in salute. "The bell — does it mean that — "

"It does," Benetan replied tersely. "The grooms are being roused now." To his private relief he felt his trained responses beginning to take over, eclipsing the sickness in his stomach. "Full complement: if we haven't enough fit men, get the unfit out of their beds. I want everyone presented and ready ten minutes from now. Where's your sergeant?"

"Here, Captain." Dark eyes in a white face, the man's rank denoted by a crimson shoulder flash.

"Ten minutes, Sergeant. It's imperative that nothing goes wrong." He added, more quietly, in the man's ear: "The rumor is for Vordegh."

Fear, yes. The same fear he had felt when Savrinor whispered the news. It stirred within him again now as he uttered the magus's name, adding a sour spice to the disquiet. And with good reason, Benetan told himself as the sergeant hastened away.

With good reason.

When the expected summons came, they were ready. Forty-nine fully armed warriors — seven times seven — ranged in silent ranks before the stable block. Inside the stable Benetan could hear the horses stamping restively; they had caught something of the pervasive atmosphere and were alerted. But the Chaos riders would have no need of them tonight.

The sky was beginning to agitate now. The spires no longer spat their shivering bolts of energy, but the lightning far to the north was almost continuous and an uneasy spectrum of dim colors marched slowly across the heavens, blotting out the stars. Though the first moon still glared down, it was haloed with a pale, ghastly corona; minutes more and its face would be obliterated as the supernatural storm, known to the cowering world as a Warp, gained power.

Benetan's senses were straining involuntarily to catch the first eerie and far-off sounds that would herald the Warp's onslaught. He was sweating again, and the black silk of his shirt and trousers clung to his skin with a cold, faintly repellent touch. He'd put on the silver circlet with its ornate embellishments that made a fearsome half mask around his eyes; it kept his unbraided hair from blowing across his face but couldn't hold back the perspiration beaded on his forehead; each time he blinked, droplets of it glittered on his lashes, breaking and refracting the moonlight on silver wristbands and on the glinting gems at his waist and shoulders. His teeth were clenched — try as he might he couldn't stop the reflex — as he listened for the first shrieking herald out of the north, and waited for the summons that he knew must come at any moment. Then a sound alerted him — the scrape of wood on stone, followed by a creak of hinges — and he looked toward the double doors at the castle's main entrance.

A shadow fell across the steps before the doorway, and a solitary man emerged. Disquieting patterns of light from the moon and other, less discernible sources distorted his figure and made him impossible to identify, but his bearing, and the long, heavy robe that enveloped him, told Benetan that he was no mere servant. For a moment the newcomer surveyed the scene, then a hand rose, gestured; and, heart quickening painfully, Benetan hastened across the courtyard and up the steps.

"Captain Liss." The voice was dry, slightly clipped; old, shrewd eyes regarded Benetan from under hooded lids. In the fine embroidery of the magus's robe, strange shapes writhed and shifted with a life of their own. "You are to be commended for your prompt response."

"Thank you, my lord." Benetan's own eyes were unfocused; he touched a hand to his breast in formal salute, and somewhere overhead felt rather than saw the sky shiver. Footsteps sounded softly on the flagstones as the magus moved back from the steps and into the silent, lofty entrance hall beyond, and Benetan followed at a respectful distance. Then the dusty voice spoke again.

"We require a full harvest tonight. Satisfy that requirement and your diligence will be commended to those whom we all are privileged to serve."

"I'm grateful, my lord. And I will discharge my duties to the utmost of my ability." Benetan fought a tic that threatened to make his cheek muscles twitch, and silently praised Savrinor.

The magus nodded. "We ask nothing more, and demand nothing less. Now: you have a full complement of riders?"

"Yes, sir."

"Very good. Then you are ready to take the sacrament."

"I — " His voice cracked; he forced it back under his control. "I am ready, my lord."

Now he could hear it: the first thin, screaming wail far out over the sea, as the Warp began to move in toward the peninsula. Ten minutes, perhaps fifteen, no more, and the huge forces unleashed by the gods would come shrieking out of the night in wild and deadly celebration. And he must face the Warp, and lead his riders out into its howling heart. . . .

He heard the magus turn away, heard the crisp snap of his fingers, the light, hesitant feet of the servant who had been waiting in the shadows and now came forward at his summons. She held a pewter tray on which were set a flask and a tiny chalice carved from a single diamond; averting her gaze, she dropped to one knee before the magus and held the tray out.

As the sorcerer filled the cup to the brim, Benetan tried to quiet the pounding of his heart. He could see the faint, darkly phosphorescent gleam of the liquid, and against his will he found himself starting to crave it and the effect it would have on him. It was a bulwark against fear, a shield for his sanity in the face of what was to come. . . . Shrewd, relentless eyes focused on him, seeming to see beyond the physical contours of his skull and into his inner mind. The magus smiled thinly and held out the brimming chalice.

Yandros, greatest lord of Chaos, strengthen my resolve tonight! Benetan shut his eyes as the silent prayer went through his mind, then drank, draining the chalice in a single mouthful. The taste of the draft burned his tongue as he swallowed, and he felt its heat pervade to his stomach. Then, his legs not entirely steady, he set the tiny vessel back on the tray.

"The Maze stands open and waiting, Captain. I would advise you not to delay." The magus gestured toward the doors. "Search well, and reap a good harvest."

Aware that the last words might be either a blessing or a threat, Benetan repeated his formal salute. The servant stepped forward and handed him the tray; the magus nodded once, satisfied, and walked away as Benetan turned numbly back to the courtyard.

Two sergeants were waiting at the head of the line of men. One took the tray, and Benetan said curtly: "See that each man takes his share."

"Sir." The sergeant nodded, understanding. With a queasy sensation that couldn't yet be due to the effects of the narcotic, Benetan watched him carry the flask down the line, watched each man drink in his turn. Then he looked over his shoulder and saw Colas waiting, wide-eyed, at the stable door. The boy was too young and too inexperienced for this; better that he be dismissed now rather than risk him before he was ready. Benetan signaled, and Colas hastened forward.

"Captain?"

"Go to your bed, Colas. You'll not be needed again tonight."

"But sir, I — "

"I said, *Go to your bed*. Or you'll face the lash tomorrow for insubordination." He didn't want to be harsh with the boy, but there was no time for explanations. If Colas lingered, his sanity could be in jeopardy without the drug to shield him.

Colas's eyes lost their focus and he touched his hand to his left shoulder. "Yes, sir!" He turned stiffly and strode away, trying to maintain his dignity in the face of stung pride.

Overhead the sky spat crimson lightning, and the distant singing sound swelled like a tidal surge, counterpointed by a far-off rumble of thunder. Without warning, the scene before Benetan warped, as though he were viewing it from another dimension. The illusion lasted only a moment, but it made him realize that the narcotic was beginning to work. He drew several steady breaths, counting, hearing the air rasp in his throat. The sounds in the sky were augmented now by a singing in his brain, an unholy, unhuman choir of joyous voices; and an arrhythmic vibration thrummed through his bones. He felt as though his body were stone, the stone of the castle, and the breaths he took tasted of fire and of wine and of other, subtler things that he couldn't name.

He looked to where his sergeant was administering the magus's draft to the last men in the line. The ranks of riders looked alien, silhouettes etched by the night's feral glow, and the world was turning, turning, the huge, dim spectrum of the Warp gaining strength as it wheeled across the sky high above. Benetan felt laughter shake itself into life deep inside him and he turned, moving in a fluid, dream-like way to the stable, past the nervous horses and toward the iron door with its heavy bar. The grooms — meaningless shadow men, not worthy of his notice — backed away from him, and the dimensions of the stable seemed to stretch into impossible distortions, walls rearing and lurching, floor undulating beneath his feet. Benetan knew he was hallucinating, but the earlier dread was leaving him now as the drug took hold of his mind and body, and he welcomed the illusions, gloried in them. The door loomed like a mouth; he stopped before it, and pulled from his belt a pair of long, black gauntlets, each finger tipped with a silver claw. His hands tingled as he drew the gauntlets over them and smoothed them on his forearms; under the moon the claws glinted and he flexed them, feeling the power and the control they granted him as they transmuted his hands into something unhuman.

The door's metal bar gave under his grip; he wrenched it aside and let it fall. Then he bunched his fist and the laughter spilled from his throat as he pounded on the door's surface.

With the seventh blow, the door smashed back onto a tunnel of utter blackness. Benetan swayed backward as a vast breath of air belched out of the dark: then a heavy, phased clopping echoed in the confined space, and something huge, blacker even than the tunnel, moved beyond the door, treading toward the physical world.

Even in his drug-heightened state Benetan couldn't fully assimilate it. It was a monstrous thing of iron and dark, horselike but not spawned by any creature of flesh and blood, quartz hooves shimmering, cold silver glittering in its eyes, the shadows of great wings rising from its back. It opened a crimson mouth, and its breath was like the touch of fire on his face as he reached up toward it, grasped the mane that writhed like snakes in his hands, coaxed it, caressed it, urged its sleek, sinuous form out into the courtyard. Behind it more were emerging; huge silhouettes, things born of Chaos, demonic and powerful. Benetan was laughing again and his men were joining in as they, too, fell prey to the sacrament. The laughter, mingling with the voices that howled their weird harmonies in the sky and in his head, was tinged with insanity. The entire world was turning to black and silver as Benetan's perceptions altered; he saw beyond the dimensions that physically held him, into places where other consciousnesses moved in dark and formless undercurrents, feeding on his excitement, imbuing him with sensations that made his blood burn and race in his veins.

In the stable, someone was screaming. A young groom, unprepared for the things that he was witnessing, unprotected by the narcotic that gripped the minds of the riders and held them steadfast in the face of Chaos. Another Benetan felt pity and regret for the youth's horror, but that Benetan was a stranger, an alien being: the Chaos captain who swung himself up onto the smoke dark back of his mount could know only contempt for such weakness.

A jolt of raw power slammed into him as the terrible fusion between man and demon beast engulfed his reeling senses. The courtyard turned and toppled about him and he uttered a high, ululating yell that was taken up by his fellow riders, a hungry and feverish celebration of energy, desire, madness. He raised his left arm high so that the gauntlet's claws caught the angry moonlight and, in his altered, churning vision, seemed to flash five searing bolts that spat upward into the night. Lightning answered from the heavens, and the northern and eastern spires crackled and sang again. Benetan felt the moment coming, felt the Warp's awesome power building to a crescendo, thrumming through his bones — on the far side of the courtyard the great gates were opening —

A titanic howl smashed against his eardrums, and the sky split open. Blinding light turned the courtyard to an inferno, and, in hideous harmony with the voice of the breaking storm, the Chaos creatures shrieked a wild challenge as the mass of riders surged forward like a black, breaking wave, with Benetan screaming at their head. Possessed, inspired, deranged, his mind was no longer his own; the gates within him had opened, as the Chaos Gate was even now opening far, far below him, and humanity was drowned in the dervishistic joy of the warrior, the hunter, the reaper, as the demonic riders streamed through the gate to be unleashed upon the world.

CHAPTER II

S avrinor had returned quietly and unobtrusively to his rooms without, he hoped, drawing attention to his earlier absence. He knew he would be summoned soon enough; although he wasn't of the magi's ranks, not even a sorcerer, his position as the castle's historian required him to attend and chronicle all major events, and for tonight's ceremony he had no doubt that his presence would be demanded.

He didn't watch the Chaos riders leave. Spectacular though their departure might have been, it was nothing he hadn't seen a hundred times before and he was no longer moved or even especially impressed by it. Instead as the Warp shrieked in from the north he sat motionless at the ornately carved desk in his study, elbows on the desktop, hands clasped before his face, pale eyes unquiet. He didn't care to probe the reason for it, but there was an uneasiness in him, a sense of tension and anticipation — not pleasant anticipation — that even the breaking of the Warp had done nothing to allay. And when at last he heard the tentative knock at his door, he wasn't sure whether relief or dread had the upper hand.

"M — Master Savrinor . . . ?" The magi had a marked preference for female servants, Savrinor thought; this one was probably no more than twelve or thirteen years old, and any promise of later beauty she might have had was spoiled by her slack mouth and empty, hunted eyes. He doubted if she would last the year out.

"What is it?"

"The . . . l-lord magus Croin, Master, he . . . that is, I am to tell you . . . if you will permit . . ."

Fear and stupidity offended Savrinor in equal measure, and he made no attempt to hide his irritation. "Speak clearly, you witless drudge. Does Magus Croin wish to see me?"

"He — the lord Croin . . . he is at the b-bedside of the F-f-f . . ."

"Yandros preserve us!" Savrinor hissed the words exasperatedly and, as the girl continued to stammer incoherently, brushed her aside and strode away down the corridor. He'd made out enough of the faltering mumbles to surmise the rest of the message, and the girl's efforts to tell him that Croin was with the First Magus confirmed it. Croin was the magi's most skilled healer; if he had issued this summons, it must mean that the end was very close, probably less than an hour away, and by now the magi would be preparing for the final procession. If he valued his skin, Savrinor couldn't afford to be late.

Tidying his hair and clothes as he went, he reached the First Magus's private chambers within minutes and, as he had expected, found the thin, aesthetic Croin waiting for him outside the iron-studded black door. The door was closed, but light swirled beneath it and on the far side Savrinor could hear the chilly, atonal sound of a dirge as the senior magi chanted an elegy for their leader.

"My lord." Savrinor's bow was exaggeratedly formal yet without the smallest hint of his usual sardonicism; it was an approach that stood him in good stead with the magi, and Croin in particular. "The First Magus — he's surely not — "

"No, no." Croin made a negative gesture, rings glinting on each of his seven fingers. "He has not yet left us. But it will be very soon. We are ready to proceed, and of course your presence is required at the time of passing."

"Yes, my lord. I'm only sorry that I must be the chronicler of the castle's loss."

Croin regarded him shrewdly, noting the genuine regret in Savrinor's tone and perhaps interpreting the reason for it all too well. "Our sorrow is the First Magus's joy, Savrinor. He goes to a reward that we all hope to earn in our time."

"Of course, sir." Savrinor averted his gaze.

"And if the great lords accept his chosen successor, we will have cause for celebration." Croin's eyes narrowed. "I advise you not to overlook that fact."

"My lord." Savrinor bowed again in a way that conveyed apology and understanding without the need for further words. The healer continued to stare at him for a few moments longer, thinking his own thoughts. Then he turned, lifted the door's heavy latch, and led the way into the First Magus's chambers.

The last journey of the dying man began ten minutes later. No lamps shone in any of the castle's myriad windows now; shutters were closed and all but those who walked with the procession had retired to their quarters as tradition demanded. The Warp had passed, shrieking into oblivion, and the cortege emerged from the entrance doors under the indifferent eyes of the two moons which now hung in a silent sky.

The first herald of the procession was a cold, glowing green sphere hanging unsupported in the air, which moved slowly from the shadows of the entrance to hover in the courtyard. Following it came the magi, dressed in flowing robes, their forms ghastly and other-worldly under the eerie light. In their midst, four bearers carried a litter draped with white hangings, on which lay a still figure.

There was no sound: no chanting, no dirge now, not even the shuffle of feet. The magi moved as noiselessly as ghosts, the shining ball of light guiding them as they advanced in slow and stately procession toward the stoa, a covered walkway of colonnaded pillars on the far side of the courtyard, and the door at the stoa's end through which they would carry the First Magus to his final earthly encounter.

Savrinor walked behind his masters. The route was a familiar one, but the occasion not so; though he knew the form that tonight's ceremony would take, he didn't know precisely what to expect and felt reluctant to speculate. He watched the shadows of the colonnade as they passed by, unconsciously counting the pillars; then the procession turned as it reached the door, and passed through it to begin the long, slow descent of the spiral stairs winding down into the foundations. At the foot of the stairs they passed through a great, vaulted room, dark and silent now, then another door gaped before them and they were on the last stage of their journey, along the sloping corridor that would bring them at last to the Marble Hall.

The Marble Hall, deep beneath the castle foundations, was a place of mist and deception. Its dimensions — if it could truly be said to have dimensions — were shrouded in an uneasy swirl of pastel-shot light and shadow, while the floor from which it took its name was an intricate mosaic of every perceptible shade, a random pattern that drew the eye yet disturbed senses constrained by the limitations of humanity. Centuries ago, when the seven lords of Chaos spoke to the sleeping minds of the world's greatest artisans, inspired them with dreams of terror and glory and guided their hands to cut the massive foundation stones on which this ancient castle was built, Yandros himself, highest of all the seven, had created the Marble Hall and with it the Chaos Gate. The Gate was a link between this world and the realm of Chaos, which no man still cloaked with the trappings of mortality dared enter; and as the procession moved across the shimmering floor Savrinor felt the deep-rooted thrill of awe and fear that no amount of familiarity could ever erode. The Gate lay at what was believed to be the Hall's exact center, and when closed it was marked by nothing more than a black circle in the mosaic pattern of the floor. Now, however, the mists about the circle were agitating, their pastel hues shot through with dark and dangerous colors; as he took his appointed place Savrinor saw a wavering column of unutterable blackness appear above the mosaic circle, flickering close to the limits of perception, and felt the pulse of the forces held but barely in check under his feet.

Chaos was stirring.

The white-draped bier was lowered with reverential care to the floor of the Hall, before the Gate. The First Magus's eyes were open and aware; but if he recognized the faces that surrounded him, or the nature of what lay ahead, he gave no sign of it. A paralyzing weakness had overtaken him that morning together with the final loss of his powers of speech; any last benisons he might have wished to grant to old friends would never now be uttered.

Savrinor watched the dying man, whilst seeming to keep his gaze focused on the floor. A good master, in his own way; vain and self-seeking, yes, but who wasn't in these times? Such faults, if faults they were, had their uses, as Savrinor knew very well. A good servant to the Seven from whom he took his power? Perhaps; though that was not for any but the Seven to say. Better, certainly, than the one who would come after him. . . . And at that thought Savrinor's gaze slid surreptitiously to the members of the small innermost coterie of magi who had taken up their positions at the head of the bier, and to one man in particular.

Vordegh. In late middle age now, but still retaining the strength and musculature of youth in his massive build. Black-haired, swarthily handsome, dark eyes calm as he regarded the Chaos Gate and waited with his peers. A sorcerer of rare skill, a demon master, ascetic, sadist . . . and the word he had stopped Benetan Liss from uttering came unbidden into Savrinor's mind.

A madman.

Efficiently, Savrinor quashed the thought. With Vordegh as First Magus he'd do well to take his own advice to Benetan and not even allow such concepts to enter his mind. Croin had echoed that same warning back to him, though not in so many words, and Savrinor hadn't missed the brief flicker of unease in the thin healer's eyes as he spoke. From now on he'd guard even his innermost thoughts with the utmost care. Whichever way the wind blew, there would still be room for him to maneuver, *if* he kept his wits about him.

A stirring in the group's midst alerted him and he looked up quickly. The dying man on his litter was trying to speak. Words were beyond his power now, but a guttural croaking issued from his withered throat, like the last cry of an old, sick raven. The other magi hastened to his side, and Vordegh leaned over the bier and took hold of the old man's hand as though to offer comfort or a last farewell. The First Magus's fingers fluttered feebly; he held something bright in his failing, arthritic grasp, and the artifact passed from his hand to Vordegh's before the arm fell back limply to his side.

Vordegh straightened, and a cold, proud smile touched his mouth. Then he raised his arm, and Savrinor saw the thin, metallic wand that the First Magus had placed in his palm. A chilly blue white radiance spilled from the wand; bands of shadow moved slowly along its length, and Savrinor sucked in a quiet breath as he recognized it.

The ultimate symbol of the power granted to the magi by the gods, and one whose use lay solely in the charge of the castle's undisputed master — the key to the Chaos Gate.

The First Magus had named his successor.

Vordegh turned to face the Gate, and raised the key high above his head. As his arm reached its full extent the wand's white radiance changed suddenly and shockingly to black, and it began to pulse like an unstable, earthbound star. The shivering column of the Gate took up the rhythm of the pulse, until the two meshed in perfect, terrible synchrony.

The old man on the bier stirred again. A crazed smile split his seamed features, and a spark of fire lit up the failing eyes as, with many hands supporting him, he raised his head a few inches from its pillow. The pulsing black light intensified in a ferocious flare — and the column of darkness seemed to invert, twisting in on itself and opening like a gigantic eye as the Chaos Gate yawned wide.

Savrinor looked into the eye and through it, to a black road that arrowed from the Gate toward a horizon so vast that he bit his tongue in shock. He could never habituate himself to this: to the vastness, the vertigo, the impossible, alien madness of the world that assailed his senses. Wild colors spun across dizzying spectra, shapes that defied comprehension shifted in constantly alternating patterns of gloom and livid brilliance; figures that were not quite tangible, and held their form only for the space of a heartbeat, moved like restless wraiths on the periphery of vision. And the Marble Hall vibrated with the anticipation of something titanic, that breached dimensions, approaching.

The magi were still again. Even the shrunken old man on the pallet had ceased his efforts and lay passive once more, waiting, only his eyes animated and eager. Then came a sound like measured footsteps or a lethargic heartbeat, felt in the marrow rather than heard. Tension became palpable; somewhere — it seemed to emanate from the vastness beyond the Gate, but that might have been illusory — a low humming vibrated in the bones behind Savrinor's ears.

The Gate shuddered and for a moment seemed to collapse back in on itself. Then a massive flash of brilliance, scarlet shot with searing white, turned the Marble Hall briefly to an inferno of light and fire, blinding the watchers and forcing them to turn their heads aside. And when Savrinor, teeth clamped down on an involuntary oath, was able to look again, Chaos's emissary stood in the shadows of the portal.

The being, which was half again as tall as any of the magi, had the body of a man and the head of a scaled, gape-jawed reptile. Colossal wings rose from its shoulders, the flight feathers fashioned from white-hot metal that spilled molten fragments about its feet. A phantasmic, golden corona of flames burned around the figure; flanking it, two eyeless and monstrously distorted chimeras strained at their chains, snakes' tongues licking at the air, dogs' claws scraping and scrabbling for purchase on the mosaic. The emissary opened its jaws, and the stench of a charnel house made Savrinor's nostrils flare. He forced himself not to flinch from it — discourtesy would be dangerous — and watched as the being's eyes, which were a warm amber brown, calm and intelligent and beautiful, slowly scanned the gathering, their gaze resting at last on the now quiescent First Magus.

The silence was profound. Blood pounded in Savrinor's ears and he held his breath, not daring to move a muscle. The emissary gazed down at the pallet; then its unencumbered hand came up, and a finger, tipped with a curving claw the color of old bronze, pointed at the First Magus's heart.

The old man smiled, and in the smile was the joy and triumph of achievement. He reared up as though to meet and embrace the Chaos being — then the chilling hiss of his death rattle echoed hollowly through the silent hall, and his empty husk fell back onto the bier.

Hastily following the lead of the magi, Savrinor dropped to one knee and traced the Seven-Rayed Star over his own heart as a mark of respect for the First Magus's passing. Only Vordegh didn't kneel or make the sign; he merely stood erect, unmoving, gazing steadily into the quiet eyes of the demon before him, and waiting. The emissary's reptilian head inclined once, and Vordegh held out his hand, displaying the darkly glowing wand on his palm. The claw reached out, plucked; and in the demon's grasp the wand turned white hot. The monstrous jaws gaped again in a parody of a smile. Then the emissary touched the tip of the wand to the exact center of Vordegh's forehead, and held it there.

Savrinor almost gagged on the reek of charring flesh, and some of the magi looked away. Vordegh, however, didn't flinch. The tendons of his neck stood out like whipcord, but he stayed his ground, eyes staring straight ahead, though unfocused now with the strain of absorbing and withstanding the agony he must have felt. He would not recoil, he would not plead for cessation. The will of the man, Savrinor thought with an inward shudder, was unhuman.

Suddenly it was over. The demon's arm fell to its side, and Savrinor saw the puckered and near-black stigma of a ferocious scar on Vordegh's brow; a scar that would never heal. Vordegh's gaze dropped — the only sign of relief that he would permit himself to show — and the emissary held out the wand, no longer blazing with heat, for the new First Magus to take. The two eyeless chimeras opened toothless mouths, shaking their chains, and the emissary stepped back a pace. Once more, though briefly, it scanned the assembly with something resembling cool speculation in its eyes. Then the molten wings rose high, clashed together, and with an enormous, silent concussion, the black eye of the Chaos Gate closed and the emissary was gone.

Through the silence of the darkest hours Savrinor sat at the table in his room, committing the night's events to parchment as his duty compelled. The window was heavily curtained, and the airlessness together with the heat from the built-up fire made the chamber stifling, but Savrinor couldn't stop shivering. The feeling of bone-numbing cold in him was partly due to the effects of the narcotics he'd been using since his return, but the real cause of his condition — and the reason why he'd turned to his drugs in the first place — was the unpleasant and unnerving track of his own thoughts.

There had been something wrong with the ceremony. He'd not dared to consider it at the time, but now the memory echoed in his mind like a recalled nightmare. On the surface, everything had gone well enough. The old First Magus's soul had been gathered to the realm of Chaos and had made its last journey gladly; his successor had undergone trial and had not been found wanting. But there were anomalies. The emissary sent by the Chaos lords had been a demon of no great rank; Chaos was perverse, and its higher beings tended to favor less bizarre manifestations than their lower brethren. Though Savrinor had never been privileged to witness such an event, he had heard that Yandros himself took the form of an ordinary man on the rare occasions when he deigned to make himself known to his human worshipers. All well and good, the emissary had been of an order warranted by such an occasion as this. But there had been no shout of fanfares, no violent assault on the senses, none of the ceremonial that usually accompanied the arrival of the lesser demons. The emissary hadn't spoken a single word, had demanded no praises or psalms in its turn. And Vordegh's trial had been simplicity itself.

It didn't fit with the accepted pattern. Despite its erratic nature, Chaos maintained a certain predictability in its dealings with the mortal world; without that stability its worshipers couldn't hope to function. And by those rules, such anomalies as Savrinor had witnessed tonight simply shouldn't have existed. They suggested, to his uneasy mind, an ambivalence on the part of Yandros and his six brethren. But ambivalence toward what? The old First Magus? The new? Or something that, as yet, he couldn't even begin to guess at?

Savrinor shook sand over the last of his parchments. He had no time for false modesty and knew that his work tonight had excelled even his usual high standard. Every detail of the ceremonial was there, and woven in among the facts was a sober tribute to the wisdom and nobility of the late First Magus, carefully balanced by several subtle paragraphs in respectful but emphatic praise of his successor. Even Vordegh couldn't possibly find fault with this. And no one, Savrinor hoped and prayed, would ever know of the other document, the few brief but succinct notes in his own shorthand code that now lay secreted in an inner drawer, and that told a different story. . . .

Feeling faintly queasy with the sense of having finally shed an unpleasant burden, Savrinor set the completed document aside. Fastidiously he turned down the cover of his bed, then moved to extinguish the lamp by which he had been working. A gaunt shape moved in the gloom beyond the lamplight, and he started nervously before realizing that it was nothing more than his own shadow disturbed by a flicker within the lamp's chimney. Jinking at shadows . . . it was a trait he mocked in others, for twilight, literal or metaphorical, had always been his natural habitat. But suddenly he felt uneasy in its embrace. And the thoughts that had been troubling his mind were still there, and they still wouldn't let him alone.

Forcing down the tension within him, Savrinor sought refuge in his bed, for once not troubling to shed his clothes. It would be dawn soon enough, and the new day would see a good many changes if he and his bones were any judge. Better to be ready at a moment's notice, in case of . . . what? He didn't know. Perhaps nothing; perhaps not. He, like all of them, would have to wait and see.

Again he reached out to extinguish the lamp — then let his hand fall away from it and instead left it burning, a small pool of brightness in the dim room. It was irrationally comforting, and there was no one else here to witness his small show of weakness.

Savrinor didn't sleep that night.

CHAPTER III

They had both dearly wished that the ceremony could have been conducted during daylight hours, under the kindlier light of the sun, but the risk of discovery was too great. So they had gathered, with the few family members and close friends who could be trusted beyond any doubt, in the cellar of the house, set apart from and slightly larger than its neighbors, which stood at the eastern end of the rough, sprawling village. It was the one place, they had decided, where the vows that were to be taken, and the pledges that were to be made, would be safe from prying ears.

Two months had passed since she had last seen Kaldar, and as the day set for their reunion drew closer Iselia Darrow had suffered agonies of fear for his safety. Visitors were a common enough occurrence at the house, for her father, as overseer of a nearby mineral mine, acted as intermediary between the laboring men and their masters, but still each caller had awakened the cold claws of irrational terror inside her. And the fatalistic dread that something would go wrong only abated when finally the moment came for her to climb down the steep ladder into the cellar where the celebrants had quietly taken their places.

He was there, waiting for her; even in the gloom she could see the bright flash of his red hair among the other shadowy figures. How and when he had arrived in the village she didn't know and didn't ask; Kaldar had his own methods, and for safety's sake they were best not discussed. But he had had the chance to wash himself, and someone had given him fresh clothing, not white but at least light in color. His eyes as she appeared from the room above were lit by more than the reflections of the seven tiny votive lamps that burned on her father's bench.

She knelt now at Kaldar's side before the makeshift altar with its draped white cloth, the lamps and the bowls of salt and wine. Behind them, the shadowed figures of her parents and sister, and two trusted witnesses — old friends, and dear ones — were still and quiet as ghosts in the darkness. Iselia had no bridal trappings; there were no garlands to be placed about their necks when the simple ceremony was done; there would be no feasting or dancing. Only a quick and furtive farewell to her family, a last kiss and embrace before she and Kaldar slipped away under cover of the night to begin a new life far from home and friends. Even Kaldar's own kin knew nothing of tonight's events: they believed, as did all but a very select few of his onetime acquaintances, that he was dead. It was far safer that way.

The moment for silent contemplation was over, and Kaldar stood, taking Iselia's hands to raise her to her feet. She turned to the altar and lifted the bowl of wine, noting as she did so how the pinpoint reflections from the lamps danced on its surface like tiny, fierce eyes. Then she turned again to face the small company, and her husky voice broke the silence.

"Be it known to those assembled that I, Iselia Darrow, do make this vow in freedom and in joy." She had rehearsed the words a hundred times in her mind; to be uttering them aloud at last sent a tingling frisson through her. She held the bowl high, and faced Kaldar. "In love and in hope do I pledge and bind myself to you, Kaldar Alvaray, to be wife to you, to be comforter and helpmeet to you, from this day until my life's end."

She held the bowl to Kaldar's lips. He smiled at her across the rim and his eyes were both fiercely possessive and fiercely proud as he looked into her face. Guessing his thoughts, knowing what was in his mind, Iselia felt an answering surge of bold defiance rise within herself. The moment for which they'd planned and schemed and worked had arrived at last. Nothing could stop the ceremony now — and when it was over, when they were truly man and wife in the eyes of Aeoris, the *real* work could begin.

The intense, private contact broke as Kaldar closed his eyes. He drank deeply, and a sigh of approval rustled in the cellar. Then the bowl was taken from her hands, and Kaldar in his turn raised it.

"And I, Kaldar Alvaray, in love and in hope, do pledge and bind myself to you, Iselia Darrow, to be provider and protector to you, from this day until my life's end."

His hands smelled faintly of sun and the mountains as he held the bowl to her and she, too, drank from it. The wine was the finest that her family had been able to procure without arousing suspicion, and Iselia found a moment to silently bless her father for his kindness. Despite the secrecy, despite the risks, he had done all he could.

Kaldar set the bowl back on the altar, and picked up the dish of salt. The room fell utterly silent as he lowered the dish to the floor, and in the gloom Iselia saw her mother reach out and take a tight hold of her father's hand. Kaldar's eyes, hooded now and lit with a new fire of fanatical devotion, scanned the gathering.

"My friends." His voice was grave, and there was an edge to it. "Before my bride and I make the final pledge that will seal our bond in the sight of one whose name cannot be spoken openly, I wish to thank you all for your goodness to us. You have opened yourselves to great danger by agreeing to be present at this ceremony, and I feel privileged to be among such company. I'm only sorry that we must part so soon, and that I will be taking Iselia from you rather than returning to my old home with her. But I promise you this: I will guard her more closely than my own life, and I will never, ever forget what you — all of you — have done for us."

Iselia's father cleared his throat, but no one spoke. Kaldar looked at Iselia. "Are you ready, love?"

She nodded, couldn't speak. Together they knelt before the bowl, and slowly she stretched out her right hand — it was shaking, but she couldn't make it stop — over the salt. Kaldar's own right hand clenched, then opened, and she saw the silver ring with its seven tiny topaz stones lying on his palm.

"As salt is to earth, so we are to earth." The words were of Kaldar's own devising, and he spoke them with such soft reverence that his voice was barely audible even in the intense quiet. "As we have drunk of the wine, so shall we drink of the water. And as we pledge our lives and our souls by this token each to the other, so do we pledge our lives and our souls to the power and the justice of Aeoris, Lord of

Order, One of Seven, that His light may scourge the taint of Chaos from our land."

Iselia held her breath and felt the ring, cold and unfamiliar, slip onto her middle finger. Kaldar's hand closed tightly over hers, then he guided her fingers down, down, until they rested on the salt crystals.

"To the power and the justice of Aeoris, I pledge my life and my soul," she whispered, and the oath was taken up by the gathering, a soft, sibilant murmur.

For a few moments the absolute quiet that followed their murmuring held, as though time itself were in abeyance. Then Iselia felt Kaldar's hand squeeze hers, and he was straightening, drawing her toward him. His arms went around her waist and he kissed her with slow deliberation before holding her to him in a powerful hug.

"It's done." His face was buried in the cascade of her corn-fair hair, and she alone could hear him. "Whatever happens now, Aeoris has blessed us, and nothing can change that!"

Iselia tried to reply but words wouldn't form. Joy and relief were at last overtaking the dragging fear of the last weeks; the ceremony was completed, they were wed — and the secret of their forbidden allegiance was safe.

She turned as the company gathered round, and wordlessly embraced her parents. Her mother had been crying; her father was red faced and overly jovial; others wanted to kiss them both, bless them, congratulate them. Wine cups clinked; and her father uncorked a bottle of the sweet, flowery mead he kept for family celebrations. The first cup was poured, splashing over the rim to laughter and approval; as Iselia reached out to take it, her hand froze suddenly at the sound of a door slamming overhead.

"Kaldar — " She clutched at his arm.

"Wait." He, too, had heard it, and was listening. Above them feet sounded on the floorboards, shockingly loud in the uneasy silence that had abruptly fallen.

"It's Arin." But even as he spoke, Iselia's father was reaching to his belt and the knife he carried there. "He's — " and he broke off as the trapdoor in the cellar ceiling opened and Arin, Iselia's younger brother, flung himself through the gap, almost losing his footing in his frantic haste.

"Father!" Arin's eyes were wild. "Clear the cellar, *quickly!*"

"What is it?" Iselia felt sick, and her voice was shrill. "Arin, what's happened?"

"There's a Warp coming." Fear showed starkly through the pity in Arin's eyes as he met her shocked stare. "It'll break within minutes. And it's bringing the Chaos riders!"

Iselia's father paled. "Are you certain?"

"I've heard them, Father. The screaming, the sounds of those demon horses they ride — " He shook his head, unable to express what he felt.

Iselia's mother hissed, *"Aeoris!"* and her husband turned on his heel, pointing to the makeshift altar. "Get that bench cleared! Scatter the salt, get the dishes out of sight — and douse the lamps!" He turned again, came face to face with Kaldar. "This can only mean one thing. They're hunting down candidates to take to the Star Peninsula. Kaldar, you've got to go. If they find you — "

Iselia cried, "No!" but her father caught her by the shoulders and shook her. "D'you want to be a widow on your own wedding night, girl? If Kaldar stays in the village, those devils will root him out for certain. He's *got* to flee!"

She turned in mute, frantic appeal to Kaldar, but he shook his head. "Your father's right, love. We've all seen enough of the Chaos riders to know their methods and their skills." His hands closed over hers. "I'll come back for you as soon as they're clear away."

"I'll come with you!"

"No, Iselia: there isn't time. I can get clear of the village quickly; I know the paths. But if you're with me we'll be slower, and they'll catch us both."

"Kaldar, *please* — " But she couldn't finish. Bleakly, dismally, she had to admit he was right.

"Aeoris protect you." He kissed her, then embraced her father, gripped Arin's hand briefly, and swung himself away up the ladder. Iselia stood helpless, her face suddenly ugly with tears as all the words she'd had no time to say tumbled into her mind, but suddenly her mother's voice, firm but gentle, cut through the turmoil. "Iselia. Come with me, child. Hurry, now."

Iselia was frozen, still staring at the ladder and the trapdoor through which Kaldar had disappeared. Around her she was dimly aware of the altar being cleared, the cloth swept off the bench and bundled hastily away, mead and cups vanishing into hiding. And now that her senses were alerted she could hear another sound beyond the house's safe and solid walls: something that turned her courage to dust. Far off still but coming closer, the shrieking, insane voice of the Warp, and the demon-inspired horde who rode it.

A distorted sense of rationality struggled to the surface of her mind as she strove to find a shield against her rising panic. "I must help them. . . ." Her voice shook, one arm reaching out toward the hurrying shadows about her.

"It'll be done in time." Her mother was implacable. "Come, now. Come."

Arin was trying to take her hand; they were leading her toward the ladder. She climbed in a sick miasma of misery and shock, and emerged into the unlit room above. It should have been dark, but there was a faint, grim radiance shining in at the windows, making shadows shift eerily in the gloom. And the appalling sound of the Warp was growing louder. . . .

Numbly, Iselia allowed her mother to bustle her through the house to the room where she had slept for twenty-four years. The wooden shutters were slammed, muffling the worst of the approaching din, and she sat stunned and immobile on her bed while her clothes were taken off and her night shift slipped over her head. Only when she lay down on the mattress and her mother tucked the covering around her did she start to shiver uncontrollably.

"The ring." There was a catch in her mother's voice. "Your marriage ring, Iselia. You'd best take it off. Just in case."

She didn't want to. It was all she had of Kaldar, and her fist clenched spasmodically. Her mother stroked her hair.

"He'll be back soon. It's just for a few hours, my dear child."

Slowly, as though in a dream, Iselia slipped the ring from her finger. It fell to the floor; her mother took a brass chain from around her own neck and threaded the ring onto it, then fastened the chain about Iselia's throat.

"There, now. It's safe but still within reach." She pulled the coarse blankets over her daughter's ears to muffle the sounds of the Warp. "Try to sleep. If the house is dark and quiet when the horsemen ride through, they'll not trouble us."

Iselia raised her head from the pillow. "Father — and Arin, the others — "

"We'll all be abed within the minute." Her mother squeezed her hand hard. "Pray to Aeoris. He'll protect us from them."

The door shut and Iselia lay shuddering, not daring to turn her head and look toward the shuttered window. She desperately wanted the comfort of light, but dared not strike flint to tinder lest even a candle should show a sliver of brightness and draw attention to their home.

Pray to Aeoris, her mother had said. She tried and tried, but for once the words wouldn't come; wouldn't break through the barrier of dread deep within her. Out there in the dark were the demon-driven elite of Chaos, masters of all the land, tyrannizers, reavers; tonight *they* were the reality, they and not her god, for her god didn't have the power to protect her from them. And out there was Kaldar, running against time to get clear of the village before the riders came to reap their harvest. Could the powers of Order safeguard him? Iselia asked herself desperately. Would Kaldar's faith and skill be enough to form the protective link with their friends, even if she could do nothing to keep him from discovery?

Her heart was hammering against her ribs, each beat sending a shaft of pain through her, and the noise of the approaching horror engendered a terror that stifled her throat and made every breath an ordeal. The Warp was rushing closer and closer, the sounds swelling like the voices of an unhuman choir as it swept in toward the village. Lightning shivered beyond the shielded window, slivers of white brilliance flickering through gaps in the shutters and dancing in crazed patterns on the wall. Nothing could blot out the oncoming turmoil now; even when she blocked her ears with clenched fists Iselia could still hear the high, insane shrieking of the storm and, in ghastly counterpoint, a deep, subsonic throb that seemed to rise through the earth and through the foundations of the house to vibrate in her bones like the pulse of Chaos itself.

Suddenly the pitch of the unholy shrieking changed. Iselia's muscles locked rigid, every nerve afire with tension, but her mind had no time to react to her body's intuitive warning before thunder smashed' the night in a shattering, deafening wall of sound that hit her like a physical onslaught. She lost control and, screaming, flung herself from the bed as a primitive instinct to run, to flee, eclipsed all semblance of reason. She hit the floor with a painful impact, struggled wildly as her limbs tangled with the blanket that had fallen with her —

And, stunned and trembling with shock, she raised her head in the dark room, to realize that the night was utterly silent.

Nausea made her stomach contract. She fought the reaction, tasting bile, and after perhaps half a minute was able, slowly, and cautiously, to get to her feet. *Silence.* At first she thought the concussion had deafened her, but when she tried her voice the small whimper that was the only sound she could make was loud against the deathly backdrop. Iselia stared blankly at the window, unable to comprehend what had happened. She listened, straining to catch even the smallest sound, but there was nothing.

Unsteadily, she moved toward the shutters. Her fingers were shaking and clumsy as she scrabbled to unfasten the catch, and an inner voice warned her not to be a fool, not to take the risk. But she had to *know*. The shutter swung back: she caught it before it could expose more than a narrow oblong of the window and, pressing as close to the wall as she could, looked out onto the hard-trodden earth of the street below.

The scene was steeped in disquieting shadows. She saw the hunched silhouettes of houses, the starker outline of a cart, shafts rearing skyward, by the side of the road. Overhead, bands of eerie, sullen colors shifted across the sky, turning like the spokes of a vast and spectral wheel. The silence was absolute.

Iselia began to shiver. She wanted to turn away, close the shutter, and creep back to her bed, where the blankets might hide her from the fear that she felt was eating her alive. But she couldn't move, couldn't make her limbs listen to the commands her mind tried to give them. Then a disembodied voice screamed shockingly from the dark, and suddenly the sky lit with a colossal white flash that for one instant bathed the street in livid and unholy brilliance. And she saw them. Black and silver in the night, moving with slow and terrible grace, they were entering the village from the northwest. The hooves of the demon beasts struck sparks from the flint road and their eyes gleamed red with greedy intelligence; under the malign shadows of their wings Iselia glimpsed the glitter of their riders' insignia, the metallic flash of weapons. The deep, subterranean pulse grew stronger until she felt it would shred the flesh from her bones: then suddenly it was no longer subliminal but physical, shattering the eerie silence, beating against her ears.

Lightning danced across the heavens again, and in the wild glare Iselia saw faces that were something beyond human; harsh bones, savage eyes, men transformed into creatures from a nightmare as their monstrous mounts halted. A dog howled dismally in the distance, cutting shockingly across the throbbing vibration, but no voice was raised to silence it. The Chaos riders were dismounting; cold gazes scanned the street. The dog's howling fell away into a void, and the pulsing went on and on.

A black-clad figure, little more than a silhouette in the darkness, walked slowly across the street. Below Iselia's window the rider halted and looked up. Feral eyes in a face made hideous by the intricacies of a metal mask focused on her and she gasped, spun away from the window with her heart pounding and bile rising in her throat. When she dared to look again, the rider was gone.

And a moment later, the house shook to the crashing, splintering sound of the door being kicked in.

She didn't scream or struggle when they took her out of the house. Desperately, mutely, she looked at her parents' haggard faces one last time, then for their sakes turned her back and allowed herself to be escorted to where the six others chosen from the village stood shivering and cowering under the silently flickering sky. The captives were all young, Iselia noticed with impotent bitterness; the flower of the village's youth. But Kaldar wasn't among them. That much, at least, she could take comfort from: her own life wasn't in immediate peril, but his would have been another matter.

There was a sudden scuffle among the group as a boy — Iselia recognized him as a neighbor's son, ten years old — tried to break away from the group and run back to his home. The Chaos riders reacted swiftly, efficiently and without a word spoken: one stepped into the running boy's path, clubbed him, then kicked him back into place with his head bleeding. Iselia looked away, sickened, and her hand went involuntarily to her breast and the topaz ring on its chain about her neck. She didn't dare so much as mouth Kaldar's name, let alone the furtive prayer to Aeoris that ran in silent litany through her mind, but she tried to hold to the memory of her husband's face, and of the promises they had made to each other such a short time ago.

The sorry little procession fell into line, and Iselia shut her eyes, preferring to risk a fall than to be forced to look at the black, unearthly creatures which were to carry her and her fellow victims away into the night. She knew that no one lucky enough to be left behind would dare to watch them go, and, trying to cling to sanity and the last traces of hope, prayed that she might be able to get a message from the Star Peninsula, to let her family — and thence Kaldar — know that she was alive.

Then following on the heels of that thought came another that struck cold dread into her and shattered the illusion of courage she'd been trying to maintain. A message to her parents? It might be possible . . . but only if, once she had made that nightmare crossing and faced the fate that lay before her, she *was* still alive.

She clamped her teeth hard on her tongue to stop a sudden violent, chattering quiver in her jaw, then stumbled forward as she was pushed with careless and indifferent efficiency toward the waiting demon beasts.

CHAPTER IV

Benetan was waiting with two sergeants under the towering black arch of the castle's gateway. His role was to supervise the harvest rather than to play any direct part in the gleaning; he had visited, though briefly, each of the seven villages from which tonight's candidates had been chosen, and now he had returned through the Maze ahead of his men to see that each small yield was brought safely in.

The night's mission had gone well. The skills of the magi had dispatched the Chaos riders on the howling back of the Warp to seven widely spaced districts, and the gleaning had been both simple and swift. Six of the raiding parties had now returned, thundering in a crackling blaze of energy through the Maze's spatial gateway, and though the captives had been terrified by the ordeal, there were no serious casualties. Benetan was glad: aside of the fact that a high number of candidates losing their minds on the journey incurred the magi's displeasure, he had no wish to inflict unnecessary torment on the innocent. In saner moments he admitted to himself that he was thankful for his rank, which no longer obliged him to tear children from parents, wives from husbands, brothers from sisters, with his own hands; but at this moment he was too bound up with his duty to feel anything beyond a mild satisfaction that all had gone according to plan.

The early mayhem of the narcotic administered by the magus had worn off and given way to the quieter but equally deadly calm of invincible authority. His mount, aware with its alien senses that the reaping was done, had modulated its form, seeming now to be nothing more than an abnormally large and abnormally black horse. Though Benetan's senses were still sharply augmented, the charge of drug-induced adrenaline was a memory, replaced by an odd sense of peace. He had removed the circlet and the mask that made his face unhuman and, with the Warp now vanished back into the unearthly realm from which it had come, he simply sat patiently and stared into the night, drinking in the silver gray moonlight and listening to the muted roar of the sea as it beat against the Peninsula cliffs.

Old memories had stirred in him tonight, creeping up through the strata of more recent years. He couldn't be entirely sure — it was so long ago, or seemed so, that he wasn't altogether inclined to trust the recollection — but he believed that one of the northern villages visited by the Chaos riders had been a part of his own home district. It meant nothing to him now, of course; twelve years in the service of the magi had changed his perspectives beyond recall. But long ago, on a night very like this, he had been dragged from his family's hearth to face the numbing terror of a future in the Castle of the Star Peninsula; a future that had yawned as black and unpredictable before his impressionable young mind as Chaos itself.

Benetan smiled absentmindedly and perhaps a little wistfully as he wondered how many among tonight's harvest would have the wit to make the best of their lot. Though they professed to look down on outsiders, the magi were pragmatic enough to acknowledge the fact that, with fewer and fewer children being born within the castle's shadow, they needed new blood if their community was to thrive. Of the harvest that was taken, those who overcame their terrors — and who had the strength — could prosper in the castle's service. As he had done. . . .

Someone cleared his throat, breaking Benetan's reverie, and one of the sergeants leaned across from his own mount to speak.

"I think they're coming, sir."

Benetan looked toward the rectangle of unnaturally bright green turf that marked the Maze. Shadows were shifting in the air above it; he felt the disturbance like a breath of wind on his face, and for a moment glimpsed the giddying vortex beyond. Silhouettes appeared in the vortex, wrenching back his sense of perspective, then with a silent flicker of vivid light the last raiding party arrived.

Benetan watched as the Chaos riders lifted their passengers down to solid ground, where they huddled uneasily together. Seven candidates, pale and helpless as lost ghosts in the night robes which they had had no time to change for more suitable clothes. Well and good; seven times seven would please the magi. Two boys, five women, none, from what he could discern in the darkness, past their middle twenties. The boys held their heads high with grim defiance; one sported smears of drying blood on his face and Benetan wondered detachedly what form his brief resistance had taken. Of the girls, three were dark and two fair, but whether they were comely or otherwise he couldn't yet judge. He could only trust that his men had interpreted their orders correctly and selected the best of what was available.

One of the sergeants spurred his mount forward to meet the returning reapers; low-pitched words were exchanged, then the captives were brought forward for Benetan's closer scrutiny. He stared down at the group — and something triggered in the back of his mind, an old memory, long overlooked —

His mount shifted, sensing his sudden disquiet. Its eyes glittered ferally and its form began to change: not wanting to alarm the captives, Benetan gripped the reins more tightly with his gauntleted hand and spoke to the creature in a peculiar, sibilant tone. It quieted, and as it settled, the object of his concern raised her head and looked him full in the face.

Twelve years fell away in the space of a moment, and Benetan hissed: *"Iselia?"*

For a few seconds she didn't recognize him. She saw only the Chaos riders' captain mounted on his hellish beast; a strong, lean, dark figure with long, sweat-damped hair clinging to his neck and shoulders and the Seven-Rayed Star emblazoned on his breast. An implacable servant of the magi, member of a feared elite, touched by the all-encompassing hand of the gods of Chaos. She was torn between a desire to plead with him and an urge to spit in his face; still undecided, she looked up, resolving at least to return his scrutiny boldly and without fear. But as their eyes met, the Chaos captain vanished and she saw instead the boy from the neighboring village, the lad of fifteen summers who had kissed her in the harvest field out of sight of their parents and peers; who, awkwardly and with callow hesitancy, had asked her to wait for him, wait until he was free of his indenture and could make a good enough living to keep them both.

"Benet Liss . . ." Her voice cracked on the second word, and she turned her head aside with a violent movement. "Oh, gods!"

Benetan made to reach toward her, then realized that the sergeants were watching, avidly curious. He couldn't afford to show any partiality. He had to fight the shock, pull his stunned mind back together and quash the torrent of feelings that this specter from his past had so dramatically awakened.

He tore his gaze abruptly away from Iselia's face and cautiously urged his mount to step back a pace. *Breathe, you fool,* he told himself. *Keep your voice level.* "A good enough gathering, Sergeant." He maneuvered the Chaos creature about, obliquely seeing Iselia's head come up again and thankful to set his back to her.

"Thank you, sir." The man eyed him with what might have been a hint of suspicion; Benetan swallowed against the pounding of his own heart, then — it had to be done, there was nothing else for it — turned again to address the riders.

"You've worked speedily tonight, and you've earned your rest." Though he tried to avoid it, he could feel her gaze on him, taut, venomous. "Take them through the gates, then consider yourselves dismissed with my commendation."

Iselia's face was a white oval in the dimness, her eyes huge, dark hollows. But she said nothing when he passed, and Benetan forced his lungs to expel pent air as the silent captives finally moved away under the black arch of the castle gates. The riders fell in behind them, and Benetan and his sergeants followed last of all. The sound of the gates closing made him shudder, and when a nervous groom came forward to take charge of his mount and return it whence it had come, he slid from its back and stood numbly in the courtyard, unable — unwilling? — to think clearly. His body ached and the muscles in his legs were numb: he wasn't sure that they would support him if he tried to walk across the courtyard.

"Captain Liss?" Benetan started, and turned to find one of the sergeants standing beside him. The man looked weary and his eyes were bloodshot, the pupils still dilated from the narcotic. He nodded toward the captives now being escorted toward a door that would take them into the castle's main wing. "The girl there; the one with the fair hair." He glanced sidelong at Benetan, his curiosity now undisguised. "She seemed to recognize you, I thought."

Benetan's heart was pumping painfully, but he forced a careless note into his voice. "Yes," he replied. "I think she did."

The sergeant wouldn't dare press the matter, but talk was cheap in the Chaos riders' quarters. Trying to recover from his shock, Benetan reminded himself that the truth could hardly harm him. He made his mouth form a smile. "It was a long time ago, Sergeant, but I believe we might have been neighbors once."

The sergeant chuckled with a hint of lasciviousness. "*Just* neighbors, sir?"

Benetan's expression masked a squirming toad of discomfiture in his gut. "We were a little young for much else."

"All the same, sir, it might be — interesting — to renew an old acquaintance, eh?" The sergeant grinned broadly. "Pardon me, but I saw the way you looked at her back there, Captain. And we're all human, whatever these ignorant commoners might think."

On the verge of delivering a reprimand to the man for his presumption, Benetan paused. It would be a chance — maybe his only chance — to speak to her, to try to explain. *Explain what?* an inner voice asked. He didn't know; she must surely understand that he didn't dare jeopardize himself by releasing her. But something inside him had made him hate himself in the moment when he looked into her eyes, and he had at least to try to earn some measure of redemption.

He forced himself to laugh, reach out, and punch the sergeant's shoulder, man to man. "Yes, Sergeant, I think it might be interesting, as you put it, to renew an old acquaintance. I imagine that I can trust to your discretion?"

The sergeant's grin broadened. "Depend on it, Captain!"

It wasn't the way he had anticipated, the way his racing imagination had told him it would be, when they brought Iselia to him in his room. She had been given no fresh clothing — the sergeant had clearly assumed she'd have no need of it — and the two Chaos riders who escorted her simply pushed her unceremoniously into the room and departed with foolish smirks on their faces, shutting the door behind them.

He had rehearsed what he would say to her, but as they faced one another in the lamplight the words in his mind suddenly crumbled. She stood before him in a flimsy nightgown stained with dirt and sodden at the hem, her shoulder-length hair uncombed, her bare feet scratched and filthy. Her face was deadly pale, expressionless; only her eyes held any animation, and in them Benetan saw both fear and contempt. Iselia was afraid; but her fear was contained within the bounds of a quiet dignity that shamed him.

Abruptly, he turned toward the bed and picked up his own night robe, holding it out to her. "I'm sorry." His voice suddenly and uncomfortably recalled the callow youth he had been when they had parted so many years ago. "They should have given you new clothes. Please, take this."

She looked at the robe; at the fine fabric, the embroidered trim. "Thank you." Her voice was remote. "I'm well enough as I am."

"Iselia — " He started toward her, thought better of it, and instead slumped onto his bed. "Gods help me, won't you just sit down? I only want to talk to you, explain — "

"Explain?" She still didn't move.

"Why I didn't — why I *couldn't* let you go! Iselia, please. . . ."

She did move now, but not toward him. Her night shift made a rough sound in the claustrophobic gloom as she took a pace toward the fire that he had ordered to be relit in the grate. "A Chaos rider," she said softly, bitterly. "I wouldn't have thought it, Benet. I wouldn't have thought it was *possible."* She turned her head, her eyes gleaming through the curtain of her hair. "But then it's been so long since you left. I've lost count of the years."

"Twelve," he said quietly. "Twelve years."

"Twelve, is it? Well, I can hardly expect to know you after all this time, can I? I can hardly expect you to be the same Benetan Liss who left his home for . . . *this* place."

Anger rose in Benetan. "I was *taken*. I had no choice in the matter!"

"As I have no choice now."

"Iselia, I couldn't stop it! I'm captain of the Chaos riders; I have a duty to perform that I can't shirk." He saw disbelief in her eyes, and added unhappily, "I *daren't* shirk it. Not if I value my life. You don't understand."

She held her hands out toward the fire, warming them. Light glowed on her face and made a golden halo of her hair. "I understand that you've prospered, Benet. I understand that you're willing to forget everyone you knew and everything you believed in, and become one of the very same warriors you used to detest!"

"Can you blame me for that? What would you have had me do — fight them tooth and nail, and end up as carrion or worse?"

Iselia shrugged. "I don't know. Which *is* worse? Death, or betrayal of everything you once thought was honorable?" She blinked, then added with sudden venom: "At least death is clean!"

"The kind of death that the magi give to those who resist them is anything *but* clean!" Benetan fired the words at her, made a violent movement to rise, then slouched back again and shook his head helplessly. "No, I can't expect you to understand that. You've never been faced with that choice. You've never seen what happens to those who won't give in to the inevitable."

"As you gave in?"

He nodded. "As I gave in. To survive."

There was a long pause. Then she said in a small voice: "You always did like warrior games, didn't you? I remember when we were children, you, and Piad, and Lirri, and — and Kaldar." She swallowed. "You used to have mock battles with sticks for swords, and you were always the leader, and — and — " Her voice broke in a sob.

Benetan was on his feet and at her side in two paces, but every angle of her body, every taut muscle, was a warning to him not to touch her. "Iselia, please don't!" he said helplessly.

She turned away from him, covering her face with both hands. Tears glittered between her latticed fingers and she cried quietly, bitterly. This time when he tried to put his robe around her shoulders she didn't spurn it, but she would unbend no further and he drew back and sat cross-legged on the floor, staring miserably into the fire until at last her weeping subsided and she sniffed.

"Iselia — " He leaned forward.

"*Stop it!*" She shrank away, though he wasn't close enough to touch her. "Don't keep repeating my name; I don't want to hear it from your lips. And don't start saying *please* again. It's meaningless, it rings hollow." She looked up, and the look in her eyes shocked him. "I'm all right. Just leave me alone."

He said in dismay: "Do you hate me that much?"

Her face was blotched but still, to him, beautiful. Calm was returning in the wake of the bout of weeping; tension and fear had found an outlet and now she felt more in control of herself.

"I hate what you've become," she said coldly. "You're not the same person who went away twelve years ago."

"How *could* I be the same person? You don't realize, you don't understand anything! Yandros, I—"

"Don't say that name to me!" Her voice went up, shrill with fury, cutting his words off. Her rib cage heaved sharply, convulsively; then she got quickly to her feet and moved away from him toward the window. When she spoke again, her voice was disturbingly controlled.

"I'm sorry. I didn't mean to shout at you." She drew another deep breath. "What's going to happen? Now that I'm here, what will your masters do with me?"

She was trying to draw back from the brink of a full-blooded quarrel; not, Benetan believed, because she didn't feel combative toward him but because she had realized that it would do her little good. He stared at the floor, wishing she could have found any other topic to divert them both. "It depends," he said.

"On what?"

"Firstly, on the magi." A pause. "Do you know why we were sent out tonight?"

"Your men didn't trouble to tell us when they dragged us out of our beds. But my . . . someone said that the First Magus was dying."

Benetan refused to take the vitriol-laced bait. "He is dead," he told her. "By now they'll have named his successor. There'll be an inauguration, certain ceremonies." His mouth was arid. "It's an old tradition, that they—"

"Bring new blood to the castle, to be used in those ceremonies. Yes, I know; I learned my catechisms." Iselia started to hug herself, then forced her arms to drop back to her sides, determined not to display the smallest sign of weakness. "It's supposed to be an honor, isn't it? That's what we've always been taught. To be *chosen*. Given the chance to lift ourselves above the midden of our lives and become something better than peasants." Her lip curled. "And, of course, if that means we must also spend our lives in daily terror of the Chaos riders, and of being snatched forcibly from our homes and our families in a random sweep, with no right of appeal, what does that matter? We're simply too ignorant to appreciate our good fortune!"

"Many do see it as good fortune," Benetan said defensively. "There's no shortage of postulants seeking advancement here."

"Is that how it was for you?"

He looked up, angry and unhappy together. "Not when I was brought to the castle. I didn't come willingly, you know that — and you know why."

"Don't try to pretend you were unwilling because of me! In those days you were as terrified as any of us of the riders!"

That was true, though he wished with all his heart that she hadn't remembered it. "All right," he said, "I won't try to deny that. I *was* ignorant then. But things change. You grow up. You learn." He hesitated. "When I came here, I was given a simple choice: to learn to become one of the elite that my friends and family feared so much, or to spend the rest of my life as a slave. Faced with that option, I found myself looking at the Chaos riders in a different light."

Iselia's eyes became contemptuous. "A very convenient change of heart."

"Maybe it was." Benetan's voice grew sharp suddenly. "But in my place, would your decision have been any different? Would you have had the courage to sacrifice your future — perhaps even your life? Because that was the decision I had to make! And, I might add, a decision you will have to make shortly."

She didn't reply but only continued to stare at him, and suddenly the contempt in her look goaded him to real anger.

"Who are you to condemn what I've done, Iselia?" he demanded. "You know nothing about the castle, nothing about the magi and those who serve them! Maybe you'll learn — maybe in a little while you'll be *forced* to learn, as I was — but until you do, you've no right to sit in judgment on me!"

Still she said nothing, still her expression didn't change, and he went on hotly, "What could I have looked forward to in my home village that would have been so much better than the life I have now? As a boy I had the choice between laboring on a farm and laboring in the ore mines. I chose farmwork, because though it paid a miserable pittance it would at least allow me to keep my health and strength beyond the age of thirty! Oh, assuming, of course, that I didn't fall foul of our overlord in the meantime. When we were children we were in fief to one of the harshest masters in the district — or have you forgotten Overlord Jestre, and his taxes, and his tithes, and his petty spites? Do you remember the boy who was publicly flogged in our village for simply looking at him in an 'impudent' way? And when one of Jestre's own nephews arranged a convenient hunting accident for him and took over the demesne, I seem to recall little improvement in our lives! But when I came to the castle, things were very different. I was barely educated; I could hardly hope to earn enough money to keep body and soul together, let alone improve my lot, or break out of serfdom by buying land of my own. But at the castle it suddenly didn't matter who my clan were, or whether they had money or not, or whether they could find me an influential patron! *Merit* is what matters here, merit and ability! I *proved* my merit and I was rewarded for it; I've been allowed to rise and prosper in a way that would have been *impossible* at home. I have responsibility, I have respect, and I've earned them both. The magi may be harsh masters, but by all the seven gods at least they're *fair!*"

Iselia said something under her breath. The word was so soft that Benetan's ears couldn't catch it, but he suspected it was a filthy oath.

"Oh, yes," she added more loudly. "I'm beginning to understand, Benet. I'm beginning to understand just how deeply these grand and splendid masters of yours have corrupted your conscience! But, then, what does mere conscience matter? You've done very well for yourself. It must be well worth the price you were willing to pay!"

Benetan flared up. In truth, his attempt at self-justification had sent a worm of disgust writhing through him, and his horror of admitting it, combined with the accompanying stab of guilt, broke the shackles on both his temper and his tongue.

"You can be as noble and ethical as you please, Iselia, and I don't doubt you're enjoying your high moral ground!" he said savagely. "But you might find your own conscience priced more cheaply when your time comes to choose between obedience to the magi and becoming a demon's plaything!"

Silence hung like a physical wall between them. Iselia's face had frozen, her body was rigid, and Benetan realized that his words had gone home with a vengeance. *Yandros*, he thought, *what have I said? I didn't mean it to come out that way; I didn't want to phrase it so brutally —*

"Iselia — I'm sorry, I didn't mean to — "

"No." She was shaking and couldn't seem to make herself stop. "No, Benet. Don't apologize. Not if what you said is the truth." Her mouth worked in a peculiar spasm. "Is it the truth?"

He couldn't answer but his face betrayed him. She nodded.

"Tell me about it. Tell me what choice I'll have and what I must expect."

He looked away from her. "What would be the point? It can't achieve anything."

"Please, Benet." Suddenly her shoulders sagged. "You were right to say what you did and make me face it. I don't want to die, any more than you wanted to twelve years ago. At least tell me how I can best protect myself from that."

The admission, and its implied apology, had cost her dearly, Benetan knew; and his resistance crumbled. He didn't want to quarrel with her. And for what little it might be worth, he wanted to help her if he could.

"All right," he said. "The candidates, they . . . well, most of them will take part in the rites, willing or not. The early ceremonies aren't so daunting, but once the Chaos Gate is opened . . ." The sentence trailed off; he shrugged, then shivered involuntarily. "Sometimes one or more of the gods chooses to attend in person. I was lucky; they sent only lower emissaries to the rite for which I was brought here. But at the inauguration of a First Magus it could well be different." Suddenly his eyes hardened. "How strong are you, Iselia? Ultimately, you see, that's all that matters. Your strength. Your ability to look on the face of Chaos and stay sane." He shivered again, a racking shudder. "That's how you'll be judged. That's how we're *all* judged here."

Iselia stared hard at him, as though seeing him from a new and unexpected perspective. Quietly, she asked, "Then you've seen it? The face of Chaos?"

"As I said, I was lucky."

"And the unlucky ones?"

"You don't want to know that."

"Yes, I do. Tell me."

Benetan sighed heavily. "Those whose minds simply break stay here as servants, put to the simplest and most menial tasks," he told her. "They're fed and clothed, but they have no life that's worth the living. Some others die. Shock, fear — there are always a few. After a time you get inured to that, and expect it. The rest . . . well, insanity is a risk that even the strongest run when confronted with Chaos incarnate. And those who are beyond help share the same fate as the ones who refuse to yield."

"Which is . . .?"

Benetan gave another shrug, trying to pretend carelessness. "There's only one destination for them. They might reach it by any of several ways — the magi conduct a lot of experiments — but it all ends at the same place. The realm of the lower demons. They're always ready to welcome a new soul to play with. Do I need to say any more?"

"No," Iselia replied softly. "I don't think you do." She clasped her hands together, stared at them. "And at the rite — if I'm to be one of the . . . lucky ones. What will I have to do?"

Benetan's expression, already strained, became grave. "Whatever you're told to do, without question and without flinching," he said flatly. "It's as simple, and as demanding, as that."

For some time there was silence but for the fire's faint, sluggish hissing. The courtyard beyond the window was pitch dark now, the sky quiet. Lights burned dimly in one or two high windows; otherwise the castle seemed utterly lifeless.

At last Iselia moved away from the window, returning to the lamplight. She looked ethereal, unreal. *A ghost*, Benetan thought, watching her. A phantom from a life he had abandoned too long ago to have any hope of recapturing. And for the first time in many years he bitterly, bitterly regretted it.

He said: "I wish I could persuade you not to hate me, Iselia."

"Hate?" She seemed surprised; then she looked away, shaking her head. "No, Benet. I hate the Chaos riders; I hate what they've done to me, and I hate the fact that you've become one of them. But I don't hate *you*." She made a brave effort to smile, but it didn't convince either of them. "I tried to say it earlier, but you didn't understand. Perhaps I was too angry then."

"Are you still angry now?"

"Yes. But not with you. Not anymore."

"Then might you not learn to do as I did? Put the past behind you, and — "

"No." Her voice was quiet but implacable. "I can never do that."

"Iselia, your family and friends are lost to you, as are mine. You can't go back. Accept it. And perhaps in time I can help you to — "

"No," she said again. Her face was tense and she seemed to be inwardly debating with herself, struggling with some unspoken dilemma. After a few moments she met his gaze once more.

"Benetan."

He noted the use of his full name and felt suddenly uneasy.

"Benetan, I may be about to make a terrible mistake. But I don't think so. I think I can trust you."

Feelings that he barely comprehended moved in Benetan like a tide. "You can. I'll do anything within my power to help you, Iselia. I swear it; I swear it by the seven gods!"

Her doubts fell away. Anathema though it might be to her, she knew that Benetan wouldn't make such an oath lightly. Even as a boy he had been faithful to the lords of Chaos, and she was wise enough to realize that now, as one of their own elite, his loyalties must run deeper still. It was a strange and piquant irony, but she *could* trust him.

"Yes," she said soberly. "Yes, I believe you. And because of that belief, I have something to ask of you."

"Ask it."

She reached to her throat. "There is a reason why I can never fully accept my fate as you've done. I may have no choice but to bow to the inevitable, but in my heart I won't ever accept it." She hesitated. "Benet, I want to entrust something to your care."

A tiny sound, the faint snapping of metal, intruded on the quiet, and a broken brass chain fell to the floor at Iselia's feet. She held out a hand to him, palm upward.

"Keep this for me. Keep it safe until I can claim it again."

He looked at her hand and saw the warm, tawny glint of the topaz stones in their setting. And something within him, a hope hardly formed, a dream that as yet had no structure, crumbled.

It was a marriage ring.

He couldn't speak. His eyes met hers, haunted by questions that he couldn't formulate, and she said:

"I took my vows only hours before your men reached the village. Perhaps now you'll understand why I feel as I do."

For Benetan it was as though the stones of the castle were moving under his feet, threatening to open beneath him. *"Who?"* His voice was unrecognizable to his own ears.

She shook her head. "It doesn't matter."

But it did. "Who?" he asked again. "Iselia — "

"No." This time the refusal was more vehement. "I won't tell you. I — can't. I simply ask you, for the sake of our old friendship, to do this one thing for me."

Hardly aware of what he was doing, he reached out and took the ring from her hand. It felt cold and alien as his fist clenched over it.

Iselia cast her gaze down. "Thank you."

There was nothing more to be said, nothing that had any meaning. She wanted to leave, and Benetan felt too dispirited to dissuade her. The servants who came at his summons to take her to the candidates' quarters might think what they pleased; they wouldn't arrive at anything close to the truth. And when she had been taken away, when the door had closed behind her and the room was suddenly silent and empty, Benetan sank down on his bed with a bewildering sense of loss in his heart.

He still held her ring; slowly, his fist uncurled and he laid the little jewel down on his table, aware of its imprint even on the weapon-hardened flesh of his palm. Iselia. Stepping out of the forgotten past, from a life he had put behind him so many years ago. Iselia, whom he had loved. Iselia, wed but refusing to divulge the identity of her — he balked at using the word, but forced it into his mind — her husband. Asking him to keep her secret, for the sake of their onetime friendship. But it had been far more than friendship, at least for him.

Iselia. Another man's wife. Snatched from her own wedding feast, maybe even from her marriage bed, and brought to the castle as a prisoner to await the pleasure of the magi and the gods. He'd tried to convince himself that it would have been impossible to let her go, that to do so would have imperiled his own position, but the arguments rang hollow. The thing could have been done; in his position he could have done it, if he had been determined enough. It would have been easy to invent a reason for rejecting her as unsuitable or unfit. The magi's only demand was that seven times seven candidates should be produced for their ceremonies; who they were or how they were chosen was of no concern to them. With one command Benetan could have had Iselia sent back to her village and another taken in her place; it had happened before and his sergeants wouldn't have dreamed to question the order. To pretend that he had had no choice but to bring Iselia to the castle was a pitiful exercise in self-deception.

The stark truth was that, from motives which he didn't care to dredge from his subconscious mind, he had let her be taken. He had betrayed her, unwittingly perhaps, but it was a betrayal nonetheless. Now it was far too late to change matters. And a part of him, a small but painfully honest part, was glad of it.

Benetan rolled over, stretching at full length on the bed and desultorily pulling the cover over his body. He was miserably tired but doubted if he could sleep. And, bleakly, he forced himself to acknowledge the fact that at this moment he didn't know whom he hated the more. The man who had won Iselia Darrow, whoever he might be.

Or himself.

CHAPTER V

Throwing stones at seagulls was a futile pastime, but on this dank, dreary morning it held as much appeal for Benetan as any other activity. He had been abroad since dawn, prowling the castle while it was still deserted but for a few servants, refusing breakfast, tempted instead to get drunk but realizing before he touched a first cup that even that form of solace had nothing to offer him. He'd thought of going to Andraia's room and trying to make peace, but that hadn't appealed either. This latest quarrel would be forgotten eventually, as their quarrels always were, but at the moment Benetan didn't want to think about Andraia, for she added an extra and undesirable complication. At last, for want of anything else to occupy his restless mind and body, he had shrugged on his oldest hide coat, knotted a jet rope into his hair to keep the long strands back, and made his way through the cellars to a narrow and very ancient stairway that spiraled down into the bowels of the huge granite stack on which the castle was built. These stairs, slippery with lichen, and lit only by a peculiar, innate phosphorescence in the rock walls, led to a cave that opened onto a sullen crescent of shingle beach at the stack's foot.

Benetan had often wondered why anyone should have taken the trouble to create a path to such a barren and worthless destination, for the beach led nowhere, and no boat's crew in their right minds would ever attempt a landing. In kinder seasons, he knew, some of his own men occasionally swam there when they couldn't get leave to visit the warmer coasts to the southwest; but for most of the year the beach was the unchallenged domain of the gulls.

The tide was out and turning when he finally reached the foot of the stairs and emerged from the cave mouth. A strong northwesterly wind was blowing, carrying the mingled smells of brine and stranded wrack. The sky crouched, lowering, on a claustrophobically close horizon, rags of black cloud running like blown smoke under the denser gray pall; the heavy thump of waves and the drag of shingle in the undertow made a hypnotic counterpoint to the wind's gusting voice. And the gulls were everywhere, wheeling, dipping, shrieking.

Benetan sat on a sheltered rocky outcrop, feeling the spindrift soak his clothes and hair, tasting the wind and trying to let its coldness cleanse the taint that he felt was on him. When the gulls' raucous cries grew intrusive he picked up pebbles from the debris at his feet and hurled them at the flapping gray bundles of feathers: his aim was good but the birds were faster, and after a while he contented himself with skimming flatter pieces of shale over the sea's surface, watching them bounce and sink beneath the heaving tide. Anything, *anything* to keep all but the most peripheral thoughts at bay.

He didn't know how long he had been sitting in that one place before the first sound of a foot sliding on shingle alerted him to the fact that he was no longer alone. Deprived of sleep, he had slipped into a reverie that had almost begun to merge into the first images of a dream, when the noise made him start reflexively and he turned to look back at the cave mouth.

A slight figure swathed in a heavy fur cloak stood at the top of the beach. For a moment neither of them moved; then the newcomer visibly relaxed, and picked his way across the sloping shingle to Benetan's vantage point. The wind whipped his unbound hair and tore at the cloak, almost pulling him off his feet; then he reached the lee of the cliff and the northwester lost its hold, allowing him to sit down beside Benetan with his dignity relatively unimpaired.

"Good day, my friend," said Savrinor. "I must say that, short of Vordegh himself, you're the person I'd have thought myself least likely to meet in this forsaken spot this morning."

Benetan eyed the historian, uncertain whether he welcomed or resented the intrusion on his privacy. Savrinor's face was abnormally pale, he noticed; and there was a foxiness to his look, an indefinable impression that every feature, every nuance, was faintly exaggerated.

Suspecting he knew the cause of the subtle change, Benetan allowed himself to smile reservedly.

"I might say the same to you, Savrinor. You've never been famed for your love of fresh air."

"True. But there are times when even the most dedicated sybarite is driven to seek a respite from life's entertainments." Savrinor turned to squint up at the monstrous cliff towering sheer above them. "Some of the younger bloods believe it improves their mettle to climb this face on the outside. Were you aware of that?"

Benetan wondered if the casual question masked a rebuke. He never felt entirely easy in Savrinor's company, for he was always aware of the anomaly in his own apparently congenial relationship with a man who ranked so far above him. Savrinor, doubtless for his own convoluted reasons, chose to disregard such protocols, but now and again a chance remark reminded Benetan sharply of their underlying presence.

He shrugged. "They've had fair warning of the danger."

"Mmm. And largely disregard it, I gather. Did you know there are rival cliques growing? Those who dare, versus those who don't?" His light blue eyes suddenly became shrewd. "I hope you've cast your lot with the wiser faction, Benetan. We'd hate to lose you."

Hints, oblique references, veiled allusions. Savrinor was playing games again. And his manner, the jerky movement of his hand as he brushed a strand of hair from his face, the dilated pupils, told Benetan that he had little hope of penetrating this particular maze.

He turned away, staring out across the angry sea. "Come to the point, Savrinor. I'm too tired to follow your labyrinthine reasoning this morning."

"Ah." Savrinor hunched his shoulders, the heavy black cloak giving him the air of some bizarre bird of ill omen. "Then I'm not the only one who had a sleepless night."

Benetan glanced quickly back over his shoulder. The historian wasn't looking at him but had leaned back against the rock, eyes narrowed to lazy slits. "I saw you return with your little flock of lambs for the slaughter," he added, "and I saw the light still burning in your window a good few hours later." A sly smile. "I must admit I was tempted to seek out your company, for I imagined that your mood must be similar to my own. But in the light of this morning's rumors, perhaps it's as well I didn't."

"Rumors?" Benetan was suddenly suspicious.

Savrinor laughed softly but not altogether humorously, the sound almost inaudible against the bluster of the wind. "Tittle-tattle is no respecter of rank, and your sergeant has a lively tongue." Suddenly his gaze flickered, gimlet sharp, to Benetan's face. "Though I must admit you surprise me, Benetan. To take such a personal interest in one of our new candidates seems a little out of character."

Benetan felt blood rise to his cheeks and a cold film of perspiration break out over his torso, clammily unpleasant beneath damp clothing. When he spoke, his voice was sharp.

"What's it to you?"

"It's nothing to me. What you do in your off-duty hours is entirely your own affair. However . . ." Savrinor picked up a smooth pebble and weighed it in his hand. "You and Andraia have been bonded to a quite tedious degree, albeit on and off, for — what, two years now? I find it hard to believe that there can be many successful rivals for Andraia's charms, so a glimmer of a suspicion tells me that there's something more behind your departure from custom than meets the eye. Something that troubles you enough to have driven you to this hellhole to seek solitude. As a similar — unease, shall we say — has brought me." Now there was an open challenge in his look. "If I'm right, your preoccupations *do* become my concern."

Benetan drew breath to deny it, then paused. He knew precisely how far he could trust Savrinor, and within those bounds the historian was more reliable than anyone else he knew. He had nothing to lose by revealing last night's events; but there was more to his reluctance than innate caution. Questions, emotions, the stirrings of an unquiet conscience . . . Even if Savrinor, who seemingly didn't possess a conscience, could have understood the feelings within him, he doubted if he could find the words to explain.

He hunched forward, resting elbows on knees. "Savrinor, have you any idea of how deeply the ordinary people hate us?"

If Savrinor was surprised by the change of tack, he didn't show it. "Us?" he queried gently.

"The Chaos riders." It wasn't what he wanted to say, but he

couldn't bring himself to approach the subject directly.

"Ah," said Savrinor.

"To the farmers, the drovers, the artisans, even to many of the merchants and nobles, we're devils. No, worse than devils; we're serpents, monstrosities, something subhuman that has no business to exist in a decent world." He looked up. "Have you any idea of how it feels to be loathed by almost everyone you meet outside the walls of this castle?"

"No, I haven't, because I have no particular wish to travel outside the walls of this castle." Savrinor steepled his fingers together and stared at them. "Should I infer from this that you had a troublesome harvest last night?"

Benetan shook his head with a sigh. "Not in the sense you mean. They didn't fight; they never do. I sometimes wish they would, rather than simply giving in and hating us."

"They give in because they have no choice," Savrinor reminded him. "You know that better than I do. You shared their predicament once, and doubtless you reacted in much the same way."

Iselia's bitter accusation came back. "Thank you," Benetan said sourly, "but I'd prefer not to be reminded of that at present."

"Whether you prefer it or whether you don't, it's the truth." Savrinor tossed the pebble away; it fell with a dull crunch into the shingle. "Very few of us actively enjoy the more distasteful aspects of our duties, Benetan; and although it may surprise you, I include myself in that sweeping generalization." His expression by now was quite unreadable, but there was an odd edge to his voice that Benetan found disquieting. "Like the flocks you shepherd through the Maze, we're not such fools as to rail openly against what we must do. But unlike them, we have the experience — or should have — to shrug our shoulders, make the most of what we have and what we are, and look to a kindlier time ahead." Suddenly he stood up, startling Benetan, and paced away toward the sea's edge. "Which, from the vantage point of this glad morning, seems extremely unlikely to materialize in the foreseeable future."

Abruptly it all slipped into place. Savrinor's peculiar mood, his unwarranted presence on the beach, the admission that he hadn't slept . . . Amid his more personal preoccupations, Benetan had forgotten about the First Magus.

He asked: "It was as you said? As you forewarned me?"

"Exactly as I forewarned you. Sometimes my powers of prediction astonish even me!" The last words were tinged with venom, and Savrinor picked up a new stone and hurled it viciously at an incoming wave. "All hail to Vordegh, First Magus, and overlord of our lives!" Another stone hurtled into the sea.

Uneasily, Benetan got to his feet. "What happened?"

The historian turned to look at him. Above the dark folds of his cloak he looked quite ill. "Nothing happened; nothing of any obvious significance. The old First Magus died, and an emissary came to take his soul. Vordegh was tested, and, as anyone might have anticipated, passed."

"And the ceremony?" Something was wrong, Benetan knew; but Savrinor seemed unwilling or unable to admit to it.

"What about the ceremony?" The historian's voice was muffled. "Did it go well?"

"It was unspectacular." Savrinor paused. A wave advanced over the shingle with sudden vigor and he took a fastidious step back. "*Too* unspectacular."

"I don't understand you."

The cold, pale eyes met his, and Savrinor sighed. "No, my friend, I don't suppose you do." He came slowly back to the cliff, pebbles crunching beneath his feet. "And I don't think I could explain, even if I thought it wise to do so." He blinked rapidly as though to clear his mind, then wiped his mouth with the back of one hand. "It seems that I've indulged myself to the detriment of prudence. That which stimulates certain areas of the senses also has the unfortunate effect of loosening the tongue at inopportune moments." His gaze hardened. "I'd strongly advise you to forget that this discussion ever took place. For both our sakes."

Benetan wasn't to be satisfied with that. "But — " he began.

"But nothing. Forget it, Benetan. Especially once you're back within the castle walls, for in the days to come I suspect that walls will have ears." He made to pull the cloak collar more closely around his throat, changed his mind when he found the fur was soaked with spray, and stared speculatively at the restless sea. "I seem to be a treasure store of good advice this morning, so I'll offer you just one more trinket from my coffers, and it's this: if you have any care for the girl you were with last night, do what you can to secure her position before the inauguration. After that, it might be too late."

Benetan stared at him in silence. After a few moments Savrinor glanced at the sky.

"I smell rain. And this damned beach bores me." He turned, started to walk across the shingle toward the cave mouth, then stopped and looked back. "Are you coming?"

Still Benetan couldn't speak. Savrinor's warning had accorded so closely with his own barely formed fears that words were beyond him. Suddenly he didn't want to stay here with only the sea and the dismal sky and the uncaring rocks for company.

They didn't make any attempt at conversation as they began to climb the stairway. Savrinor, though his lack of physical stamina made the climb hard, seemed less encumbered by the darkness than his companion; Benetan almost lost his footing several times and couldn't shake off an irrational urge to keep looking back, half convinced that something more solid than shadows prowled in their wake. At last — he judged that they must be halfway to the top, though it was impossible to be sure — he had to break the silence.

"Savrinor — "

The historian stopped. "What is it?"

Benetan drew breath between clenched teeth. "I do care for her. But I don't know how I can help her."

"Ah." Savrinor turned round, and sat down on a stair. "At last we come to the root of it. Who is she? Someone from your past?"

"Yes."

"Her name?"

"Iselia Darrow." Benetan smiled wryly. "We were betrothed, after a fashion, when I was fifteen and she twelve. I'd all but forgotten her these last few years, but — "

"Suddenly she was there among your candidates. Yes, I quite see how that must have disquieted you." Savrinor studied a fingernail. "Why didn't you simply send her back and take another in her place?"

"I — " But the explanation died on Benetan's tongue as he realized that it was both glib and dishonest. He shook his head, and Savrinor grinned humorlessly.

"So the plausible excuse you've been working on since last night doesn't convince you any more than it does me. All right: the simple fact is that you didn't release her, and now it's too late to reverse your decision."

"I thought about reversing it," Benetan said.

"Then thank our lord Yandros that you had the wisdom not to act on that thought. It would have been the deed of a self-destructive fool. Besides, you don't *want* her to leave, do you?"

The younger man scowled. "Damn you, Savrinor, it isn't like that!"

"Oho, it — "

"*No!*" His shout echoed in the confined space, and the sound sent a chilly shiver along his own spine. He drew breath. "It can't be; not anymore. I can't tell you why."

"I think you can, and must," Savrinor countered. "After all, you have my momentary lapse on the beach as a safeguard against any indiscretion you might commit." In the dimness his eyes gleamed. "The even slate, Benetan."

The even slate . . . Slowly, Benetan reached into an inner pocket of his shirt. He had carried Iselia's ring with him rather than risk leaving it in his room, and now, wordlessly, he held it out to Savrinor.

"Pretty." Savrinor took the ring between finger and thumb, and peered at it. "Cheap; but it has a certain charm." His fist closed briefly over the little jewel, then he tossed it back to Benetan. "So she's wed to someone else. Who's the favored man?"

"She refused to tell me."

"Mmm." Speculation crept into Savrinor's eyes, then he masked it. "Doubtless she has her reasons. But it's not something the magi would look on kindly, were they to discover her little secret. You know how highly virginity is prized by certain of the Chaos beings who attend our major rites."

Benetan looked away, angry. "Don't say such things, Savrinor!"

"Would you prefer a comfortable lie to soothe your finer feelings? She's young and ripe; if she's pretty into the bargain, then unless she has some especial talent that's useful to our masters, we both know what her role at the inaugural ceremony will be." A pause. "*Does* she have any such talent?"

Benetan shook his head. "I don't know. She had some education; she can read and write. . . ."

"As can the vast majority of people in the castle; even you, if I remember rightly. That's of little use. Isn't there anything else that sets her apart from the average peasant?"

Benetan flinched inwardly at Savrinor's disdainful choice of words but bit back an angry urge to jump to Iselia's defense. "No," he said miserably. "Not that I know of."

Savrinor considered this for a few moments. He recalled the molten-winged demon with its reptilian head, the emissary that had conducted the old First Magus's soul to Chaos. The image of a human woman prey to the lusts of such a creature didn't overly trouble him, but he could see that for Benetan — not to mention the girl herself— it would be another matter. And if one of Chaos's favored demons found itself cheated by the fact that the girl was not virgin, someone would suffer. Iselia Darrow's future did not, at this moment, look anything but bleak.

Not wanting to reveal his thoughts as yet, he said, "You'll not be required to attend the rite, of course."

"No."

"But, as one of the choice fruits of your gleaning, the girl will; that is, unless a very plausible reason can be found for excusing her. I hardly think you'll be able to invent one at this late stage."

"I know. But I've got to *try*, Savrinor! If she — "

"Wait; hear me out. You're not in a position to protect her, your rank doesn't carry sufficient weight. But *I* may be able to help."

The atmosphere was suddenly charged. "You?" Benetan said.

"Yes. There'll be a price, of course." Savrinor smiled, vulpine. "You know me well enough to realize that my services are never given charitably."

"Of course I know that." Benetan met his gaze. "And I also know that when you give your word, it can be relied on."

"A very foolish assumption. Nonetheless, I'll apply my mind to the problem." Savrinor stood up, flexing a cramped leg. "There's no more to be said for the time being, Benetan. I'll take a look at the girl — unofficially, of course — and see what can be done." He glanced at the stairs spiraling on ahead of them. "Gods, this is a tedious climb. Best to get it over with, I suppose."

"Savrinor — "

The historian looked at him. Benetan swallowed. "What can I do?"

"Pray to Yandros." The hard contours of Savrinor's face softened momentarily. "It's sound advice, my friend. You might be surprised by the interest our gods take in the petty deeds of mortals." He took a step upward, gazing again at the dark vortex of the stairwell above his head. "Especially when those deeds might have some bearing on their own affairs."

They continued to climb in silence.

The morning light couldn't penetrate the maze of galleries that led from the mine adit to his lair, but an inbuilt sense roused Kaldar Alvaray from the doze into which he'd fallen, and when he opened his eyes he knew instinctively that the sun had risen. He raised his head, aware of stiffness in his muscles, a dull aching in his skull, and by the light of his fire's fading, sluggish embers he looked about him at the cave, just another one of so many that were the nearest thing he'd known to a home for the past three years.

It was some seconds before his mind cleared and he remembered the events of the night. But when he did, the twin agonies of grief and rage were like a vicious physical punch to his stomach. Luck had been with him at first. By the time the Chaos riders thundered through the village street he'd been clear away into the foothills of the northern mountains, and there he had waited, watching the second moon's slow decline until it set and the greater darkness gave him the cover he needed to return. But in the space of a few more minutes his eager anticipation had been shattered, for on the edge of the village he met Arin and his father. They had set out to search for him and, their faces haggard under the cold starlight, they told him that the Chaos riders had taken their tithe and that Iselia had been caught up in the harvest.

Kaldar could remember little of what they had said to each other, and anyway it was irrelevant, for no words could have expressed their mutual grief. He had wanted to stay, comfort them if he could, but Iselia's father said no, the family would bear their sorrow in their own way and Kaldar must look to his safety. So he had turned back, shock blotting out any ability to assimilate or even comprehend his loss. Numbly he had retraced his steps back through the foothills and into the higher peaks, finally traversing the defile that led to the played-out and abandoned mine workings. Only when he had walked, like a man in a dream, through the crumbling galleries to his private, secret cave in the mountain heart had coherence returned and the barriers within him finally shattered.

Tears sprang into Kaldar's eyes and he let them fall. He had cried last night when the realization had finally come: it was a uselessly inadequate expression of his guilt and his misery, but he couldn't stop himself, then or now, and those who thought it unmanly to weep could be damned. For a few brief hours he had let himself believe that all would be well, but he should have known that faith and determination weren't enough. What was it he had said in that brave, hollow speech he'd made only minutes before the Chaos riders' arrival? That he would guard Iselia more closely than his own life. What a bitter joke *that* had been. He'd done nothing; he'd failed her, failed himself, failed everyone who had had faith in him. Neither he nor his god had been strong enough to protect Iselia, and she was lost.

Kaldar tried to rise, and cramp seized him. He hadn't meant to fall asleep, hadn't thought it possible in the midst of his grief, but exhaustion had overtaken him after the first emotional storm and he had slumped down by the fire and succumbed. When the cramp eased a little he prodded at the embers and added more fuel; the chill had got into his bones and wouldn't entirely relax its grip even when the fire flared up and dried the tears on his face. For some minutes he stared into the blaze, rejecting the unholy pictures his imagination conjured in the flames while he forced his thoughts into coherence. He had to pull himself together and set grieving aside. Tears couldn't help Iselia: he had to *act*.

At last he rose to his feet and, ignoring the pain that still snatched at his thigh and calf muscles, crossed to where several bags and bundles — the sum total of his belongings — lay at the far side of the cave. As he rummaged among the bags it occurred to him, unbidden and in an unpleasantly detached way, that this would have been no place to which to bring a new bride. Iselia had deserved far better than a rolled-up pallet for a bed, a bare rock floor for a chair, nothing but a few crude utensils as his contribution to her dowry chest. She deserved a home, the good things of life, a husband who was something better than an outlaw, a —

The curse erupted from him, shocking in the empty quiet, and he smashed a fist against the wall in impotent fury. Pain shot through his arm; he hissed on an indrawn breath and pressed his forehead to the bare rock, sucking at his bleeding knuckles until the throbbing receded. The pain was a focus, an ally, clearing his mind like ice-cold water. He had to *think*.

Kaldar ran through a rapid mental exercise to calm himself and turned back to his bags. This time his search was more systematic as he gathered together what he needed, and as he pulled out the last object — a small brass censer half filled with charcoal, its outlet holes smoke blackened and in want of cleaning — the weary confusion slid away and his mind felt suddenly and completely clear. He knew what he must do; it was a contingency he'd planned for in his darkest moments, never dreaming that events would make it necessary. And if Iselia was still alive, then his dead hopes might be rekindled.

Kaldar carried the censer back to the fire with the other items he'd garnered from the shelf, and sat cross-legged before the flames. As he sprinkled pinches of several powders into the censer, his lips moved in a silent exhortation, a preparation for what he was about to attempt. Until recently he had been under no illusions about his skills as a sorcerer. He had a natural aptitude for the ways of magic, but his early life as a miner in these barren hills had given him little opportunity to pursue the craft. Besides, the law on such matters was adamant and inflexible: any man, woman, or child who showed a talent for sorcery had no choice but to enter the castle, where he would be schooled and used as the magi saw fit. Kaldar, however, had had no intention of taking that path, and for some years he had tried to train himself in secret. But a foolish lapse of discretion had revealed his aptitude to the castle's spies — together with the fact that his loyalties and priorities were not those expected of a faithful servant of Chaos. With a price on his head Kaldar had fled into hiding, and had remained in exile ever since.

But though exile meant a life of danger and hardship, it had brought its benefits, for it had given him the time to devote to more intense study. At first his power had been random and unreliable, but that was changing. He had a mentor now, someone who, though they had never met face-to-face, was helping him to hone and develop his talents and put them to efficient use. Now Kaldar had *real* power; he had put it to the test often enough, and dangerously enough, to have no doubts on that score.

He closed the censer and set it on the fire. Smoke began to rise as the brass bowl grew hot, and a sweet scent that recalled summer hay meadows filled the cave and made Kaldar's nostrils flare with headily nostalgic memories. He forced himself to concentrate. Time was of the essence, for he dared not risk the smell of the incense escaping through the adit and coming to the notice of some of the creatures — and not only creatures of flesh and blood — that haunted the mountains. Chaos had eyes everywhere, and any untoward activity would be of great interest to the devils at the castle. He thought of Iselia, formed an image of her face in his inner eye, held it. Slowly he began to rock back and forth, and, as he had hoped, the disembodied countenance in his mind began to change. Hair as white as the first winter snowfall, cascading over broad, strong shoulders. Features that combined mercy and compassion, power and understanding, in an unhumanly beautiful form. Golden eyes, warm and knowing and loving. Kaldar's body was racked by a long shudder as the trance took deeper hold, drawing his mind up, up, through rock and stone and grass and air, into a place of freedom where no darkness could enter.

He couldn't speak Iselia's name aloud, but the syllables vibrated silently, powerfully within him. He would find her. He would call on the strength of his forbidden allegiance, take the mantle of the Lords of Light upon his shoulders, draw into him the strength of his lost and exiled gods. And when the rite was done, when he had drunk of the bright power of Aeoris, he would be ready.

He would be ready.

CHAPTER VI

Savrinor's proposal, when it came, wasn't delivered at an opportune moment for Benetan. Four days passed without a word from the historian following their encounter on the beach, and the continuing silence was a constant source of unease to the young captain as he waited for news that he was beginning to fear might never come. He was sorely tempted to seek Savrinor out, but prudence warned him to caution, and he didn't dare to inquire how Iselia herself was faring lest he should alert Andraia to his interest in her.

He and Andraia had patched up their latest quarrel, though for once it was she and not Benetan who had made the first conciliatory move. Since then she had been particularly affectionate toward him, at times almost deferential, which certainly didn't fit her usual nature, and Benetan suspected that she'd put the wrong interpretation on his distracted and preoccupied mood. Though Andraia's love — and her way of showing it — was quirkish and often mercurial, their feelings for each other were genuine, and her misunderstanding added to Benetan's growing sense of guilt. He couldn't tell Andraia the truth, for she simply wouldn't have understood, and any attempt to explain would only have led to another and probably far more serious quarrel. He didn't want to risk losing her, so he told himself, though with some discomforting qualms, that she shouldn't even know of Iselia's existence.

To add to his tensions there was trouble in the ranks of the Chaos riders. One of his younger officers — like himself, an unwilling candidate from the villages who had made the best of his lot — was caught attempting to smuggle a blood mare out of the castle, intending to sell the animal and pocket a healthy profit. The crime was too petty to be brought to the attention of the magi, but the penalty was statutory, and responsibility for its execution rested on Benetan's shoulders.

The young rider's screams as the multibarbed lash flayed the skin from his naked back still reverberated in Benetan's head as he left the stable where the punishment had been administered, and his right hand ached as though the whip handle had made an indelible imprint. As the unconscious youth was dragged away, his blood leaving an ugly, trailing pattern on the stone floor, Benetan shut his eyes, sharply aware of the resentment directed at him by the miscreant's peers who had been obliged to watch, and wishing that the ground might open and swallow him. Turning his back on the row of accusing eyes as he stalked out into the sunlit courtyard, he felt lower than a worm.

He crossed to the east wing where his own quarters were situated, his thoughts as bitter as those of the men who had silently condemned his action. To try to justify himself, explain that the laws were the laws and he'd had no choice in the matter, was useless, and would do nothing to reinstate him in the eyes of his subordinates. The resentment would pass in time; until it did he must live with his conscience if he couldn't silence it. After all, he reflected savagely, recalling Iselia's accusation, it was one of the currencies with which he had bought his rank.

Breakfast was still being served in the great central dining hall, but though he'd eaten nothing since the previous night Benetan's stomach rebelled at the thought of food. He headed down the corridor to his room, ignoring someone — his overtaut mind didn't register a name or an identity — who signaled a greeting as he passed. His door stood slightly ajar; as he approached, it opened and Andraia emerged.

"You have a visitor." She still looked as she'd done the previous night; her heavy chestnut hair a mass of tiny braids, and gold-and-black curlicues painted around her lively green eyes. As their gazes met he saw intense curiosity mingling with another, less definable emotion in the look she gave him.

"A visitor?" His heart seemed to stop momentarily. "Who is it?"

Her brows went up. "Who were you expecting?"

"No one. . . . I just thought . . ."

From inside the room came a familiar, mocking voice. "No one? Such compliments from my friends!" The door swung fully open and Savrinor rose from Benetan's best chair. "Good morning, Benetan. I'm sorry to disappoint you, but whoever you were hoping to see, I'm afraid you must make do with me."

Benetan hesitated on the threshold, then stepped into the room. Andraia followed, still watching him curiously, and suddenly his feelings boiled over and he slammed the door ferociously at his back, only just giving her time to get clear.

Savrinor raised an eyebrow. "Trouble?"

Benetan shook his head. "A disciplinary matter." His voice was tightly controlled. "Some men relish the delivering of summary justice. I don't."

Andraia moved to an alcove at one side of the room and took from it a stone jar of wine and three pewter cups. She'd shared Benetan's bed last night and was well aware of his distaste for this morning's punishment detail, but she privately thought that he made too much of it. Only the fact that she wasn't in the mood for yet another altercation persuaded her to keep her opinions to herself.

It seemed that Savrinor shared her view, for he said, "Benetan, you really are a slave to your misplaced guilt." Andraia handed him a full wine cup and he bowed to her with great courtesy. "Thank you, my dear." And to Benetan: "Your lady clearly knows the universal remedy for a poor temper. Good health and long life to you both." He drank deeply, though his gaze didn't stop flicking shrewdly from one to the other of his two companions. Their faces gave nothing away, but Savrinor had a rare talent for seeing what wasn't apparent to others, and he read the tension between them and guessed who was responsible for it and why. Under some circumstances he might have enjoyed prolonging Benetan's discomfiture for a little longer; at the moment, though, the entertainment didn't seem worthwhile.

"Benetan, my friend," he said when he lowered the cup from his lips, "I have some business to discuss with you. But it's just a small thing, and no matter if it isn't convenient now." He smiled at the girl by Benetan's side. "I wouldn't wish to put Andraia out in any way. . . ."

As the daughter of a high-ranking official Andraia knew enough about political machinations within the castle to recognize the difference between a slight hint and a strong suggestion. She was also wise enough to have no wish to cross Savrinor, and she smiled her most charming smile, masking her pique at being excluded, however politely.

"I have a number of things I must do today." She offered no further excuse; it was unnecessary. "I shall leave you gentlemen to your discussions. Benetan, I'll see you later." She let her smile modulate a little, leaving Benetan in no doubt that he'd have some questions to answer on her return, then bowed formally and with faint asperity to the historian. "Good morning, Savrinor."

Savrinor watched her leave, his eyes frankly appraising her slim body through the silk shift she wore. As the door closed, he said laconically, "I wouldn't risk losing her if I were you, Benetan. There are many others ready to appreciate her qualities if you don't."

"I'll bear that in mind," Benetan replied acerbically.

Savrinor sighed. "By the gods, you're sour this morning. Drink your wine, and let's see if that puts you in a better mood." He picked up Benetan's untouched cup. "And when you've drunk it, you may be interested in a proposal I have to put to you."

Halfway to the cup, Benetan's hand froze. "Proposal?"

"Your peasant girl." An eyebrow went up. "Don't tell me you've forgotten our little discussion of a few days ago? Really, Benetan, I — "

"Savrinor, what have you done?" Benetan's tone was suddenly dangerous.

"I've *done* nothing. Yet. Here, take this cup; I've better things to do than stand here all day holding it out to you."

Benetan took it and immediately set it down again, spilling a good quantity over his own hand, though he didn't notice. "You've some news about Iselia?" he asked sharply.

"Yes," Savrinor told him. "It's a simple suggestion, and one that will effectively ensure her safety not only at the celebrations but thereafter." He moved away, pacing slowly across the room. "It's so simple, in fact, that I really can't comprehend why I didn't think of it at the time of our original discussion." A pause. "However, I rather suspect that you won't like it."

Benetan's skin crept. "Tell me."

Savrinor told him. And when he heard the proposal, when its implications sank into his mind, Benetan turned sharply away as icecold sweat broke out on his neck, his arms, his torso.

"No." He felt sick to the pit of his stomach, and in the poor light his eyes burned with disgust and loathing. *"Never."*

Savrinor shrugged, unmoved. "Which would you prefer? To give Iselia into my care, or to see her in the hands of whatever may choose to grace our celebrations three nights from now?"

"There's a difference?" Benetan's voice was vituperative.

The historian laughed softly. "My dear Benetan, I at least am *human."* Then his pale, sly eyes hardened. "You might serve yourself by remembering that, and also by remembering that a civil tongue has a better prospect of remaining intact. I think you're intelligent enough to take my meaning?"

They stared at each other for a long moment, and Benetan realized that he'd gone too far. His last retort could have cost him far more than his rank, had Savrinor chosen to take insult.

Though his shoulders remained rigid, defeat showed in his eyes, and Savrinor smiled.

"We understand each other." His voice was sweet reason and he patted Benetan's arm, a gesture to show that — this time — there was no ill feeling. "Besides, the lady should surely be granted the opportunity to weigh the options and decide for herself?"

Benetan slumped down onto a chair, his face gray as cold logic struggled to assert itself. Savrinor was right: the final choice must rest with Iselia. He had no right to sway her, no right to demand anything of her. If she chose to give herself to a man who, however bizarre his tastes, however perverted his pleasures, was at least human, who could deny her that chance when the alternative was something beyond imagining?

But there should have been a third option. There *should* have been.

He forced the thoughts back and said indistinctly, his voice tightly controlled: "What I said was uncalled for. I apologize."

Savrinor's smile broadened. "Accepted. I like to think that whatever else I may be, I'm never less than gracious."

That night, lying sleepless in his bed with Andraia breathing softly and evenly beside him, Benetan sweated at the thought of what Savrinor could have done had he chosen to take offense over that savagely unguarded remark. They had finally parted without overt hostility, and tomorrow Iselia would be brought to meet the historian and her fate would be sealed.

He refused to let himself dwell on what that might ultimately mean. Savrinor's sybaritic inclinations were legendary, but although speculation was rife, gossip didn't extend to the detail of how he took his pleasures. With a smooth reason that Benetan found chilling, Savrinor had insisted that Iselia must be allowed to choose her own path: but how could Benetan warn her, when his own doubts were so unformed? All he knew was that when the historian put his proposal, something had moved in him that made him feel as if a stinking disease were eating at his vital organs. And at the root of it, though no power in the world would have made Benetan admit to the truth, was blind jealousy.

He turned his head to look at Andraia, and felt guilt swamp him yet again. She'd returned to his room later in the morning, avid to hear what Savrinor's mysterious business had been, and with a subtlety unnatural in him Benetan had affected bafflement. Savrinor, he said, had apparently wanted only to ask him a few oblique questions about the Chaos riders' last sortie, and that for no obvious reason. Andraia had jumped immediately and eagerly to the conclusion that some reward or promotion must be in the wind for Benetan, and Benetan hadn't had the heart — or the courage — to protest the idea too strongly. He had forced himself to make a pretense of celebrating with her, and only when she at last fell contentedly asleep had he been able to set aside the mask he'd worn all day and open his mind again to the thoughts that preoccupied him.

The night seemed endless, a dark miasma of nightmares punctuated by long and dismal periods of uneasy wakefulness. But at last the first light of dawn broke, conjuring shadows from the receding gloom, and Benetan rose, dry throated, to face what must be faced.

Andraia was still sleeping. He dressed quietly, anxious not to wake her, then wrote a hasty note telling her that he'd been called out early by one of his sergeants; some problem with the horses; he'd see her later in the dining hall. Gently and guiltily he kissed her coppery hair, then, leaving the note on his pillow where she would be sure to see it, he made his way to the north wing and Savrinor's apartments.

Savrinor's sense of timing was uncanny. He was waiting for Benetan as though he'd known the precise moment at which the younger man would arrive, and Benetan hadn't been in the room for three minutes before a respectful if faintly furtive knock at the door announced the arrival of two men escorting Iselia.

She looked desperately tired, Benetan thought, but otherwise well enough. However, she was unwilling to meet his gaze, instead gazing mutely at her surroundings with eyes that had a hunted look to them. She said nothing beyond a murmured response to his greeting, and wouldn't sit down when Savrinor invited her to do so. She was still dressed in the same rough shift, crumpled and dirty now, and Benetan saw that her hands were shaking, though she strove to control the spasms. He wanted to offer her some comfort or reassurance, but knowing what he knew, and with Savrinor in earshot, he couldn't bring himself to do it. Instead he embarked on an attempt to explain the historian's plan. But his voice faltered and the words wouldn't come; and after listening with an exaggerated air of patience for a minute or two, Savrinor intervened.

"My friend, if you continue as you've begun we'll still be here at sunset," he said. "If I may clarify the matter . . . ?"

Benetan subsided unhappily into silence and, turning to Iselia, Savrinor outlined his proposal in a few concise and courteous sentences. Iselia listened, her face very still and a faint frown creasing her brow. And when Savrinor finished speaking, and Benetan heard the awful calm in her voice as she gave her answer to the proposition, something within him turned to ash.

She said, quite simply: "Yes. I am willing."

Savrinor looked up from where he sat relaxed in his chair, and smiled an old, sardonic smile.

"You're to be complimented, Benetan." Silk rustled, the sound obscene to Benetan's ears, as he shifted his position slightly. "I find your judgment sound; the lady is all you implied, and more." He rose, smiling at Iselia, though the smile didn't touch his eyes, which were thoughtful. "My dear, if you will be so good as to wait outside briefly, I crave a few moments alone with your champion."

Iselia nodded wordlessly. She looked Benetan, once, then with tense dignity walked from the room. As the door closed behind her Savrinor touched his tongue to his upper lip.

"She's quite charming in her own way." His voice was detached, remote. "And something of a beauty, considering her low birth."

Benetan's jaw muscles clenched. "Damn you, Savrinor, have done!"

"Done?" My friend, I haven't yet started!" Savrinor pivoted on his heel, pointing a finger at the younger man. "You forget that I've needed to call on all my diplomacy, all my influence, to bring matters to this pass! You should be thankful that your precious Iselia has more wit than you, Benetan." He eyed the door speculatively, then laid a hand on Benetan's arm. "The lady has chosen. Have the good grace to accept it, and be thankful."

"Thankful?" Benetan said haggardly.

"Indeed. Even though she's barely uttered a word yet, I'm convinced that there's more to this girl than either of us realizes, and I'll consider it a privilege to discover her true mettle. Who knows, I may find enough in her to reduce the debt you owe me." Thin fingers squeezed Benetan's biceps, making him recoil. "Now, I'm sure you'd like to make your farewells, so I'll retire to my bedchamber and give you a few moments alone with her." Savrinor moved toward the inner door, then looked back with another of his enigmatic smiles. "Only a few moments, mind."

The door closed quietly behind him, leaving Benetan staring at the empty space and feeling that a black void existed where his heart should have been.

As she watched Benetan walk away toward his quarters, Iselia found that she was not, as she had feared, in danger of losing her hold on her carefully nurtured self-control. When Benetan had disappeared from view she turned back to the room, quietly closing the door, and as she waited for Savrinor to reappear from the inner room she tried, with what little information she had, to assess him. In the few minutes that they had spent alone, Benetan had attempted to warn her against the historian, but to Iselia it had seemed that both the warning and Benetan's motives were garbled and uncertain, and her first impressions of Savrinor had confused the issue further. Benetan's swift, urgent words gave the impression that Savrinor was a despot, an overt sadist, the epitome of everything she loathed and dreaded within the walls of this castle. She, though, had thus far seen only a man of elegant taste and punctiliously courteous manner, not handsome yet by no means repellent, a powerful intellect, a sardonic sense of humor. A man of standing. A man who was willing and able to protect her from the perils of her captivity.

At a price.

Iselia clasped her hands tightly together against a sudden chill. There lay the worm in the bud, for as yet she had no clear understanding of what Savrinor's price would be. His offer had been couched in clear enough terms: in order to safeguard her from the fate of her fellow candidates he was willing to take her under his patronage, which meant that from now on every moment of her existence, waking or sleeping, would be his to dictate. It was a form of slavery — Savrinor hadn't for a moment made any bones about that — but it offered her the security of at least knowing who her slave master would be. And under Savrinor's wing she could prosper. He had made it quite clear that willing service would be meticulously rewarded, and even Benetan had been unable to deny that that was true. All he hadn't told her was what manner of service he would expect from her. . . .

She stood motionless on the flagged floor, and her heart began to thump painfully as that thought took hold. For the first time fear was beginning to creep up on her; she thrust it forcibly down and tried to concentrate on her surroundings as a defense and a distraction. This was a large room, far larger than Benetan's, and though the furnishings were tastefully sparse by the castle's standards, to Iselia it seemed opulent, almost unreal. The table glowed with the warm sheen of frequent and diligent polishing; the rugs were plush, almost new; the curtains heavy and rich, the lamps neatly trimmed and with no trace of soot on their glass chimneys. There were several long mirrors on the walls, each clear as water and each tinted a different subtle color. Near the window was a desk on which parchments were tidily stacked, an inkwell, a silver sandbox, and a horn containing a selection of quill pens were arrayed neatly beside the pile. The chamber, she thought, of a man who knew his own mind, and who had a firm idea of his own worth.

"A cup of wine, Iselia?" The gentle, confident voice spoke from behind her and she jumped, turning quickly. Savrinor had emerged. He was smiling, and walked with quiet assurance across the room. "This seems an appropriate moment to toast our new alliance."

Collecting her wits and her composure, Iselia nodded. "Th . . . thank you."

He poured. The sound of the liquid splashing made her feel claustrophobic, and when she took the cup he proffered, her hand shook. They drank in silence and Iselia quelled the temptation to drain the cup in one draft, telling herself that she didn't need false courage. Carrying his own drink with him, Savrinor returned to the inner door, which swung open at his touch. From the corner of her eye Iselia saw through to the other room, which was dominated by a wide, low bed with a rich velvet cover thrown over it.

"That is where we shall sleep." Savrinor spoke carelessly, then his gaze locked quickly on her face as he saw her tense. He smiled. "Does it displease you?"

She swallowed, her knuckles whitening, and he came to stand at her side. One slim hand closed lightly over hers and he steadied the cup as she almost spilled its contents.

"My dear girl, you may as well know that Benetan has told me your secret. As a married woman, you're surely not so naive as to think our relationship is to be entirely chaste?"

Iselia shut her eyes tightly. "I . . ." She swallowed again. "I didn't . . ." She paused, then, realizing that he wasn't going to help her, forced the words out between parched lips. "I was married on the very day the Riders came." Her eyes opened again and she looked at Savrinor with a mixture of mute defiance and desperate appeal. "There was no time. . . ."

"Ah. I understand." The hand moved from her knuckles to her wrist to her forearm, traced a line to her shoulder, and rested there, lightly stroking her bare skin. "You've adhered to that eccentric little convention some villagers have of staying chaste until they tie themselves to one lifelong spouse, is that it?"

Her cheeks flamed. "Yes."

Savrinor smiled, and there was something underlying the smile that made Iselia shiver. "I wasn't aware of that. . . . Well, then, it appears Benetan has unwittingly delivered to me a greater prize than either he or I realized."

She turned her head away and he took her chin between his fingers, forcing her to face him.

"You're not afraid of me, Iselia? Are you?"

"Nnnh . . ." She took a grip on her unruly tongue. "No." And thought: *Kaldar — ob gods, Kaldar . . .*

"I'm glad to hear that." Savrinor bent his head and his lips touched her shoulder blade, the tip of his tongue making her flesh tingle. "For I believe we may each find much in the other to intrigue and to enjoy. Isn't that so?"

The veins in her throat stood out rigidly. "Yes . . . ," she whispered obediently.

For a moment they formed a bizarre tableau, something that contrasted obscenely with the mellow light flooding in at the window. Then Savrinor raised his head, and his smile took on a humorous edge as he patted Iselia's arm in an almost avuncular manner.

"Benetan tells me," he said, "that your little fraternity of farmers and miners boasts a scholar or two. Do you count yourself among that happy band?" Iselia looked blankly back at him and he laughed, a soft chuckle as though at some private joke. "I mean, lady, can you read a manuscript, and can you form your letters in such a way that the result doesn't look like the staggerings of a drunken spider?"

She tried to fathom the change of topic, failed. "I went to school, sir."

"School? Do you mean one of those threadbare and sorry little arrangements that they have in the peasant communities?"

She flushed at what seemed a deliberate slight. "It served our needs," she said. "I attended for five years, and I learned to read and write well enough to teach the younger children in my turn."

"Good." Savrinor smiled in a way that suggested she should learn not to take his challenges too seriously, and indicated the neat pile of parchments on his desk. "Then you'll earn my unstinting gratitude by relieving me of a tedious task. I need a fair copy of that document.

There's a drawer below the desktop; you should find enough fresh parchment in there."

She continued to stare at him, not comprehending, unable to grasp the mercurial twists in his nature. For a moment she wondered if he was playing some joke on her, but if he was, the jest was too subtle for her and at last she turned obediently toward the desk, torn between confusion and relief.

Savrinor watched as she took her seat and gathered new parchments from the drawer. He'd arrange clothing for her, he thought; a few things to reflect her new status and to mellow that gauche and stilted demeanor a little. There was a certain woman with an excellent eye for such things, who owed him a favor or two. Yes; a few subtle changes and Iselia Darrow would make a more than presentable asset. . . .

As Iselia bent her head, a quill clasped in her hand, he stepped forward, lifted the heavy bob of her hair and kissed the nape of her neck. She froze, and Savrinor smiled with the pleasure of a small triumph.

"You don't understand me, do you?" His voice was soft, gentle, yet to Iselia's shuddering mind it seemed that there was a hint of menace in his tone. "In time, Iselia, you may learn a great deal. In time."

His fingers lingered briefly, coolly, on the skin where her neck joined her shoulders. Then, quiet as a cat, he went out of the room and left her to her solitary task.

CHAPTER VII

On the morning of the inauguration ceremony, dawn came amid an unnatural stillness, and the sun, when it rose, was haloed by an eerie purple corona.

The phenomenon was short-lived but spectacular, and nowhere more so than from the vantage point of the Star Peninsula. Many of the castle dwellers witnessed the bizarre phantasm, the brooding and unnatural shadow that reached out from the northern horizon and spread like a vast, cold wing across the sea, the eldritch, sickly light about the sun's disk. Some took it as a excellent omen; others — among them Savrinor and several of the magi — differed, but took care to keep their opinions to themselves.

Preparations for the events of the coming night began early. Every castle servant knew the penalties for laxness or neglect, and was aware that today, of all days, those penalties would be ferociously exacted. Nothing less than perfection must be achieved, and nothing must go amiss. Tension was high, too, among the Chaos riders when Benetan made a morning inspection of the men under his command. All would have some part, however small, to play in the festivities following the inauguration itself, and while the older hands were stoical enough to trust in the gods and their senior officers to guide them through, the nerves of some of the younger and less experienced warriors were dangerously close to breaking point. Benetan did his best to calm and reassure them, singling out one or two of the worst cases for individual attention, but his mind wasn't fully on the task. In truth he felt as tightly strung as they, and only ingrained training and habit enabled him to hide the fact. It wasn't the prospect of the ceremony itself that had woken him in a cold sweat time and again during the past night, for he wouldn't personally be present in the Marble Hall when Vordegh received the blessing of the gods. But when the ritual was over, the magi would return to the great hall where their new lord, and whatever denizens of Chaos had chosen to grace the castle with their presence, would preside over a night of wild celebration. *That* was what turned Benetan's blood cold. For when the castle dwellers gathered in the vast hall, Iselia would be among their number.

Three times last night he had dreamed the same dream, in which he had seen Iselia plucked from the throng and given as a gift, a plaything, to one of Yandros's grimmest creations, while he and Savrinor could only stand by and watch. To Benetan's fevered imagination the dream had had the inexorable ring of prophecy. Logically he knew that was foolish; he'd learned enough about arcane matters to be aware that the gods didn't send truly portentous dreams to unimportant and untrained minions. But the fear had lodged itself deep in him like a maggot burrowing into an apple, and he couldn't exorcise it. Again and again the questions tormented him, and always they were: *what if?* What if Savrinor should grow bored with Iselia, as he'd done with so many other women, and capriciously choose to renege on his promise to protect her? What if a demon should take a liking to her and demand her as tribute? What if the magi themselves —

No, Benetan told himself fiercely, *no*. This couldn't go on, or before the night was out he'd have more cause to worry about his own neck than about Iselia's. He must continue with his work, perform his duties, prepare himself for the celebrations and *forget* his fears. Savrinor wouldn't let him down. Whatever his vices, the historian was scrupulously reliable. And didn't the gods always protect the innocent? Iselia had nothing to fear from tonight's revels, and neither had he. It would go well. It *must*.

Benetan's efforts to drive out the demons in his mind met with some success at last, and when the morning ended he was able to face sharing a hasty and belated meal with Andraia in a corner of the disrupted dining hall. The sun was past meridian when they sat down, and they exchanged wry smiles with a group of minor castle officials at an adjoining table as the few servants who weren't occupied with the preparations scurried to scrape up enough food to satisfy them.

Andraia was in an ebullient mood. She loved festivities of any kind, and tonight's celebration promised to be the greatest that she could remember. She'd been too young to enjoy the last inauguration of a First Magus, and seemed oblivious to the tension that Vordegh's elevation had awoken in some quarters. As they ate cold meat and shared a loaf of the previous day's bread, faintly stale now, she affectionately berated Benetan for displaying, as she perceived it, a level of modesty that didn't befit his status.

"You should have a servant." She mumbled the words through a mouthful of food, swallowed, then washed all down with a gulp of wine from her cup. "I've told you time and again, you're not living in your childhood village anymore. You're at the Star Peninsula, my love; you're a captain now, you have rank and you have appearances to maintain! You should have a personal servant to see to your needs." She refilled his cup and her own, then plucked at the front of his shirt. "Look at you — your clothes are creased, your hair is left to do whatever it pleases, and you don't sport so much as a single adornment from head to feet! What sort of example does that set to the men under your command?"

Wine and food were having a mellowing effect on Benetan; he pulled a face at her and tweaked a tendril of her piled-up hair. "I've spent the morning grubbing around the stables — how do you expect me to look? Stop trying to organize me, sweet. I'm well enough as I am!"

"You are *not*." She turned her head in a quick movement and nipped his fingers playfully before he could withdraw them. "For example, what do you intend to wear to the celebrations tonight?"

The question caught him unawares and he dissembled. "I — oh, I don't know. I'll decide later; there's time enough yet."

"There is not, and you will not!" Andraia was indignant. "I'll decide for you. I'll come to your room, and I'll make you presentable. In fact, I'll make you *magnificent*." She paused, and mischief glinted in her eyes. "Because, you see, if you let me down tonight, if you *dare* to look less than your best, then you might find yourself in want of a lover when the revels are over!"

Benetan gave in. "All right, all right. Do your worst to me; I'll suffer it. But — " He yawned. "I'm going to need some sleep if I'm to be fit for anything."

She was suddenly alert. "You didn't sleep well? No, I thought not; you were twisting and turning half the night like a cat in a trap. What was wrong?"

He shook his head. "Nothing that I can put a finger on." *Liar*, said an inner voice. "Tension. Anticipation. Nervousness."

Andraia sighed, but the sigh was sympathetic. "Don't worry, Benet. It'll go well." She reached out and clasped his hand, and a frown creased her small, feline face. "I've been thoughtless and selfish, haven't I? These past few days . . . you've had so much on your mind, preparing your men for tonight. I should have been more understanding. I'm sorry."

Her concern was so genuine, and so misguided, that Benetan felt guilt stab him afresh like a knife between the ribs. His fingers tightened on hers with a strength that made her start in a mixture of surprise and gratification.

"I'll make it up to you, Andraia." He meant it; he *wanted* to mean it. "When tonight's over — "

She laughed huskily, and with the laugh came a return of confidence and the fiery coquettishness that had charmed and ensnared him for the past two years. "That," she said, "is not to be discussed, but to be anticipated!" She rose to her feet, pulling her hand free and snatching at her wine cup to take a last drink. "Now, if I'm to make you presentable later, I must go and look to my own preening! Have your sleep, and be ready for me an hour before sunset. Yes?"

He smiled warmly. "Yes. Whatever you say."

She blew him a kiss and was gone.

Benetan returned to his room feeling calmer than he'd done all that day. Though she didn't know the real source of his unease, and that in itself was cause enough for discomfiture, Andraia had brought him back to earth, banishing the fears to a quiet and untrammeled region of his mind. A few hours' sleep, he thought, and perhaps a few more cups of wine, and he could face the prospect of tonight's celebrations with equilibrium.

He opened the door of his room, and went in. He'd neglected to draw the curtains before leaving this morning; the air smelled stale, and with the fire out there was a dank edge to the atmosphere. He crossed to the window, pulled the curtains back, and thumped on the casement to force it open. Daylight and fresh air streamed in —

And from behind the door, a voice that stripped twelve years from him and propelled his memory back into childhood, said,

"Benet."

Benetan swore an oath never used in the castle, and spun round.

He'd changed. Gods, how he'd *changed!* It was only to be expected, of course; the transition from boy to man was powerful and far-reaching, and Benetan knew that he himself must be barely recognizable from the lad of the northern mountain village who had been dragged screaming from his home so long ago. But there could be no doubts. The awkward, rangy frame was just the same, albeit gaunter than it should have been. The mouth still had that familiar lopsided quirk which made him look as though he were laughing and disapproving at the same time. And the hair — red as a sunset, cut sharply below his ears in the fashion of the miners yet still as unruly as a hay field in a gale, and instantly recognizable —

Benetan said, *"Kaldar Alvaray!"*

Kaldar was sweating despite the room's chill. He threw a rapid glance over his shoulder, then pushed the door shut. "You remember me?" His voice was tense, clipped. "I'm flattered, Benet. I'd have thought that after all this time you might have forgotten!"

Benetan stood helpless in the middle of the room. He was stunned beyond the ability to say anything that made any sense. Kaldar, here, now, in his own private sanctuary, in the magi's stronghold? This was *insanity.* He was dreaming. He *must* be.

As though reading his churning thoughts, Kaldar flashed a searing and humorless grin at him. "Surprised, old friend? You shouldn't be. I gather that my name and my crimes are known to your masters these days."

Recollection came back. Benetan had heard Kaldar's name bandied in the castle several years ago, and at the time it had awoken a cold frisson within him. As a child and a youth he had known Kaldar well; the odd, temperamental, red-haired boy had been one of his own small coterie of friends, though, being Kaldar, always with a hint of the maverick, the born outcast never fully accepted into the ranks of his peers. When the Chaos riders had snatched Benetan from that old life and carried him to the Star Peninsula, he'd forgotten Kaldar as he had forgotten so many of his childhood companions. But, briefly, the name had come back to haunt him when a price had been set on the head of a troublemaker from a northern village; one who publicly defied the magi, and who had fled from the magi's retribution and hidden himself in the bleak mountain fastnesses of the mineral mines. Kaldar Alvaray had caused a brief but intense furor at the castle. But it was widely known — or rather, Benetan corrected himself; it was widely *believed* — that Kaldar had died three years ago, when a creature of Chaos, conjured by the magi, had pursued him to his hideout and had separated his soul from his body before consigning both to oblivion.

Kaldar's smile became harshly cynical. "They failed to eradicate me, Benetan. Your masters may not know the truth or they may not want to broadcast it to the likes of you, I don't know which. But they failed. I'm no ghost. I'm alive."

"I didn't — " Then Benetan gave up. Words had failed him and he shook his head helplessly at the sheer impossibility of explaining the thoughts and feelings that ramped through him. It wasn't the fact of Kaldar's appearance here in his room, nor shock at seeing a supposedly dead man restored to life. It was . . .

He found his voice again at last. "How, Kaldar? How did you get *in*? And, in the name of every demon ever created by our lord Yandros, *why*?"

Kaldar's wakeful gaze flicked around the room. "We're not likely to be interrupted?"

It was less of a question than a statement, as if he knew without the need to ask, like a hunting animal testing scents on the wind. "No," Benetan said. "But you must be out of your *mind*! One instant, that's all it would take. Don't you realize that? One instant for me to call out, and it won't matter what tricks you might have worked on the magi before; you *will* be a dead man this time!" He shook his head again, violently, and his sword rattled in its scabbard at the movement as though emphasizing his explosive confusion. "For the gods' sakes, I needn't even do *that*! You're not armed, I could take you myself, cut you down before you could speak another word — "

"I know," said Kaldar. "But you won't."

Benetan stared at him, and abruptly his mixed emotions of shock, outrage, and bewilderment were crushed under the weight of cold understanding. Kaldar was right. Loyal captain he might be, skilled Chaos rider he might be; but there were older ties that could suborn his fealty to the masters he now served. Kaldar had judged him, and had gambled on his judgment. His old friend was, Benetan thought, either a madman or something else; something, perhaps, to be feared.

His voice cracked on a strange, ugly note. "What do you want with me? After all these years — I don't understand, Kaldar!"

"No. No, perhaps you don't." For a brief, disturbing moment something in Kaldar's demeanor reminded Benetan of Savrinor. "I tested your mind, Benet. I doubt that even after twelve years in this place you entirely comprehend what I mean by that, do you? After all, you never did show any innate talent for sorcery, and if you had done, then I imagine you'd be something more than a military man by now." That harsh smile; it was like a corpse's rictus. And the words, the vocabulary, the phrasing; this wasn't the speech of the miner's son who had followed his father's trade and consigned his life to dreary slavery. He sounded more like Savrinor.

Benetan's hand, blindly groping, found the back of a chair, and he used it to support himself as his legs seemed about to fail. "Kaldar. Kaldar, listen to me. I don't know what kind of insanity possessed you to come here, I don't know how you did it or why you did it, but you've got to go. *Now*. You know what's happening in the castle tonight — if you're discovered here, you'll end your life as a sacrifice in the Marble Hall, and so will I!"

Kaldar made a dismissive, almost contemptuous gesture. "I'm not afraid of your masters, Benet, nor of anything they can conjure! I got in here by sorcery — "

"*What?*"

" — by sorcery, and I'll leave the same way." Kaldar's lip curled cynically. "You needn't fear for your own skin. I just want one thing from you, and then I'll leave you to the pleasures of your corrupt new life."

Benetan was oblivious to the bait. Feeling sick, he demanded, "What is it you want?"

"My wife."

Benetan felt as though his heart had stopped beating as the words sank in, as he understood what Kaldar was telling him. Iselia's ring, which he still carried inside his shirt, suddenly seemed to press hard and ice-cold against his skin, and he heard himself saying in a help-less, foolish voice, "Your wife . . . ? Oh, gods . . ."

Kaldar's eyes, which looked a far darker blue than he remembered them, grew abruptly gem hard. "You've seen her, haven't you? Don't try to deny it; your face gives you away. You know about us."

"*No!* No, I — " Benetan felt as though he had broken glass in his throat. He swallowed, trying to choke down the obstruction. "I've seen her, yes. We were able to talk, privately — just for a few min-utes. She told me she was married, but she wouldn't say who her . . ." He couldn't bring himself to utter the word *husband*, and finished helplessly, "I didn't know, Kaldar. I didn't know it was you."

Kaldar smiled sourly. "And you didn't expect Iselia ever to have looked twice at me, did you? No, you wouldn't. But a lot of things have changed in the past few years, Benet. I'm not the same nuisance who used to tag along after you and your little coterie of friends. I've learned things that you can't even *dream* of!"

I got in here by sorcery, and I'll leave the same way. . . . "Yes," Benetan said. "Yes, I believe you."

Abruptly Kaldar's smile faded. He reached out, and a hand whose strength surprised Benetan clamped around his right wrist. "Your masters knew what they were doing when they set a price on my head," Kaldar said. "You see, I've been studying the arts that they like to keep strictly to themselves, and I've proved a very good student. I've learned enough to have come safely through the Maze tonight, and through the castle gates, and to have found your room." The grip shifted and tightened slightly. "I want your help, and I know you'll give it and not betray me. Your motives don't matter; your actions are all that count."

With a jerk Benetan pulled his hand free. "You're presuming a great deal!"

"No, I'm not. I told you, I have power. And that power enables me to judge exactly how far I can trust you. You'll help — not for my sake, but for Iselia's."

Benetan couldn't deny it, but the fact that Kaldar had divined the truth made him irrationally angry. He looked sharply away. "If you're so sure of that, then don't you think that if I could have done any-thing I'd have done it by now?" *I should have let her go,* he thought. *Yandros help me, I should have let her go!*

"I'm not asking you to take any risks." Again there was a hint of contempt in Kaldar's tone. "Just tell me exactly where Iselia is, tell me how to reach her, and then you can forget that you ever set eyes on either of us."

For the first time Benetan fully comprehended the nature — and the sheer lunacy — of what Kaldar had in mind, and he turned back, his face ashen. "You're not going to try to get her out of the castle?"

"I'm not going to *try;* I mean to succeed."

"Kaldar, you can't! It's impossible! She's — " He bit the words off, but too late; Kaldar was alerted.

"She's what?" He darted forward so fast that Benetan couldn't evade him, and grabbed his forearms, shaking him. "*What? What's happened to her?*"

"Keep your voice down!" Benetan's arm came up in a furious, prac-ticed movement and knocked the clawing hands away. Kaldar backed off, but his eyes were wild.

"If any harm's come to Iselia — "

"It hasn't! For all the gods' sakes, Kaldar, listen! She's safe, I *promise* you she's safe. But you can't reach her. She's under the protection of a high-ranking castle official; he's taken her for his — his attendant."

Kaldar hissed a hard, rapid breath. "What do you mean, his *attendant?*"

Cold sweat broke out on Benetan's torso. "He needed an assistant, a scribe — he's the castle's historian, and when he discovered that Iselia can read and write, he agreed to take her under his wing." He paused, swallowed again. "It was either that, or watch her take her chances at the inauguration ceremonies tonight. I think you know what that could have meant."

Very softly, Kaldar swore. His voice was too low-pitched to be clear, but Benetan thought he said, "*Aeoris!*" and an icy shiver went through his bones. Then the red-haired man spoke again.

"It makes no difference. He's a historian, not a magus. I can still — "

"*No.* You can't, Kaldar. Savrinor's wiser and more cunning than half the magi together; you'd never succeed in spiriting her away from under his nose. Besides, I told you she's safe and I meant it. He has enough rank to protect her, and he's promised to do so."

"*Promised* — " Kaldar began scathingly, but Benetan interrupted. "Savrinor never breaks his word. Never."

Perhaps it was the intensity of his tone, or perhaps Kaldar's heightened intuition made him sense that what Benetan said was no less than the truth. Seeing him waver, Benetan desperately pressed the small advantage he'd gained.

"If you try to reach Iselia now, you'll kill us all — her, yourself, and me. In a matter of hours the Chaos Gate will be opening, and however powerful you think you are, you can't hope to hide from the beings that are going to gather in the castle tonight. You may be strong, they're stronger. Believe me, I know, I've seen them. They'll *annihilate* you, and Iselia with you! Is that what you want?"

"Damn you, you know it isn't! But — "

"Then put this precious wisdom of yours to good use for once! *Go*, Kaldar — go quickly, and go now. Or I swear by all that's ever been held sacred that you'll put us all on the execution block before tonight's over!"

For several seconds that seemed to Benetan like half a lifetime Kaldar was silent, staring down at his own feet as prudence and instinct warred. Loud against the sudden quiet, footsteps pattered down the corridor outside, past and away too quickly to be anyone other than a servant hurrying on some errand. Remembering Andraia's promise, Benetan allowed himself to breathe again. Then Kaldar looked up, and for the first time Benetan saw the depth of his feeling for Iselia, his love for her, in the stern blue glitter of his gaze.

"Yes," Kaldar said, "You're right. I won't imperil her. Or you for that matter, although, by . . . by . . ." He thought better of speaking his god's name aloud, for Benetan's savage warning had gone home. "I shouldn't give a curse for you, because you're a part of this corruption now. But I trust you, Benet, and I believe what you say. I'll go." He paused. "On one condition."

Cross currents of emotion were moving in Benetan. "Name it."

"That you meet me. Tomorrow night or the night after, it doesn't matter which, just as soon as you can get away." His mouth jerked spasmodically, a smile that had no humor. "Are you allowed to leave the confines of these walls?"

"Yes," Benetan said whitely.

A nod. "All right. Do you remember the twin crags that are visible from the far end of our village, to the west? Yes, I see you do. Come there, where the pass runs between the two peaks. Tell me what took place at the inauguration. Tell me how Iselia fares, and what I can do to get her out." Another long hesitation. "If you can see her alone before then, bring me a message from her." A shudder racked Kaldar and suddenly his face looked like the face of a living skull, his skin white and fleshlessly drawn over stark bones. "Do that, Benet, and I'll know that your soul isn't entirely damned. Fail, and I'll come back for you. Don't doubt that. Don't doubt it for one *instant*."

Benetan didn't doubt it. It was mad, preposterous, but he felt that he was being carried on tides which he could barely yet comprehend. Kaldar's love for Iselia; his own love for her, which he hardly dared acknowledge yet which had awoken currents of guilt and set them flowing like vitriol through his veins. . . . For Iselia, he would take the risk that Kaldar demanded of him. And for Iselia, he would no more betray Kaldar's trust than he would take his knife from its sheath and open his own arteries to let his life's blood flood him into the arms of the gods.

"I'll be there." He didn't recognize the voice as his own.

"Yes." Suddenly, strangely, Kaldar's tone was gentle. "I think you will."

Benetan had closed his eyes; a sound, impinging, made him open them again, and he saw that Kaldar was moving toward the window.

"It's how I came in. Don't worry, Benet. No one will see me leave."

But there was something else, something that had to be done. Benetan didn't want to do it, but his conscience — again, his conscience — impelled him. He reached to the inner pocket of his shirt, and his fingers closed round the ring that Iselia had given into his safekeeping.

"Kaldar." He held the ring out, struggling to ignore the feelings surging within him. "She asked me to look after this for her. It's yours by right. Take it."

Kaldar stared at the ring, at the seven small topazes glinting in the fading light from the window. Then he came back and plucked it from Benetan's palm. The ring fitted his little finger; he clasped his other hand over it, hiding it from view.

"Thank you." For a moment there was a catch in his voice, then the emotion was gone. "Tell her it's safe. Tell her . . . it's still sanctified." An expression that Benetan couldn't interpret, or perhaps chose not to interpret, flicked across his face. "Tomorrow night or the next, Benet. I'll be waiting."

Benetan turned his head away. He didn't want to see, didn't want to know, how Kaldar would make his escape. He heard the creaking sound of the stiff casement opening, and a breath of cool air blew into the room. When at last he turned toward the window again, he was alone.

Her hand ached. Her fingers were ink stained and felt as though they had been cramped around the pen for a day and a night without cessation. But for now, at least, her work was done. The final document was completed and he'd asked nothing more of her save that she should sit quietly and wait while he attended to some minor business elsewhere before preparing himself for the events of the coming night.

He was, Iselia thought with a strangely detached part of her mind, an elegant man. Not handsome by the standards she set, for his skin was too pale, his form too slight, and his demeanor too precise—perhaps a little too unwholesome — to produce anything but a half-formed yet deep-rooted shiver of revulsion within her. But in the three days since she had given herself into his keeping, Savrinor had behaved toward her with scrupulous kindness and courtesy. He had made no demands on her other than that she should set to her work with silent goodwill. He saw to it that she had good food, fresh clothes, fine wines if she desired them (though more often than not she declined), and in all ways he had treated her more like a friend than a servant. Contrary to his early intention he had even provided a separate bed for her in the outer room and had made no attempt to touch her. The desperate warnings that Benetan had tried to impart to her had proved unfounded.

Strange and wonderful though it seemed to her, Iselia *liked* Savrinor. In truth it was hard not to, for when he chose to exercise it he had a personal charm that went a long way toward overcoming and allaying her fears. He treated her almost as an equal. He was witty, entertaining, a thoroughly pleasant companion, and despite her early misgivings Iselia couldn't help but feel both admiration and respect for him. From the seeds of doubt and fear, a root of trust was beginning to grow.

She looked up from her reverie at the sound of the outer door opening, and smiled tentatively as he entered the room.

"Master Savrinor." She'd learned quickly that he preferred her to address him by name rather than by any more formal title, and she made the small, obeisant gesture which also seemed to please and amuse him. For once, though, Savrinor didn't respond with his customary smile and soft chuckle. His expression was speculative and the look in his eyes impossible to read. Suddenly Iselia felt the first stirrings of disquiet.

"My dear." He crossed to where she sat at her table, and one graceful, thin-boned hand riffled through the papers she'd been working on. "Yes; very good. As always, very good." She heard the faintly reptilian rustle of his sleeve close to her face; gray silk, his favorite fabric. It gave a cold cast to his eyes.

"I am faced, my dear Iselia, with a small problem."

She tensed. Something in his voice; she couldn't pinpoint it, for she didn't yet know him well enough. But something, some intuitive sense, made her feel as if ice were forming in her stomach.

Apparently indifferent to her disquiet, Savrinor continued as calmly as though he were discussing the weather. "You must be aware of what is to take place in the castle tonight, Iselia." The sleeve brushed her cheek a second time. "I have certain duties to perform, which will mean that I can't guarantee to be at your side for the duration of the festivities." Abruptly his fingers caught in her hair and turned her, gently but forcibly, to face him. "Knowing, as I do, the . . . *tastes*, shall we say, of some of the beings which will grace us with their presence tonight, I am a little concerned for your safety."

"My safety?" She didn't understand.

He smiled. "I wouldn't like to lose you, Iselia. And I made a promise to Benetan. I never break my promises; foolish of me, perhaps, but true nonetheless. So, my dear child, I'm afraid that I find myself obliged to take certain precautions."

She realized then what he meant. He saw it in her face, saw her eyes widen in horrified understanding as the knowledge dawned on her. In a perverse way that pleased him, for Savrinor had always believed that there was a certain piquancy to be found in fear, and the knowledge that she was afraid of him, and of what he intended to do, added spice to the feelings that were already alive and stirring in his veins.

"Iselia." He spoke her name as though it were something sacred, and the hold his fingers had taken on her hair tightened suddenly, his other arm slipping around her waist so that she could not — or dared not — move. "Iselia, you'll learn to thank me for this. I promise you, you'll learn that lesson, if no other. Answer me, sweet child — which will be better? Do you want to die virgin, with your soul sucked from you by a being so low that even Yandros himself can't recall why he created it? Or will you give what you have and what you are to me, to your mortal lord, and rejoice at your salvation?" So slowly, so deliberately, his cool lips touched her shoulder, her neck, then moved to linger on the smooth skin an inch from her mouth, with an implicit hunger that made the ice within her turn to a glacier.

"Choose, Iselia. Choose, my pretty, clever girl. For your soul's sake, what will it be? Savrinor's small and private pleasures, or the hands of a demon to carry you away from this mortal world forever?"

She knew now, in a screaming, cowering part of her mind, what Benetan had been trying to tell her. In her inner eye an image rose like a vision of justice incarnate. Kaldar . . . her own love, her own husband, to whom she had pledged her body and her life. But Kaldar couldn't save her. He couldn't reach her, couldn't come to her, couldn't stop this nightmare. She was alone, with no one and nothing to offer her sanctuary. And though no other living soul knew of it, Iselia had made a silent, secret vow when dawn had broken on her first morning in the castle. A vow to Kaldar, to herself, and also, most sacred and solemn of all, to Aeoris, her god whose name she dared not speak aloud. She had promised that whatever befell her she would never lose hope; and while hope still burned, then however fearsome the price she might be forced to pay, she would do anything and everything within her power to stay alive.

Her body felt frozen to the marrow. But suddenly her mind was colder still, and the face of her husband which had risen before her inner eye was replaced by another face, too beautiful to be human, wise and compassionate and forgiving. Above all, she prayed desperately, above all, *forgiving*.

She turned with slow, sinuous grace, the smooth fabric of the dress Savrinor had procured for her slipping through his encircling arm with a soft, almost intimate sound. She had no beguiling skills to come to her aid, no knowledge of the castle women's sophisticated ways. All she could rely on was her own naive and untutored instinct, and the memory, like a goad now, of the promise she had made.

She whispered, her voice so low that it was barely audible, "My lord . . . I am yours to command. . . ."

She had pleased him. She saw the flicker of keen stimulation in his half-hooded eyes, felt the brief but emphatic tightening of his fingers where they held her. Savrinor smiled, and with a colossal effort Iselia forced herself not to look away.

"Sweet child, you are as intelligent as you are charming." He released his grip on her hair, and his hand moved to the pocket of his long velvet jerkin. From it he brought something which for a numb moment Iselia couldn't identify. Then, as he shook it out, she saw that it was a scarf, a fine, shining scarf made from exquisitely woven silk threads, with tiny pearls threaded among the fine strands.

"Turn round, Iselia." The arm that held her waist released her. "Turn away from me."

Not understanding, but feeling fear like a deep, running wound within her, Iselia obeyed him. She sensed him drawing closer, though his movements were noiseless; then the room blurred before her and light vanished as something cold, gem-encrusted, folded over her eyes.

Savrinor tied the blindfold, catching a strand of her hair in the knot and allowing his fingertips to linger like an insect's touch on the sensitive bones at the back of her skull.

"It's better this way, Iselia." His voice was sibilant and hungry; she seemed to hear his words as though they were spoken from another, nightmarish dimension. "This way, there is more . . . *delight*. And this is just the beginning, my sweet, pliant, lovely peasant girl. Just the very beginning. . . ."

She moved like a zombie, like a dead thing without a will or even a life of her own, as, with exquisite tenderness, he steered her toward the door of his inner, private sanctum.

CHAPTER VIII

There was a cool, contented glitter in Savrinor's eyes as he waited among his peers in the castle's vast entrance hall, and a private smile touched his narrowly handsome face, though so faintly that to outside scrutiny it was barely discernible.

One observer, though, was more perceptive than most, and an extraordinarily tall, lithe, but heavy-boned woman moved with apparent carelessness from her position near the back of the hall and crossed the floor to stand beside him. Savrinor made a deep bow to her and she gazed down at him, taking in the smooth sheen of carefully combed hair, the fastidious neatness of his clothes — gray silk and black velvet, and worth three years of a farmer's or miner's labor. She smiled.

"Black suits you, Savrinor. You should wear it more often."

He inclined his head. "You're too kind, my lady."

Pirane, lady magus, shrewd manipulator, and, by repute, sometime lover of half the high-ranking men in the castle, allowed the curl of her full lips to become a shade more cynical. She was a striking, almost unnerving figure, close on seven feet tall with thick, blue black hair which tonight she had piled up in an elaborate style to accentuate her height still further. Her face was beautiful, and her heavily elegant features and slanting eyes had a slightly unhuman cast, emphasized by a silver tinge to her skin that did not come from a cosmetic phial. Tonight she wore a shimmering robe that appeared to be formed from the skeletons of a myriad of human hands, each skeleton sorcerously transformed and ossified into quartz of seven different colors, to honor the seven gods of Chaos. As she moved, the robe made not the slightest sound. Savrinor knew of the tale circulating in the servants' quarters that Magus Pirane's mother had been a succubus sent by the gods to pleasure a favored worshiper, and that she might be anything from fifty to five hundred years old. He was also aware of another rumor, which claimed that Pirane had once had a liaison with Yandros himself. The thought aroused in him a strange mixture of fascination, excitement, and dread, but he was wise enough never to show his feelings in Pirane's presence.

She said, her voice a languid drawl, "Dear historian, I simply state what's obvious to any discerning eye." One hand, the middle finger far longer than the rest and the curved nails gleaming with a greenish nacre, lifted a fold of his sleeve and she critically studied the jet beads sewn along the seam. "They're from that last northwest coast consignment, if I'm not mistaken? Yes, I thought so. I wonder how it is that you so often manage to inveigle a share of the highest quality tithings?"

Savrinor always trod a careful path with Pirane, but he also knew that she despised sycophancy and liked her teasing to be reciprocated. "By a sharp ear and a keen eye, madam," he told her. "And a favor or two conferred in the right place."

"We'd all expect nothing less of you, my dear. So: no paramour tonight? What a shame. Perhaps I should find you a choice morsel from among my own little flock of doves." She nodded toward the back of the hall, where some thirty or more young men and women stood together in a tightly huddled group. All were naked, but their skins had been tinted gold and then painted with intricate, elaborate scenes like living human tapestries, shining in the soft light that permeated the hall. The pickings from Benetan's harvest, Savrinor thought, and not such a sorry herd as usual. Even Vordegh couldn't fail to be pleased; and Pirane, whose responsibility it was to oversee the preparation of these offerings and drive the spike of obedience into their hearts, looked positively smug as she gestured negligently in their direction.

"The Riders excelled themselves this time," she said, reading Savrinor's thoughts with intimidating accuracy. "I must convey my personal congratulations to that young captain with whom you're so friendly. He's still Andraia's lover, isn't he? Mmm, yes, so he won't be wanting one of these creatures to divert him. I shall think of another reward." Then abruptly her head turned, and her huge eyes, to which Savrinor had never quite been able to put a color, focused intently on his face.

"Then again, you won't be queueing for one of my gifts either, will you, Savrinor? How *is* that little fair-haired girl you've taken under your wing? I understand you have plans for her."

Savrinor was surprised, but quickly masked the flicker of disconcertment that showed momentarily on his face. He should have realized that Pirane, of all the magi, would have learned about Iselia. Pirane made it her business to know everything that went on between the castle walls. In that if in nothing else, they had much in common. But as for what lay behind her interest . . . that was another matter entirely and he couldn't yet fathom it. He'd be well advised to be cautious, Savrinor thought. It would never do to underestimate this magus, or to mistake her motives.

"Thus far I'm greatly pleased with her, madam," he said lightly, and his eyes watched her while seeming not to. "But as for my plans . . . it's a little early to be sure."

Pirane's expression remained inscrutable. "Then you're not about to hand her back to that young captain of yours. Very wise, Savrinor. She is not, I think, suitable material for him."

Ah, so *that* was it. Pirane had wind of Benetan's interest in Iselia — though the gods alone knew how she had gleaned that piece of information — and she was delivering, via Savrinor, a gentle but emphatic warning. Andraia's mother was senior lady-in-waiting to Pirane, and Pirane took a proprietorial interest in Andraia. She tacitly approved Andraia's choice of Benetan as a lover, and would take a very dim view indeed of any serious attempt on Benetan's part to pursue another woman.

Savrinor's long eyelashes came down in a slight movement that conveyed his understanding. "Indeed, Lady Magus, I agree entirely. And so, I believe, does Benetan Liss."

"Good." Her sensual mouth curved with satisfaction. "Then I shall go and tend my flock whilst we await our summons to the Marble Hall. My compliments, Savrinor — and a felicitous night to you."

Savrinor gazed obliquely after her as she stalked away from him back to her cowed and frightened charges, and his mental tally slate stored another snippet for later use. Benetan would indeed be in his debt for this warning, for to cross Pirane was to invite disaster. He was just beginning to speculate on whether or not Andraia herself might have had a hand in this matter when abruptly his attention was diverted by a faint but unmistakable sensation beneath his feet, as though the floor had begun to quiver. Savrinor's pulse quickened with excitement, and all around him he caught the echoes of rising emotion as others, too, felt the signal. Down below in the castle's foundations the Chaos Gate was stirring from dormancy, the great powers that controlled it awakening, preparing. A shiver of eager and exquisite anticipation ran through Savrinor like the delicious touch of ice against his skin — and then the air seemed to explode with the sound of a thousand unhuman voices singing in flawless harmony, one huge, perfect chord that filled the hall, filled the entire castle, bursting between dimensions as its supernatural notes heralded the arrival of the First Magus.

He came, as so many predecessors had come before him, down the great carved staircase, borne on a cloud of light that billowed with a hundred impossible colors. Furious crimson spheres of ball lightning spat and danced among the cloud, and above Vordegh's head a cold, white star, its seven points slowly and majestically puls-ing, hung like a celestial crown. The First Magus's handsome face was set in a look of rapt ardor, and his eyes stared fixedly beyond physical confines into another and more glorious world. In his hands the wand of Chaos which he had earned at his trial shone with its own inner radiance, and behind him seven huge, gaunt shadows glided in silent formation.

Reverently, Savrinor made the sign of the Seven-Rayed Star over his heart, and resisted a compelling urge to fall to his knees in sheer devotion. All thought of the perils that might beset the castle under Vordegh's rule vanished, all fears of a madman's reign of terror fled from his mind. This man was the gods' own choice. Yandros had set his hand and his mark upon Vordegh, and for that, for that alone, Savrinor would love the new First Magus and lay before him his undying loyalty.

As the wonderful vision drew nearer, the singing sound increased in volume, until it was almost unbearable. Savrinor's eardrums ached as they strove to absorb the incredible frequencies; then, like a wave breaking on the shores below the castle stack, the congregation bowed low as their temporal lord came among and past them. Savrinor wanted to cry out with the sheer ecstasy of his emotions, but he fiercely held the desire back and made his deepest and most fervent obeisance. The entrance hall doors swung back as Vordegh and his entourage approached them; outside, the courtyard was a glittering blaze as unearthly light flared in every one of the castle's myriad windows, rivaling the power of the two moons and the stars that stared down from a cloudless sky. Again the floor shook as though with an earthquake, and at the summits of the four towering spires green-and-blue lightning flashed out with a thunderous noise that momentarily drowned the supernal choir. Vordegh's radiant panoply emerged onto the courtyard steps; and in one huge, concerted movement the congregation swept in his wake, a tide of power and energy and celebration moving like a river out into the night and away toward the Marble Hall.

And there, in that Hall, before more than a hundred chosen witnesses, the gods of Chaos came to give their sanction and their blessing to their new avatar in the mortal world. If he were to live for another century, Savrinor would never forget the moment when Vordegh stepped toward the pulsing column of black light that throbbed at the Marble Hall's very center, when he raised the wand, when he spoke the names. For one instant the watchers were engulfed by a silence so profound, so complete, that the historian's own heartbeat was like thunder inside his skull. Then, with no warning, a colossal flash hurled his senses into mayhem. When his vision cleared, when his eyes could see again, a solitary figure stood where the vibrating black column had been.

His hair was gold. Molten gold, on fire with an inner radiance that lit the Marble Hall as brilliantly as a midsummer sunrise. But the face framed by the hair and the form he had chosen were human. He was tall, spare; cheekbones almost gaunt above the smiling, thin-lipped mouth. He wore no splendid robes but was clothed in plain, simple garments, with a cloak of pale smoke cast over them and sweeping the floor in his wake. Only the light in the golden hair cascading over his high shoulders marked him for what he truly was. That, and his eyes.

Savrinor looked, once, at those catlike eyes, at their ever-changing colors, at the pride and the assurance and the knowledge which reduced humanity to a craven shell, and he could no longer control the riot of emotion within himself. He dropped to one knee, and as he covered his face with both hands his lips soundlessly mouthed a name, a prayer, an exhortation.

"*My lord Yandros . . .*"

Yandros of Chaos gazed at Vordegh. The First Magus, too, was kneeling, his head bowed in honor of the highest of his gods.

"My lord!" His words echoed Savrinor's own silent invocation, but his voice rang clearly through the Hall. "You are a thousand times welcome!"

Yandros smiled, and Savrinor felt as though a million needles were pricking his skin. To witness this encounter, to see the greatest of the gods in person, was a privilege and a joy almost too great for his mind and heart to contain. He had hoped, he had dreamed, that Yandros might deign to grace the celebration with his presence, but until this moment he had never dared believe that the dream might be fulfilled. Savrinor hadn't cried since he was four years old, but now he felt tears starting to his eyes as Yandros spoke.

"Greetings, Vordegh. Chaos conveys its felicitations to its new instrument in the mortal world." His voice was mellifluous, like molten silver. Savrinor had never heard a sound that could compare with it, and he wiped ferociously at his eyes to clear his blurred vision, desperate not to miss one moment of Yandros's visitation.

The Chaos lord moved smoothly from the Gate's portal and looked around him at the gathered company. His gaze lingered a little on Pirane and her quailing prisoners, and he smiled faintly; then he returned his attention to Vordegh.

"What delights do you have in store tonight, Vordegh?" he asked. "What offerings and pledges will you make to Chaos?"

"My lord." Vordegh still knelt reverently. "I pledge to you simply the one gift that, if you will it, shall be within my power to offer. I pledge to you the lives and the souls of every living thing within the realm of mortals." Now he looked up, gazing into the Chaos lord's face, and his voice became fervent. "I believe, Lord Yandros, that a worthy avatar can do nothing less. I am yours — and if you will grant me sanction to rule in your name, then this world and all it contains shall be yours also. That is my one desire, and that is my sacred promise to the gods I serve. State your will, great master — state your will, and it shall be done!"

For some moments Yandros held the First Magus's gaze, his expression quite unreadable. Then, softly, he laughed.

"No lengthy speeches; no flowery protestations," he said. "Simply the unadorned truth." His ever-changing eyes flickered as he gazed about the Hall again. The scrutiny was longer and more measured this time, and with a twist of excitement Savrinor realized that in those few moments the Chaos lord was assessing every soul present, from the highest to the lowest. Tension filled the Marble Hall, so acute that Savrinor imagined he could reach out and touch its physical presence. Even Pirane's little flock no longer trembled and wept but stood still, their terror giving way to captivated wonder. Then Yandros smiled. White light flared at his heart, a blinding, seven-rayed star that briefly dimmed the Marble Hall's illumination, and he said:

"I approve, First Magus."

He turned, and spoke a single word in a language that no mortal tongue had ever uttered or could ever utter. Behind him the Chaos Gate flashed into life once more. Savrinor had a momentary impression of vast doors within the surging column of black light, swinging open on silent hinges — and then the barrier between the mortal world and the realm of Chaos was shattered, and Yandros's legions entered the Hall in a triumphant, shouting tide.

In one single, ecstatic moment the historian opened his mind and his soul to the sheer power and beauty and glory of Chaos unleashed. He was blinded by an explosion of color as a hundred different beings, the highest and the lowest creations of the gods, surged through the Gate. He glimpsed the faces of animals, the bodies of birds, the forms of all creatures within and beyond imagination, as light and sound engulfed his senses in a joyous meld. Two worlds had become one, and Savrinor was lost to them both. He saw Yandros, proud and assured, presiding over the sudden glorious mayhem. He saw Pirane laughing, her wild hair unbound as her huge body swayed to the rhythms of unhuman music that filled the Hall. He saw Pirane's flock overwhelmed by beings that mimicked human form and yet were too alien and too beautiful ever to have been human. Some screamed as they were chosen, too ignorant or too afraid to understand the honor bestowed on them; some fainted dead away, their minds broken; but a few, a very few, were made of stronger stuff. Savrinor saw a slight, dark-haired girl caught up in the arms of a creature twelve feet tall, with hair on fire and eyes that were vortices onto nothing; the demon kissed her hands, her breasts, darted to kiss her thighs and her feet, and she flung her head back, a look of wild bliss on her face that made Savrinor rejoice for her. Then a woman who seemed to be made of water, exquisite beyond belief, her eyes glittering diamond-brilliant and her voice a shrill, sweet symphony crying alien words, rushed at him like an incarnate dream, and as he reached out to embrace her Savrinor was a man blessed, hurled to new heights of strength, of passion, of frenzied euphoria. Her arms enfolded him, twin rivers sweeping him into their current — but then, even as her essence engulfed him, his senses were suddenly attuned to something else, something far greater even than the dizzying glory of her promises.

The Chaos Gate was pulsing like a huge, black heart, throbbing out a titanic rhythm that shook the Marble Hall and rocked his mind. And through its portal, out of the warp between dimensions, new figures were materializing.

The first was Yandros's own dark twin, his wild hair blacker than a storm cloud, his eyes two blazing emeralds, his face a cold and savagely aquiline sculpture. He smiled, and a ripple of raw power rocked the Hall from end to end. Behind him came a vision of fire, hair and eyes burning, unhuman venom in his look. Then a third, draped in the nacreous green and silver white of rotting weed; and Savrinor had to look quickly away, for the eyes of this being promised insanity. Three more followed: one white-haired, an eagle's profile, proud and disdainful; the next dark and beautiful with an air of peace so profound that it almost stopped Savrinor's pulse; the last a silhouette, faceless, a shadow darker and deeper than the furthest reaches of space etched upon the air.

As the seventh lord of Chaos materialized from the Gate, Savrinor fell to his knees again. The woman of water was forgotten, for her beauty and her enchantment meant nothing in the face of this. The gods — all of the gods, *all* of them — had graced their worshipers with their presence, and the historian's mind reeled giddily. On the floor, shivering, his knuckles pressed hard against the cold mosaic, he saw Yandros's six supernal kin gather beside their great brother, and above their heads a huge, glowing star began to pulse as Yandros held out his hand toward the bowed figure of Vordegh. Wordlessly, knowing what was required of him, Vordegh surrendered the wand of Chaos. As Yandros took it, the wand began to throb with urgent, brilliant life, throwing a cold, blue white light onto Vordegh's face.

Yandros raised the wand. Through the Marble Hall's dimensions all sound and all movement ceased as every gaze present turned to the tableau of the magus and his gods.

"Vordegh." Yandros spoke quietly, but his molten silver voice carried to every ear. "Chaos sanctions you as its avatar among mortals, and names you First Magus and overlord of this realm. Do you accept the honor and the burden that are set upon your shoulders?"

Vordegh fell forward, his hands sprawling across the floor at Yandros's feet. "My lord." There was triumph, controlled but intense, in his tone. "I accept the honor and I accept the burden. I am yours to command." With the wand's light still glowing on him, he raised his head. "A new age is dawning, my lord. A new age of Chaos — and I swear to you that it will be like no other age this world has ever known!"

"The man's a tiresome bore." Yandros looked disdainfully about him at the tall windows, the vaulted ceiling, the swirl of movement and color that filled the castle's vast dining hall under the dance of a hundred flaring, phosphorescent witch lights in their iron sconces. "And he's as vain, arrogant, and overweening as any of his predecessors, despite the fact that he professes to be such an ascetic." He watched a servant, carrying wine, approaching them. "Still, I suppose he's no worse a choice than any other, and at least his austere tastes have saved us from the tedium of the usual lengthy ceremonies and speeches."

The servant was passing by; the Chaos lord snapped his fingers, and when his cup was refilled the attendant bowed hastily and went on his way, not knowing whom he had served. It amused Yandros to indulge now and then in the human habits of eating and drinking, and it also amused him to move anonymously among his worshipers when the mood took him. Both he and his black-haired, green-eyed brother, who stood beside him near the double doors, had shed the signs of their Chaotic nature and now looked to all intents and purposes like any other high-ranking human guests at this feast. The servant had probably placed them as select visitors from some outlying part of the world, for many favored emissaries had been brought through the Maze to participate in the night's more secular celebrations. Only the magi knew that Yandros and his brother had chosen to join the throng gathering in the castle, and Yandros had made it clear that he wished the knowledge to go no further.

The other Chaos lord regarded the gathering with cool, speculative eyes. "There's disquiet about the choice in some quarters," he said. "Whatever his merits as a sorcerer and leader, Vordegh isn't popular."

Yandros shrugged. "That's something the magi must resolve as they see fit. They elected him, so the responsibility is entirely theirs. I'm not about to hold their hands and make their decisions for them—that's never been our way."

Expressively the other raised a dark eyebrow. "Free will?"

"Something like that." Then Yandros smiled wolfishly. "Or as near as makes no difference to the mortal mind, for they can't lament the lack of something they don't even comprehend. No, Tarod, whatever the merits or otherwise of Vordegh as First Magus, it's up to him to hold on to the reins of power in whatever way he chooses. If he can't control what he's taken on, so be it. I shan't interfere." From an adjacent table he selected a piece of heavily spiced fish. "I'm not sufficiently interested in his well-being to worry about it. There are plenty more fish in the sea. . . . Speaking of which, this food is good. I'm glad to find that, whatever manner of master they may have chosen for themselves, our subjects still know how to make the most of their subtler pleasures."

Tarod was still scanning the hall. Colors flickered and shifted and merged under the unearthly lights, and the sea of faces, some human, some unhuman, others a disturbing hybrid, moved like a living tide among the dazzle. In one corner near the vast fireplace something blue and silver and strange was dancing, attracting an appreciative audience, while other denizens of Chaos, permitted by their lord to taste mortal festivities for one night, mingled silently among the guests, some in company with a boy or girl chosen from Pirane's "flock" for a brief alliance. But amid the revelry Tarod noted a number of bemused or even frightened faces, and his lips twitched with faint amusement.

"Pleasure, I think, is a relative concept," he said. "Some of Vordegh's outland guests look as though they'd prefer to be alone in their beds at this moment, with the door bolted and barred."

Yandros laughed. "The loss is entirely theirs. They'll either learn to swallow their terrors, or be less eager to push themselves to the forefront of the magi's favor in future. Well, if they are unwilling to enter the fray, I'm not. Let's divert ourselves and sample the entertainments. If what we see pleases us, I'll consider deferring the breaking of dawn for a few hours, so that everyone might benefit from our enjoyment."

Somewhere among the press of people but, fortunately, far enough from the high dais to escape the First Magus's notice, Benetan and Andraia were on the verge of another quarrel.

This time it was entirely Benetan's fault, and he knew it and was silently upbraiding himself for a fool. The night had begun well enough; in an amber-studded gown that clung to her willow-slim body but revealed her long, painted legs, and with the hundred tiny braids of her hair threaded with gold like a great, glittering mane, Andraia looked lovelier and more desirable than ever before. And thanks to her family connections they'd had privileged places in the throng that made formal obeisance to the First Magus when he returned with his entourage from the Marble Hall. Several people had remarked in their hearing that Benetan and his consort were among the most striking couples in the hall, and when Savrinor, who had briefly left the gathering, returned with Iselia on his arm, Benetan was determined to pay no heed to the fair girl. But one look at the dead-white mask of her face had undone his resolve. He'd been drawn reluctantly into a small group that had congregated around Lua, Andraia's mother, and was making stilted small talk with them when the historian and his "protégée," as it now pleased Savrinor to call her, had entered the hall. Benetan glanced briefly at Iselia, and his voice trailed off in the middle of answering a question Lua had put to him.

Andraia nudged his hip savagely and painfully with her elbow.

Hastily Benetan snapped his mind back to attention, but the damage was done; Lua was clearly put out by his lapse and others were looking askance at him, suppressing wry smiles. Worse still, Andraia's sharp eyes hadn't failed to focus on the object of his sudden distraction.

She also noticed the surreptitious glances he kept casting over his shoulder when she asked him to fetch her some food a few minutes later. Weaving his way between the bright, noisy clusters of celebrants, Benetan couldn't keep his mind on Andraia's request. All he could think of, all he could concentrate on, was Iselia.

What had Savrinor done to her? Speculations and possibilities tumbled through Benetan's head, each one wilder and more sickening than the last. He couldn't have taken her to the Marble Hall. He had promised to shield her from that, and Savrinor never broke his promises. *What,* then? For something within Iselia's mind had broken, Benetan knew it as surely as he knew anything. Her hair was too perfectly dressed above that ashen face and her clothes too neat and smooth, a careful disguise to mask a terrible darkness. Her mouth smiled mechanically but the smiles were rigidly controlled and there was emptiness behind them. And her eyes held no animation, no emotion, but seemed to look into a world from which all warmth and all hope had been eradicated.

Benetan knew he shouldn't have done what he did then, but at that moment the restraining hand of Yandros himself couldn't have prevented him. Forgetting the food, forgetting Andraia, he turned from the tables and walked straight across the hall, apologizing absently to those he barged into, until his path crossed that of the approaching couple.

"Savrinor . . ." He didn't know what to say, but the look on his face made the need for words redundant.

"Good evening, Benetan." The historian's voice was perfectly calm, although his eyes looked heavy, as though drugged with a narcotic or with some peculiar intensity of feeling. Then he turned to the girl at his side. "Iselia, my dear, here is Benetan come to pay his respects." He was holding Iselia's hand; he squeezed it.

Iselia smiled another of her meaningless, contrived smiles. "You look very fine tonight, Benet. Are you enjoying the celebrations?"

Gods, Benetan thought, she didn't even *sound* like the Iselia he knew. Now that they were at close quarters he could see that her eyes weren't simply emotionless, they were also cold. Cold and hard as metal, distant, uninterested. She looked at him as though she had never met him before and had no wish ever to meet him again.

Benetan said sharply, chokingly, "Savrinor, what —"

Savrinor interrupted, and his gaze flicked over Benetan's shoulder and past him. "And here is Andraia coming to join us. How delightful."

Benetan's head whipped round and he saw the vivid copper gold flicker of Andraia's hair among the crowd, the shimmer of her gown as she moved with lithe but aggressive grace toward them.

"*Savrinor* —" He had to ask, had to know —

"Not now, you bloody fool, and not here!" Drugged or not, Savrinor was suddenly alert as a hawk, and he hissed back savagely. "Lua is watching you, and Pirane's with her!" Then swiftly his voice and the focus of his pale, angry eyes changed and he sidestepped around Benetan, holding out a graceful hand. "My dear Andraia! How lovely you look — come here and stand at my side, and then I can pretend that you're consorting with me instead of with this overgrown young hound you're so inexplicably fond of!"

His manner took Andraia by surprise in just the way he'd intended, but after a moment she collected herself and laughed her warm, husky laugh.

"As always, Master Savrinor, your observations are both accurate and timely," she said, and flashed Benetan a glare that warned him to look to his own salvation the moment they were alone. "And if I may return the compliment, you are handsome enough to grace any woman's bed tonight, from the highest to the lowest."

The word *lowest* was faintly emphasized and accompanied by another swift and venomous glance, in Iselia's direction this time. But if Andraia expected a reaction she was disappointed. Iselia only continued to gaze into the middle distance, unmoved.

"Be careful, lady, or I might be tempted to put your claim to the test," Savrinor warned, and even in his distraught state of mind Benetan noted the comment and wasn't sure whether or not the historian was joking. For a moment or two Andraia's green eyes held Savrinor's thoughtfully, then with an abrupt movement she linked her arm with Benetan's.

"Well, we must both be disappointed for the time being, Master Savrinor, as it seems we're both spoken for. I'll take my overgrown hound away and put him back on his leash for a dance or two" — Benetan felt the pressure she applied to his biceps — "and wish you a joyous night."

This time Benetan had wit enough not to demur in any way, and he let Andraia lead him away through the crowd. Music had started to play, soft and subtle, drifting down from the gallery above the dining hall's vast hearth, though whether the musicians were human or lent by Chaos to grace the occasion Benetan didn't know, for they were invisible behind the gallery's heavy curtains. As though responding to an instinctive signal, people graduated toward the sides of the hall to create dancing space at the center. Couples began to pair up; a short distance away Benetan saw the striking and unmistakable figure of Magus Pirane, with Lua at her side, and he spared a cautious glance toward the dais where Vordegh sat in solitary splendor. Vordegh did not dance — he eschewed almost all of what might be called the ordinary pleasures of life — but his dark eyes were alert and intent as he watched the festivities, and his full-lipped mouth smiled with satisfaction.

Benetan would have led Andraia out to join the couples forming up in the middle of the hall, but Andraia had other priorities. She pulled him out of the main press of people, then looked him straight in the eye.

"All right, Benet," she hissed, keeping her voice low. "Who is that girl?"

Benetan's cheeks flamed, paled, flamed again. "She's Savrinor's protégée."

"I can see *that*." Andraia's tone was scathing. "But what I *can't* see is why you're so interested in her all of a sudden!"

"I'm not interested in her."

"No?" Andraia's eyes narrowed. "So why have you done nothing but stare like a moonstruck oaf at her since she walked into the hall?"

"I haven't!" Then, realizing that the protest sounded hollow, Benetan tried to explain without giving too much away. "It's just . . . she was brought to the castle in our last gleaning, and I — I used to know her, many years ago. She's from my home district." He paused. "Gods, Andraia, this is ridiculous! Iselia's nothing to me and she never was." *Liar*, said his conscience. He pushed it forcibly down.

Andraia didn't answer, though she stored the name, Iselia, securely away in her memory. Discomfited by her long silence, Benetan said tentatively, "You're not *jealous*? Of her?"

"Jealous? Me?" Andraia tossed her hair back with a brittle, affected laugh. "No." Her eyes narrowed still further, and there was a dangerous glitter in them now. "Should I be?"

"Of course not!"

"Good. I'm glad you see it that way, Benet, for I'll tell you here and now that I have no intention of comparing myself to that — that vacuous *baggage*. Take a fancy to her if it amuses you; take her to your bed for a night and do whatever you like to her; neither of us is averse to the occasional dalliance and that's all well and good. But do not — I repeat, *do not* — insult me by making a spectacle of yourself with her in public, or I shall have no hesitation in finding a new consort!"

A few people nearby were watching them, some covertly, others openly and smiling with amusement. Benetan felt his face redden again, and sharply he turned Andraia away from the impromptu audience, telling himself that against the background of music and chatter no one could have overheard more than a few words of their skirmish.

"You're making fire out of ashes, Andraia." His voice was clipped, strained with the twin warring pressures of guilt and anger. "I am *not* interested in Iselia in any of the ways you think, and *you're* insulting *me* if you believe for one moment that I am! She's simply a face from my past, and I wouldn't be human if I didn't have some care for her wellbeing."

Andraia's teeth nipped at her lower lip, and the expression in her eyes became thoughtful. "I see. And I suppose that explains your business with Savrinor a few days ago, does it? You persuaded him to take her, to save her from the Marble Hall ceremonies?"

"Yes. That's exactly what I did."

"And now you're having second thoughts."

"*No!*" Behind them someone sniggered, and Benetan hastily lowered his voice. "No, I am *not* having second thoughts. I simply sought to inquire after her, to make sure that she prospers." He sighed heavily, exasperatedly. "Andraia, will you please stop this? It's pointless, it's meaningless, and I've had enough! We're supposed to be celebrating the inauguration of First Magus Vordegh, not squabbling like two cats over one bird!" He caught hold of her hand, gripping it so hard that she winced. "Dance with me, and let's forget Savrinor and Iselia. Dance, before we both lose our tempers and say things we might regret later!"

For several seconds they stood motionless, their mutual challenge unresolved. Andraia wanted to pull her hand away but didn't; Benetan wanted to kiss her and hit her, and didn't know which emotion was the stronger.

Then a new voice broke the deadlock.

"Andraia, my delight. D'you have an embrace for your father, or must I join the queue for your favors?"

The tall, thin, patrician man had moved up on them so quietly that neither had been aware of his approach, but on hearing his voice Andraia turned and, with a cry of delight, reached up to hug and kiss him. Benetan had rarely met Qenever, who was one of the magi's highest-ranking secretaries, responsible for setting the tithes that the Star Peninsula exacted from their vassals throughout the world. Andraia's parents had tired of each other and moved on to other lovers fifteen years ago, but Qenever was proud of his daughter's beauty and intelligence; and, Benetan suspected, not entirely in favor of her liaison with a man who wasn't castle bred.

Nonetheless, Qenever greeted Benetan with punctilious courtesy. "Captain Liss. Felicitations on this happy occasion — and my compliments on what I understand was a splendid gleaning for tonight's celebration."

Benetan made a bow in the formal manner adopted by the Chaos riders. "Thank you, sir. I'm gratified by your praise."

There was a girl at Qenever's side, a small, dark, and sallow creature, probably no more than thirteen years old but with a spirited eye and a willful tilt to her chin. Ignoring her, Qenever caught Andraia's hand; the hand that Benetan had reflexively released.

"Sweet child, you look delectable enough to eat. Grace your sire with a dance, or send him away a broken man."

Andraia's vivid green eyes raked Benetan, and then she smiled her sweetest smile. "Yes," she said. "I'll be glad to dance with you, Father. *More* than glad. And perhaps your little plaything can keep Benet happy in my absence, as he seems to have a roving eye tonight!"

There was nothing Benetan could say. In a single, cutting sentence Andraia had made it quite clear that he wasn't forgiven, and he stepped back as Qenever led her away to where couples were forming up in the cleared space at the center of the hall. A shimmering fanfare in a minor key announced the first set, a formal walking dance, and a small, dark hand closed on Benetan's arm.

"Captain." Qenever's paramour was looking up at him with the eyes of a knowing and hungry coquette. "Will you favor me with your company?"

Her voice was as light and thin as a reed pipe; the voice of a child. Benetan looked at the lines of dancers. Andraia laughing as her sire whispered some private word in her ear. And, further down the line, Savrinor and Iselia. He couldn't look at Iselia's face. . . .

"No." The refusal was sharper than he'd intended it to be and he tried to soften it, though the result was more of a rictus than a smile. "No — thank you, but I . . . don't dance."

She laughed, a silvery sound. "Like our First Magus!" Her body touched against him, briefly but in a way that made her compliance abundantly clear. "But I'm sure you don't scorn *all* pleasures?"

Suddenly Benetan felt sick. He took two breaths, and the mingled smells of food, wine, smoke, and the girl's heady perfume oppressed his senses. With an effort, he forced another smile.

"You're very astute," he said. "But at the moment I have other things to concern me." He bowed over her hand. "Good night."

Whether she was watching him as he walked away, and whether she was offended by his rejection, he neither knew nor cared. All that concerned Benetan at this moment was the prospect of finding a servant, and sending for wine, and getting more drunk than he'd ever been in his life.

CHAPTER IX

Six cups of wine later, Benetan still hadn't achieved his goal. The trouble was, he reflected as he beckoned a servant to refill his cup for the seventh time, he'd developed too good a head for drink during his years with the Chaos riders; one of the hazards, perhaps, of the profession. There'd been that time a year or two back, just after his last but one promotion, when one of the sergeants — couldn't remember his name now, but he'd drowned a few months later, during that stupid escapade with the commandeered fishing boat which had led to six men being stripped of their ranks and sent to menial posts at some forsaken hole in the east — when that sergeant had challenged him to a drinking contest, and against everyone's expectations Benetan had won. . . .

Ah, better. Trivial thoughts and inebriated memories; the wine must be having some effect on him at last. He looked up from the reflections in his cup and saw with gloomy satisfaction that the lights in the hall looked over bright and that there were faint, fuzzy halos at the torches' edges. Andraia's father had gone back to his child lover now and Andraia was dancing with someone else. Two or three more cups and he'd put a stop to that, he'd ask her — no, *tell* her — to dance with him. Show her that he wouldn't be trifled with. Or maybe instead he'd ask Iselia for a dance, and if Savrinor didn't like it, he could —

"Not joining in the fun, Captain Liss?"

Startled by the unfamiliar voice, Benetan turned round. The tall, blond-haired man had moved up behind him and was leaning against the wall, smiling with faint, ironic humor. Wine or no wine, Benetan was still in control of himself, and though he didn't recognize the newcomer, he sensed immediately that this was someone of rank. The man's handsome, sharp-boned face had a patrician look, and his clothes, though not elaborate, were of a very fine quality. Benetan quickly straightened his shoulders, and made the formally courteous bow of the Chaos riders.

"Sir. Pardon me — I wasn't aware of your approach."

The stranger laughed and gestured toward Benetan's hand. "By the look of it you weren't aware of anything much beyond the contents of your cup. Is the wine so good that you can't bear to abandon it, or are you drowning your sorrows?"

Despite his wariness Benetan couldn't suppress an answering wry grin. "A little of both, perhaps, sir."

Pale brows over eyes whose color was hard to judge in the torchlight went up expressively. "I see. I wouldn't have thought that a young man of your rank and attributes would have reason for sorrow on a night like this." He paused. "Didn't I see you with Secretary Qenever's daughter a little earlier?"

Benetan wasn't sure that he liked his business being known and probed into by strangers, however high ranking, but he dared not show his displeasure. "Yes, sir. We . . . ah . . . had a small disagreement."

"Ah well, these things happen. Here, refill your cup again. Then you can tell me how the Chaos riders view the appointment of their new First Magus."

Benetan was suddenly coldly alert. The stranger had spoken quite casually, but he detected a hint of greater interest underlying the apparent negligence. Was this man some agent of Vordegh's, sent among the guests to test the attitudes and loyalties of key members of the castle hierarchy? The thought that he himself might be viewed as a key figure made Benetan's blood chill. But it was horribly logical. After all, as captain of the Chaos riders he had a crucial role to play in carrying out the First Magus's will. And Vordegh's rule promised to be very different from that of his predecessor. . . . Gods, he thought, he'd have to tread as though he were walking on broken glass.

The fair man had summoned a servant; more wine splashed into

Benetan's cup. "So," the stranger said. "What is your opinion of First Magus Vordegh, Captain Liss?"

Benetan was no actor, but he needed an actor's skills now as never before. Praying silently to Yandros that his face wouldn't color and give him away, or that his voice wouldn't quaver, he said, "I'm proud to serve our new First Magus, sir. We all are. He's . . ." He fought back an urge to lick his lips, which were bone dry. "He is a . . . formidable leader, a fine man . . . and a true servant of our gods."

"A formidable leader, and a fine man." The stranger repeated the words thoughtfully, as though neither concept had occurred to him before now. Then he smiled, an enigmatic smile. "That's very well spoken, Captain. Well, I shall leave you to your solitary cup — and wish you a happier night than you seem to have had thus far."

He started to turn away, then stopped. Following the direction of his gaze Benetan saw Savrinor a short way off. The historian was talking to a portly, overdressed, and sweating man with a swarthy face, a visitor from the south, and Iselia stood beside him, her eyes cast down and her expression introverted. Benetan felt the wine in his stomach curdle as all his earlier fears for her came crowding back. Then the stranger called out crisply,

"Master Savrinor."

Savrinor turned, and his face froze.

The stranger smiled. One hand made a slight gesture, and, leaving Iselia and the swarthy southerner standing and staring after him, Savrinor approached. As he drew close, Benetan saw with astonishment that he was trembling.

"My . . ." Savrinor's voice was soft, awed. "My lord . . ." And he made a bow of the deepest reverence.

The stranger laughed gently. "Well well, Savrinor; so you're a good deal sharper than you like to pretend. . . . I'm complimented that you recognize me. In that, at least, you have the advantage of your friend Captain Liss."

Savrinor shot Benetan a look of pure horror which Benetan didn't understand. What did the stranger mean? Why should he have recognized him when they'd never met before? And why, in all the Seven Hells, was Savrinor so obviously terrified of this man?

"But, then," the stranger continued, "Captain Liss wasn't among the privileged few in the Marble Hall tonight, so it's hardly fair to expect him to have your insight."

Savrinor tried desperately to speak, but the effort was stumbling, garbled, barely coherent. "My lord, I — I can hardly — that is, I don't — "

Benetan, who had never known the historian to be at a loss for words, was nonplussed. But the tall man only laughed again, a kindly laugh without any malice.

"There's no need for speeches, Savrinor, and no need to justify yourself. I know the strength of your allegiance and the depth of your fidelity, and I assure you that that is worth far more than any words." He turned then with a graceful movement, and made a slight but explicit bow. "Good night to you both."

Savrinor didn't move a muscle. He could only stare, transfixed, as the fair-haired figure moved away into the press of the crowd. Benetan, still not comprehending anything that had happened, drained his cup again and swayed slightly on his feet. Then, so suddenly and violently that he started, Savrinor turned on him.

"*What did he say to you?*" His voice was a hiss, and his face was corpse white.

Benetan shook his head, waving one hand in a negating gesture. "He simply approached me and engaged me in conversation. It's all right; I wasn't indiscreet. Damn it, Savrinor, what kind of idiot d'you take me for?"

"I don't know," Savrinor said through clenched teeth; then his eyes widened. "But, then . . . you don't know, either, do you? You still haven't realized. *Gods* — " He snapped the oath off and made the sign of the Seven-Rayed Star before his own face. "*You still don't know who it was you were talking to!*"

The latest onslaught of wine was starting to rush to Benetan's head, and he blinked at the historian. "I don't know his name, if that's what you mean. But I'm not so drunk, yet, that I haven't the wit to realize when I'm being tested by one of the First Magus's spies."

"One of the — " Savrinor's voice went up the scale in harsh incredulity before he was able to snatch it back under some semblance of control. "You fool!" he said. "You blind, stupid, thrice-cursed and thrice-exalted *fool!*"

Suddenly then, for the first time, an inkling of the truth began to dawn on Benetan. His fingers clenched round the empty wine cup, and his face and his voice were pallid as he said,

"Savrinor . . . who *was* he?"

Savrinor shut his eyes and silently swore anathema on Benetan's witlessness. "He's here," he said, and his voice was barely audible. "He's here, among us. And he spoke to me." His eyes opened again and he met Benetan's gaze with a look in which joy, terror, and bewilderment mingled. "That," he whispered, "was Yandros himself."

The castle's battlements were a good refuge tonight for anyone who wanted to be alone. It was impossible to escape the celebrations entirely, for the courtyard below was bathed in light from the dining hall's tall windows, and wild music and wilder laughter drifted up on the night air, but still Andraia found something approaching isolation on the high black wall.

She leaned on the parapet, staring out at the dark sward of the castle stack and idly trying to glimpse the faint, telltale shimmer that would tell her where her elaborate gold shoes had landed. The search was academic, simply a device to keep her mind away from other matters; she didn't want the damned shoes back and didn't regret the instant of corrosive fury that had made her kick them off her feet and hurl them away. In fact if it wasn't for the east wind biting across the battlements, she'd have have been sorely tempted to tear off all her finery, clothes, jewels, and ornaments alike, and fling it piece by piece in the shoes' wake.

A short way from where she stood the castle's south spire towered into the night, a vast, ominous bulk looming above her head. Normally Andraia didn't suffer from vertigo, but now she carefully avoided looking upward. She'd drunk far too much; one glimpse of the spire in its entirety and she'd probably be sick, which would set the final, ignominious seal on a thoroughly hideous evening. She was glad that the second moon had set and only a faint scatter of stars lit the sky now. Moonlight made it harder to hide from herself or from anyone else, and all she wanted, all she wanted in the world, was to be left undisturbed.

Either that, or to be in Benetan's room with a knife in her hand. Fortunately for Benetan, two of his own sergeants had managed to get him out of the hall without drawing attention to the condition he was in. Andraia had never seen him in such a state before, and really that revelation was what had triggered her own headlong rush into the refuge of wine. Not the *fact* that Benetan had drunk himself all but insensible, but the *reason* why he'd done it. The sergeants had been baffled, or at least professed to be, but she knew. She'd seen the reason with her own eyes. And the reason was still down there in the hall, trailing about on Savrinor's arm like a half-trained puppy on its master's leash.

Why? Andraia asked herself. That was what she didn't understand. *Why* was Benetan so fascinated, so infatuated, with that empty-faced peasant girl? She felt her temper rising again and forced it back with a great effort. If Benet had simply taken a passing fancy to the creature, then he could have had her and forgotten her, as she had already told him. Savrinor wouldn't have objected; in fact it might have been amusing for the four of them to make a game of the whole thing. But Benetan hadn't been playing games. Aware of Andraia's feelings, aware that he was publicly slighting her, he'd still been ready to leave her side and run sniffing after that worthless *slut* as though she were the love of his life!

Andraia had been determined not to cry, but suddenly hot tears were spilling down her cheeks and she couldn't control them. Savagely she tried to convince herself that they were a sign of fury and not of grief, but the pretense didn't last, and she hid her face in her folded arms, biting at the soft flesh of her forearm in an effort to make the tears stop. All right, she thought; she'd had far too much wine and doubtless that was making her overreact. But surely, *surely* Benetan didn't have so little regard for her? He loved her, or so she'd thought for the past two years. And she, idiot that she was, loved him. So how was it that some grubby, uneducated, whey-faced *trollop* from the back of beyond could snatch him away from her as though she were nothing? She should have listened to Qenever, her father. He'd always said that Benetan wasn't good enough for her, that she should find herself a consort who was at least castle bred. Or Magus Pirane, who was always so generous to her; she should have accepted her offer of a less formal meeting with Garvid, newly elevated to the magi's ranks. Damn Benetan Liss. *Damn* him.

But even in the depths of her bitterness Andraia knew that she didn't want and never had wanted to listen to Qenever or to be a party to Magus Pirane's matchmaking. She wanted one thing and one only: Benetan, and the old intimacy, the old relationship, which had been so inexplicably uprooted by tonight's events. And she wanted to know exactly, *precisely*, what that peasant girl meant to him, and why.

The tears were stopping. She raised her head, rubbed at the painful marks her teeth had made in her arm, then tore off a piece of her sleeve and blew her nose on it. Then as she tossed the scrap of fabric over the battlements, a voice spoke out of the darkness and made her jump like a shot hare.

"Well, well. I thought I was the only one seeking a respite from the celebrations."

Andraia turned sharply. She had a momentary impression of the spire's titanic silhouette as it seemed to topple from the sky at her. Then she saw the darker shape, tall and lithe, black etched on black, barely visible.

Instinct and a lifetime's habit rallied her, and she straightened in a quick, fluid movement, tilting her chin proudly and praying that the starlight didn't show the tear streaks on her face.

"And I, sir, didn't expect anyone to impinge on my solitude." Her tone was acid; she hadn't recognized his voice, didn't know who he was, but suspected that some outland visitor had glimpsed her alone up here and was trying to take advantage of an obvious opportunity.

"I apologize, lady." Suddenly, though she still couldn't so much as glimpse his face, she could see his eyes. Green eyes, like emeralds, lit from within. . . . A peculiar intuition moved in Andraia, and she drew breath into a throat that was suddenly constricted.

He moved, then, out of the spire's deep shadow. He was wearing black, she saw, plain and unadorned black; and his hair was black, too, curling over high, narrow shoulders like smoke curling from a quiet fire. Gods, she thought, there was something about him. Whatever he might be, she had a peculiar intuition that mortality was an alien concept to him. . . .

"I — " She stopped, licked her lips. "I meant no offense. I simply wanted to . . . be alone for a while."

He made a small bow. "Then I'll leave you in peace."

"No!" The denial was involuntary; Andraia tried to make sense of it and failed. "No — please, stay. If you will." She turned her head and stared down over the parapet, and abruptly felt an overwhelming urge to strip away pretense and be honest. "Solitude loses its appeal after a while," she said. "Especially when I didn't *want* the night to end this way."

"Ah." There was, or seemed to her disordered mind, a wealth of sympathy and understanding in the one word. He moved closer; she thought he was going to touch her, but instead he turned and rested his elbows on the parapet, staring out into the night.

"There's little real solace to be had in wine. That's hardly an original observation, but it's true nonetheless."

The starlight sketched his profile against the sky; sharp, high boned; a thoughtful and faintly humorous quirk to his thin mouth. Suddenly Andraia felt very small.

"I didn't mean to do it. But when he — "

The stranger turned his head and looked directly at her, and the rest of what she'd been about to say died on her tongue. What did it matter? What did he care about Benetan, or their quarrel, or her problems? She'd never met him before, and doubtless after tonight she'd never meet him again. This was meaningless.

But then perhaps the very fact that it *was* meaningless could be her saving grace? A combative spark awoke suddenly in Andraia, shifting her self-pity to a new perspective. She wanted both to hit back at Benetan and to salvage her own pride. If a total stranger offered her the means, why should she refuse? And if that stranger also happened to have caught at some deep current within the rivers of her imagination, then the spice would be all the greater.

She glanced obliquely at her companion, then abruptly turned away as she realized that it couldn't be that simple. Something about this man precluded any of the customary bantering hints and games of manners that would otherwise have made her interest clear. Somehow, she felt, such rules didn't apply to him, and that conviction made her uneasy.

She was still debating, still unsure, when a hand closed over hers. The fingers were long, the bones gaunt, but there was strength in his grip. No, not so much strength as *power*. It startled Andraia and she made a small, involuntary sound, like a kitten's mew. But even now he didn't turn to her, didn't reach out for her, but only said,

"And is there no one else in the great hall tonight who might offer you solace?"

Her blood seemed to stop flowing and turn cold. It was as if he had read her deepest thoughts. Wide-eyed, she stared at him, and in the darkness his smile was the smile of a lazy, patient predator. Then, to her astonishment, he laughed.

"No; perhaps not. It's a dull celebration by the magi's standards, after all. I must say I'm surprised by our good Vordegh's restraint; but then he's always considered himself something of an ascetic."

She tried to swallow, but her throat was dry. "You . . . know the First Magus?"

"Yes." The vivid green gaze flicked keenly to her face. "Does that make a difference?"

"No . . . I simply thought — wondered . . ." Andraia faltered, then took refuge in a challenge of her own. "You haven't told me your name."

"And you haven't told me yours; though I've heard it spoken by others."

She was oddly gratified by the thought that he had, perhaps, asked about her, and suddenly, involuntarily, she gave him one of her natural and brilliant smiles, a look of sheer, unaffected warmth. He laughed again, but pleasantly, almost affectionately. "Well, Lady Andraia, I'm glad to see that you're not entirely downcast! So tonight isn't a lost cause."

Her confidence was returning. "For you, sir, or for me?"

"Perhaps for both of us." His hand was still holding hers; abruptly though subtly the grip increased. "Do you want to return to the festivities?"

Andraia looked directly into his eyes. *Sweet Yandros*, she thought, *but if he only chose, this man could have the power to turn the sea from its course! But, then . . . but, then, I don't believe he is merely a man. . . .*

"No," she said.

Very slowly, very deliberately, he raised her fingers to his lips and kissed them. The kiss felt like fire on her skin, and in that moment she knew the truth.

Hesitantly yet eagerly, barely able to contain the thrill of giddying, terrified delight that coursed through her, she whispered, "My lord . . . ?"

Still holding her hand to his lips, Tarod of Chaos raised his forefinger in a silent and conspiratorial gesture. Andraia understood, and she nodded. No one else would ever know of this. It would be a fleeting interlude, a brief bridging of the gulf between the mortal and the supernal. Though she knew that for him it was no more than a moment's dalliance, yet she felt the wound of betrayal healing, and for that kindness and that alone she would love him above all the gods.

A dark wing of shadow seemed to move over her as he drew her toward him, and she felt the psychic touch of a power that thrilled her to the core of her being as he said softly,

"Not only kindness, Andraia. Not only that."

The stars gazed down, tiny eyes in the vast bowl of darkness, silent and secret witnesses who would never tell what they had seen, as she walked away with him toward the south spire.

CHAPTER X

How many hours passed until the last, die-hard revelers finally sought the relief of sleep, no one would ever know. Yandros of Chaos had been pleased by the celebrations, and so he used the power which, long ago, he had invested in the fabric of the castle, to shift the great black building fractionally out of phase with the normal spectrum of time. Had he chosen to make it so, the night could have been endless; but at last the power was revoked, and the gods and their denizens departed from the mortal world as the first cold glint of dawn showed on the eastern horizon.

Barring those servants who had no choice in the matter, few of the castle's inhabitants stirred until the morning was well on. Benetan Liss woke to find himself facedown on his own bed, still fully dressed and with sledgehammers pounding in his skull. For a minute or two he had only vague recollections of his last hour at the revelries, but then, like mist clearing to reveal a dismal landscape, memory came back with awful clarity, and he covered his head with his hands, suppressing a groan of self-recrimination. What had he done? An image haunted him of Andraia's face, tight with disgust and betrayal, swimming before him just before his senior sergeant had helped him from the hall. She'd looked furious and miserable together, and he hadn't wanted to hurt her, hadn't wanted her to believe for one moment that he — that Iselia —

He cut the train of thought off, not knowing what he did want or what Andraia might or might not believe. Until he could clear his system of last night's poisons he'd be fit for nothing. With an effort he raised his head, but immediately his stomach protested and he thought better of the rash impulse to sit up. He needed more time, more sleep. If he made any attempt to see Andraia in his present condition, he'd deserve all she was likely to give him, and more.

"Oh, *Yandros*..." Then, horribly, the unthinking oath brought the other thing, the one fact that had stayed buried in his subconscious, surging to the surface. An image of the tall, fair-haired man who had spoken to him in the hall was suddenly sharply and urgently clear in his mind. He'd thought the man was an agent of Vordegh's, a player in some devious game the First Magus had devised. But Savrinor had said . . .

Benetan's stomach churned again as he sat up, but he couldn't heed the warning this time. If he was sick, so be it; better in fact that he should be, for it might sweep the miasma away. He *had* to clear his head. Revian, the castle's general physician, must be abroad by now; he'd surely have something to stop the giddy nausea and at least keep him upright. He couldn't wait. He *must* see Savrinor and find out the truth.

Fighting against retching spasms, Benetan rose to his unsteady feet and made dizzily but determinedly for the door.

Savrinor had not yet risen, but neither was he asleep. He lay in his bed, as he had lain for several hours, gazing at the shadowed ceiling above him, his eyes half lidded and his expression one of peculiarly peaceful contemplation. At his side Iselia slept, her face turned away from him but her body relaxed. Last night, when they had left the celebrations and returned to his apartments, she hadn't spoken a word but had simply taken off her finery and shown by her posture and the downward tilt of her head that she would not fight him but was ready to submit to whatever he desired. Savrinor, however, had no thought of further pleasures, and had coolly but courteously told her that while her presence would be pleasing to him, tonight he wanted nothing more from her. He'd seen the uncertain, fearful glimmer in her eyes as she climbed dutifully into bed at his side, but he made no further comment and after a restless while she had fallen asleep and left him to his private reverie.

Now, irritatingly, someone was disturbing that reverie by knocking at his door, and though he'd tried to ignore it the unknown visitor was proving persistent. At last Savrinor gave up. He rose, pulled on a fur-trimmed robe against the cold, and went through to the outer chamber to answer the summons.

"Benetan." He looked the younger man up and down, making no effort to temper the displeasure in his voice. "Dear gods, you look an abysmal sight. What do you mean by calling on me at this hour?"

"It's nearly midday."

"It may well be, but I'm not nearly ready to be dragged from my warm and peaceful bed by an unwarranted intrusion. What do you want?"

"I must talk to you, Savrinor. It's urgent."

The historian eyed him shrewdly for a few seconds, detecting something in his look which, perhaps, Benetan would not have wanted him to see. Then he relented.

"Oh, very well, if you must. Come in, and shut the door behind you; there's a draft in the corridor fit to freeze granite." He walked across the room toward his wine cupboard. "I trust you'll remember this favor in the future."

Benetan ignored that and said with a new sharpness in his voice, "Where's Iselia?"

He had noticed her neat, empty bed on the far side of the room. Savrinor glanced pointedly and a little malevolently toward the inner door, which was sufficiently ajar to show a glimpse of his own bed, though not whether it was occupied. "That," he said, "is none of your business — as you'd have done well to remember last night. But I in my turn won't be so vulgar as to ask you where Andraia is today, as I don't suppose you're any better informed on that subject than I am."

The jibe went home and Benetan had the good grace to flush.

"Sit down," Savrinor told him. "You're not a pleasant sight standing there swaying on your feet like a dog just rescued from drowning. Have you seen Revian, and has he given you something for your hangover?"

Benetan's color deepened. "Yes," he said, his voice clipped.

"Well, that's one mercy at least. Some wine?" He proffered a bottle and Benetan winced. "As you please. I thought you had a good head for drink."

"There are limits."

"True; and from what I saw last night you've learned how to surpass them. Well, then; now we've put the pleasantries behind us, and I've tactfully failed to inquire after Andraia's welfare, I'll ask you again: what do you want?"

Benetan subsided heavily onto the nearest chair. He couldn't cope with Savrinor's sharply bantering tongue; he had to speak bluntly or hold his peace and go away.

"Last night," he said. "Look, Savrinor, I know I was drunk and the memory plays tricks, but . . . the man. The tall man, with the fair hair . . ."

"Ah." Savrinor's tone and manner changed immediately; he was suddenly attentive, and serious. "Yes. I wondered if you would remember."

"I remember. You said . . ." But he couldn't get the words out. He swallowed. "Was it true, Savrinor? Was that man . . . Lord Yandros himself?"

There was a long pause while the historian poured himself a small cup of dark wine. Then, without looking round, he spoke.

"Benetan, you know my reputation, but I think you also know me well enough to be aware that I would not, under any circumstances, tease you or mislead you on such a subject as this." Another pause, then he turned to face the younger man. "Yes. The one who approached you and spoke to you was Lord Yandros. And I hope for your own sake that you will never, *ever* forget the privilege that has been bestowed on you."

Shafts of searing heat and withering cold chased each other through Benetan's blood and bones. "Gods . . . ," he whispered at last. "I thought . . . I told myself . . . it wasn't possible." There was no color whatever in his face now; he looked up at Savrinor helplessly. "But *why*? Why should he have chosen me?"

"I can't fathom Lord Yandros's reasoning, and I wouldn't presume to try." Savrinor fingered his cup but didn't drink from it; his expression had grown introspective. "I saw him in the Marble Hall. That alone would have been worth bartering my life for; I didn't dream to have the greater blessing of seeing him mingling among the celebrants in the castle, let alone dream to imagine that he might . . ." But Savrinor didn't want to speak of his own encounter with the greatest

Chaos lord; his feelings were private and to be savored privately, as he had done through the slow dawn and morning hours. He brought himself back under control and continued, almost carelessly, "The gods have their own means and their own motives, Benetan, and it isn't for us to speculate about either. Be content that Lord Yandros considered you fit for his notice. You're a very fortunate man."

That was the nub of it. Benetan said, "But *am* I, Savrinor?" He ran his tongue over dry lips. "If I displeased Lord Yandros in any way, if I said the wrong thing — "

There was a moment's hesitation, then Savrinor uttered a sharp bark of a laugh. "Oh, by all of the Seven Hells! Your peasant origins are showing, my friend." He shook his head, quelling the laughter. "You may have been bred to believe that the gods hear every word we mortals utter and that they're constantly and fearsomely poised to punish the smallest transgression; but twelve years here should have taught you to throw off that childish nonsense! Grow up, Benetan. Our gods aren't ogres, and it would take far more than a few of your drunken and tactless slurrings to move Yandros to anything but amusement!"

Benetan turned his head sharply away. "Is that meant to be a reassurance?"

"Yes, of course it is; and if my words have a sour edge it's because I don't take kindly to having my private hours interrupted without notice or permission." The historian sighed exasperatedly. "Take my word and accept it, Benetan. You haven't offended Lord Yandros. Far from it, I suspect, or would he have troubled to single you out from among so many? Now, calm your unease and clear your head." He paused. "Then you can tell me the *real* reason why you're here."

He saw immediately that his guess had been accurate, for Benetan's chin came up sharply and there was a clear glint of guilt in his eyes before he could mask it.

"Yes." Savrinor smiled and took a long draft from his cup. "I thought so. It's Iselia, isn't it? Your question of a few minutes ago wasn't quite as careless as you'd have me believe." He set the cup down, pulled his robe more closely around his slight frame, and crossed to the window, where he pulled back the curtain sufficiently to let a little daylight in. "You really are a fool, Benetan. Here you are, the envy of half the men in the castle — or at least you were until last night — fretting like some lovesick pup after a girl who you know full well is not and could never be Andraia's equal. And who, I might remind you, is no longer available to you."

The warning note in his voice didn't escape Benetan, and he tried to dissemble. "It isn't that, Savrinor. I'm not trying to — to — "

"To usurp the place I've taken? I should hope not. After all, you were the one who effectively foisted the girl on me in the first place, so you'd be hypocritical in the extreme to carp about it now."

"I know that. I know. But . . . last night, when you brought her into the hall, she looked . . ." Benetan hesitated, swallowed saliva. He didn't dare say exactly what he thought, but had to express his fears somehow. "She looked ill, frightened. I feared that you might have been . . . unable to keep her from the . . ."

"Oh, I see." Savrinor's tone made it clear that he inferred a good deal more than Benetan had intended. But his mouth curved in a smile. "Then I'll give you your second reassurance of the morning and tell you that your fears are misplaced. Iselia spent the hour of our First Magus's inauguration alone and safe in my chambers, with nothing to threaten or alarm her. Does that satisfy you?"

Benetan nodded. "Yes. Yes . . . it does. Thank you." And thought: *but that's a lie.* Something *bad* happened to Iselia, something that had changed her, darkened her spirit. He hadn't the right or the courage to demand an answer, and Savrinor wouldn't have given one, but he felt a sickness that had nothing to do with the night's excesses as his mind surmised the truth.

The historian walked delicately toward him and laid a hand on his shoulder. Benetan couldn't bring himself to meet the pale gaze.

"I'll give you a little advice," Savrinor said softly. "Clear your head, revive your body, and concentrate on making your peace with Andraia. Knowing her, I'd say that it probably isn't too late despite your behavior last night. Stop fretting about Iselia. She's no longer your concern." The hand withdrew and Savrinor stared thoughtfully, over Benetan's bowed head, at the bedchamber door. "Nor is she quite the wilting flower that you believe her to be. Don't cling so closely to your fond notions of being her champion. I'm not sure that she needs one."

Benetan wasn't in the mood for advice, from Savrinor or from anyone else, and the historian had the distinct impression that his words were falling on deaf ears. He made an impatient sound, a faint hiss between clenched teeth.

"Listen or not, as you please; it makes no difference to me. Now, I'll be pleased if you will go away, Benetan. You've had more than enough of my time, and I'm not in the mood to see any more of your long face. Take it out of my sight, and let me return to my peaceful contemplations."

Benetan started to rise, then a last spark of rebellion flickered. "I want to see Iselia."

Savrinor looked him in the eye and said, quietly but very emphatically, "No."

It was no use. Savrinor was adamant, his temper was beginning to shorten, and Benetan knew that he was in no position to argue. He straightened his shoulders, walked to the door with what dignity he could muster under the circumstances, then nodded a formal farewell.

"Thank you for setting my mind at rest about . . . the other matter." There was a hint of defeat in his voice and the words were coldly distant.

"Don't trouble to thank me. It wasn't what you came for, after all. Good day, Benetan." •

The door shut firmly behind him.

Shortly after Benetan had returned to his room with his mind in a discomfiting tug-of-war between dejection and anger, Magus Pirane found Andraia fast asleep in her mother's private chambers.

Pirane hadn't seen her own bed that night, but that was nothing unusual. She seldom slept; an hour or two every seven days or so was more than enough to sustain her, and after the celebrations ended she had indulged her fancy for two youths of her "flock" who had not been chosen for other purposes, before dismissing them and preparing herself for the new day. The young men had promise; she had detected a latent psychic talent in one, which was something the magi were always quick to nurture within the castle walls, while the other, with education and training, would in time make a secular but useful addition to the ranks of senior servants. Now, bathed and refreshed, and changed from her festive finery into a plainer but still startling green robe in which wraithlike shapes moved and curled,

Pirane was seeking Lua with a view to instructing her on the placing of her two new protégés under suitable tutelage.

She was amused rather than surprised to find that Lua was not in her rooms. Few of the castle's inhabitants had gone to their own beds at the end of the revels, and even fewer shared Pirane's ability to go without sleep. Content to shelve her business until her lady-in-waiting returned in her own good time, the magus was about to leave when a glimmer of gold in one of the deep, comfortable couches by the fireplace caught her eye.

Andraia was curled on the couch, face buried in cushions and oblivious to the world. She was still wearing her amber gown, but her gold-plaited hair and the paint on her face and body looked draggled, giving her the air of a helpless and rather lonely kitten. Her feet silent, Pirane crossed the room to gaze down at her, and her lips curved in a faint, fond smile — then something else, something about the sleeping girl's aura, caught at the edges of her powerful mind. For a brief moment the magus's strange eyes flickered with an unnatural light; then the smile took on a shade of amusement. So *that* was where the land lay. Good, she thought; good. A great compliment to Andraia, and timely under the circumstances. But then Yandros and his brother gods were never less than subtle.

Pirane leaned down toward the curled, sleeping figure. Her extraordinarily long middle finger reached out, and lightly she touched Andraia's brow.

Andraia stirred, twitched violently — then abruptly her green eyes opened.

"Madam!" Shocked and chagrined, she floundered into a sitting position as Pirane's presence and her own disheveled state registered in the same moment. "Madam — oh, forgive me; I didn't mean — "

"Hush, child," Pirane said. "There's no need for any apology; I doubt you're in any worse state or any more unlikely place than many others this morning."

A little reassured but still nervous, Andraia pushed both hands through the wild tangle that the night had made of her hair. "I was seeking my mother," she said uncertainly.

"Yes, I imagine you were. And when you didn't find her you were simply too tired to do anything but sleep in the first chair you could reach. Quite understandable, my dear. Especially after such a very . . . demanding night."

Despite the fact that she still wasn't fully awake, Andraia didn't miss the slight hesitation, and the emphasis it conferred on the word *demanding*. Hectic color flared in her face as she began to comprehend what Pirane was implying; then as the realization went fully home the color drained abruptly to a sickly pallor.

Pirane raised a perfect eyebrow. "There's no need to look so horrified, Andraia." She crossed the room to where she knew Lua kept a good selection of wines, deliberated for a moment before making her choice, then filled two cups. Returning, she gave Andraia one of the cups, and with it a conspiratorial smile. "Did you imagine for a moment that I, of all people, wouldn't divine your secret? Here, now; drink this, and we'll toast our great lord Yandros and his noble brother."

Andraia's cheeks flamed anew, but she obeyed. She shut her eyes as she drank, and Pirane knew that she was remembering her hours with Tarod and savoring the memory. They set their cups down, and abruptly the magus's demeanor sobered.

"Andraia, my dear, I have a small piece of advice for you." Her strange eyes regarded the girl thoughtfully. "Don't make the mistake of seeing more than was intended in the honor that has been bestowed on you." She smiled again, but this time the smile was poignant. "The gods are good to us, but you must never, ever forget that the ways of gods and men are not the same. You have been granted a great and rare boon, but for Lord Tarod it was nothing more than a moment's diversion. You may never see him again. And you must live with that knowledge, and never for one moment regret what has been or wish that it might be again. Do you understand what I am saying?"

Andraia looked steadily back at her mentor. There were images in her mind: visions of a sculpted face in its frame of pitch-black hair; of eyes like living emeralds; of a voice and a body that transcended all concepts of mortality. . . . And yet, and yet . . . though there had been wild magic in the small hours of that night, the love that she had given to that being was too pure and too sacrosanct ever to truly fulfill her. As Pirane implied, love for a god and love for a man could never be one and the same. And despite all that had taken place, Andraia's very human heart was still pledged elsewhere.

She lowered her gaze and said, "Madam, I understand you." Then, quietly, she began to cry.

Pirane moved forward. Her arms slipped around Andraia and she held her as though she were a small, helpless child, stroking her disordered hair and careless of the tears that soaked her shining, shifting robe.

"There, my dear; there." Her voice was as kind and soothing as honey, for she loved Andraia, with all her confused passions and fierce loyalties, as dearly as if she'd been her own daughter. "Your captain will return to you soon enough. Take my promise on it, for I know the ways of lovers. But you have strength now, Andraia; and you must learn to use it." Oh yes, she thought; Lord Tarod had granted a greater boon to Andraia than she knew. The god of Chaos had given her a power of which she was, as yet, unaware. . . .

"Benetan Liss is a fool," she said softly. "He has yet to learn where his loyalties truly lie. You can teach him, my child. You can teach him. And I will help you."

Two hours later, Benetan came in search of Andraia.

He had recovered from the worst of the night's megrims. A visit to the bathing rooms below the castle cellars, a shocking but reviving plunge in the saltwater cold pool, and then a change of clothing had completed at least a physical transformation, so he resolved to bite on the knife, as his senior sergeant would have put it, and brave Andraia's wrath in an attempt to be reconciled.

Andraia wasn't in her room. Disappointed but not entirely surprised, Benetan steeled himself for a visit to Lua's chambers. Often after their past quarrels Andraia had sought refuge with her mother, whom she could always count on for a fiercely sympathetic ear; it was likely as not that he'd find her there now. He was as ready as he could be, or so he fervently hoped, for a possible confrontation with Lua; but he wasn't prepared for the shock, when the door opened to his tentative knock, of coming face-to-face with Magus Pirane.

Pirane stared coolly down at Benetan's neat but still pallid figure. "Captain Liss. Do I assume you are looking for Andraia?"

Sweating, Benetan recovered enough to make a hasty bow. "Yes, madam. That is, I — ahh — "

"She is busy." The magus's gaze seemed to eat into him like white-hot metal. "And I imagine she will be busy for the rest of the day." Her lip curled with faint sardonicism. "Do you wish me to convey a message?"

"N-no, madam. . . . I — wouldn't dream to impose. . . ."

"Good." She started to close the door, then paused. "Young man, I have a very simple suggestion to make. It is this: use your remaining free time until you're recalled to your duties to consider your behavior and its possible consequences with great care. Only when you have done that, and are quite certain in your own mind that there will never be a repetition of last night's display, should you have the courage to show your face to Andraia again. Do I make myself clear?"

Benetan stared at his own feet. "You do, Lady Magus."

Pirane continued to study him for a moment more, then nodded. "Yes, I see I do. You're very intelligent, Captain Liss. It would be a regrettable thing to see such an asset wasted." And the door shut in his face.

Benetan stepped back. For several seconds he stared at the door's paneling, then abruptly he turned on his heel and walked away along the corridor. His skin prickled icily as the short but trenchant encounter resounded in his memory. Pirane was very powerful in more ways than one; even Savrinor never took risks where she was concerned, and the fact that she had a fond interest in Andraia's well-being made her doubly formidable as a potential adversary. Benetan had hoped that his excesses of last night had escaped her notice, but clearly he was wrong. He only prayed, privately and silently, that Andraia hadn't spoken to the magus about Iselia. . . .

As that thought ran through his mind he turned a corner of the corridor, into the passage that led toward the main staircase — and stopped.

Iselia was coming toward him. She wore a plain gray robe — gray, Benetan remembered with a sudden mental stab, was a color Savrinor favored — with an embroidered jacket over it, and her fair hair was unbound. Her gaze was downcast, introverted. She hadn't seen him.

Benetan spoke her name. She looked up quickly, and in the instant before her expression froze he saw the drawn lines on her pale face, the haunted shadows in her eyes. Then, quickly, she collected herself.

"Benet." That remoteness again; it had been in her voice last night and had disturbed him then; it disturbed him the more now.

"I . . ." His mouth was dry, and suddenly he felt like a gauche boy again. "I tried to . . . I came to see you. Earlier . . ."

"I know. Savrinor told me." Her eyelids flickered, looking at the stairs, the wall, the floor; anything rather than meet his gaze. "He said you were concerned for me."

Wondering precisely what Savrinor *had* said, Benetan nodded more curtly than he'd intended. "At the celebrations, you seemed . . ." He searched for a word, found one that was inadequate but the best he could conjure on the spur of the moment. "You seemed troubled."

A muscle in Iselia's neck tightened. "Why should you think that?"

She wasn't about to unbend. Benetan made another effort. "Iselia, please don't turn away from me! There's something wrong, I know there is; any fool could have seen it last night and could see it now. I want to *help* you!"

At last she did look at him, but it was no more than a brief glance than seemed to mix resentment and fear with something else that he couldn't interpret.

"You have already helped me, Benetan." She used his full name, which disconcerted him still further. "You made sure that my fate would be different from that of my fellow prisoners, after all. Isn't that enough?"

What did she mean? Oh, gods, Benetan thought; what had Savrinor *done* to her? A stampede of emotions surged in his mind, but before he could speak again they both heard approaching footfalls, and Iselia's head whipped nervously round.

One of the senior castle stewards was approaching, climbing the stairs toward the upper floor. Benetan would have ignored him, but Iselia tensed and what little color there was in her face vanished.

"I must go," she said sharply. "I am on an errand for Savrinor; he'll be growing impatient."

"Iselia, wait — "

But she wouldn't wait; she was already turning away. The steward reached the top of the stairs, looked at them both with mild but momentary interest, then walked away along the passage in the opposite direction. Iselia hesitated, then suddenly her eyes in the white face were animated by a terrible, burning passion. In a hissing whisper she said,

"I want only one thing, Benetan — my freedom. If you claim to care one whit for me, and if you would save my life and sanity, think on that!"

And she turned and fled away down the corridor.

There was no one in the stables when Benetan entered. In the wake of the celebrations the grooms were probably all nursing hangovers, and no one came to disturb him as he fetched his own black mare's saddle and bridle from their places and began to harness her. The mare was pleased to see him, whickering a greeting and snuffing at his hands in the hope of tidbits, but Benetan barely noticed. His fingers moved mechanically, tightening buckles, checking girths, but his face was grim and his thoughts locked into a dark plane far removed from the task at hand.

With her parting words, Iselia had confirmed his worst fears and shattered beyond recall any hope of regaining his lost peace of mind. For more than a minute after she'd disappeared from sight he had stood alone in the corridor dumb and immobile as a stricken dog as the ramifications of what she'd said burned into his brain. Only when a menial servant had hurried past, head dipping respectfully and veering a little to avoid him, had he at last found the wit to shake off his paralysis and return to his room.

And there, for the first time since the celebrations had begun, he remembered Kaldar Alvaray, and the promise he'd made.

Benetan didn't want to meet Kaldar in the mountains. At the time he'd agreed to it simply as an expedient to dissuade Kaldar from his suicidal resolution to rescue Iselia, and to get him out of the castle before his presence was discovered. He didn't ever want to see Kaldar again, and despite his own conscience and Kaldar's threats he had already begun, at least subconsciously, to push the promise far away into a corner of his mind where it could be conveniently forgotten. Not now, though. Though she knew nothing of his meeting with her husband, Iselia had seen to it that the rendezvous must be kept. Not for Kaldar's sake, not even for Benetan's own, but for hers.

If you would save my life and sanity . . . Again the desperate words reechoed in Benetan's head, and again he felt a clenching in the pit of his stomach. The rift with Andraia was forgotten, Pirane's disapproval and warning were forgotten. All he could think of, all he could concentrate his mind upon, was Iselia's plight. He had brought her to this; he *had* to help her. Even if he could do no more than bring her the comfort of a message from Kaldar, then however confused his motives, and however clouded by jealousy, he must do it.

The magi were good masters to those servants who pleased them, and Benetan's rank and loyal service had earned him the right to take leave from the castle at any time when he and his men were not on immediate call. In fact he rarely took advantage of that privilege, for although the entire world was in theory open to him, there were few districts — and least of all his home village — ready to offer a genuine welcome to a Chaos rider. Occasionally he enjoyed hunting or sailing with a party of his own peers, but more often than not there were better diversions to be had within the castle walls. Now, though, it was time to break with habit. Summoning his duty sergeant, he had placed him in charge of the riders' affairs until further notice, and when the surprised man ventured to ask why, he was simply and curtly told not to question an order, and that Benetan expected to return by morning. A brief visit to the kitchens to collect a few emergency rations, and without another word to anyone Benetan was ready to leave.

The black mare whickered her pleasure at emerging into the daylight. Benetan mounted, and as he rode across the deserted courtyard toward the main gates he squinted at the sun, darkly crimson and streaked with cloud above the castle wall. Three hours, perhaps a little less, until sunset. Time enough to find Kaldar before dark. . . .

The guard on duty at the gates had found himself a patch of sunlight, sheltered from the wind, and was drowsily passing the long watch with a solitary game of cross stones. Hearing the clop of approaching hooves, he hastened to activate the gates' mechanism, and Benetan nodded his thanks.

"Is the Maze open?"

"Yes, sir. The First Magus has given orders that it should stay open until all our visitors have left." He grinned. "Though none have gone yet, and I imagine there'll be few of them in a fit state to travel today."

Benetan smiled dryly but made no comment, only touched his heels to the mare's sides and rode on through the gate.

A strong, clean westerly wind met him as he emerged on the far side of the wall, and he drew in his breath with an involuntary gasp as, suddenly and shockingly, the huge panorama of the outside world opened before him. Though he'd seen this vista countless times before, still it had the power to awe him. The rock stack on which the castle was built towered more than a thousand feet high, and it was as though the entire world, land and ocean alike, lay spread below Benetan's giddying vantage point in a tiny microcosm. Dominating all was the ominous gray vastness of the sea, unbroken but for the silhouettes of a few small islands and vanishing to a colossally distant horizon. Southward, the mainland lay like a bank of dark cloud, a harsh coastline of bays and promontories and high, forbidding cliffs stretching away into the sun's haze.

The sound of the castle gates closing made the black mare jink suddenly, and brought Benetan out of the trance which the view had momentarily engendered. He shook his head, pushed back some strands of hair that the wind had already teased free of its customary braided knot, and focused his gaze on the ground ahead. The sward sloped gently away for some thirty yards before reaching the edge of the stack, and here a narrow rock bridge, just wide enough for three horses to cross abreast, spanned the dizzying gap between the castle and the mainland, where the foothills of a hostile mountain range reached out like fingers. Benetan spared only a glance for the causeway; his attention now was fixed on a patch of ground just a short way on. Here the grass grew lusher and darker, and the air above the patch shimmered faintly, distorting the view beyond. The mare started to dance eagerly; Benetan reined her in; then as she quieted he tried to conjure a picture in his mind. The Maze had the power to carry anyone who entered its portal to any destination; as the Chaos Riders' captain Benetan had been taught the techniques of visualization and will necessary to negotiate the Maze's complexities, and the right to use it for his own purposes was a privilege of his rank. Now he reached inside his jacket and shirt, and his fingers closed on the small, star-shaped amulet on its iron chain. He wore this star constantly and had come to look on it as his personal touchstone; but it was also the vital key which allowed him to enter the Maze without the need for a magus's sorcerous skills. Holding the talisman, he shut his eyes and formed a mental image of mountains; not the range confronting him on the far side of the causeway but another, gentler but bleak and barren; the mineral-rich peaks of the far north, his own homeland. The twin crags, Kaldar had said. Benetan remembered them well, for they overshadowed his village like sentinels, and legends of the monstrous creatures that haunted their dark caves and gullies were rife. His mind fine-tuned the image, closed in on a clear picture of the pass that bisected the two peaks; sunless, dank, hemmed in by towering rock walls.

Abruptly the image came strong and clear; Benetan breathed out in relief and, gripping the star amulet securely, pressed the mare forward. He felt a lurching disorientation; energy crackled in the air about him, seeming to set his bones briefly on fire. Then the Maze swallowed him, and he and the mare vanished from the stack.

CHAPTER XI

A wave of nausea and a blast of ice-cold air hit Benetan simultaneously as he and his mount burst from vertiginous limbo into the gory light of a northern afternoon. With a practiced reflex he hauled on the reins, dropping his hands to the mare's withers and bringing her under control. She circled, dancing, then with a shivering snort settled and quieted, moving a few paces clear of the small, scorched patch of earth that marked their point of arrival.

Benetan took a deep breath. His head was still spinning and his stomach wouldn't right itself; a hazard of using the Maze and one that he suspected he'd never become inured to. Usually he only *felt* nauseated, and that briefly. This time, though . . .

He slid hastily from the saddle, and was wretchedly sick among the thin, sere grass at the side of the track. It wasn't a pleasant experience, but when at last he straightened he felt a good deal better. The ravages of last night again, he suspected, and, thrusting away a fierce desire for water, he returned to the mare's side and took stock of his surroundings.

He was surprised by the sheer familiarity of the scene around him. After so long an absence he'd expected his memory to be at best unreliable and at worst downright faulty; instead, he felt suddenly as though the past twelve years had dissolved and he had returned to his old home territory after no more than a day's absence. He was on the pass road — though *road* was too grandiose a term, for it was no more than a rutted and potholed track — through the mountain spur that curved westward from the village where he had been born. Though the sky here was clear, daylight was waning and only the higher mountain slopes were still touched by the sun, the light creating strange, murky colors among the veins of mineral ore. Benetan himself stood in the deep, cold shadows of a gully, while ahead of him the pass itself burrowed between towering walls of rock. And in the distance, where the pass reached its northerly end, two tall crags rose stark against the sky; Kaldar's landmark, and his own destination.

Benetan studied the crags for a few moments, then gazed at the gully and at the yawning black mouth of the pass beyond. Where and how he'd find Kaldar he didn't know, but he felt a strong instinct that that needn't concern him. One way or another, he surmised, Kaldar would find him.

The mare didn't like the look of the pass when he remounted and turned her head toward it, but he ignored her sidestepping and head-shaking protests and pressed her firmly on. It was ironic to reflect that in the distant days of adolescence he would have felt just as she did now. But a captain of the Chaos riders had nothing to fear from any supernatural denizens of these crags; rather, they had cause to fear *him*, for he carried the authority of their creators.

The flicker of disquiet within him, last remnant of an old but now meaningless memory, died, and he spurred the mare forward into the gloom.

Benetan had forgotten how cold these latitudes could be. Living amid the comforts of the castle and surrounded by the warming influence of the sea, he was unaccustomed now to the harsh, dry chill of autumn air in the northern mountains that heralded the bitter and snowbound winter to come. By the time he'd ridden a mile into the pass he fervently wished that he'd worn his fur coat instead of merely the quilted leather jacket, and his hands, gloveless, were nearly numb on the mare's reins. And there was no sign of Kaldar.

Where in the Seven Hells was he? Benetan knew he hadn't mistaken the instructions he'd been given, but he was beginning to wonder if this whole affair had been some momentary whim on Kaldar's part, a reckless assignation which he now had no intention of keeping. That would be typical, Benetan thought sourly; in the old days

Kaldar had been notoriously unreliable, doubly so when he was in one of his obsessive moods, and nothing short of —

He was shaken from his preoccupation as the black mare suddenly shied, throwing her head high and whipping her long mane painfully across his face. Benetan swore and gathered in the reins, and the mare came to a standstill, tense beneath him.

"Come on." He spoke adamantly but not unkindly. "There's nothing to be afraid of."

She shook her head, trying to deny him; but Benetan wasn't about to be bested by a horse, and he dug his heels hard into her sides. "Forward! Come on!"

From the darkness above and ahead of him, a voice spoke tautly.

"Don't be a bloody fool, Benetan. There's a devil cat on the upper path, not three yards ahead of you."

Shocked, Benetan almost lost his hold of the reins altogether. *"Kaldar?"* His voice echoed between the rock walls.

"Yes. Stay still, and stop shouting!" A pause. "It's seen us both. It can't make up its mind which of us to attack, but you and your horse will probably make the better meal."

Benetan touched his tongue to his lips, gentling the mare as she started to dance again. "Where? Left of me, or right?"

"To your left. It's moving now."

Benetan saw it a moment later; a shadow among shadows, gaunt and lithe, gliding along a ledge too narrow for any human and about a man's height above his head. In the old days he, like everyone hereabouts, had been terrified of these creatures; they were voracious predators and it was widely believed that the gods sent them to devour any man, woman, or child who transgressed against the magi's laws. Benetan didn't know the truth or otherwise of that, but since joining the Chaos riders he had learned to both admire and respect the devil cats. As his old weapons master had once pointed out, they had more than a little in common.

Benetan hissed a soft reassurance to his nervous mare, then spoke to the still invisible Kaldar.

"It's all right, Kaldar. It's only interested in me, and I've no reason to be afraid of it. Move back, and it'll be on its way." The cat took another pace then, emerging from deep shadow into what little dusky light was left in the pass, and slanting, green gold eyes gazed coolly into Benetan's own as it regarded him. It was a big animal, possibly twelve feet from nose to thickly furred tail, and as he stared steadily back at it Benetan recognized an extraordinary, almost preternatural intelligence in its look. Its dense coat was a brindle of bronze and charcoal and silver gray; its build heavy, paws huge and soft, concealing the deadly claws. He knew it had the power and the skill to disembowel him with one blow, but even as his mare pranced wildly he only smiled and said, under his breath:

"Beautiful . . ."

The cat blinked slowly, as though acknowledging the compliment. An odd sound came from its throat, a rumble midway between a growl and a purr. Then, with one disdainful flick of its long tail, it bunched its muscles and sprang away up the rock face, vanishing into another wing of shadow.

The black mare's head dropped and she snorted as though sighing with relief. Benetan found he was grinning, close to laughter, and there was a hint of it in his voice as he called out, "All's well, Kaldar. The cat's gone, and there's nothing to fear. Where are you?"

For a moment no answer came. Then there was a brief hissing sound, and a chilly blue light sprang into being a short way ahead. Etched by the glow of the small flare he held, Kaldar Alvaray stood on a ledge, staring down at his old friend.

"I'm impressed," Kaldar said with rancor. "There aren't many who'll stand up to one of those creatures without flinching. Your masters have obviously trained you well."

Ignoring his tone, Benetan slid down from the mare's saddle. "Are you coming down here, or do I come to you?"

"There's a path up to this ledge; it's wide enough, and there's room in the cave for your horse."

"Cave?" Benetan raised his eyebrows but made no further comment. The path was easy to negotiate, and within a few minutes he was following Kaldar under a rock overhang and into a surprisingly spacious cavern, lit by a small fire in the center of the floor.

Benetan stared at the fire in surprise. "Where do you find fuel in a place like this?"

"There are ways and means, if you know where and how to look." Kaldar smiled humorlessly, then turned to give Benetan a hard-eyed, sardonic scrutiny that seemed to strip him to the bone. "Well, the traitor's life doesn't seem to have done you any harm. You look fit enough, for all your showy trappings."

Reminded of Iselia's accusations, Benetan said acidly, "If you didn't bring me here for any better reason than to trade insults, I'll leave now. I've taken enough of a risk as it is."

"Nothing to the risk I'm running by simply trying to stay alive," Kaldar retorted. "And you know full well why I wanted us to meet."

"I'm surprised you thought enough of me to trust me to come — or not to bring a full force of my men with me."

"Ah, well." Kaldar crouched down by the fire, holding out his hands to the small circle of flames. "That comes down to ways and means again. And something else." He looked up, his gaunt face challenging. "You were betrothed to Iselia once, weren't you?"

Benetan turned his head away. "That was a long time ago."

"So it was; but if it hadn't been for the band of reavers that you're now so proud to lead, you and she would have been married these past ten years." He smiled without humor. "In that sense if in no other I suppose I owe you a debt, don't I?"

Benetan didn't answer that but looked for a relatively clean place on the cave's grimy floor, brushed the dust aside as best he could, and sat down. Noting Benetan's fastidiousness, Kaldar allowed his smile to grow more cynical. "I'm sorry I haven't a padded chair and a flask of vintage wine to offer you," he said. "For one of your status — "

"*Kaldar.*" Benetan had had enough, and his expression grew dangerous. "I'll say this once, and once only. Either we submerge any differences we might have and concentrate on the business that we're both theoretically here to discuss, or you put your challenge in clear terms and we'll resolve it here and now." His eyes, hard and suddenly bleak, raked the other man dangerously. "And I wouldn't give much for your chances."

He thought for a few moments that Kaldar would rise to the bait. In the old days there'd have been no doubt of it, for Kaldar's temper and rashness had been legendary in their village. But time had either mellowed him a little or taught him to understand when enough was enough. He stared back furiously — then abruptly held up his hands in a calming and acquiescent gesture.

"Peace on it." It was the phrase they'd used as children, an acknowledgement of a hiatus and as close as Kaldar could bring himself to come to an apology. "You're right; this isn't relevant." He hunched his shoulders and twisted round to reach into a pile of bags and animal skins that lay behind him, just out of the firelight's reach. "I've got a bottle of some brew here somewhere. Tastes disgusting, but it helps to keep out the cold." The blue eyes still held resentment and mistrust. "Will you drink with me?"

Benetan nodded, his own resentment lessening though not yet entirely gone. "Yes."

It was, at least formally, a breaking of the ice. Kaldar produced the leather bottle, and offered it, settling himself cross-legged on the floor as he did so. Benetan drank, handed the bottle back, watched as his onetime friend did little more than sip at the contents. This was another new development; years ago Kaldar had been renowned and privately mocked for his fondness for liquor, and also for his inability to hold his drink. Whatever had brought the change about, Benetan suspected that Iselia had played little part in it.

"So." Kaldar set the bottle down between them, and his posture grew suddenly tense again. "Have you told her? Have you told her that I've been to the castle?"

"No."

There was a blur of movement, a clenched fist coming up, and for a split second a ghastly aura seemed to flicker around Kaldar's frame. *"If you've betrayed —"*

"Listen to me!" Instinctively Benetan's hand had gone to the knife at his belt and he was half on his feet. They both froze, and Kaldar's aura — or the illusion of the aura, Benetan couldn't quite judge — died. Slowly, he took his hand away from the knife's hilt, and sank back. Kaldar had power. He'd claimed it before and, though he was no sorcerer himself, Benetan had believed him. Now he'd seen the truth of it for himself in that small, brief, and probably unconscious display. His hackles rose.

"Listen, Kaldar, before you jump to conclusions. No, I've not told her of our meeting, because I haven't yet had the chance to speak to her alone." He paused. "You know about Savrinor."

"Her patron." Kaldar's tone was ferocious.

"Yes. He kept his promise; I told you he would. The inauguration took place, and she was safe; her only part in it was to attend the secular celebrations afterward." Benetan forced down memory of the blank, shocked mask of Iselia's face as Savrinor had led her into the castle's great Hall.

Kaldar sucked in a painful breath. "You're sure of that? Because if you're lying to me — "

"Yandros's eyes, why *should* I lie? Once and for all, Iselia was, and is, safe!"

"With him?"

Benetan nodded. "With him." Perhaps as desperate to convince himself as to convince Kaldar, he added, "Savrinor is the castle's senior historian; his work obliges him to record significant events for the magi's archives, and for that he needs assistants to copy documents and carry out secretarial duties. That's what Iselia does for him."

Kaldar's thin rib cage heaved. For several seconds he stared into the fire. Then:

"He's a married man? This Savrinor?"

"No. Damn it, Kaldar, even you must know that marriages are only conducted in the villages. Savrinor's castle born and bred; it isn't the same for them as it is — or was — for us."

Kaldar's tension didn't relax, but he forced himself not to flare up again. "And you," he said at length. "What about you?"

"What about me? What do you mean?"

Kaldar looked at him. His expression was bitter and unyielding, almost fanatical. "You know perfectly well what I mean. If you've so much as *thought* of touching her — "

"Seven Hells, what do you take me for?" Benetan was furious that Kaldar should have dared to cast such a slur, but even as he vented his fury, he felt a black worm of guilt writhing in some deep pit of his mind. How great, or how small, was the divide between desire and deed? It was a question he didn't want to contemplate.

Jaw muscles clenching, he pulled his temper and the guilt back under control. "For your information," he went on in a clipped, tightly controlled voice, "I have an attachment. She is the daughter of one the castle's highest secular officials, and she is also very beautiful. Without wishing to offend, and bearing in mind that I still have *some* scruples" — this with considerable sarcasm — "what would I want with your wife?"

The barb found its mark and Kaldar had the good grace to color slightly. "I had to know," he said, wavering between defense and aggression. "Forgive me, Benet — and I didn't intend to give offense — but I had to *ask*." He rubbed one hand across his face. "If you love your woman, then surely you must understand the terrors I've been suffering since Iselia was taken? Knowing nothing, always fearing the worst. And the *nightmares* . . ."

Kaldar's guard had begun to crumble. Whether it was his reference to Andraia that had breached the wall Benetan couldn't say, but abruptly he felt a surge of sympathy for Kaldar's plight, and with it a desire, impetuous perhaps but strong nonetheless, to put right the wrong he'd already done and salvage some hope from this unholy mess.

"Kaldar." He reached across the sluggish fire and his hand closed on the other man's arm. Reflexively, from mistrust or revulsion or both, Kaldar started to flinch away, but the impulse was aborted, though a muscle twitched under Benetan's fingers. "Kaldar, you asked me to come here, and I came. I don't know why I did, but — "

"Don't you?"

A pause. "I don't understand."

"I think you do." Kaldar drew a long breath, then let it go with a sound that set odd echoes chasing across the cave. "I maligned you, Benet, and I admit it, when I challenged your intentions. I know you better, and I also know that even in — in *that* place, a man's basic nature doesn't change. You were always honorable. Probably too honorable for your own good, though that's neither here nor there now. All right, I'll be blunt. I asked you to meet me because I want to entrust you with a task. No," as Benetan started to protest, "no, don't say anything, not yet. Just listen. I want you to do something for me. And I know that you'll do it, for one reason and one alone." He raised his head, red hair glinting dangerously as it reflected the flames, eyes suddenly very intense. "You'll do it because you'll know that if you fail, you'll destroy Iselia. And for all your protestations about your official's daughter, I don't think anything will prompt you to do that."

Kaldar knew. He knew what Benetan was thinking, what he was feeling. It wasn't *possible*. But —

"I told you I have power." The statement was flat, unarguable. "Your magi don't have quite the stranglehold they claim on the sorcerous arts, and not all who have the talent go running to the castle for training and indoctrination. Oh, don't look so surprised, Benet. I know what you're thinking, such sophisticated language from a peasant miner who hadn't even learned his letters when you were called to greater things. Well, education can be had in other ways than through the Star Peninsula's good graces." He hesitated, then a sharp, cold smile curved his mouth. "Yes, I see you understand. You saw it when I came to you at the castle, and though you didn't want to believe it then, I think you believe it now. Or do you? Would you like a demonstration?"

As he spoke, he reached out toward the fire, holding one hand, palm downward, over its heart. The flames wavered, then abruptly changed from red gold to a strange, sickly green. A shape began to take form —

"Kaldar, no!" Panic swelled in Benetan. "Don't be such a fool!"

The flames flickered, resumed their normal color. Kaldar regarded him steadily, faintly amused. "What's wrong? Afraid of a little sorcery?"

"No!" After some of the things he'd seen in the castle, that was a ridiculous question. "But the magi scent sorcery as cats scent fire on the wind!" Benetan shuddered. "Sweet gods, if you flaunt your power like this it's a miracle you've stayed alive until now!"

Kaldar laughed. "You fear that I was about to bring the wrath of Yandros down on both our heads? Don't worry, my friend. Your magi aren't omnipotent, and some of us know a few tricks which they're not privy to." The laughter faded and his expression grew deadly serious. "Which brings us back to the nub of the matter. I have power. Power enough to see into your heart and know that the flames of your old love for Iselia are very far from dead. No, you won't take advantage of her. I accept that, I believe it, and I won't question your honor any further. But I'm going to use that honor, Benet. And I know that you'll have no choice but to agree to what I ask." The smile grew grim. "For Iselia's sake."

Something turned cold in Benetan's stomach. "That's blackmail."

"Yes. And there's nothing you can do about it. Is there?"

It was true. Benetan pressed a clenched fist against his mouth to stem the tide of savage words that were forming on his tongue, and only managed, indistinctly, "You unscrupulous bastard. . . ."

Kaldar laughed again, a staccato bark. "Bastard? I thought your masters spurned such concepts — but then, old habits die hard, don't they? Oh, yes; I can trust you, Benet. Whatever the castle may have made of you, you're still one of us at heart. Anyway, you've already committed yourself beyond the point of no return, haven't you? Firstly by not arresting me when I visited you at the castle, and now by coming here in secret to meet me. There's a price on my head; or rather there was and there would be again if the magi were to find out that I'm still alive. But you didn't do anything then and you won't do anything now, and we both know why." He waited for an answer but didn't get one, and after a few moments he sat back, gripping his own ankles and rocking gently back and forth. "Very well, then, let's get down to business. I want you to carry a message to Iselia for me."

Benetan was surprised. He'd expected Kaldar to want, at very least, his complicity in some plan to smuggle Iselia out of the castle, and had been prepared to argue over the feasibility of such an idea. This, though . . . He felt greatly relieved, and nodded.

"Not easy with Savrinor watching her, but possible. What do you want me to tell her?"

"Simply this. I'm going away." Kaldar looked up quickly, perhaps sensing Benetan's astonishment. "No, I'm not abandoning her; very far from it. But I took your words to heart at our first encounter, when you told me that any rescue bid would be suicidal. You're right, and I'm not about to sacrifice Iselia's life and my own for the sake of an ardent but doomed cause." His smile had a hint of grim humor. "Even I'm not quite *that* foolish. So tell her this: I'm going south. She'll understand. It was what we planned to do as soon as the marriage ceremony was over, and but for you and your riders we'd have been well on the road by now. Tell her that I've made contact, and I'm going to join our friends."

Benetan's spine prickled uneasily. "Made contact? With whom?"

There was a long pause. Then Kaldar said, very quietly: "Do I need to spell that out to you, Benet? You must know, or at least you must have guessed, what Iselia and I are committed to."

The prickling turned suddenly to ice as abruptly the missing piece of the puzzle slipped into place. Benetan had forgotten what had lain behind the magi's search for Kaldar, the real reason why he had been a hunted man. A troublemaker, yes, and suspected of practicing sorcery; but there'd been more to it than that. *Far* more.

"Yandros . . ." Quickly, reflexively, he touched the star amulet at his throat. "You're with the heretics!"

Kaldar's lip curled. "That's what they call us, is it? Heretics? We look at it differently, Benet. We're not heretics but willing servants of the *true* gods — and we're fighting for freedom from the tyranny of the magi and the devils they serve!"

Horror moved in Benetan as the import of Kaldar's words sank in. History was littered with the many attempts that had been made to revolt against the magi's rule. Stories were legion of the bands of disaffected rebels who had risen to brief glory, like meteors in a summer sky, and vanished as swiftly and violently as those same meteors as the magi crushed them out of existence. As a youth — and perhaps, remembering this, Benetan could hardly blame Kaldar for calling him turncoat — he himself had had some sympathy with the rebel bands, for the life and conditions imposed upon many in the peasant villages was at best unjust and at worst barbaric. Despite the changes that twelve years had wrought in his outlook, that sympathy, or at very least its fundamental principle, was still alive in him. But this revelation of Kaldar's . . . this was different. Benetan knew of the heretics. And he knew that their cause was rooted in pure evil.

The rumors had been about in the castle for some time now. Officially they were ignored, and the magi took a dire view of anyone who publicly gave them any credence. But his duties as the Chaos riders' captain, and his uneasy half friendship with Savrinor, meant that Benetan was better informed than most. This newest rebel faction was something more than simply another disorganized village rabble driven by desperation and fragmented rhetoric into making some suicidal protest. It was known that they had existed, and that their numbers had been growing, for some years. They had done nothing, made no move. But they were *there*, and now it was beginning to be whispered that they were stronger, better organized, and far more dangerous that any who had risen before them. Word had reached the castle recently that they had united under the leadership of one man, and rumor claimed that that leader was himself a sorcerer of such power that he had thus far eluded all the magi's efforts to identify him, let alone find and destroy him.

Here lay the crux of it, and the thing that set the horror moving through Benetan like a slow glacier. For these rebels, these heretics to whom Kaldar had pledged his fealty, were bent on overthrowing not merely the magi, but the gods themselves. They had raised the banner of blasphemy in the world, and worshiped the seven demons who were in every way anathema to all that Yandros and his brothers represented. Centuries ago, so the catechism ran, Chaos had fought a titanic battle against the forces of Order, who sought to overthrow their power and impose their own monstrous and stultifying control upon the mortal world. Yandros had triumphed — a fact for which heartfelt thanks were still given by the magi at the ending of each day — and Order's power had been shattered and its seven evil wielders exiled to a dimension beyond the borders of space and time. Now, though, the heretics were turning to those exiled powers again. And their avowed intention was to bring the seven demons back to the world of men, to challenge and overthrow Chaos, and set up the terrible regime of the lords of Order in its place.

"Kaldar . . ." Benetan's voice caught in his throat. "You can't mean this . . . you can't believe in it. . . ."

Kaldar continued to regard his old compatriot steadily. His blue eyes glittered like sapphires, and for a moment his emotions almost got the better of him. Part of him wanted to sneer in Benetan's face, wanted to spit back at him: *Can't believe that Yandros and his filthy kin should be wiped from the face of this world? Oh, but I do, Benet, I do!* Yet time and necessity had taught Kaldar some hard lessons; and one of those lessons was that of judgment. Benetan Liss was no longer the boy he'd known in the villages, the restless spirit cut out for neither farming nor mining yet condemned to be broken, body and spirit, by one or the other. Benetan had found a kind of freedom in the castle, freedom to grow strong and to fulfil his potential. Kaldar might despise his shift of allegiance, but in truth could he say with certainty that, had their positions been reversed, he would not have taken the same course and grasped the opportunity with both hands? Perhaps, he thought, there were more similarities between them than either had imagined.

"Benet." His voice changed, became quiet, calm. "I don't think this is something we should discuss; not here, not now. I think we're too far apart. But we share one common cause, if no other, and that is Iselia." The mania in his eyes had faded; all that remained was a deep emotion. "I've put my trust in you. I ask nothing more than that you carry my message to her. I'm going south, to join . . . our friends. Who they are, what they stand for, isn't important to you. Go back to your exalted world, be content in it if that's what you want. I don't hate you, I don't blame you. Only carry my message to my wife. And . . . something else, if you will." He turned with a sharp movement, as though trying to hide his feelings, and rummaged again in the bags beside him. After a few moments he held something out to Benetan. "This."

It was a small, withered posy of leaves. Benetan stared at it, feeling that circumstances had run away with him and that he was no longer in control. "What does it . . . ?" The question trailed off.

"It was a part of her marriage garland." Kaldar's gaze didn't waver. "Remember such things, Benet? In the village, in the old days?"

He did. His own mother had had one, dried and shriveled but preserved, pressed beneath her pillow. It had meant much to her. . . .

"Yes." His last thoughts of the heretics fled; this was something else, something more personal. And it hurt. "I'll give it to her, Kaldar. And your message." He blinked, met the steady gaze. "You have my promise."

Kaldar didn't watch him depart. Benetan had seemed reluctant to divulge the castle's secrets, and anyway Kaldar had no interest in learning how the magi's servants traveled. That knowledge could wait for a later date, when it would be more useful. They clasped wrists, briefly, at the cave entrance, then as the black mare's hooves clopped away through the darkness and diminished in the pass Kaldar withdrew into his sanctum and began to gather his belongings.

He didn't believe for one moment that Benetan would betray his whereabouts to anyone, but he hadn't survived thus far by taking chances. If the least hint of suspicion had attached itself to Benetan's absence from the castle tonight, it was quite possible that the magi might have sent a servant, elemental or otherwise, to watch his movements, and Benetan wouldn't have the skill to be aware of the surveillance. Kaldar had his own ways and means of hiding from such powers as the magi used. An hour from now, and no trace of him would be found by anything that came sniffing.

He finished packing his belongings, secured the straps of his packs, and then went about methodically extinguishing the fire. Whatever else might or might not result from tonight's encounter, its primary, vital purpose had been served, and Kaldar smiled a small, private smile as he thought of what Benetan was unknowingly carrying back with him to the magi's stronghold. The verbal message, the overt one, told Benetan nothing that he couldn't have worked out for himself easily enough. But the message contained in the bundle of withered leaves was quite another matter. Marriage garland, indeed. . . . Did Benetan imagine that Iselia's wedding had been conducted in full panoply, with half the village cheering and waving and throwing flowers to the happy couple? Was he genuinely that remote, now, from the realities of his old life? Well, Kaldar thought, if that was so, then Benetan deserved to be used as he had used him tonight, and as he intended to use him again as and when the time came. In truth he was privately pleased by the ease with which he'd duped the other man. Iselia would receive his gift, his ostensible sad little love token, and she would know exactly what it meant. They'd concocted the message code between them a long time ago, when the rebel movement was only just beginning to unite under its leader, and now, not for the first time, it had proved its worth. Iselia would know where he was going, whom he would meet, and what they intended to do when they reached their final destination. The thought of leaving her behind was like sour milk curdling in Kaldar's gut, but there was no other choice. Another sortie to the castle in an attempt to get her out would indeed be sheer madness. Iselia wouldn't expect that of him, wouldn't *want* that of him. She would say — he could hear her voice in his mind, clear and strong — she would say that the cause must be advanced, no matter what obstacles might temporarily stand in their way. And she was right.

The fire was out, the last ember dead. Kaldar straightened and stared for a few moments at the small circle of ashes, but didn't trouble to scatter them and smooth the dusty floor. The chances of anyone coming upon this cave were remote, and even if the traces of habitation were found, nothing could be deduced from them. Time to be gone. He had a long, long journey ahead of him, and one fraught with all too many risks. But he'd get through. He *must* get through, not just for Iselia's sake and his own, but for the sake of the cause.

Kaldar stared into the darkness, and his blue eyes glittered with renewed intensity as the old zeal came creeping back into his bones, lending him strength. For the cause, he would succeed in his endeavor. The cause was all. *Nothing* would stand in its way.

CHAPTER XII

It was fortunate for Savrinor that he didn't habitually keep
regular hours, and so was awake and working at his papers
when the First Magus's summons came. Outside clouds
obscured the sky and it was drizzling with rain, but Savrinor's instinct
put the hour at shortly before second moonrise.

He left his quarters, where Iselia was sleeping, and tried to quell
the sick uneasiness that roiled in his gut as he made his way toward
Vordegh's apartments. The was the first time he had been called to
attend on the new First Magus, and he wasn't looking forward to the
experience. As the castle's senior archivist his duties did, of course,
include the provision of information to the senior magi whenever the
need arose, and Vordegh's predecessor had often made use of his services. Vordegh himself, though, was likely to prove a far more critical
and demanding master, and the timing of this first summons left Savrinor in no doubt that he was about to be tested.

The studded door that led to the First Magus's sanctum was
closed. That in itself was intimidating, but Savrinor, knowing the
form, knocked lightly on the ancient wood and waited, well aware
that the knock would have been heard. After perhaps a minute soft
footsteps sounded on the far side, and the door was opened. A tall,
lissome female servant, coldly and virginally beautiful and swathed
from neck to feet in a dark gown, gestured for him to enter, then
padded away through an inner door to inform her master of his arrival. Savrinor waited again, striving not to fidget, and at last he was
ushered into the chamber beyond the door.

The room was elegantly but sparsely furnished. The curtains were closed against the wet and dismal night and a fire burned in the hearth, but somehow the flames' warmth was a peripheral thing, a mere physical property that did nothing to dispel the prevailingly icy atmosphere. Vordegh sat in a high-backed and uncushioned chair, before a large table spread with papers, ink stand, and other paraphernalia. Without looking up he signaled the servant to leave, then unhurriedly sprinkled sand over the parchment on which he'd been writing, set the document aside, and, finally, raised his head.

Calm brown eyes, self-contained and fearsomely intelligent, looked the historian over, and the First Magus said, "Good evening, Master Savrinor."

"Good evening, my lord." Savrinor bowed with the severest formality; no flourish, no embellishment, not with this man.

"Your response to my summons is refreshingly prompt. If this is an indication of your general efficiency, I shall have no cause for complaint."

The knot in Savrinor's stomach slackened a little. "Thank you, my lord."

"I have read your account of my predecessor's passing." Vordegh indicated one of several manuscripts on the table before him. "I will say, Master Savrinor, that I was impressed. Your reputation as an accurate chronicler is well founded; the facts of the sad event are all meticulously recorded, and you are to be commended. However" — a faint, dry smile caught at the corners of the First Magus's mouth — "there is, I think, a slight tendency to hyperbole. Quite understandable, of course, as the document is intended for what I might term a broader audience than the magi's inner coterie. You've done nothing other than what was expected of you; but I think that when it comes to writing the account of my own inauguration, I shall require something a little less flamboyant. Embellishment is both unnecessary and tiresome; for me, Master Savrinor, you will write the plain truth, no more and no less." The smile grew a shade less wintry, though it was still remote. "I don't think I'm underestimating you when I suggest that that will probably come as something of a relief."

Fire and ice washed over Savrinor in rapid succession as he realized that Vordegh looked on him with favor; or as close to favor as was possible with such a man. He hadn't expected this, and the implications were terrifying. He stared down at the floor. "You compliment me greatly, my lord. And I'll confess that to be freed from the demands of . . . of . . ."

Vordegh raised his dark eyebrows. "Necessity?"

"As you say, sir. Necessity." Sweat trickled down Savrinor's spine; he was treading a narrow path and whatever appearances suggested, he was well aware that at any moment it might crumble under his feet. Praying that he'd read the signals aright, he continued, "My calling, Lord Vordegh — and, I hope, my talents — incline me to one strict principle." He dared to glance up. "Whatever else may be required of me — or have been required of me in the past — I wish only to chronicle the *facts* of our history, so that future generations may know the truth."

There was a pause. It was brief, but in its duration Savrinor felt as though he'd suffered through a hundred lifetimes. Then, at last, Vordegh spoke.

"You are a very intelligent man, Master Savrinor. It's a pity, perhaps, that you haven't the innate sorcerous talent to become a magus, for I think you would have made a valuable addition to our ranks. . . . But, then, the gods bestow their gifts as they see fit. Which reminds me — I noted that our lord Yandros made himself known to you at the celebrations."

The thrill of that memory coursed through Savrinor's head like strong wine. "He granted me that honor, my lord. It's a moment I shall never forget."

"You were with Benetan Liss at the time. The Riders' captain."

Savrinor's pleasure vanished abruptly and completely as he saw that Vordegh's apparently casual question had been nothing of the kind. *Sweet gods, what was behind this?* Keeping his voice level, he replied, "He was, sir."

"Mmm." A pause; Vordegh glanced carelessly over one of his parchments. "Benetan Liss left the castle this afternoon, via the Maze."

"Yes, my lord, I believe he did."

"Why?"

The query was mild, but Savrinor knew Vordegh's reputation too well to be taken in by his tone. "In truth, sir, I don't know," he said.

Vordegh grunted noncommittally. "Well, when he returns you

may tell him that he'll be well advised not to make a habit of it in the future. I shall want the Riders on call at shorter notice from now on; there'll be a great deal of work for them. And that brings me to my primary reason for summoning you here."

Savrinor allowed himself to breathe again, though cautiously. "Sir?"

"I have a task for you. You may complete your account of the celebrations first, but don't waste time over it; this new commission is more important and must be carried out thoroughly and quickly. I want you to scour the castle's records for all information we have on the heretic factions that have troubled us from time to time, and in particular anything that relates to their activities over the past three years. Find the details, collate them, and present a full report to me."

Savrinor was surprised. He was aware that the steps taken to wipe out the growing rebel movement hadn't been entirely successful. Some key individuals had evaded the traps set for them and slipped through the magi's net, but the old First Magus had shown no interest in intensifying the hunt and Savrinor had assumed that Vordegh would follow his example. It appeared he had been wrong.

Vordegh regarded him astutely. "Clearly you're taken aback by this commission, Master Savrinor. It's high time, then, that you and perhaps a good few others thought again." His brows came together ominously and he shifted his bulk slightly in the chair. "My predecessor, though an excellent man, believed that this movement, like many before it, would be short-lived and present no threat to us. I do not share that belief. And neither, if you are wise, should you."

Savrinor's eyes grew suddenly intense. "My lord . . . are you saying that these rebels, these heretics . . . could pose a threat to us?"

Vordegh looked back steadily. "Yes, Master Savrinor, that is precisely what I'm saying."

"But the gods —"

"The gods don't intervene in mortal affairs, as you know very well. That is a measure of our lord Yandros's trust in us, his servants, to rule in his name. We have had trouble with insurgents many times before, and we have dealt with them. This newest faction, though, is a little different." He steepled his fingers, continuing to watch Savrinor over them. "Tell me what you know of the heretics."

Savrinor frowned. "Little enough, my lord, save that they've dared to renounce the gods. I hear, though I don't know the truth or otherwise of it, that they have given their allegiance to — " the words stuck in his throat with revulsion, but he forced himself to utter them — "to the demons of Order."

"Your ears are as reliable as ever, Master Savrinor," Vordegh said dryly. "And what other facts have they transmitted to your resourceful brain?"

Savrinor flinched slightly at the phrasing but tried not to show it. "Few others, sir. Except . . ."

He hesitated. Vordegh prompted with a raised eyebrow.

"Well, my lord . . . I understand it's put about in some districts that this faction has a leader." He paused, observing the First Magus from under carefully hooded eyelids, then added, "A somewhat unusual and . . . singular man."

The corner of Vordegh's mouth twitched. "Unusual and singular. Your choice of adjectives is tactful — and apposite. Do those who put these rumors about give this man a name?"

Briefly Savrinor felt on safe ground. "No, my lord, or at least none that I've heard."

"Mmm. Well, in that at least we're ahead of you, for what little it may be worth. We have three names for this rebel leader, Master Savrinor, none of them previously known to us, and any or all as likely as not to be a product of sheer fancy. But amid all the conjecture there are one or two hard facts. Firstly, this man, whoever he is, exists. Secondly, he has thus far evaded all our efforts to discover his identity and his whereabouts. And when I say *all* our efforts, that is precisely what I mean."

Savrinor realized abruptly what the First Magus was implying. He'd heard it whispered that this rebel leader, this heretic worshiper of the demon cult of Order, was a sorcerer, and no mere dabbler but a man of supreme skill. Now Vordegh confirmed it — and the confirmation was a clear and shocking admission.

"Yes, I see you understand." Vordegh sat back in his chair, his eyes glinting and dangerous. "We — even *we* — have been unable to touch this man, which means that he has a command of sorcery to match, or even outstrip, our own. I very much doubt that his talent is entirely natural, or he would have come to the attention of our agents many years ago and would have been brought to the castle."

Savrinor coughed delicately. "With respect, my lord, it's possible that he was overlooked. There have been precedents. . . ."

Vordegh's faint answering smile told him that he had been tested, albeit in a small way, and had passed the test. In this at least, the First Magus wanted frankness above tact.

"You're right, of course. But I still think it unlikely. My belief" — again he pressed his fingertips together — "is that this heretic's powers, at least in part, have an external source."

Savrinor saw where his thoughts were leading and, before he could stop himself, said a word he'd learned from one of Benetan's sergeants. Vordegh's mouth pursed censoriously and the historian made a hasty apology.

"Forgive me, my lord; I didn't mean to utter such a profanity. But—"

"But you are sharp-witted enough to comprehend my meaning without the need for further words. Quite, Master Savrinor. In essence, then, it seems that this heretic, name, identity, and whereabouts unknown, is being shielded from us by the demon Aeoris. Yet Aeoris, together with all his infernal legions, was exiled from the mortal world by our lord Yandros, many centuries ago." The First Magus's hands unfolded once more and he began to tell off on his long fingers. "Question one: how have the forces of Order found a means to break their exile? Question two: how did this heretic make contact with Aeoris? Question three: by what means, and to what degree, is Aeoris able to exert his influence? And question four, perhaps the most important of all: what does he hope to gain by it?"

Savrinor stared at the four fingers held up before him. "As to the first three questions, my lord, I can't begin to offer an answer. But the fourth . . ." He suppressed a shiver. "I think it's all too clear."

"Then your thoughts match my own. Aeoris's intention — and that of the rebels who have joined together under his banner — is to challenge the rule of Chaos. And that, Master Savrinor, no matter what the cost in effort, in resources, or in lives, must be *stopped*."

The First Magus's voice took on a new and pitiless note as he uttered these words, and for the first time Savrinor found himself witnessing, at first hand, Vordegh in his true guise. No mercy here, no tolerance, no reason. Only the relentless, inflexible, and monstrously powerful will of a man whose word must be law, and who would crush the world under his feet rather than brook the least opposition.

"It must be stopped, Master Savrinor." Vordegh rose to his feet and turned to face the window, his stare seeming to penetrate through the heavy curtains to the cold night beyond the glass. "And it will be stopped. I don't want merely a few peripheral followers of this cult to make a public example of; that might have contented my predecessor, but it doesn't content me. I will have this leader, and his closest cohorts. Whatever the price of their capture, it will be paid."

Savrinor watched his master's broad, powerful back, and touched his tongue to his lower lip. "I understand you, my lord. I'm at your command."

For a second or two Vordegh didn't respond. Then suddenly, and with a litheness that belied his age, he turned to face the historian again.

"Very well, Master Savrinor." The ferocity had vanished from his voice as swiftly as it had risen; now he was brisk, businesslike. "For the present, concentrate on your report. I want it within three days."

Savrinor blanched a little. "In addition to my account of the celebrations, sir?"

"Yes. One draft will suffice; copies can be made later."

Savrinor swallowed and nodded. "As you say, Lord Vordegh."

The First Magus's gaze flicked briefly but knowingly to his face. "If you haven't sufficient supply of your favored narcotics to keep you awake, speak to Magus Croin. He'll have my sanction to provide you with whatever you need. And don't dissemble about it; I'm as aware of your predilections as anyone else in the castle, but how you choose to abuse your body is of no interest to me unless it should affect your efficiency."

Whey-faced, Savrinor pressed his lips together and nodded.

"Then that's all I have to say to you for the present." Vordegh reseated himself at the table and reached for the parchment he'd set aside earlier. Aware that formal farewells weren't required, and still perspiring in the wake of the First Magus's careless comment on his proclivities, Savrinor made a bow and prepared to withdraw.

As he reached the door, Vordegh looked up again. "One last thing."

"My lord?" Hand on the door latch, Savrinor paused.

"I don't need to remind you, I believe, that the details of this interview are not for other ears?"

"No, my lord."

"Good." Vordegh smiled. "Discretion is a valuable commodity, and I would prefer not to hear that it had been squandered. Good night, Master Savrinor."

"Good night, my lord." Savrinor bowed again, and departed.

Iselia heard him come in. She'd woken to find herself alone in the wide bed, and for a short but precious while had felt a sense of intense though, she knew, illusory freedom. Now at the sound of the outer door closing, her body tensed and the mask she was fast learning to wear imposed itself once more. She waited, expecting him to come through to the inner room, but when after a few minutes he hadn't done so she slipped out of bed and padded to the dividing door.

Savrinor was standing by his ornate desk. He held a glass in one hand, and with the other was measuring something into it. He must have sensed rather than heard her, for she made no sound, and his head came up sharply.

"Savrinor . . . ?" She'd dropped the *Master* now, at his order.

"Go back to bed." He spoke mildly enough but there was an underlying edge to his voice.

"Can I fetch you anything?"

Savrinor's mouth hardened. "If I give you a clear command, I expect — " Then the reprimand trailed off. He had no cause to be angry with her, and he disliked displays of petulance, especially in himself.

"No." He put the cup down. "I want nothing. And in truth, my dear Iselia, you'd be well advised to sleep while you can. I'll have a great deal for you to do in the morning."

She emerged from the bedchamber, aware that he was observing the curves of her body through the thin folds of her night shift, but no longer shrinking from his gaze. "Is something amiss?" Her eyes were wide, ingenuous.

"Amiss? No; I wouldn't put it as strongly as that." Savrinor stared for a moment at whatever he'd mixed into the cup, then drank it in one draft, grimacing at the taste. That would put paid to any ideas of sleep for a few hours, at least. "I shan't have the pleasure of your company tonight," he added. "I have a new commission from the First Magus, which means I must spend the hours until dawn writing my account of the celebrations, and you must spend tomorrow making copies of the document for wider circulation."

"You've been to see the First Magus?" She looked both surprised and a little unnerved.

"Yes." He set the cup down and crossed the room to where she stood. One hand covered her left shoulder, the other traced lightly across her forehead, nose, chin, down to the cleft between her breasts. "And he is an impatient man. So, sadly, I must deny myself the delights of your body tonight and for several more nights to follow."

Instinct made Iselia want to flinch from his touch, but she didn't; she was beginning to learn how to control her reactions.

"For how long?" She pitched her voice softly.

Savrinor appeared to misinterpret her meaning, as she had hoped he would.

"Three days." The hand that touched her shoulder caught suddenly in her hair and he tilted her head back, his searching, pale eyes looking into her own. "Only three, my dear. Can you contain your impatience for that long?"

Iselia realized at once that she'd miscalculated; he wasn't fooled by her apparent regret but knew perfectly well that she was thinking only of the respite. She flushed and her gaze slid away.

"I . . . think so."

"Yes. So do I." He kissed her mouth, not fondly, then turned her to face the inner door. "Go back to bed, Iselia, and leave me to my solitary labors. I'll want you refreshed and sprightly and ready for work one hour after dawn and no later."

She held his gaze for a moment. Something was afoot, she knew it; small nuances in his posture, in his voice, in his eyes, gave it away. But she didn't dare ask. In time, she thought, in time he'd tell her. She'd persuade him. Despite this small setback, she was learning a good deal about the ways and means by which Savrinor could be persuaded.

She gave him a smile that was warmer than he might have expected. "I shall be ready, of course," she said, and was gone.

***

The First Magus summoned his servant ten minutes after Savrinor's departure. The tall, cold-faced woman entered the inner room silently, bowed, and stood waiting for his command. Vordegh had resumed his scrutiny of the documents on his desk; after a few moments he looked up, his eyes coolly and distantly appraising as he regarded her. The girl's mother had been a pretty child of fourteen, one of Pirane's gaggle of candidates from a sweep in the southeast twenty-five years ago. Chosen for a Quarter Day rite, the woman had been used by one of Yandros's emissaries and later enjoyed by a visiting noble; she'd lost her mind and died, but not before bearing a daughter. Magus Croin, Vordegh recalled, had been greatly interested to discover that the infant carried the sparks of two separate fathers, and had wanted to experiment on her to further his store of knowledge. Vordegh, though, had been against the idea, arguing that the child would be more valuable to the castle alive than dead. He'd won the dispute, together with jurisdiction over the infant, and time had proved him right. The girl's characteristics as she grew toward maturity were almost entirely human but carried just enough of Chaos's influence to give her unusual grace and intelligence. Vordegh had meticulously trained and molded her until she had become, even by his exacting standards, as close to the perfect amanuensis as he could rationally expect to find. She was also aesthetically pleasing, and the First Magus was aware that a good number of his fellow magi coveted her for her beauty and envied his possession of her. The knowledge amused him and also gave rise to a certain degree of contempt, for Vordegh had chosen long ago to live the life of a celibate ascetic; pleasures of the flesh, he considered, were a crude preoccupation that could only detract from higher matters. But he knew perfectly well how many of his colleagues would have treated such a creature were she to fall into their hands.

He addressed her at last, dismissively. "I shall have no further requirements tonight. You may retire."

She didn't speak, only made another bow and withdrew as noiselessly as she had come. Vordegh heard the soft sound of the outer door closing, heard her enter the adjoining quarters where his other four women servants were doubtless already asleep. When the small sounds had ceased, the First Magus put his papers aside once more and altered his posture in the chair, straightening back and aligning knees and feet until he looked as formal and still as a carved statue. All expression had been banished from his face, leaving it like stone. Only his eyes held animation now, seeming lit from within by some dark and unnameable fire.

His focus changed, his pupils dilated momentarily. An aura of cold, nacreous light shone briefly around the inner door before him as he psychically and astrally sealed the room. He wanted no interruptions, physical or otherwise. A great deal of work lay before him, and it was time for the preparation and purification to begin.

Vordegh raised his left arm, holding it out before him. He focused his will and a black flame appeared, hovering in midair a handspan from his outstretched fingers. There was a hollow *thump* of displaced air as the flame's enormous heat sucked oxygen from the room, and Vordegh felt the backlash of the heat on his face, bringing a rush of blood to his skin. Slowly, every muscle under rigid control, he rose to his feet and his hand made a beckoning motion.

The flame responded. With a flowing, almost graceful motion it surged toward him as though impelled by a strange intelligence of its own. Black tongues licked at Vordegh's fingers, spread across his palm, over his wrist and forearm. The pain was staggering, as real as though his arm had been immersed in physical fire, but Vordegh didn't flinch. He smiled, a proud smile, a contented smile, as the black flames licked to his shoulder and began to surround his head and torso, until he stood wreathed in a blazing, flickering corona. By will alone his skin was unscathed, his hair and clothing unscorched. There was only the ecstatic agony of power, filling him, renewing him, strengthening his body, mind, and soul.

The First Magus tilted back his head. Through the black fire the room roiled and twisted, its planes distorting in the heat as he welcomed and absorbed the savage energies of Chaos which he had conjured. He spoke no word, uttered no sound, but in his mind and heart, like a litany, a pledge and a promise took form.

My lord Yandros, all you lords of Chaos, hear me! My will is as this fire, and it burns like this fire with hunger and with certainty. A new age is dawning, my lords, and this age will carry the mark of Vordegh. I am strong, I am ready. Let those fools who dare rise against my will — there will be no mercy for them. No mercy and no quarter. I wield the wand of Chaos. AND I WILL PREVAIL!

CHAPTER XIII

The drizzle still hadn't abated in the predawn hour when Savrinor emerged from one of the castle's lesser doors and started across the courtyard toward the west wing. His fur cloak was slung over his shoulders, but he'd put it on only to protect the rolled parchment which he carried under its folds; he felt the need of the rain to refresh him and clear his head, and for once his customary fastidious dislike of the elements could go to the Seven Hells.

His gait wasn't entirely steady. Savrinor knew it, and it angered him. Normally he could predict the effects of the drugs he used with fine precision, but this time lack of sleep had been his enemy and, as the narcotic wore off, sheer weariness was washing over him in waves, a tide ebbing and flowing. He could have taken a second dose, but he was rational enough to know that sleep would be a wiser answer before he set his mind to the new task with which the First Magus had charged him. Only let him deliver this first damned document to Vordegh's apartments, and he could snatch a few hours' oblivion to refresh himself before the real work began.

The courtyard was deserted, only dimly silvered with a spectral glow from the second moon as it struggled to break through the rain clouds. Even so, Savrinor's senses were alert enough and his eyes keen enough to catch a glimmer of movement by the stable block. He stopped, watching. Then a foot slid on stone and the latch of one of the stable doors clicked.

"Benetan?" Quite how he knew that the featureless silhouette emerging from the stables *was* Benetan, Savrinor had no idea; his drug-heightened senses, perhaps. Anyway, he was right. The younger man hesitated briefly, then came toward him. The set of his shoulders, Savrinor thought, had a defeated look.

"Yandros preserve us all." Savrinor raked him with a sour glare. "We meet again at an unlikely hour and in an unlikely place. This is getting to be a habit."

His reference to their encounter on the beach produced nothing more than a humorless twitch of Benetan's lips. "Not comfortable in your rooms with Iselia?" he said acidly.

"No. Not comfortable in yours with Andraia? Obviously not. Well, then, it seems we've both been unfortunate tonight. When did you get back?"

Benetan shrugged. "An hour ago, perhaps a little more. How did you know I'd left the castle?"

"I miss nothing; you should know that by now. But I neither know nor care where you've been — that's a matter entirely between you and your conscience. So, you returned an hour ago. You must have been a long time in the stables. Do you find horses' company preferable to that of humans, or " — Savrinor sniffed the air ostentatiously— "are you too drunk to remember where your room is?"

"I'm sober, thank you. My mare has a shoe loose and I think she's going lame into the bargain, so I've treated the strain and bound up the leg. It didn't seem necessary to wake the grooms for something so trivial."

"Very noble of you." Savrinor wondered privately why Benetan appeared so anxious to explain himself, and stored the question away for later consideration. "Well, if we're going to stand passing the time of day — or night, to be accurate — I'd suggest we do it in more clement surroundings. I have an errand to the west wing, and you may accompany me or not, as you please."

He started off across the courtyard again. Without any real motive, Benetan fell into step beside him. "What's your business in the west wing at this hour?"

Savrinor glanced obliquely at him. "An errand for the First Magus. One of many more to come, if I'm any judge." He rubbed at his eyes suddenly and savagely, aware that he shouldn't have said that, but Benetan seemed too preoccupied with his own private thoughts to comment or even to notice the lapse of discretion. Perversely that annoyed Savrinor, and there was a hint of vitriol in his voice as he added, "Some of us aren't likely to have the time to go gallivanting through the Maze in pursuit of pleasure in the foreseeable future."

That did provoke a reaction. "Pleasure?" Benetan said challengingly.

"Pleasure or folly or anything else." They had reached the colonnaded walk on the castle's west side; under the shelter of the roofed pillars the rain was reduced to nothing more than an occasional spatter of droplets carried by the wind. Savrinor brushed meticulously at his cloak, then eyed the other man acerbically. "You really are a fool, Benetan. Drowning your sorrows in the arms of outland whores when, if you'd half a modicum of common sense, you'd know that Andraia is only waiting for you to make the first move toward reconciliation."

Benetan's mind had been elsewhere, but the historian's biting words jolted him back into the reality of the present. *Outland whores?* Just in time he stemmed the instinctive angry reaction. If that was what Savrinor, or anyone else, believed, then he was out of danger. . . .

He lifted his shoulders eloquently and said, "A lesser man would think you were jealous."

"Of your liaison with Andraia? Half the castle's jealous of it, my dear friend. She's worth better than you."

Benetan's hackles rose. "And Iselia —"

"Iselia's no longer your concern, as I've attempted to get through your skull on more than one occasion." Something in Savrinor's tone then, Benetan didn't miss it and sensed instinctively that it wasn't merely the narcotics speaking. What he didn't anticipate, though, was the sudden tensing of Savrinor's posture, the quick turning to face him, and the look almost of challenge in the historian's eyes.

"Iselia *is* no longer your concern, Benetan. And I don't mean that quite in the sense that your gutter-born mind will have interpreted it."

Perhaps it was the combination of tiredness and confusion that conspired to make Benetan's mind grasp at more than a fraction of what Savrinor implied, or perhaps, simply, something far less tangible communicated itself between them in that moment. But either way Benetan's sour levity dropped from him like a discarded mask.

"What do you mean?"

Savrinor turned away and stared at the black wall. "Nothing."

That was a lie. Benetan reached out, touched the historian's arm. "Savrinor. I don't know how the slate stands between us at the moment, I can't remember. But tell me. What's afoot?"

Well, he'd know about it soon enough, Savrinor's drug-sodden mind reasoned. Benetan was captain of the Chaos riders, one of the elite, one of the privileged. . . . *Tell him*, a fierce inner voice said. *After all, he'll be the one who has to carry out the orders.*

"Our new First Magus doesn't intend to waste any time," he said, then his voice dropped to a near-whisper. "He has plans. And I, who am responsible for the castle's archives, and Iselia, who spends the great majority of her waking hours diligently copying the reports I prepare, and you, who spearhead the purely physical aspects of our masters' commands, are going to be a part of those plans whether we relish the prospect or whether we don't." He turned, hunching his shoulders, staring at the wall. "If we all achieve the goals he sets us, well and good. If we fail . . ." A small, negating gesture with one hand conveyed the rest.

Benetan stared at the historian's back. Whatever his own preoccupations this was vital news, and he didn't like the sound of it.

"What *are* his plans? Do you know?"

"In essence. The First Magus was good enough to call me before him and apprise me of his intentions a few hours ago." Savrinor swung round again and briefly showed the parchment in his other hand. "Hence this. It's the factual report of the inauguration ceremonies; just one of the small, bothersome necessities that must be disposed of before the real work begins." He tucked the parchment away again, then his pale eyes looked hard into the younger man's face. "Tell me, Benetan, do you ever kill people?"

Benetan's eyes narrowed in response. Savrinor knew the nature of the riders' duties as well as anyone. "Yes," he said shortly.

"Do you enjoy the experience?"

Now Benetan's expression became dangerous. "No, I do not."

Savrinor smiled a strange, bleak smile. "Then you'd best start hardening your heart and sharpening your weapons, my friend. You and your men are about to become the honed blades in our lord Vordegh's hands. And Lord Vordegh wants blood."

Suddenly, Benetan's throat felt dry. "Blood?" he repeated. "Whose blood?"

"Heretic blood. You've heard about the movement in the south? Yes, obviously you have. Then you must also be aware that this faction, unlike those that have gone before, have evaded all our masters' efforts to unmask and destroy them. Lord Vordegh intends to put matters to rights."

The dryness became a searing ache; Benetan could barely swallow. He must have succeeded, though, in hiding his reaction from Savrinor, for the historian continued without appearing to notice anything untoward.

"My unenviable task," Savrinor said, "is to provide our First Magus with every scrap of information in the castle's records which might aid him in his search for the rebels. Listed, collated, documented, and commented upon in detail. I have precisely three days in which to complete this undertaking, which means that neither I nor anyone who serves me is likely to enjoy the benefits of sleep until it's done. Then, when our work is finished, yours will begin."

"Mine . . . ?"

"You're uncommonly fond of repeating my words tonight. Nothing original to say?" Savrinor's tone was sour and a little self-pitying. "You will be the one to act on the information that I unearth. I hope for your sake that you're ready, because my bones tell me that what our First Magus has in mind will be no pleasant and idle diversion for anyone." He scrubbed hard at his eyes, which were growing sore with tiredness and the aftereffects of his drugs. "Now, if you've quite finished keeping me from my errand, I shall complete it and steal a few precious hours in my bed while I still can."

He turned and started to walk away. For a second or two Benetan's mind was too numb to react, but suddenly a feeling that was partly due to the night's events and partly sheer instinct goaded him. Consciously, he couldn't have explained his reasons; but there was a question he had to ask.

"Savrinor. Savrinor, wait — "

Savrinor halted and looked back. "What?"

"You said . . ." He licked his lips, trying to induce enough saliva to allow the words to come. "You said that Lord Vordegh means to stamp out the rebel movement."

A pale eyebrow quirked. "Oh, you *were* listening? I'm flattered."

Benetan ignored that. "You must surely approve?"

"Of course I do."

"Then . . ." *What was he trying to say? What was it that nagged at the back of his mind?* And suddenly it came.

"Then what are you afraid of?"

Savrinor stared back and realized that he'd given himself away. He hadn't intended to speak so freely, certainly hadn't intended to betray his inner feelings. Now, though, it seemed that Benetan had a degree of subtlety that he'd not previously been aware of.

Aloud, he said: "Don't be ridiculous."

It wasn't convincing. Savrinor knew it and he saw immediately that Benetan knew it, too.

"Savrinor — "

"*Damn* you for an idiot child!" The historian took three strides and was back at Benetan's side; a hand, thin-fingered but surprisingly strong, gripped Benetan's arm and shook it sharply. "All right. All *right.* I'll tell you what's in my mind — and if you utter a word of it to another living soul, I'll have the skin flayed from you and your stripped remains thrown from the stack! Do I make myself clear? Very well, then. I've no quarrel with Lord Vordegh's intentions. No man or woman who loves our gods and to whom the taint of heresy is like the stench of the Seven Hells in their nostrils would *dream* of quarreling. No, my friend, no. Lord Vordegh is right. These evildoers must be found and destroyed. But there are ways and ways of achieving this end, Benetan. Ways and ways. Some are proper and justified in the eyes of our lord Yandros, but others are not." Savrinor sucked in a harsh breath. "Wholesale slaughter is not justified. Unfettered violence is not justified. Taking systematic retribution against the innocent in order to flush out the guilty is not justified." His eyes flicked to Benetan's face with a trace of angry resentment. "Must I endanger myself still further by spelling it out to you in greater detail?"

The chill of the night and the rain seemed to be seeping into Benetan's bones. "That is what Lord Vordegh intends?"

"Yes." Suddenly Savrinor felt a surge of feeling that he didn't want to acknowledge, was almost afraid to acknowledge. A sense of kinship with this midden-born peasant who had risen through his own merits and now, against unlikely odds, he counted as a friend. He *trusted* Benetan Liss. And — ludicrously uncharacteristic, he knew;

maybe the narcotics were having a less controllable effect than he'd thought — he wanted to confide in Benetan. *Sweet gods*, Savrinor thought, *I have to confide in someone. . . .*

His voice had a savage edge. "Lord Vordegh rules in Yandros's name, and so by carrying out Lord Vordegh's orders we are, in theory, carrying out the will of the gods. But you and I have both been granted the ineffable honor of standing before our lord Yandros and speaking directly with him. Can you recall that experience, Benetan, and tell me that this planned carnage is what Lord Yandros wants?"

There was silence for several seconds. Then Benetan said softly: "No . . ."

Savrinor looked steadily at him. "Then, my friend, we share a common dilemma." And he turned and walked away.

The battle that Benetan fought with his conscience during that dismal dawn was fierce but short-lived. Deep down, he knew from the start that whatever wisdom and self-preservation might dictate, there was only one choice he could — or rather would — make. However strong his fidelity to the gods, the gods were remote and impersonal. And despite the fact that, as Savrinor reminded him, he had spoken face-to-face with Yandros, Yandros was not involved in the realities of his life. Those realities, loves and hatreds and rivalries and concerns, lay in the human dimension, and human loyalty was a stronger force than his dedication to the deities he served. Whether or not it was a betrayal of his principles, Iselia had to be warned of what Savrinor had told him tonight.

But then the image of Andraia rose in his inner vision, and his conscience rose again with it, sharply and painfully. In even considering a meeting with Iselia, was he not also betraying the woman he claimed to love? Andraia, surely, was a vital part of his much-vaunted "realities of life," his precious "human dimension"; he had already lied to her about Iselia more than once, and now here he was planning another piece of subterfuge. It was dishonest. He should speak to her, try to explain, try to convince her that she had nothing to fear. . . .

But even as the thought entered his mind Benetan knew that he couldn't and wouldn't do any such thing. Whatever he said, however hard he might try to convince her, Andraia wouldn't understand. Better to risk further hostility than make matters worse by a misguided attempt to salve his conscience that might, anyway, put Iselia in jeopardy. Her safety must be his first and only priority, and he would just have to live with his discomfort. Any other course of action simply wouldn't *work*.

If it occurred to him that the question of Andraia's feelings had been resolved a little too easily and glibly for comfort, he ignored the perception as he considered how best he might contrive a private meeting with Iselia. Unless Savrinor had been exaggerating, which was unlikely, Iselia would have no time to call her own over the next few days — and even without that complication the historian's increasingly proprietorial attitude toward her presented another barrier. Benetan was still pondering the problem, and getting nowhere, when a tentative knocking at his door heralded the appearance of one of his junior men.

"Beg par'n, Capun Liss." The big, gangling youth had been inducted into the riders' ranks less than a year ago and hadn't yet lost his heavy southwestern accent. "Thur's a bit' trouble, sir. Coupla men be tooken sick hour-two after breakfast, and Sarn't says I'm to come ask you what's to be done."

An hour or two after breakfast . . . ? Surprised, Benetan glanced toward the window and realized that the morning was half over. The hours had slid away while he sat ruminating, and he hadn't had a wink of sleep.

Habit and his sense of duty elbowed away a flash of irritation, and he got to his feet. "Sick? What's wrong with them?"

"Don't prop'ly know, sir. Sarn't thinks they've ate sunnat bad, like. Several others is down with same thing, and he wonders if physician should be tolden."

"All right, I'll come." Benetan shoved his feet into his boots and pulled on his quilted jacket, which still felt damp after his foray into the mountains. "Where are they?"

"Sick dormitory, sir. We did call for herballer, but she ant arrived 'fore I was sent tellen you."

As they walked together down the corridor and toward the main stairs, Benetan quickly racked his memory for the young messenger's name. Lotro, that was it. With more than seventy men under his command it was sometimes hard to match every face to every name, but Lotro had caught his attention early, almost from the day of his gleaning. In fact, Benetan recalled, he had personally singled the youth out for the riders' ranks, seeing beneath that pleasant-faced, slightly shambling exterior a hint of untapped qualities only waiting for an opportunity to bloom. Thus far he hadn't been disappointed; Lotro had a quick mind that belied both appearance and speech, and had shown a skill with weapons that before too long would threaten to outstrip Benetan's own. Lotro promised to be a credit to the Chaos riders.

And yet another honed blade in Lord Vordegh's hands. . . .

"Lotro."

He had stopped without consciously intending to. Surprised, Lotro halted, too, and turned to look at him. "Sir?"

Dear gods, what was he doing? But the words came nonetheless. "Do you enjoy your work, Lotro?"

The young man's face blossomed into a broad smile. "'Es, sir, I do!"

A reckless instinct drove Benetan. "Then answer me a question. Whom do you serve?" He paused. "Whom do you *really* serve?"

Lotro's smile didn't waver. "I serve the gods, sir." He made a religious sign over his own heart. "And I serve our magi, and I serve you, too. After all, tes all one and same, ant it, sir? All one and same; and that a rare privilege for anyone as gets the chance."

Suddenly Benetan could no longer meet his eager, open gaze. He looked away. "Yes, Lotro," he said. "Of course, it's all one and the same."

His sergeant was right; the two sick men were suffering the ill effects of bad food. By the time Benetan arrived in the sick dormitory the herballer, who was one of the castle's senior servants, had already made her diagnosis and was grumbling about lax kitchen standards which had led to the improper salting of meat, rendering it unfit for human consumption. It was always the same at this time of year, she said; the autumn tithes hadn't yet arrived and the castle's cooks were obliged to make the best of what little they had left at the season's end. Benetan listened courteously to her complaints and extracted from the tirade the knowledge that his men's illness wasn't serious enough to warrant the attention of Magus Croin or even the castle's general physician, Revian. A purging draft and a few days' rest would see the sufferers on their feet again, the herballer said, and stern words would be had with whoever had been responsible for this lapse.

It was almost noon when Benetan started back to his rooms. The rain had finally petered out, giving way to watery sunlight that lifted the day's bleakness a degree or two. A few hurrying figures were about in the courtyard as Benetan left the dormitory above the castle's armory in the south wing, and as he passed the central fountain a glint of fair hair caught his eye.

He stopped. Iselia was walking along the pillared stoa on the castle's western side, heading toward the door that led down through the foundations to the library. Briefly, almost subconsciously, Benetan's mind registered the elegance of her clothing, the cream fur wrap she wore against the day's chill. Then, goaded by instinct rather than reason, he quickened his pace to intercept her.

"Iselia!"

She paused, turned, saw him, and instantly her expression became guarded. "Benet." She nodded as though he were a very distant acquaintance.

The distractions of the past hour collapsed and vanished from Benetan's mind as he came up to where she stood waiting, her posture uneasy. He glanced swiftly, surreptitiously, around. Lotro was following him from the south wing, but he had paused to speak to a girl servant.

"Where are you going?" Benetan's voice was tense.

Her gaze flicked toward the library door. "I'm busy, Benet."

"I have to speak to you."

"We've nothing to say to each other. You know my position." Then her blue eyes hardened. "You should, you of all people. Savrinor has work for me. He's waiting in the library."

Trying to tell himself that it wasn't hatred or bitterness he saw in her face, Benetan shook his head. "You don't understand! Iselia, I *have* to talk to you — it's vital!"

She gave him a searing glance that almost unhinged him. "Vital? It's a little late for that, Benet! You should have thought about what was vital before you had me snatched from my home and brought here!"

Something in Benetan seemed to shatter as he saw that the frail bridge he had tried to build between them on the night she had come to the castle had collapsed. Whatever Savrinor had done, Iselia had changed.

"Please, listen to me!" On the edge of vision he glimpsed Lotro starting toward him again. There was so little time. "Iselia, you *must* meet me!"

She didn't unbend; her face was stone. "Why?" It was a bitter challenge.

"Because . . ." *Damn it, that fool boy would be with him in seconds. . . .* Benetan threw caution to the four winds. "Because I've seen Kaldar."

Her expression, her posture, everything about her, froze. *"You've . . ."*

"The dining hall." His mind was racing, flying like a hawk. "This evening —"

"We *can't!*" she said. Her face was suddenly flushed with hectic color. "We'll be in full view of everyone — it's too dangerous!"

"Not if we get there early, before the crowding begins. No one will think anything of it; besides, the more public we are, the less likely we'll be to arouse suspicion. Try, *please*. For all our sakes."

"Capun Liss?" Lotro's voice impinged like a dog's bark against restful silence. A part of Benetan's mind that didn't feel entirely real made him turn to face the young rider. On another level he was aware of Iselia hastening away.

"Your jacket, sir." Lotro was beaming, eager to please. "Looks a bit the worse of wear, if you'll pardon the liberty. Shall I take un, sir? Go and get un cleaned up proper, like?"

Oh, gods . . . , Benetan thought. *So anxious to please. . . .*

"Yes." He heard his own voice as though from a very long way off. "Yes, Lotro. Take it." He was sweating; relieving himself of the jacket was a blessed, almost animal relief, like shedding an unwanted skin. "Thank you. I appreciate your thoughtfulness."

As soon as he entered the dining hall he saw her. She had taken a place at one of the most out-of-the-way tables, between two north-facing windows where the declining evening light couldn't reach. For appearances' sake she had a plate of food before her, but it was untouched.

A background hum of voices swam around the huge chamber. Some early diners had already arrived and one group in particular was making its presence felt with occasional bursts of laughter. But as yet there were no senior officials in the hall, nor any of the magi. A few Chaos riders, but they would only assume that their captain was playing games behind Historian Savrinor's back and not for a moment suspect any other motive. Benetan felt a slight lessening of his fearful tension as he made his way toward the table, trying to appear a good deal more casual than he felt.

"Iselia?"

She looked up, then slid a little way along the bench to make room for him. "It wasn't easy to come here, Benet. Savrinor is still in the library; he gave me leave to snatch a meal but he expects me back soon."

A servant approached and Benetan curtly told the man to bring him a plate of whatever was most plentiful tonight.

"Wine, sir?" The servant still hovered. "Or ale, or — "

"No." Benetan bit back his unstable temper. "Just the food."

The man glided away and he looked at Iselia. At the celebrations she had been haggard, haunted. That was gone now, though his imagination still saw echoes. Instead, her face was peculiarly composed.

She broke the silence first. "So you've seen Kaldar." A muscle twitched in her throat. "You know, then."

"Yes. I know." Hidden under the tabletop Benetan's hands twitched in a sudden, helpless spasm. "I gave him your marriage ring. It seemed only right."

Whether or not the words were deliberately intended to win her favor he didn't know, but they had the desired effect, for her expression changed. "You . . . ?" Then she bit her lip. "Thank you, Benet. Thank you."

Suddenly Benetan found himself telling her the whole story of his first, unexpected encounter with Kaldar, and of the promise he had made to rendezvous in the northern mountains. Iselia listened without saying any more until at last his flow of hesitant and uncertain words led him to the one thing he had meant to say from the start, the fulfillment of his promise to her husband.

"He entrusted me with a message, Iselia. And he gave me something — a token — to hand on to you."

From under his jerkin Benetan drew the dried and withered remains of the marriage garland. For several seconds Iselia stared at it before, very slowly, her hand reached out and took it from him. Very quietly, she said: "Ah . . ."

"I'm sorry that you've had to receive it through me; that circumstances didn't allow . . ." Benetan was floundering, the words threatening to die on his tongue. "Something like this, it's — it should be private, personal — "

She didn't answer. He struggled on. "I tried not to damage it on the journey back. It's withered, but . . ." He swallowed. "Kaldar must have saved it for you when — when — "

Iselia looked up sharply as she realized suddenly what Benetan meant and what he had assumed. A marriage garland — of course, it was only natural that he would think that. But there had been no garland to commemorate her marriage. This little wreath, Kaldar's gift to her via Benetan's good offices, had another significance entirely.

Offering silent thanks for Benetan's mistake, and for the fact that her initial puzzlement didn't seem to have caught his attention, she cast her gaze down and tucked the garland into a linen reticule that she wore at her waist, which already contained several quill pens and a small bag of drying sand. "Thank you," she said. "It was . . . kind of you to bring it back."

For a few moments an awkward silence fell. Then: "You said there was a message?" Iselia asked.

This was the moment Benetan had been dreading. What to say, how to explain to her that he knew the truth about her allegiances yet convince her that she was in no danger from him. He had turned it over and over in his mind and still didn't know, couldn't begin to predict, how she would react.

"Kaldar's going south." He heard her draw in a quick breath at that. "That was his message. He told me that it was what you both originally planned to do. . . ." Something caught in his throat; he coughed. "His exact words were: 'Tell her that I'm going to join our friends.' But . . . Iselia, there's more." Suddenly he knew that he had to find the words and utter them within the next few seconds, or his resolve would fail him. He sucked air into his lungs. "I know about your allegiance to the cause of . . ." A nod finished the sentence; even though no one else was sitting close enough to overhear them he didn't dare to speak the name *Order*. "Kaldar told me last night. And though my head will be on the block if anyone should find out that I've said this, there's something you have to know."

The hall was beginning to fill with people now. One group some half dozen strong had just entered through the great doors, their voices swelling the background hum of sound, and had taken places at one of the tables nearest the hearth, which were reserved for those of high rank. Among the group were Magus Pirane — and Andraia.

At first Andraia didn't notice the couple who sat together in the shadows. But as she took her seat at Pirane's left hand there was a flicker of familiarity at the border of her vision, and she looked up in time to see Benetan walking away from the table at which Iselia now sat alone.

A tight, ugly sensation clutched at her stomach. *That girl again!* Benetan wasn't aware of her presence; she stared at his departing back and then, as he reached the doors and went out, her gaze swung venomously to the solitary figure of Iselia. A serpent in the clothes of sweet piety, Andraia thought savagely. The image of meek virgin, Lady Purity; and she found little consolation in the knowledge that with Savrinor for a master the image undoubtedly belied the reality by now. Had Benetan's little peasant girl told him about Savrinor's appetites and tastes? Unlikely. After all, it might shatter his fond illusions and tarnish her in his eyes, and doubtless she wouldn't want *that*.

"Andraia?" Pirane's voice at her side snapped her from her furious thoughts. She blinked and looked up.

"What will you choose tonight?" A servant was hovering behind Pirane's shoulder, bowing to all and sundry. "Fowl, or red meat?"

Andraia wanted to cut a choice fillet of red meat from Iselia's body and wash it down with a cup of her blood, but with a great effort she forced her composure back under her control.

"Ah . . . the fowl I think, madam, thank you."

Pirane gave her a long, shrewd look but made no comment on what she saw. "The fowl, then," she said to the servant. "And bring three flasks from the last season but one's southern tithe. The white grape, not the red."

Andraia was fingering the knife set beside her plate, making small, stabbing motions at the table with its sharp tip. Pirane waited until the servant was out of earshot and their other companions engrossed in conversation, then she said quietly and mildly,

"If her presence is truly intolerable to you, I'll have her assigned to Magus Croin for his experiments, or make a gift of her to one of the lower demons. Savrinor could find himself a new assistant with no difficulty.. But really, my dear, is it worth upsetting yourself?"

Andraia felt the tide of her fury ebbing before the cool words of reason. Pirane was right, she had no worthwhile cause to be jealous of Iselia. Benetan's infatuation would fade or not, as his nature dictated. If it didn't fade, she was well rid of him. If it did, he would come back to her soon enough pleading for forgiveness and, if she still wished to, she would forgive him — though at a price which she would dictate.

That last thought restored her appetite, but still as the food was brought and she began to eat she continued to cast frequent covert glances in the direction of the fair girl at the table under the window. No one had come to join Iselia and she had eaten none of the food in front of her. She simply sat there, fiddling with something that she held in her hands as though carefully nursing it. Then suddenly she rose to her feet and left the hall almost at a run, and as she departed Andraia had one glimpse of whatever it was that she seemed to find so precious. A small, withered bundle of leaves. Herbs? Andraia wondered. The ingredients for some potion or remedy or mind-changing drug? And what connection could that little posy possibly have with Benetan?

Her meal was going cold. Andraia returned her attention to her plate and attacked the food with renewed energy. *Something* was afoot with that little baggage, she told herself; something in which Benetan might or might not be involved. She wanted to find out more. Perhaps, she thought, a word in Savrinor's ear when the time was right wouldn't go amiss. And in the meantime she would begin to keep a very close watch on little Lady Purity.

CHAPTER XIV

It took only five days of journeying southward from his mountain hideaway for Kaldar Darrow Alvaray to learn three invaluable lessons. The first lesson was the wisdom of relying on his own instinct. The second was that, in his precarious situation, theft was a safer option than barter. And the third and most vital lesson of all was the value of extreme caution.

The first two days had been uneventful. The sere, unproductive land of the far north, populated only by the occasional sprawl of dwellings that had grown up around the mineral mines, were easy enough for a careful traveler to cross without meeting another human soul. The weather was also in his favor, cold but dry, and — as far as it was possible to judge such things with no map and few milestones to guide him — Kaldar thought that so far he was making good time.

On the third day, the nature of the countryside began to change as the scree and litter and bare slopes of the mining areas gradually gave way to more fertile land. Animals grazed in scrubby fields and in the increasingly frequent areas of bush and shrubland; root crops and even a few acres of hardy northern oats began to appear. The area was more populous, dotted with small steadings and a number of rough-and-ready villages, and by the fifth day of his journey Kaldar realized that, unless he traveled only by night, it would be impossible for him to avoid human contact for much longer. He'd planned for this, resolving to adopt the guise of an ostler given leave by his master to walk to a family wedding in the south country. It was a reasonably safe identity, for Kaldar's apprenticeship in the mines had taught him enough about horses, or at least about mine ponies, to fool anyone but an expert. And so he stood at the edge of the belt of trees on the fifth evening, shading his eyes against the sun that glowered on the western horizon, and gazing at the village that lay a few hundred yards ahead. It was a good-sized village, straddling the road and spreading away from it on both sides, and to avoid it would mean taking a long and difficult detour through dense forest. Instinct urged Kaldar not to take the chance, but logic and a few other considerations were rapidly overcoming his intuition. Kaldar was hungry for a taste of fresh food rather than the nutritious but repellent strips of dried meat which had been his only sustenance since his wedding day and the precipitous flight into the mountains. He was also running short of water and didn't relish the idea of yet another lengthy search for a stream or spring from which to refill his two leather flasks. He had a few coins, enough to pay for his needs. There was no rational reason why the village shouldn't oblige.

He emerged from the trees and walked along the last stretch of road toward the cluster of houses ahead. As he drew level with the first house a dog started barking, and moments later a door in one of the larger dwellings opened.

"Who is it?" The voice was belligerent and the accent strange to Kaldar's more northerly ears. "Who's there?"

Kaldar stopped. "Just a traveler. I'm looking to buy some food."

The dog began to bark again, was silenced with a curse, and a silhouetted figure emerged from the house into the shadow-filled street. A man, heavily built by the look of him, with a large, long-coated hound straining and growling on the end of a leash.

"I'll see your pass token." The voice didn't unbend. "And the toll's two coppers, or a quarter silver if you're leading a pack animal."

"Toll?" Kaldar was nonplussed.

The man swore roundly at the dog as it began to bark again. "Quiet, you bastard!" Then: "There's a toll to be paid by any outlander using this road."

Kaldar had never heard of such a thing, and his innate combativeness prompted him to challenge it before tact could stay his tongue. "By whose decree?" he demanded.

"Our overlord's decree, what else?" the man snapped back. "And it's no damned business of yours to argue. You pay, or you leave the road."

Overlords were a constant and unpredictable factor in the lives of everyone born and bred to a peasant's existence. They were the pivot around which each district revolved, secular tools of the magi appointed by the Star Peninsula to govern everyday matters on the rulers' behalf. In theory they had no true power, but in practice, to a farm laborer or miner or herdsman, even to the better-placed overseers and craftsmen, their overlord's will — or whim — was absolute law. Providing the Star Peninsula received each seasonal tithe in full, and providing trouble was kept to a minimum, the magi considered the question of the methods used to achieve those ends too trivial to be worthy of their notice. If an overlord demanded further extortionate tithes to keep himself and his cohorts in luxury, if justice came only to the highest bidder, if the smallest offense brought savage reprisal, and land, livelihood, and life could be forfeited on a moment's caprice, the magi neither knew nor cared. And the overlords, secure in their fortresslike stone towers, could always find enough men ready and willing to enforce their rule.

Kaldar had encountered both good and bad overlords in his own home village, and common sense came to his rescue in time to stem any further retort. This self-styled toll keeper might or might not be telling the truth, but if he was, then to argue would be foolish in the extreme. Besides, the size of the man and the gleam of the dog's teeth in the half-dark were enough in themselves to still his tongue.

He fished in his belt pouch. "I've no animal," he said. "Two coppers, was it?"

The coins changed hands and the toll keeper peered suspiciously at them in the gloom before pocketing them. "All right." He yanked viciously on the hound's chain, causing it to give a strangled yelp, then held out his hand again. "And the pass token."

Nonplussed, Kaldar stared at him. "Pass token?"

"Pass token, *pass token!*" The outstretched hand beckoned impatiently. "You've been to the overlord's holding, haven't you, you've paid the fee?"

"But the toll was — "

"Not the toll, dolt! The *fee.*" Then, seeing that Kaldar still didn't understand, the toll keeper said something foul under his breath before adding, "If you want to buy food or water or get a bed for the night, you've to pay the overlord's fee! Damn it, are you so pig ignorant that you can't understand plain speech?"

The sound of a door opening saved Kaldar from diving headlong into trouble with a furious retort. He turned, and saw that a newcomer had emerged from one of the houses on the far side of the street. Lamplight spilled out from the house, showing a tall, slim man of about Kaldar's own age, dressed in clothes that no peasant could have bought with a year's wages.

"What in the Seven Hells is all this din?" There was a hint of a swagger in the newcomer's walk, and Kaldar saw the dull glimmer of a blade at his hip. Reaching them, he stared at Kaldar with an expression that suggested he'd discovered a bad smell under his nose and wasn't about to tolerate it for long. "And who are *you?*"

The toll keeper touched his forelock respectfully, seeming to shrink into himself as he did so. "Beg your pardon for the disturbance, Steward. This one here's a stranger; he's paid the toll but he doesn't understand when I demand his pass token."

The tall man ignored him and continued to stare at Kaldar. "Name?" he demanded.

The house door had closed again, but before it did Kaldar's sharp eyes had seen a half-dressed girl of about fourteen or fifteen peering nervously out.

"I said, name!" A forefinger jabbed against his breastbone and snapped him back to earth. Kaldar fought an urge to spit in the tall man's face and replied, "Skand Arlan."

"From?"

"Northward, two days." He gestured vaguely over his shoulder. "I'm traveling south, for a family wedding. My cousin — "

His explanation was cut off. "With or without your master's permission?"

"With his permission." It nearly killed Kaldar to say the word, but he forced himself to add, "Sir."

"He's paid the toll, Steward, no trouble there," the toll keeper repeated, hunching still further. "But the pass token — "

"All right, all right, I don't need the likes of you to keep stating what's obvious to anyone. Either he's trying to evade the fee or he's got dung in his head instead of a brain." Another jab sent Kaldar staggering back a pace. "Well, dung brain? No pass token means no food, no water, and no bed for the night. Clear? If you haven't paid the fee, then your pig's trotters had better carry you straight through this village and away from our district." The steward paused, making a pretense of considering, then abruptly his expression modified into an unpleasant grin. "Or on the other hand I might be generous and allow you to pay the fee to me. Let's set it at . . . say, two silvers, and another half silver if you want someone's daughter to grunt and rootle with for an hour or two." The grin broadened. "That suit you, dung brain?"

In his mind, silently, Kaldar prayed: *Lord Aeoris, grant me strength if you can!* Aloud, his voice steady but only just, he said, "I haven't that sort of money."

"No? Well, then, there's no more to be said, is there?" With one hand the steward fingered the hilt of his long-bladed dagger. "There's the southward road, my peasant friend; and if a wild cat or dog pack doesn't get you in the meantime, you'd be well advised to be a long way away by morning." With a flourish he turned to the toll keeper. "Give him to the count of twenty to be out of sight, then if he's still in view, loose your hound. And see to it that I'm not disturbed again, or you'll spend the next season stone-clearing in the fields."

The toll keeper made a further obeisance. "As you say, Steward; and I ask your pardon for the nuisance." From under lowering brows he glared at Kaldar. "You heard the steward, dung brain. On your way — and be thankful to have been so generously treated!"

As though to emphasize the order, the dog snarled ominously. Kaldar didn't look at either of the two men; he didn't dare, for fear that his self-control would snap. Forgetting dignity, but with rage blazing in his gut, he ran away down the village street.

Kaldar spent the night hunched ten feet above the ground in the fork of a gnarled tree trunk, his back uncomfortably wedged against a bough and his ears unpleasantly attuned to the rustling, snuffling sounds that came intermittently from below. He was reasonably certain that the animals down there on the woodland floor were only pigs, turned into the forest to graze on the autumn bounty of nuts and seeds, but when he'd first heard them approaching he hadn't been inclined to take any chances. Besides, even pigs could be dangerous, and his knife, which was his only weapon, would be of little use against a fully grown boar or even a large sow if it should decide to turn aggressive.

Sleep was impossible under these circumstances, and so Kaldar had a good deal of time to think . . . and for the seething fury within him to abate. Though it galled, he was forced to acknowledge that he had been extremely lucky to have escaped from the village with his hide intact and only a few coins the poorer. Despite his arrogance, the overlord's steward had been nothing more than an idle bully, bent only on bolstering his self-esteem at the expense of an inferior who wouldn't dare to answer back. Far more dangerous would have been a zealous and eternally suspicious petty tyrant with an instinctive mistrust of strangers. There were many men of that ilk in the employ of the overlords, and Kaldar might easily have found himself imprisoned and held on the smallest pretext, with little hope of talking or buying his way to freedom.

Well, then, he thought, *tonight's experience must serve as a severe but fortunate lesson.* He'd escaped lightly, but next time he might not be so lucky: better to take no chances, and avoid all human contact unless forced to it by necessity. It would make traveling all the harder, but all the safer, too.

So when dawn broke he resumed his journey, keeping now to the forest tracks and only venturing out into open country when no village or farmstead was in sight. Water, at least, was plentiful if not always palatable, for even when he couldn't find a woodland stream there were dew ponds, or even the irrigation channels that fed the farmlands, where he could refill his flasks when they were empty. And when his dried rations ran out three days later, Kaldar set aside his scruples and began to learn how to steal. Nothing that would bring hardship to the loser; he had unshakable views about that; but enough to sustain him, taken whenever and wherever he could tiptoe in undiscovered. An egg from a fowl coop on the edge of an orchard; a small loaf of bread from a new-baked trayful set to cool in an empty farm kitchen; a piece of cheese from a dairy; a game bird brought down by a hunter's falcon and spirited away before the retrieving dog could find it. One way and another he survived well enough, but his progress was now frustratingly slow, for the forests made arduous going and he only dared to venture into the open during the hours of darkness.

Then, fifteen days after his journey had begun, Kaldar heard the first snippet of news from the north.

Again, the countryside had been changing. As the land became lusher and more fertile, isolated farmsteads were giving way to villages, rough settlements to organized townships under the looming protection — or shadow — of an overlord's high, inviolable towers. With more and more acres under cultivation, forest cover was becoming harder to find, but after an uneasy day or two Kaldar convinced himself that there was no longer any real need to hide from his fellow humans. This country was more populous, its roads busier, and its settlements more lively, and he reasoned that the people hereabouts had enough business of their own to attend to without being overly curious about a passing stranger.

All the same, unable to forget his earlier experience, he had to steel his nerves before he summoned the courage to make his first daylight foray into one of the larger settlements. In any event, he needn't have worried. A livestock market was in full swing in a roped-off enclosure, and amid the shouting and bawling and churning clouds of dust he was only one more obscure figure in the general jostle.

A number of stalls and booths had been set up around the enclosure, and a motley collection of hucksters were shouting their wares, striving to be heard over the hubbub. A one-eyed grandfather peddled his skill as a pot mender, a fat woman was selling garishly dyed horse hides for making winter coats, and a man with a disease-pocked face and the scars of countless knife fights proclaimed the carnal delights to be had from his three surly-looking daughters who were ranged in a pouting row before him. Between the stalls, armed men sporting the insignia of the local overlord patrolled like carrion crows around a carcass, alert for any transaction and ready to demand their master's tithe. Kaldar was fascinated by the haphazard bustle. It was quite alien to anything he'd known in his homeland; the northern people were by nature self-contained almost to the point of coldness, and fairs such as this were unheard of. But for all the liveliness and color, there was nothing here that he wanted to buy, so after a short while he made his way to an area of hard-packed earth where, under makeshift canopies in case of rain, food was being cooked in three large roasting pits and sold to the fairgoers. Kaldar queued for a slab of meat on a trencher of thick, dark bread, filled his own cup from a water barrel for which there was no charge, and found a place on the ground between four chattering women with young children at their knees and a group of farmers bemoaning the unseasonably dry weather.

He was preoccupied with his meal, which was surprisingly well cooked and succulent, when he heard the word *heretic*, and his muscles seemed to lock, paralyzing him.

It had been a woman's voice. . . . Cautiously, his expression hidden, he hoped, behind his cup, Kaldar glanced sidelong at the gossiping group beside him, and his ears attuned to the pitch of their voices against the deeper background rumble of noise.

". . . only saying what I've heard, mark you. But her sister works in Overlord's kitchen and one of his men-at-arms is being obliging to her, so she would know, wouldn't she?"

The other women made shocked noises. *"Here, though? No! Not here."*

"I didn't say here. Did I say here? No, well, then. But you never know, do you? That's what I think, and she thinks same as me. If this creature's about and abroad, and getting followers, who can guess where he might find them and where they might all go next? He's down in the far south now, they think, but who's to say he'll stay there?"

There was more muttering, and Kaldar, listening, cursed the unfamiliarity of the southern accents, which he found hard to follow. But after a few moments the first woman's voice cut clearly through the rest.

"Now, I won't say it's true and I won't say it's not, because I don't know the all of it and that's a fact. But I've *heard*" — she left a significant pause — "that the new First Magus himself has ordered every overlord to muster his men and start searching for this heretic. And until he's found and made a proper end of, there'll be no rest for any man-at-arms, and no safety for the rest of us!"

Her companions stared, wide-eyed, and one of them made a religious sign. A child started to grizzle; without so much as a glance its mother slapped it and it fell silent again.

"Well, then." The first woman nodded ominously. "Now you've heard it all, and I dare say you won't sleep easy tonight any more than I will. And I also say we'll do well to pray to our good lord Yandros that our overlords find this evil monster, and all the hideous creatures he's got about him, before we're all strangled in our own beds by him and his henchmen!"

The child started to grizzle again at that moment. This time the reflexive slap only caused it to howl more loudly, and the women immediately launched into a debate over whether the brat should be disciplined or consoled. Kaldar had heard enough, and the distraction gave him the opportunity he needed to leave without making his departure too obvious. He got to his feet, pushing the remains of the food into his pack — he had no appetite now — and, ignored by the small group, walked away from the eating area, away from the noise and activity of the market, and out of the town.

He told himself over and again that it was just one isolated rumor and not to be taken seriously, and at first he almost managed to believe it. But his fragile conviction was soon shattered. Fresh news was sweeping down from the north, outstripping his slow pace, and within two more days rumor had blossomed into certainty. The new First Magus had made his mark, given his orders, and the hunt was on for Kaldar's friends; or, more accurately, for one friend in particular.

It appeared that, despite their formidable skills, the magi hadn't yet been able to discover their quarry's identity, and for that Kaldar gave desperate and heartfelt thanks. Lord Aeoris's power in the mortal world was tenuous and unreliable as yet, but he had the strength to protect his most vital servant, and Kaldar prayed that that protection would hold. He knew very little about Vordegh, the First Magus, but through one tidbit of information and another he was starting to build up an impression of a man who was a stark contrast to his predecessor. In past years the ruling cadre at the Star Peninsula had taken little concerted action over matters of heresy. They'd rooted out troublemakers, or potential troublemakers, where they found them and their reprisals had been cruel, but until now their operations had been perfunctory almost to the point of carelessness. In fact, Kaldar reflected ironically, it was that very carelessness, born of the magi's faith in their own invulnerability, which had allowed his friends' secret alliance to grow to its present strength. Now, though, there had been changes. A new regime at the castle; a new magus in the seat of power. Lord Vordegh, it seemed, was not content to let matters run on as they had done for decades. He wanted war. He wanted to see all traces of opposition wiped from the face of the world and consigned to the Seven Hells, and nothing less would satisfy him. And as the news flowed and the picture became clearer, Kaldar began to realize, with a cold and dreadful feeling in his gut, just what manner of enemy he and his friends were facing.

He made his decision on the third day after the incident at the town fair, and though he knew he was running a risk, the thing had to be done. He was now in the heartlands, where much of the natural forest had been cleared to make way for agriculture and secure cover was hard to find, and so when he came upon an unexpected tract of dense, uncleared woodland stretching mistily south and west, he felt that it might afford him his one and only chance.

The first moon cleared the eastern horizon an hour after sunset, a thin, pale crescent that cast a dim glow through the trees and created uneasy pools of shadow. Kaldar had made camp on the edge of a small glade. He hadn't lit a fire, for he was anxious not to attract human or animal attention to his presence, but as the moonlight grew stronger he set flint and tinder to a small pile of damp leaves and grasses. The pile began to smolder and a faint, pungent smell tickled Kaldar's nostrils. He shivered slightly — the clear sky made the night cold — and from a leather bag in his pack measured seven crystalline grains of incense. The smoke changed color as he dropped the grains onto the leaf pile, and the smell changed, too, becoming heady and acidic.

Kaldar stared into the smoke, knowing that he had to work quickly. He'd spent the hour since sunset working on the mental exercises that would attune his mind; now he could only hope that the preparations had been enough and that his skills were up to the task. He leaned over the smoldering leaves, inhaling deeply, and within a few seconds felt the first stir of disorientation as his consciousness began to sideslip out of kilter with his surroundings. Turning his thoughts inward, he listened to the rhythm of his own breathing, matching it to the regular beat of his heart and hoping to great Aeoris that someone would be ready to forge the link with him. A sentinel should be alert at all hours of the day and night, but safety and secrecy were precarious, and any one of a hundred things could have gone wrong.

Gathering his will, and drawing the incense smoke deeper into his lungs, Kaldar projected his psychic call.

Brothers of Aeoris. Sisters of Aeoris. The night is silent but the day brings a flash of lightning. Hear me and answer. Hear me and answer.

He used the code known only to the innermost coterie of Order's followers, and repeated the call a second time, a third, a fourth, over and over again until it became a silent, singing litany in his head. He still stared into the smoke and could see nothing else, but he felt that the forest around him was turning, revolving like a giant wheel with his own body a single pinpoint of stillness and power at the hub.

Hear me and answer. Hear me and answer. Again and again the call went out; then at last, suddenly and without warning, Kaldar felt the first tentative touch of an answering consciousness. It took him by surprise and he almost lost the fragile link, but with a quick effort he got a grip on his excitement and concentrated harder.

A face formed in the smoke. Its outlines were uncertain and it wavered, fading and reappearing; but Kaldar's eagerness surged again as he recognized the broad, heavyset features, the hazel eyes, the dark hair like a nimbus around face and jaw.

Simbrian! His fists clenched unconsciously at his sides. *It's Kaldar— Kaldar, from the north.*

The image shivered and broke apart, but the answer was just audible. *Kaldar. All's well here. What news?*

Danger. Kaldar emphasized the word with a mental image of something twisted and bloodied, knowing that his telepathic abilities were sorely limited and that, in addition, he had little time to get his message across. *There's a new First Magus, and he isn't like the old one. He wants you, Simbrian. He doesn't know your name, but he knows you exist, and he'll stint nothing to find you.*

There was a pause, so long that Kaldar began to fear that his projected thoughts had failed to break through. Then:

The link is weak, Kaldar, but I understand. Where are you?

On my way to you. Another seven days, perhaps more. But where?

The image of Simbrian's face grew stronger momentarily. This time there were no words as such; but the sense and location of a particular place slid into Kaldar's mind as surely and clearly as though someone had slipped a metaphorical knife into his brain. His breath caught and he suppressed a cough, then, unconscious of the gesture, he nodded.

I understand. It's safe?

For the time being, yes. But don't delay. I thank you for your timely warning, Kaldar. Good fortune — and our lord Aeoris defend you.

There was a sound in Kaldar's ears like a small implosion, and a quick, sharp pain flared momentarily in his skull. The ground under him seemed to lurch; then suddenly the link was shattered and Kaldar sat, bewildered and feeling as limp as a child's rag doll, on the hard, damp ground in the dead of night, with the last remnants of incense smoke drifting away and dispersing among the trees.

After some seconds he let out a long, pent breath. He was exhausted; the rite had taken an enormous toll on his energy and he wanted only to sleep until sunrise. Nonetheless, with the double impetus of caution and training, he put his small paraphernalia away in his pack and took care to ensure that the pile of half-burned leaves was scattered widely enough to show no telltale traces before climbing into the lower boughs of the largest tree he could find. The forest was silent but for the occasional distant hooting of nocturnal birds, but Kaldar knew better than to trust to luck alone to keep him safe.

Wedged firmly between two great branches and with his pack hanging beside him, he was soundly asleep minutes later.

Unlike the great majority of the settlements through which Kaldar had previously passed on his journey, the sprawling but substantial township which he reached two days later had a name. Chaun had grown up on the eastern borders of a dense deciduous forest, where the belt of trees was bisected by a broad, slow river. The town had no wall and no toll-gate; only a wooden pack bridge wide enough for a timber wagon with two horses hitched abreast marked the boundary. Forestry was the staple industry here — the town was named, so Kaldar discovered, for a method of cutting wood against the grain — and a great quantity of timber was carted near and far, much of it to satisfy the demands of the magi at the Star Peninsula. The area was prosperous by comparison with many of its neighboring districts, though the local overlord was reputed to exact harsh tithes, and as he approached the town's boundaries Kaldar saw that Chaun was alive with bustling activity.

. The bridge was busy despite the early hour; two carts, one wagon, and upward of a dozen people on foot passed Kaldar in one direction or the other as he walked across. No one challenged him, indeed no one gave him so much as a second glance, and he soon found himself walking on a surprisingly good, firm road into the center of the town. In the typical pattern for larger communities hereabouts, the heart of Chaun was an open arena, and here almost all of the town's business, official and otherwise, was conducted. Dominating and sharply contrasting with the surrounding wooden houses and marts, a single building in dark gray stone — not a local material — towered starkly on the north side of the arena. This building, Kaldar surmised when he saw the armed militiamen guarding the open double doors, served a dual purpose as the town's tithe house and also as a base from which justice, in whatever form the overlord chose to interpret the word, was dispensed.

He had the distinct and immediate impression that it would be easy to be and remain anonymous here. From the variety of hair and clothing styles sported in the streets it was clear that Chaun attracted a wide range of incomers and, ignorant as he was of fashion and custom beyond his home district, Kaldar was both fascinated and bemused. Several men with hair cropped close to their skulls looked distinctly bizarre to his eyes, and he was shocked to the core by the sight of an obviously respectable woman clad in a woolen skirt whose hem only just covered her knees. The general tide of movement steered him at length to the arena, where from the confusing jumble of dialects he finally gleaned the fact that this was a Claim Day; a monthly event when tithes were gathered in and grievances heard by the overlord or his representatives. Already a queue of petitioners had formed outside the gray stone building, and three of the militiamen were none too gently clearing the way for the first of the tithe wagons. The usual market-town jumble of stalls and sideshows were doing a brisk early trade, watched over by the usual patrols of militia, who, in addition to collecting the overlord's tithe, coolly helped themselves to any item that took their fancy. Surreptitiously watching one pair, who were going from stall to stall taking their pick of the wares and deriving, it seemed, still more pleasure from intimidating the stallholders, Kaldar felt disgust well in him like acid. Even in his own home district, where the overlord was harsh enough, such blatant thievery by the stewards wouldn't have been tolerated, yet here it seemed it was accepted as the norm, for not one voice was raised in protest or complaint. Though a small inner voice warned him that he was being very rash, Kaldar's indignation impelled him to move closer to the pair as they made their round and eavesdrop on what was said. As he watched and listened, indignation swelled into outrage — and when the two stewards reached the stall of an elderly man, his headstrong nature got the better of him.

The booth was a sad little affair, and it was obvious at first glance that the old man was among the poorest of the poor. Once, perhaps, he had been a skilled woodcraftsman, but now his eyesight was failing and his hands crippled, and the spoons and bowls and other artifacts he sold were pitifully crude. But he had a granddaughter. Probably twelve years old at most, she sat beside him on the threadbare mat, eyes cast down, dark hair looped with an attempt at modest grace, face and body thin from the lack of good food. And she was pretty.

The stewards moved leisurely toward the booth, and halted. The taller of the two prodded an unevenly shaped dish with a well-shod toe, while his companion disdainfully scanned the few other wares on offer.

"Nothing of any worth here." The taller one's voice was contemptuous; the boot moved to dig against the old man's leg. "Lost your talents, have you, old scrag? Age got the better of you?"

The old man's hands trembled but he didn't answer. The granddaughter seemed rooted, frozen.

The shorter steward grinned. "Overlord won't see much tithe from this miserable heap. Seems hardly worth the bother of turning out for Claim Day — eh, filth? Eh? Unless of course you've got something hidden away. Something nice, eh? Something you're not quite so ready to sell?"

The other uttered a short, snorting laugh. "Maybe he has at that." Taking a sidelong step he suddenly reached out and grabbed a hank of the girl's hair, wrenching her head back so that her face was clearly revealed. "Oh, yes," he said. "Oh, *yes*."

The girl shut her eyes and her teeth clamped down hard on her lower lip. The taller steward nudged his companion.

"You're the scholar. What's *this* worth, d'you judge?"

The other man made a brief pretense of careful consideration, then sniggered. "Four coppers or an eighth silver." His gaze slid over the girl like a snake sliding over barren rock. "It all depends on how long we want the payment to take."

His companion's grin grew more feral. "Well, now, the overlord won't miss an eighth silver's worth, will he? Anyway, when we've had our share there'll probably be enough left to be put to his use if he feels the need. Right then, old carrion!" Another savage yank on the girl's hair made her whimper briefly and involuntarily. "This is your tithe. Any argument?"

Shaking like an autumn leaf now, the grandfather held up his twisted hands in a gesture of supplication. "Lords, no! Please! She is but a dozen years old, an innocent child, a — "

A well-aimed kick caught him full in the mouth, cutting off the plea, and the old man fell back coughing and spitting blood from a torn lip. The girl squealed like an animal in a snare; the tall steward wrenched her to her feet and held her half dangling in his grasp.

"I *said*, offal, any *argument*?"

It was at that moment — and later, in retrospect, he knew just how foolish he'd been and how close he had come to wrecking everything for himself — that Kaldar's self-control snapped.

"*You!*" The power and savagery of his own voice took him by surprise, but he couldn't stop himself; fury had got the better of him and it was far too late for prudence.

The stewards turned, and for one single and, to Kaldar, unutterably sweet moment they looked afraid. Fired by that, buoyed by their fear, sense and reason fled.

"Touch her, and you're carrion." His hand went to his hip, though it was nothing more than an instinctive gesture, for his only knife was secure inside his pack and was, in any case, not a fighting blade. At this moment, however, it didn't matter to Kaldar.

"Release her." Breath sawed in his throat. "*Do you hear me?*"

The stewards exchanged a glance. Their initial fear had evaporated when they saw that only one solitary man opposed them, but they were still cautious.

Then, before either they or Kaldar could decide on their next move, a new voice broke in, shattering the hiatus.

"What's afoot here?" The voice was female, and from the small press of vaguely interested spectators which had already begun to gather, a newcomer — little more than a blur to Kaldar's overheated senses — pushed forward.

"What are you doing with my servant?" Hands on hips, a well-built middle-aged woman with two heavy coils of fair hair wound around her head strode into the midst of the contention. Her eyes, which Kaldar noticed in a brief and startling moment were as blue as his own, raked him with a fearsome glare. "Simbrian! What in the name of our good overlord d'you think you're about?"

Kaldar felt as though he'd taken a cudgel blow in the midriff. *Simbrian* — the name of his mentor, his leader —

He had no time to think further, for the woman had turned instantly to the two stewards. "Sirs — " Her tone altered, taking on more than a hint of ingratiation. "I ask your pardon if this fool has offended." She stepped forward and, to Kaldar's bemusement, dealt him a blow across the cheek that sent him stumbling back. "He's no more than a boy, and a half-wit into the bargain — only give him one measure of ale too many and show him a pretty face, and he takes it into his head to champion every whore's get in the district!" One stride took her to Kaldar's side; she gripped hold of his left arm. "Why I offered him a month's work in the first place great Yandros only knows; though in my straits I'm lucky if I can afford even idiots these days! With your goodly consent, sirs, I'll take him back to the midden where he belongs and give him the right punishment for his stupidity." An eyelid flickered then in a conspiratorial wink. "And if you've the taste for it, sirs, I've a new killing of fowls to be made over and beyond the overlord's rightful tithe. Good plump birds, fed on the best of the land. Anyone will tell you where to find Shammana Oskia Mantrel's steading, and I'll be glad to make you a gift of two of the finest hens if you'll come to my door an hour past sunset."

Kaldar was still too stunned to react. He saw the stewards relax, heard their laughter, but the whole scenario was too bizarre to make sense. Who *was* this woman? He'd never set eyes on her before —

204 • LOUISE COOPER

had she mistaken him for someone else, or was this some kind of mad joke?

"All right, dame." The taller steward made a mock bow in Shammana Oskia Mantrel's direction, though he didn't relax his hold on the girl's hair as he spoke. "Make it four fowls, and we'll be generous enough to overlook your servant's insolence." Then his expression changed. "But we'll remember his face, and we'll remember your name. Keep him under tighter control from now on, and teach him how to behave in the presence of his betters, or you'll find you no longer have a roof over your head."

"I understand, sir, and I'll see to it all as you say." Shammana Oskia Mantrel made an obeisance, but as she lowered herself Kaldar saw a momentary flash of savage loathing in her eyes. His fury flared again and he opened his mouth, but before he could utter a word his "mistress" turned on him.

"Not a sound from you, cur! You'll think yourself the luckiest of groveling worms if you've a scrap of skin left on your back by the time I'm done with you!" The hand that clamped his arm gave him a fierce shake and she raised her other hand as though to strike him again.

Kaldar's gaze was drawn quickly and involuntarily to the threatened blow — and his gut froze. So briefly that the two grinning stewards couldn't possibly have glimpsed it, Shammana Oskia Mantrel's thumb and middle finger joined to make a circle. It was a clear and unequivocal sign, and one that he knew very well. The circle of light. The symbol known only to the inner coterie of the devout followers of Aeoris.

CHAPTER XV

S hammana Oskia Mantrel unfastened the last of the many
locks that secured the door of her steading house and,
with Kaldar following, stepped inside.

The large room in which Kaldar found himself smelled harshly
clean, with a faint and more pleasant scent of cooking food lurking
somewhere in the background. Light streamed in at the big south-
facing window, and the furnishings, though plain, were both sturdy
and neat. Shammana saw to it that the door was bolted, then walked
to the foot of a ladderlike staircase that led to the top floor.

"Nanithe!" There was a soft note in her voice, gentle, almost cajol-
ing. "It's only me, child. No need for alarm. Come down when you
will."

She moved to the wide grate and raked up the fire that burned
there, adding a log from a basket set ready in the hearth, then addressed Kaldar without looking at him. "Sit down. There'll be a meal
ready before long, and I don't doubt you're hungry."

Kaldar obeyed reflexively, choosing an uncushioned chair at a
distance from the window. She hadn't given him the opportunity to
speak since she'd hustled him away from the town arena, and now
that they were under her roof he couldn't find a single word that
would express his feelings. Sweet Aeoris, he thought, he didn't even
know if he could trust her. What if the symbol, the sign, had been
learned by their enemies? After the tales he'd heard during the past
few days it was more than possible that this woman was an agent of

the magi, set to root out the rebels' followers and lure them into a trap.

His train of thought was truncated as he realized that Shammana was watching him. Still at the hearth, one hand resting against the mantel as she bent to watch the new log blaze up, she had turned her head and her blue eyes were calmly assessing. Then she said, "You're wondering how I knew about you. It's simple. I've had your description from Simbrian Tarkran. I know your name — Kaldar Alvaray — and that you were on your way south, and I've been looking out in case you came by this route." For a moment her stiff manner unbent and she gave him a small smile. "I have seeing skills, so I can judge the real man from the impostor. You're welcome in my house, Kaldar. I only thank Aeoris that I was able to reach you before you wrecked your part in our cause with your hotheadedness."

Kaldar felt himself relax. The fact that Shammana knew his name had been enough to dispel doubt; if he could be sure of anything, it was that, as far as the magi and their agents were concerned, Kaldar Alvaray was long dead. He rose to his feet and made a bow to her.

"Lady, I'm in your debt. And I humbly thank our lord Aeoris for your wisdom in the face of my folly."

Shammana's mouth twitched. "Simbrian warned me that you had a temper on you and were inclined to be rash, but he also seems to feel that you have qualities to outweigh that disadvantage. I hope for all our sakes that he's right."

Kaldar flushed. "I won't make the same mistake again, lady."

"I trust you don't make that promise lightly." She got to her feet with a grunt and moved toward the scrubbed table in the middle of the room, then abruptly paused, darting him a quick, curious glance.

"But weren't there supposed to be two of you? I'd been given to understand that you planned to bring a girl with you."

All the tension that had ebbed from Kaldar came back in an instant. He nodded, then looked away from her and said, "Yes. My wife."

"Ah." He hadn't intended his tone to give him away, but Shammana was shrewd. More gently, she asked, "It's not my business, I know, but do you want to tell me what went amiss?"

He shrugged. There was no reason for secrecy, and in a few bleak sentences he gave her the story; the interrupted wedding, the gleaning by the Chaos riders, Iselia's abduction to the Star Peninsula. He didn't mention his own later actions or the meetings with Benetan Liss; the bare bones were quite enough. Shammana listened to the tale without interruption, then when Kaldar fell silent said simply: "I'm sorry."

He realized immediately that there was something more behind her sympathy than mere courtesy, but before he could decide whether or not it would be impertinent to ask a question of his own, a floorboard creaked overhead and a shadow moved on the stairs.

Shammana looked up quickly. "Nanithe?" She moved toward the staircase. "Yes, child, it's all right; come down now and meet our guest."

The girl who appeared a few moments later was some seventeen or eighteen years old, small, dark, modestly dressed with her hair in a single plait wound about her head. She reached the foot of the flight, saw Kaldar, and stopped. A pale, narrow face, not quite plain but not quite pretty, turned toward him, and Kaldar felt an inward shock as he looked into her brown eyes. On the surface those eyes were unremarkable. But behind them, and hollowing their gaze as surely as if they'd been burned from inside her skull, something within her was dead.

He dropped his own gaze swiftly, silently praying that she hadn't seen his reaction. Shammana had taken the girl's hand and was leading her forward, though she came with obvious reluctance.

"There now, child; this is Kaldar Alvaray, whom we've been expecting. He's a friend, as Simbrian has told us, so there's nothing to fear. Kaldar, this is Nanithe Lowwe."

Kaldar bowed. "Lady." He could think of nothing else to say and he didn't want to look at her face again.

"Nanithe won't answer you, for she doesn't speak." Shammana said it as negligently as though it were a trivial, everyday matter, but Kaldar heard and noted the warning in her voice and managed not to seem disconcerted. Shammana turned to the girl.

"Nanithe, I think we shall eat our meal in here; this table has more space to accommodate us all. Will you go and see what's to do in the kitchen?"

The girl nodded, glanced covertly at Kaldar again, and fled through an inner doorway. Shammana waited until the door had shut behind her, then went to a linen chest and took from it a brown cloth which she spread over the scrubbed table. Her manner and movements were brisk, and Kaldar had the impression that she wanted to say something but didn't know how to begin. He cleared his throat.

"Can I be useful?" Clutching at straws, he added, "If I'm playing the role of your servant, you may as well make the best of me."

She gave a short, snorting chuckle. It was rapidly quelled but her expression eased a little. "No, there's nothing for you to do. Better and quicker if it's left to those who know where everything is." A pause. "I trust you've got a better appetite than your bony shape implies. Nanithe will be disappointed if you don't do her cooking justice."

She'd given him the opening he needed, and he asked a little diffidently, "You said Nanithe doesn't speak. Does that mean she can't, or simply . . . doesn't?"

Shammana stopped, stared at the cloth. There were a few silent moments, then:

"She can speak, if by that you mean she has a tongue and is able to use it. But as to whether she *will* ever find a way to use words again . . . in all truth, Kaldar, I don't know. She's been with me a little over three years now, and — "

"Three years? Then she isn't your daughter?"

"Oh, no. No, no. I never had a daughter. Three sons, but they . . ." She stopped abruptly, her mouth setting into a savagely hard line. "Three sons, but no daughter. I found Nanithe two years after my sons and my husband died, you see, and as there was no one else to care for her I took her in."

Kaldar didn't know how to respond to that without seeming either churlish or artificial. For perhaps a minute there was silence as Shammana continued with her work, then she stopped again and looked at him. When she spoke her tone was unemotional, almost careless.

"I'll tell you the whole story if you want to hear it. It doesn't pain me to repeat it, because I've already done so over and over again, to the militia, to the stewards, to the justices. So you needn't fear that you'll be asking me to revive memories better forgotten. I don't forget and I never will. It's only your discomfiture you need worry about, not mine."

Kaldar looked back at her for a few moments. Then, quietly, he pulled a chair out from the table and sat down.

"Please," he said. "Tell me."

So he heard Shammana's story. Her husband had been a small farmer, law-abiding and reasonably prosperous. He and their three sons — the eldest twenty and the youngest fourteen when they died, she said — worked their land, paid their tithes and whatever bribes became necessary from time to time, and had enough left over to maintain a comfortable household. They lived well, despite ever increasing demands from overlord and greedy stewards alike, until five years ago.

"There were brigands in the district," she said. "It may be different in the north where you come from, but here that's nothing unusual."

Kaldar's lip curled cynically. "We never had too much trouble with reavers, except in the gem-mining areas. I don't doubt they prefer to go where the pickings are rich — or the overlord lazy."

He'd touched a raw nerve, he realized immediately, for muscles stood out suddenly in Shammana's jaw and her eyes took on a stone glint. "I know nothing about your overlord. But ours . . ." Her hands, resting now on the tabletop, clenched and unclenched spasmodically, then she drew a deep breath as though to calm herself. "Well, this band weren't content with mere robbery. They wanted *entertainment* as well. Isolated farmsteads burnt down, and their crops with them. Wagons ambushed in the forest and set ablaze with the horses or oxen still in the shafts. Men beaten. Girls raped. Older women, too — there was one, a woodsman's widow; she lived alone in the forest and she was over seventy — " She gave a sharp little hiss, shaking her head. "Then the trouble stopped. We thought they'd left the district for good, moved on the way these scum do, and that we'd hear no more of them . . . but we were wrong. They came back in the winter, when the days were at their shortest. It was a Claim Day; we had some trouble with our tithe wagon and so my husband and sons decided to take the levy direct to the overlord's fortress rather than to the tithing house." Her lip twitched. "Latecomers at the tithing house must pay a penalty. The clerks decide on the spot what it shall be and there's no leave of appeal."

Kaldar nodded sympathetically. Everyone knew clerks' tricks.

"By dusk they'd not returned. I thought little of it at first, only that there was some delay or dissatisfaction; and I was angry to think that for all our efforts to avoid a penalty we'd be fined anyway because something had displeased the overlord. I completed the farmstead chores; I milked the cattle, shut up the hens for the night. . . ." Shammana's hands started to clench and unclench again. "Such small things, comfortable things. It's strange how I've always remembered that hour so clearly. . . . Then I realized that the first moon was well risen — it was a clear night — and the second showing on the horizon. I walked to the town, to the arena. I thought perhaps they'd come back and been tempted into one of the taverns, and that I'd find them there grumbling with their friends. But no one had seen them. Not a sign, not a word, nothing." She drew another long breath. "I think it was then that I began to suspect the truth. I asked some militiamen to search. They wouldn't, of course; they wouldn't trouble themselves. But others did. Some good men, neighbors, *decent* people. And their women; they insisted; they came with us. We found the wagon on the forest road, less than a mile from the fortress. One of the horses was gone and the other had been doused in something — wine maybe, I don't know — and set alight in the shafts. It was a hideous sight; unimaginable to think how the poor creature must have suffered. . . . Then we found my husband and my sons."

She looked up, looked directly and steadily into Kaldar's eyes. "They were hanging from ropes in the trees. Their eyes had been burned away, and their tongues and manhoods cut off. There were small knife wounds all over their bodies. They must have bled to death very slowly." Then she blinked, breaking the mesmeric spell that held Kaldar rigid. "My neighbors told me later that there were signs of a struggle. I suppose that reavers are less . . . *gentle* with those who make a show of resistance."

Kaldar looked away. "*Aeoris* . . . ," he whispered.

"I'm sorry if I shock you." Shammana's voice was level.

Kaldar couldn't answer. It wasn't the barbarity of the act she recounted, for he'd heard worse of some overlords and far worse of the magi. What appalled him the manner in which Shammana related the murder of her family. She was so calm, so quiet and self-possessed. Either she was indifferent to their deaths now and thus unmoved, or she had an inner strength that verged on the superhuman. He ventured to looked at her face once more . . . and something in her eyes gave him the answer to his question. He felt suddenly very insignificant.

"That, I think," Shammana said gently, "was how our cause began for me. Oh, I've always resented many of the things that the overlords and their men do. They are greedy, they are arrogant, they live on the best fruits of our labors and give little or nothing in return — who among us doesn't resent them? But I believed that underneath the greed and self-interest there was still a spark of justice. I believed that justice would be granted to me in my trouble."

"You were mistaken?" Kaldar asked gently.

"I was mistaken. I tried . . . sweet Aeoris, how I *tried!* I went to the stewards, and when the stewards refused to listen I went to the justices. I brought a petition, a formal petition, pleading that the murderers should be hunted down and brought before the overlord for retribution. It was my right to ask that, and it was the overlord's duty to grant my plea. But the overlord refused me. Word came from the fortress . . ." Her voice caught abruptly, a quick shudder of anger. "Word came from the fortress that as my family had failed to pay the new season's tithe, the overlord had no obligation to help me."

Kaldar's expression changed as he realized what she was implying. "Failed to pay?"

Shammana reached out and laid a hand over his, silencing him. "The tithe wagon didn't reach the fortress. They were attacked on the way there, not on the way back, and so the tithe wasn't paid. I was informed of this, and then five days later, on the day my men went to their funeral pyre, I was also informed that the tithe was still owed and a penalty would be exacted from me because the payment was late."

Kaldar went white about the lips. "The overlord did that? He had the insolence to — "

Her fingers squeezed his. "I appreciate your ire on my behalf, Kaldar, but it achieves nothing against men like our overlord." She smiled, though the smile had no humor in it. "Didn't you learn that lesson in the marketplace today?"

Kaldar recalled the old peddler, the child, the two bullying stewards. But for Shammana he would by now be lying battered and bleeding in some windowless hole, awaiting his fate for daring to defy his betters.

"Yes, I see you understand me." Shammana released his hand at last and, chastised, he nodded.

"But what did you do, Shammana? Did you pay?"

"Of course. What else *could* I do? I and my beasts had meager rations for a while, but we made the best of it. After all," she added, and suddenly her voice grew bitter, "there were no men to feed anymore."

Kaldar said something under his breath and, catching the drift if not the substance of it, Shammana smiled another of her cold little smiles.

"You've not yet heard the end of the tale. Do you have the stomach for that, too?"

"Oh, I've the stomach," he said. "Yes. Don't doubt it."

"Well, then, I may as well tell the rest now and have done. I paid the tithe, as I said, because I had no choice. For two more years I lived on alone here, managing as best I could. I had some help from my neighbors for a time, but as the seasons went by, their help faded away. It was inevitable and I don't blame them for it; they have their own lives to live and their own families to feed. And memories are short. They're good people but my grief wasn't their grief, no reason why it should be. I did well enough, and at harvest times and breeding times I had enough to pay for the extra hands that were needed. I might even have come to reconcile myself with what the overlord had done . . . but for Nanithe.

"The brigands hadn't troubled us again. Again we all thought they'd departed for good, but again we were wrong." She made a half-angry gesture. "Or perhaps they weren't the same band, I don't know; though the marks they left behind them suggested they were. . . . Anyway, one night there was another attack. A carter's train from the west, on its way here. They'd made camp for the night in the forest about eight miles distant, and they were set upon. There were two survivors. One was a woman. They'd broken nearly all the bones in her body, but she lived just long enough to tell of the attack. The other was Nanithe." Shammana cast a quick glance over her shoulder as though she'd heard the latch of the inner door click unexpectedly. Then, finding nothing untoward, she turned back to Kaldar.

"I won't tell you the details of what they'd done to her. The woman, the other survivor, had talked to her on the road; said she was bound here to take work on the farms because there was nothing for her in her own home district. Fourteen, she said. Just fourteen years old. They'd used her . . . they'd used her in every way a man can use a woman, and so *brutally* . . . and when they were done with that they beat her, sliced off her hair, and slashed her wrists, and left her to die."

At that moment the inner door's latch did click, and Nanithe returned. She was carrying a tray with a pitcher and three kiln-fired cups on it; she set it down in the center of the table, then hesitated, glancing at Shammana and raising her eyebrows in a silent question.

Shammana leaned forward to peer at the pitcher, then smiled. "As well as the water, my dear, I think we should drink mead tonight in honor of our guest. I know there's little of it left and this year's brew has all gone in tithe, but that won't matter now. Tonight, we shall celebrate."

A strange mix of expressions flitted across Nanithe's face. First doubt and uncertainty; then, slowly, a dawning of understanding. And last of all, lighting her unremarkable features and transforming them unexpectedly into something that was almost beautiful, a look of profound pleasure and relief.

Kaldar watched her walk back to the kitchen with the empty tray, then stared down at the tabletop. "She's so young," he said.

"To have suffered so much? Yes, that's true; though I'd wager she's not so many years younger than you, and you also have your burdens to bear."

He returned Shammana's smile pallidly, grateful for her kindness yet at the same time feeling awkward and perhaps a little compromised because of it. He didn't want to dwell on that and returned to the subject of Nanithe.

"So you took her in? She didn't return to her own people?"

Shammana shook her head. "How could she? We knew only her name and that she came from the west; someone else on the convoy might have told us more, but they were all dead." She grimaced. "I went to the justices again. Fool that I was. I appealed to them, I begged them — this time, I said, something *must* be done." The stony glitter came into her eyes again. "Again, of course, they refused to listen. I was angry then, so angry. Perhaps what had happened before had hardened me, but I could *not* simply turn my back and bow my shoulders and accept their indifference. So I prayed to Chaos — "

"To *Chaos?*"

She lifted her eyebrows. "Why should that surprise you? What reason did I have, then, to hate Chaos's gods?"

"Every reason!" Kaldar was shocked. "Your own family murdered, then Nanithe's ordeal, and the overlord denying you both even the merest justice — "

"The overlord is only a man. Yandros didn't choose him, and was not responsible for his corruption. At that time, I had no cause to blame the powers of Chaos for my troubles."

"Oh, but — "

"Wait; listen. I said, *at that time.* I prayed to Chaos because I believed that Yandros would grant me justice where men had failed. And I thought my prayers had been answered, for on the next Claim Day a magus came to our town.

"I don't doubt you know how the magi travel. The citadel appeared one night, without any warning, on the edge of the forest. The conflagration it made destroyed fifty head of cattle and a plantation of young saplings, but that's a minor matter. . . . I don't know the magus's name, but I saw her, once, when she came with great ceremony into the town itself." Shammana shuddered. "A devilish creature, not wholly human. So tall and so strange . . . but I suppose beautiful in her way. . . ."

Kaldar snorted. *"Beautiful!"*

"Oh, yes. Oh, yes. At least I thought so then, for I believed her presence was my answer from Yandros. I went to her to plead my case and ask her to grant me justice."

"You spoke with the magus?" Even the word, *magus,* was like acid burning in Kaldar's mouth.

"I spoke *to* her. She didn't deign to reply, not directly." Shammana shivered as though at an old and cruel memory. "I was arrested by two of the overlord's men as I tried to reach the magus. I fought them — a farmer's wife, and perhaps especially a farmer's widow, has strong arms; I threw them off, I ran toward the magus, and I groveled at her feet, begging for her help. She looked at me with her inhuman eyes, and then she turned to the overlord — he was at her side, you understand — and demanded to know what I was about. I babbled out my story, my plea. She looked at me again, and she . . . she *laughed.* She turned to the overlord, and she said: 'Is this some entertainment you have devised for me? If so, it is highly original!' "

Kaldar stared, stunned. *"Entertainment . . . ?"*

Shammana shrugged. "That's what she said. The overlord mumbled and muttered and then confessed that I was not an entertainment but merely a stupid peasant woman with a grievance who had somehow evaded his sentries and was now making a nuisance of myself. He apologized profusely; he said that those responsible for the interruption would be severely punished. . . . And she said — oh, I remember her face now. I remember her words. She said — 'Ah, just a peasant. Well, I have better things to do than listen to peasants. Give her a flogging for her presumption and send her home to look to her own midden.' "

Shammana had memorized the magus's words to the letter and she repeated them like a litany, with a fine-honed savagery that could only hint at the emotions seething and suppressed beneath her calm exterior. Steel in her expression, she added, "That is what she said. The stewards locked me in the tithe house until she was gone, then they brought me out into the square, stripped the clothes from my back, and gave me twenty strokes of the lash. I was told . . . I was told to give thanks to the gods that the magus had been so lenient and hadn't ordered me turned out of my home, or sent to the Star Peninsula to be given to a demon as a plaything." She blinked rapidly several times "That, I think, was what finally made me realize that Chaos in all its forms is more evil and corrupt even than the overlords. It was the goad which turned me to the cause of Order.

"I'd heard of the movement forming in the south, all through rumor and hearsay, but that was enough to quicken my interest. I knew I had seeing power — I've known it since I was a child, though I always took the greatest care to hide it even from my own family — and so I started to use my talent, hoping I might make contact with them. Then, one night, Simbrian answered me." She smiled, and for a moment her face was transformed. "Perhaps I don't need to describe to you how I felt at that moment."

Kaldar returned the smile, remembering his own first, faltering efforts and their eventual success when he had all but given up hope. "No. I understand very well."

Shammana nodded. "Simbrian trusted me from the beginning. I think he must have some especial power that enables him to read people; I think perhaps he's a far greater sorcerer than anyone yet realizes. . . . He gave me a great deal of comfort in those early days, despite the distance that separates us. And he strengthened my faith in the cause. He told me that the movement is growing far faster than our enemies know; that my own story is only one of many, *many* similar reports he and his followers have heard from all parts of the world. He believes that our strength and our numbers are almost great enough for the real work to begin. So I — "

She broke off at that moment as Nanithe returned with the tray, now laden with a large bowl and three wooden trenchers. As the girl set her burden down, Shammana smiled again at Kaldar.

"I don't think I'm telling you anything that you don't already know, and Nanithe has heard my tales of Simbrian more times than either of us can count. We'll have more to say later, but for now let's leave matters of the spirit for matters of the body, and eat."

Although Shammana's house gave the impression of comfort and small prosperity, as they began to eat it became clear to Kaldar that the truth belied outward appearances. The stew Nanithe had prepared was good but meager and contained no meat. In the north that was unheard of even in the miners' households, and Kaldar felt a pang of guilt as the small portions were doled out and he realized that the two women were suffering scant rations to feed him. Awkwardly, torn between fear of giving offense and anxiety to make even a token contribution, he offered the little food he had left in his pack, but Shammana waved the offer aside with a cryptic statement that they might all be in need of his supplies before too long.

They began to talk again, and although the subject of past tribulations was carefully avoided, Shammana was willing to speak quite bluntly of present circumstances. In truth, she said, she and Nanithe were poor and had little hope of bettering themselves, for with no men to do the heavy work of the farmstead, and paid labor now beyond their means, they barely had the strength and time between them to produce enough for the overlord's tithes, let alone look to their own comfort. Perhaps she had been a stubborn fool to insist on trying to run the farmstead alone, she added wryly, but it simply wasn't in her nature to admit defeat. However, with the tithe demands growing greater with every season — and the levies were reckoned by a farmstead's size, not by its manpower — she had finally been forced to accept that matters could not go on as they were for much longer.

"We may last another year if the weather is kind and harvests good, but no more than that. And even in that time one mishap, one bad season, would finish us."

"What would happen to the farm then?" Kaldar asked.

Shammana made a small, resigned gesture. "The next tithe wouldn't be paid, and the overlord's men would seize the house and land and turn us out. The farm would be given to whoever was willing to pay the overlord the highest fee for it."

Kaldar's expression was disgusted. "But your neighbors, your friends — surely there's someone who'll help you?" He glanced covertly at Nanithe, then, with the hand further from her, made the sign of the circle, the symbol of Aeoris, to convey his real meaning.

Shammana, though, shook her head. "There's no one here I can be sure of, Kaldar. I believe our movement has its friends in this district, but I don't know who they are and I daren't take the risk of trying to find out. No, I must accept the inevitable. It is time for Nanithe and me to leave our home, while we may still do so with some dignity."

Kaldar sighed and looked down at his trencher, which he saw with chagrin was empty. He hadn't intended to eat all his share of the food; he'd meant to claim that he wasn't truly hungry and insist that the two women should take more. But, distracted by the conversation, he'd eaten every morsel . . . and could have eaten the same again and more.

It was a sharp illustration of Shammana's point, and he nodded soberly. "Yes. Yes, I understand, and I see that you're right. But where will you go?"

Shammana gazed at him for a few moments as though privately assessing him. Then she turned to Nanithe.

"Child, will you go and fetch the mead?"

Nanithe rose and left the room, and Shammana looked at Kaldar once more.

"I've been considering this for some time, Kaldar. Simbrian has asked me again and again to go south and join the gathering of our friends but I've put off the decision — deluded myself, perhaps, into believing that Nanithe and I could continue to get by here. Now I know that isn't possible. And you've given us the opportunity we need."

"I have?" Kaldar was momentarily nonplussed — then suddenly he realized what she was suggesting.

"It's the simplest and safest of solutions," Shammana said as she saw his expression change. "Two women traveling alone would face all manner of risks which I don't need to detail. One young man traveling alone may not face those same risks, but he arouses suspicion; all the more so now if the rumors concerning the new First Magus and his plans are true. But three together — mother, daughter, and son, let's say — can make their journey on proper roads in the safety of daylight, and be that much more likely to reach their destination without mishap."

Kaldar stared at her as mixed reactions assailed him. On the one hand the idea made excellent sense; but on the other he was used now to traveling alone and, even avoiding roads and all but the largest towns as he had done, could make faster progress without the presence of two women to hamper him.

Shammana smiled thinly, aware of his dilemma. "I know you think you'd reach the south more quickly without us, Kaldar. But I still have one good horse, and there's nothing wrong with the farm wagon that hammer and nails a little axle grease won't put right in less than an hour. We can all ride together in comfort — and, our lord Aeoris willing, we'll be with Simbrian before you could hope to walk the distance."

Kaldar's face began to relax — then, surprising himself, he laughed. Nanithe, returning with the mead, looked at him curiously, then, catching the mood without knowing or caring why, she gave him a sweet, open smile that dispelled his last doubts.

"It's settled, then." Shammana reached for the mead jar and unstoppered it. "We'll leave in the morning; no point in wasting more time than we must." Her lip curled with faint contempt and she glanced round the room. "Our two fine stewards from the marketplace will be coming for their bribe tonight; for all it matters to me now, they may take every fowl on the steading and anything else they can carry away. By this hour tomorrow, I shall be too far away to care."

Mead gurgled into the pottery cups. Shammana raised her own

measure, Nanithe did the same, and suddenly the atmosphere in the room seemed to change subtly but significantly. Kaldar felt as though a new presence, intangible yet imbued with enormous power, had stepped into their midst and touched them with an invisible hand. Gravely he lifted his own cup, and the three vessels clinked together with a faint ringing sound.

"In homage to our lord Aeoris," Kaldar said softly. "And in the name of our holy cause."

The fire seemed to burn more brightly as they drank.

CHAPTER XVI

Savrinor delivered his report to Vordegh within the allotted three days, and for three days afterward he heard nothing more from the First Magus. It was an uncomfortable hiatus during which he had no means of knowing whether or not his efforts had met with approval, and in the privacy of their shared apartments Iselia quickly learned to be guarded in every aspect of her behavior. Being in Savrinor's presence was like walking barefoot on broken glass, and she was thankful that he still spent most of his waking hours in the archive library deep in the castle's vaults.

She had hoped to steal a look at the report before it was delivered to the First Magus, but that had proved impossible, for Savrinor had been unusually reticent about its contents and she hadn't dared take the risk of prying in secret. However, the nature of the books and parchments which Savrinor had set her to fetch from the library for his researches sounded an alarm in her mind. Bundles of old and musty records from overlords' strongholds in all quarters of the world, reports from detachments of Chaos riders sent to enforce the rule of law in troublesome districts, and, perhaps most significant of all, two ancient and obscure volumes containing legends both allegorical and literal of the gods and their deeds. Iselia had been able to examine those volumes, but their faded, stylized script and archaic phraseology were hard to decipher. Nonetheless, she was convinced beyond doubt that Savrinor's commission was directly connected with the warning Benetan had passed to her in the dining hall.

Since hearing what Benetan had had to say, she had lived with the constant, gnawing ache of anxiety in the pit of her stomach. She had seen the First Magus only as a distant and ephemeral figure at the inauguration festivities and had gained no real impression of him, but Savrinor's attitude, fueled by small snippets of conversation overheard in the dining hall or library, had enabled her to piece together an idea of the kind of man he was. Even as a newcomer to the castle she had sensed a change in the prevailing atmosphere since his reign began; there was a constant undercurrent of tension, a sense of unease that at times touched on outright fear. She'd heard no one speak ill of Vordegh — far from it — but though his name was uttered with a respect bordering on reverence, she had the strong impression that most of the castle's inhabitants, including many of the magi themselves, lived in dread of their new ruler. If what Benetan had said of the First Magus's intentions was true, then Kaldar and their allies in the south were in far greater danger than they knew. And she, a prisoner without hope of release, had no means whatever of warning them.

Then, just before dawn on the fourth morning after Savrinor had delivered his report, a visitor came to the apartments.

Iselia hadn't slept that night. Savrinor had been absent for most of the previous day but had returned in the evening and, with a lazily carnal smile that she recognized all too clearly, told her to change her wool dress for the silk he'd given her and accompany him to the dining hall. Passively she went with him and, feeling too sick to eat, sat at his side while he drank wine and exchanged bantering small talk with several acquaintances in turn. It was late by the time they returned to their rooms, and when the door was secured behind them Savrinor augmented the wine with a cocktail of drugs, as she had known he would, and led her into the bedroom, as she had known he would, and experimented with some new pleasures that had occurred to his fertile imagination. When he finally drifted into a deep, sated sleep, Iselia crept from the disordered bed and went to sit shivering by the window in the outer chamber. Light from a number of other windows still spilled across the courtyard and there was a faint blur of sound from the direction of the dining hall, but Iselia only watched the slow track of the two moons across the clear night sky, and nursed the hatred that burned like a disease within her.

She'd feared that she would be sick in violent reaction, as had happened so many times before, but it seemed that her resolve was hardening. She had prayed for that, prayed she could learn to become inured to Savrinor's demands and tastes, and although she was realistic enough to know that the lords of Order hadn't the power to answer her prayers directly, slowly but surely a core of strength was developing. How she could use that strength to aid Kaldar and their cause Iselia didn't yet know, but her resolve to use it, to find a way somehow, was the one flame that lit her dark world. For her husband and her gods she would bear anything, do anything, and the cost to herself was irrelevant.

Her lips were moving silently but intensely in a private litany to buoy her courage, when the unexpected caller arrived. A peremptory knock at the door brought Iselia starting out of her chair, then before she could collect her wits, let alone move to answer the summons, the bolt which Savrinor had drawn snapped back without a hand to touch it, and the door opened.

Iselia had never seen the tall, cold-faced young woman before, but her demeanor, and the fact that she was both able and willing to make a mockery of privacy, sent a shaft of icy disquiet through her. The visitor looked her up and down, a mere acknowledgment of her presence, devoid of any interest, and said,

"You are Iselia?"

"Yes." Iselia felt herself tense inwardly; she had taken an instant and intuitive dislike to the woman and the fact that her identity was known alarmed her. "You — "

"I am Verdice, amanuensis to the First Magus." Her voice was startlingly deep. "I have a message for your master."

Iselia didn't know what an amanuensis was, but the invocation of the First Magus's name made it clear that Verdice had influence.

"Savrinor is asleep," she said, a faint edge to her voice. "He — "

"Wake him, and give him this." Verdice held out a small, tightly rolled parchment, tied with a black ribbon. Then without waiting for a response she turned and stalked back toward the door. On the threshold she looked over her shoulder. "The message is for Savrinor's eyes alone. If the seal is broken by anyone else, that person will be severely punished."

And she was gone.

For the better part of a minute Iselia stood staring at the closed door while Verdice's last words boiled in her mind. Battling with a sense of insult at the woman's assumption that she was likely to pry into another's private papers was a sudden overwhelming desire to do that very thing. She was certain that there must be a connection between this scroll and Savrinor's recent researches, and there was a chance — a very good chance, she realized — that the First Magus's message would provide the answers to some of her own urgent questions.

The room was cold but her palms were slick with sweat as she gripped the small roll of parchment tightly. It would be so easy. The scroll bore no seal, only a flimsy ribbon which would take only moments to retie. And Savrinor was sleeping soundly. . . .

That person would be severely punished. . . . Verdice had uttered the warning casually, but suddenly an alarm sounded in Iselia's mind. Was the very fact that the parchment was not sealed an indication of a trap — and had the tall woman's warning been a deliberate goad? She told herself that the idea was too petty to be rational, that the First Magus could neither know nor care that she even existed; but abruptly that assumption collapsed. Verdice had known her name. And it was rumored that no event or individual in the entire castle was too trivial to escape Vordegh's attention, if he had reason to show an interest.

Sweet Aeoris, Iselia thought, *do they suspect something?* Panic assailed her in a sick wave and she dropped the scroll, for a moment irrationally convinced that Vordegh could read her thoughts through her physical contact with it. Then common sense returned as she realized that even the magi could have no such power. But the trap, the test, that threat still remained, and that surely was within a high magus's scope. Who was she to know whether, by some arcane means, Vordegh might not be alerted if the scroll was opened by the wrong hand? And if she *was* under suspicion . . .

With a great effort Iselia thrust down the nausea that churned in her stomach, and crossed the room in four quick strides to bolt the door again. There was only one way to allay her terrors — or confirm them, though she didn't dare think about that. To read the scroll would be too great a risk. She must obey Verdice's instructions, wake Savrinor, and try to maneuver him into telling her what the message contained.

She picked up the scroll, holding it gingerly now between thumb and forefinger, and returned to the bedchamber. A candle sconce stood on a table beside the bed; she struck flint and lit the stub of the candle, then moved to look down at Savrinor's face and pale hair on the pillow. Asleep, he looked younger than his years, and with his mouth relaxed and sly eyes closed he had an air almost of innocence. Iselia's own lips twisted bitterly at that thought, and she wondered fleetingly how she could have been gullible enough to believe at first that she liked him. But then he was a monster in the mask of chivalry, and for a while she had been beguiled by the mask. Now, though, she knew better. Now she believed that if a human equivalent of a demon could exist, its name would be Savrinor. And that belief was the king-pin of her resolve.

She composed her face into a bland expression and reached out to shake him by the shoulder. "Savrinor. Savrinor, wake up."

He stirred, turned over, and opened drug-laden eyes. "What . . . ?" Vision cleared and he recognized her; his gaze hardened.

"Damn you, what hour is it?"

"Near dawn. A message has just come for you." She thrust the scroll toward him. "From the First Magus."

The vicious reprimand that had been on the tip of Savrinor's tongue subsided and he sat up, shaking strands of hair from his face. "Oh, gods . . . ," he said. "At *this* time of day?" He took the parchment, and his voice became sharply animated. "Who brought it?"

"Her name was Verdice. She said she is the First Magus's anam . . . aman . . ."

"Amanuensis. It means that she performs the same services for Lord Vordegh as you do for me. Or rather I should say, *some* of the same services." He flicked a quick, vulpine glance at her face; then his expression altered. "I hope to Yandros you showed her the proper courtesies."

"I barely said a word to her," Iselia told him. "She entered the room without waiting for me to open the door. She — somehow she made the bolt draw back without — "

Savrinor interrupted. "Yes, I imagine she did; and that's by no means the only trick she's capable of." He looked at her again. "I advise you to be very wary of that one. She isn't entirely human, and Vordegh has trained her extremely well."

"She warned me . . ." Iselia's voice trailed off.

"Mmm?" Savrinor was untying the black ribbon; then abruptly he took in what she'd said and his eyes narrowed. "What? What did she warn you of?"

Iselia stared toward the window. "She warned me against prying into the message. As if I couldn't be trusted."

"You're a clerk, a servant; of course you can't be trusted." From his look she couldn't judge whether or not he was joking. "No one with half a grain of sense relies on the integrity of anyone else in this place, and while you're memorizing the word *amanuensis* you'd better learn that lesson into the bargain."

The cold, sick feeling started to rise afresh in Iselia. What did Savrinor mean? What was he implying? She made to speak again, truly frightened now and looking for a way to gain reassurance without giving her motives away. But before she could say a word, Savrinor had scanned the message and preempted her.

"Go to the cabinet in the outer room. You'll find a brown phial on the top shelf, and a bag of white powder beside it. Measure six drops from the phial and two pinches of the powder into a cup of wine, and bring it to me." Eyes still on the scroll, he pointed to the table beside him. "The key's there somewhere; be sure to lock the cabinet again when you've finished."

By a quite unwitting chance he had given her her reassurance. Though her knowledge was scant as yet, Iselia was rapidly learning about the properties of many of Savrinor's drugs, and he was aware of it; indeed he encouraged it. If she *were* under suspicion, and the First Magus's message had referred to the fact in any way, then Savrinor wouldn't be unwise enough to send her on this errand. Breathless with relief she said, "Yes, Savrinor," found the key and all but ran from the room.

Outside, dawn was breaking. Watery light washed the sky above the castle walls, and the raucous screeching of gulls carried on the cold, still air. Iselia shivered as she measured the drops and the powder into a cup, filled the cup with the strongest wine — she knew that Savrinor preferred to disguise the drugs' tastes as far as possible — and carried the cup carefully back to the bedroom. Savrinor was half dressed by this time, and he took the cup from her before picking up her own wrap, discarded at the end of the bed, and tossing it to her.

"Put this on, or you'll find yourself in Physician Revian's tender care with a rheum."

"Thank you." Iselia put the wrap about her shoulders.

"My purpose is entirely selfish, I assure you. Firstly I find ailing women intolerable, and secondly I have work for you to do." He gestured, impatiently she thought, toward the parchment. "A great deal of work."

Iselia's heartbeat quickened. If she moved just a step or two closer, she might be able to see. . . .

Savrinor's voice cut across the tentative thought, making her jump. "Read the damned thing if it pleases you. It'll be your concern soon enough anyway."

Trying not to appear eager she picked up the document, but, as with the old tomes from the library, the First Magus's script was almost impossible for her to decipher. He formed his letters in a way unfamiliar to her, and joined them with flourishes that she had never learned. . . .

"Defeated?" Savrinor had drained the wine cup and was looking at her with a faint smile on his face which might have been either disparaging or conspiratorial. "You should take some time to study a few of the scripting books in the library. They'll improve your understanding and probably your own hand into the bargain."

The seed of an idea began to germinate in Iselia's mind. Her voice carefully neutral, she said, "I don't have sanction to enter the library unless it's at your bidding."

"Mmm?" He was distracted again, debating between a choice of two coats. "Oh, that's too trivial to worry about. I give you sanction here and now, and if anyone questions it you may refer him to me. The more you learn, the greater use I'll be able to make of you." To her surprise he then turned round and gave her a broad and completely unpremeditated grin. "Although I'll say that it's only in your clerical capacity that there's room for any improvement."

Iselia stared at him. To pay her such a compliment — and by Savrinor's lights it *was* a compliment, however she might view it — was quite untypical of him, but the fact that he had phrased it in such an extraordinarily open way, without acerbity or artifice, dumbfounded her. This simply didn't fit with the man she had come to know, and abruptly a new and unexpected thought crept out from a dark corner of her mind. She dismissed it instantly as too wild a surmise and only returned the grin with a forced smile.

"As to the message," Savrinor said, changing the subject as lightly as though his brief lapse had never taken place, "it means, in essence, that free time for both of us is likely to be a rare commodity in the foreseeable future. The First Magus is apparently pleased with the results of my first report to him, but he now wants more. *Much* more. He lists six questions to which he wants detailed answers by sunset tonight, when he proposes to call a conference of the highest magi to discuss his strategy. So, my dear, we must resign ourselves to a tedious morning incarcerated in the vaults among dusty books and dustier scholars, and an equally tedious afternoon copying out our discoveries for the magi's use."

The thought that her handiwork would be subjected to the magi's scrutiny was unnerving. "What are the questions?" Iselia asked.

"They're largely concerned with unrest· in the more populated southern districts."

"Unrest . . . ?" She hesitated. "Is that why the magi are meeting? Is there some trouble?"

"No, no. Not in that sense, anyway." Savrinor frowned suddenly as he remembered his last, predawn encounter with Benetan. He had been in a very dark mood then; overtired and overdrugged and seeing threats in every shadow. But the discipline of several days' hard work, with a night of pleasure to celebrate its completion, had done a great deal to restore both his spirits and his sense of perspective, and Vordegh's preoccupations no longer seemed so ominous. The frown cleared and he gave Iselia another pleasant smile.

"It's an old and stale matter newly resurrected, my dear Iselia, and of no more interest to you, I'm sure, than it is to me. I'm going down to the bathing rooms, and then to the dining hall. Dress yourself in something warm, and we'll snatch a swift and early breakfast before we set ourselves to work."

He went out of the room, taking the First Magus's document with him, and moments later Iselia heard the outer door open and close. She waited until she could be sure he wouldn't return, then shed her wrap and nightgown and began to dress. The queasiness had returned and her heart was thumping with an irregular, painful beat, for despite her inability to read the First Magus's message in any detail a few words had been recognizable to her eyes, and one was now set in her mind like a flint embedded in softer rock. Just one word: *heretics*. Benetan's warning had been right. And she, knowing it, was powerless to pass on that warning, to let Kaldar and their friends and allies know the nature of the peril that they were about to face.

Despite the early hour, there were already three other people in the library vault when Savrinor and Iselia arrived. A middle-aged woman was combing the shelves in search of some elusive document, while Revian, the castle's general physician, sat alone at a cluttered table, leafing through a pile of medical texts.

And at another table, bowed over and apparently engrossed in a single large book, was Andraia.

She glanced up as the newcomers entered, and Savrinor noted that although she had taken great pains with her appearance her face beneath the expertly applied cosmetics looked haggard. For a moment her green eyes lit cordially. Then she saw Iselia, and instantly her expression hardened.

"Andraia." Savrinor crossed the floor to her table and bent to kiss her cheek. She offered him her lips instead, and he didn't miss the swift, malicious flick of her gaze in Iselia's direction as she did so. "You *are* an early riser."

"So are you, Savrinor." She smiled sweetly. "Quite unhealthily early, I'd say. But as handsome as ever for all that."

Savrinor knew perfectly well why she was flirting with him, but for some reason he wasn't as amused by it as he would customarily have been, and that surprised him. He took hold of her hand and said, "You flatter me, my dear, and such kindness from you is far more than I deserve." His fingers squeezed gently. "How are you?"

"Very well, as you can see." Her eyes belied it; she was wretched. "So, what brings you down to the vaults?"

"Work, as always." He could have asked her the same question, but he had a suspicion that he already knew the truth, for he'd seen what she had been studying so earnestly before his arrival. A volume of romantic legends . . . Andraia had never struck him as the kind of woman to seek solace from her own troubles in this kind of pointless diversion, and it indicated the depth of her depression.

Iselia was waiting for his instructions, standing a discreet few paces back and pretending an interest in the stonework of a nearby pillar. Savrinor released Andraia's hand and turned to her.

"Iselia, my dear." Her head came up quickly, giving her the look of a startled young animal, a look which had pleased him since their first encounter. "I want you to search out these documents for me." He produced the First Magus's scroll, to which he'd added his own notes over breakfast. "You'll find the first three on the lower shelves in that section," pointing. "I'll join you shortly, but I want a private word with the lady Andraia."

Iselia nodded mutely, took the parchment, and walked demurely away. Like two predators with greatly differing intentions, Savrinor and Andraia both watched her go, then Savrinor slid gracefully onto the bench on the opposite side of Andraia's table.

He didn't mince words; he said simply and bluntly, "Well, now. Have you resolved your quarrel with Benetan?"

She looked surprised, then resentful, then defensive. "Without wishing to be discourteous — " she began stiffly.

He interrupted her. "It's none of my concern, I think you want to say; though of course you were looking for a more subtle way to phrase it. Perfectly true. However, I have a pertinent motive for asking an impertinent question, so I won't be put off. I consider Benetan a friend, as I'm sure you know." He saw the sudden skeptical glitter in her eyes and returned it with a sere smile. "Yes, I know you're wondering what my friendship's worth; I make no secret of the fact that I choose my acquaintances carefully, and I see no reason to be ashamed of it. But it may surprise you to know that, as well as finding him useful, I *like* Benetan. He's a good man, far better than many of his theoretical superiors. He's honest and he's honorable. And above all, he loves you."

Savrinor was almost the last person in the entire castle with whom Andraia had any desire to discuss her personal troubles, and as he spoke she had been tempted simply to get up and walk out. But this last statement was too much for her combative nature. She rose to the bait, as Savrinor had judged she would, and said acidly, "I think, Master Savrinor, that I'm in a better position to know the truth of that than you are. Benetan might have deceived you and he's doubtless still trying to deceive himself, but his real feelings are perfectly clear to *me.*" Her gaze flicked toward the far side of the vault, and Iselia's back view. "He has discovered, it seems, that old habits die hard."

Savrinor sighed. "I truly don't know," he said levelly but wearily, "which of us is the biggest fool. Benetan with his misplaced notions of chivalry, you with your unfounded jealousies, or me for making any attempt whatever to help either of you."

Andraia's cheeks flamed angrily. "You're under no obligation to me, I assure you! I didn't ask — "

"You didn't ask for my opinion or my advice, no. But I intend to offer them all the same, and I think you're wise enough not to flounce out of this chamber without at least hearing what I have to say."

Something in his tone made her stop short of pushing her bench back as, this time, she had been resolved to do, and a warning inner voice reminded her that Savrinor made a dangerous enemy. She subsided, though her posture was tense and hostile. "Very well. If you've nothing more diverting to do than play matchmaker this morning, who am I to argue?"

Savrinor disguised his amusement behind a delicate cough. He couldn't claim to know Andraia well, but the more he saw of her the higher he esteemed her. Benetan really didn't deserve the affections of a woman like this, he thought. But for her sake — and also as a matter of personal convenience, though that was a peripheral consideration — he would, as she put it, "play matchmaker."

"Andraia." He laid a hand lightly over hers. "I'm aware, as you are, that Benetan has some . . . interest in Iselia."

"Interest?" She repeated the word in a short, sharp bark, then hastily lowered her voice. "I'd put it a good deal more strongly!"

"Then you'd be wrong, my dear. Iselia is an old acquaintance — one might indeed say an old flame — of Benetan's, but whatever there might once have been between them is twelve years in the past. However, as I mentioned a little earlier, Benetan has a great if often misguided sense of gallantry." He smiled an intimate and faintly stealthy smile. "He feels personally responsible for the fact that the girl is here at all, which of course he is, albeit only through a chain of unfortunate circumstances."

Andraia looked back at him thoughtfully. "Ah," she said. "An old flame. I see. Benet said she was simply . . . now, what was the phrase he used . . . ? 'A face from the past,' that was it." Abruptly she slid her hand away out of his reach. "What was she to him, Savrinor? Do you know?"

"No, lady, in truth I don't. But whatever their relationship may once have been, it *is* in the past, and Benetan knows and accepts that." Suddenly, surprisingly, his face took on a hard look that she'd never seen before. "And you have my assurance that even if it were otherwise, he would have no choice but to accept it."

Andraia wasn't the most empathetic of mortals, but she was a fine judge of women, and of the effect women could have on their lovers, and she was shocked. She'd always thought of Savrinor as a master of cold pragmatism, but unexpectedly and perhaps unknowingly he had revealed a vulnerable streak. He was, she realized, as besotted with Iselia as Benetan seemed to be, perhaps even more so, and suddenly all her dark thoughts about the peasant girl took on a new perspective. What was it about her that had enabled her to ensnare two such intelligent and utterly disparate men, both of whom could have had the pick of almost any unattached female who took their fancy? First Benetan, trailing about the castle with a whipped-dog look in his eyes, and now Savrinor, suddenly jealous and proprietorial at the prospect of a rival. The old Savrinor, the Savrinor of repute, would have laughed at Benetan's infatuation and suggested that they should share the girl, with Andraia joining in the fun if she felt so inclined. Instead he was communicating a clear message that, to Benetan or anyone else, Iselia was out of bounds. *Why?* Andraia asked herself. A plain, uneducated peasant, gawky and unsophisticated and without three words to say for herself. *Why?*

Savrinor spoke again. "Andraia, Benetan has no ambitions towards Iselia. He may have deluded himself into thinking otherwise, but it is just a delusion, and a transient one."

"I wish I could believe you."

"You can, because I know it's the truth." Savrinor paused, then lowered his voice to barely more than a whisper. "I am not the only impediment, you see. Iselia also has a husband."

"A husband?" Andraia stared at him.

"Yes. The lower orders have the notion that to stay virgin until they tie themselves to one lover for life is somehow inherently virtuous, though the gods alone know how such an idea grew up. By a delightful irony it seems that Benetan's men snatched Iselia on the very day of her marriage but before she could face the hazards of her nuptial bed. That, of course, adds fuel to the fires of Benetan's conscience, and so complicates the situation still further — but at the same time, by his peculiar code, it also means that under no circumstances would he consider trampling on what he considers to be another man's territory."

As a child Andraia had once seen a marriage ceremony, when her mother had taken her on a visit to the demesne of a distantly related overlord who had given permission for two of his servants to wed. Her companions had been loftily amused while she'd thought the whole thing dully futile, but Benetan might well take a very different view. Whatever changes the castle had wrought, he couldn't entirely shake off his origins.

Savrinor saw her wavering, considering, and said, "You yourself pointed out that old habits die hard. All Benetan needs is a little . . . *persuasion* is perhaps the best word, to temper his natural but inappropriate desire to champion an old friend."

Ah, yes, Andraia had no doubts now. Another implicit warning, and less subtle than Savrinor believed it to be. An image came into her mind of Iselia sitting alone in the dining hall after what had appeared to be a private meeting with Benetan. She recalled the posy of drying leaves Iselia had been clutching tightly in her hand, and her own suspicion — no, more than a suspicion, a *certainty* — that something secret had passed between them. And she also recalled her resolution to speak quietly to Savrinor when the moment was right. . . .

She glanced covertly toward the shelves where Iselia was still hunting for documents, then leaned forward across the table. "You said the girl is married. Do you know anything about her husband?"

The question seemed to take the historian by surprise. "No," he said. "I can't say that I do. Benetan claims not to know his identity, and I've never troubled to inquire." He smiled thinly. "It's hardly relevant now, and of no concern to me."

Andraia wanted to say, "Then perhaps it should be," but prudence made her cautious. How could she warn Savrinor to be wary in his dealings with Iselia when she had no concrete evidence but only a prickling intuition to back her suspicions? Yet there was something else, something she could say. . . .

She licked her lips thoughtfully. "I'd like to find out who he is."

Swiftly, ingenuously, she met his inquiring gaze. "If he's someone that Benet used to know, it might go some way to explain . . ."

That hadn't occurred to Savrinor, and the possibility interested him. "Well, then, my dear, I'll find out for you." Iselia would tell him, he thought. She might pretend reluctance in that as she did in certain other areas, but he was coming to know her ways and her moods, and manipulate them to his own advantage.

"I'd greatly appreciate it." Andraia gave him such a dazzling smile that his annoyance with Benetan abruptly and briefly redoubled. Then she reached out and, as he had done to her earlier, laid her right hand over his.

"You've given me a great deal to think on, Savrinor. I will think on it. And I thank you."

He made a self-deprecating gesture. "I claim nothing. I've only tried in my own humble way to put right something which appears to be wrong."

"Yes." Her green eyes were keen. "Yes, you have." She withdrew her hand. "I'll see Benet. I'll try to understand, and I'll try to help him." For a moment her look became a strange mixture of the wolfish and the demure. "For both our sakes."

She walked gracefully out of the library.

The task was fulfilled and there was nothing more Savrinor could do. At this moment the senior magi were meeting and debating in the castle's north wing, and the outcome of their conference was no longer of any direct concern to him. As a pragmatist, Savrinor knew that the only sensible course was to make the most of his leisure while he could.

He had ordered a meal to be brought to him and Iselia in their rooms. It was one of the privileges which his rank could command, and though customarily he preferred to eat in the more public and thus more fruitful climate of the great hall, for once he wasn't in the mood to socialize. Andraia's question, or to be more accurate the tone of her question, had intrigued him. He'd made her a promise, and Savrinor never broke promises; but at the same time he felt a new and more personal curiosity to learn the answer.

A deferential servant brought the meal. Iselia still found it hard to meet the eyes of servants, a legacy of her own humble origins and one which Savrinor intended to remedy in good time. She picked uneasily at her food while Savrinor watched her for a while, then looked up in her usual charmingly startled way when he suddenly spoke.

"Iselia, my dear, there's a question I have never troubled to ask you until now."

She didn't answer but only continued to look at him. He smiled.

"Your husband. What is his name?"

Iselia felt as though someone had kicked her in the stomach. A wave of terror rose; she struggled to quell it, struggled to keep her voice even and not give her fear away. "His . . . name?"

"Yes. Tell me all about him. I'm intrigued."

Her mind reeled and raced; never before in her life had she had to think so fast, and never had so much depended on the answer she must give him now. Desperately playing for time she said,

"There's nothing about him that would be of interest to a man like you, Savrinor. He's a miner in the northern mountains." That was safe enough, she thought; mining was a common trade in her district and no one could possibly make the connection with Kaldar.

Savrinor's smile didn't change. "You underestimate me, my dear. Even the dullest people have something to interest an inquiring mind, and you know my boundless thirst for knowledge. So, he's a miner. Not well off, I imagine."

The comment was careless but it provided Iselia with a sudden inspiration. She pushed her plate of food aside, rose to her feet, and stretched her arms. Her slim body moved enticingly under the folds of her gown and she saw Savrinor's gaze sharpen.

"Yes," she said, drawing the word out languidly in a manner she'd copied from him. "Not well off at all. In fact, *very* poor." Across a lifted shoulder she gave him a look that blended frankness with a hint of the coquette, then she continued, "When I was first brought here, I wanted only to be allowed to return to my home and be reunited with my husband. I railed against Benet — he's told you that, I know — and I blamed him for shattering my life. Or that was how I saw it then."

The ploy was working. She saw the gradual shift of interest in Savrinor's eyes, following the trail she was trying to create. He leaned back in his chair, then asked with lazy amusement in his tone, "And now?"

"Now . . ." She let her shoulder drop — *oh, sweet Aeoris, how have I learned this, how have I brought myself to do it?* — and turned away from him as though in chagrin.

"Is it very wrong of me," she said, "to compare what I had then with what I have now, and find my old life wanting?" The words came easily and glibly; a far cry, she realized with an inward shiver, from the Iselia of only a month ago. She paused, then sighed. "I used to be very afraid of the castle. We were never told what became of the ones who came here in the gleanings, and there were so many rumors, so many tales. . . . But now I know better." She turned again. "You have taught me, Savrinor. You've opened my eyes to a life that I could never have *dreamed* of in my own village." She fingered the skirt of her gown as though to emphasize her meaning. "And — and I can't pretend anymore that I want to go home."

Savrinor said gently: "Come here."

She did, and stood beside his chair. He took hold of her right hand, stroking it, his fingers moving lightly. She was young enough for her skin not to have been roughened beyond recall by menial work, and already her face and arms were losing the tan that years of exposure to sun and wind had ingrained. Gradually, under his tutelage, the finer qualities hitherto smothered by her lowly breeding were emerging. She had a keen natural intelligence and discernment that pleased him; and as her tastes and manners grew more refined she was becoming almost a beauty. But something of the peasant still remained, and she couldn't yet entirely shake off the pangs of conscience engendered in her by her upbringing. Curiously, Savrinor found that quite touching; he might tease Benetan for exhibiting the same flaw, but in Iselia the flaw had its own charm and novelty — and it was, in an obscure way, a compliment to himself.

He drew her down until she was sitting on his knee, and one arm slid around her waist.

"My dear child, of course it isn't *wrong* to want the best that life can offer you. Perhaps it was only natural that you should have wanted at first to return to your village and your drudgery and your miner. They were, after all, the pinnacle of your hopes. But — as you yourself have said — you've learned better now."

She moved against him, awakening a small, pleasant savor. "Yes," she said quietly.

"And which *is* better, my fair village girl? To be a miner's bride, or Savrinor's mistress? Which of your two men do you love now, Iselia? Tell me."

One word, just one, seared into her mind. *Mistress.* It was a term which in the castle meant just a little more than lover and certainly far, far more than servant. Instantly she recalled her earlier, extraordinary intuition. At the time she'd dismissed it as impossible, but now she began to wonder anew. *Which of your two men do you love now?* As though her answer was greatly significant to him. . . .

Her blood suddenly felt thick and heavy, throbbing in her veins. She had to give Savrinor an answer, the answer he wanted, for he'd offered her an undreamed-of chance to win further advantage for herself, and to dissemble now would be to fail in her commitment to the cause.

Iselia drew breath, bringing her runaway pulse under control. Oh yes, she had learned a great deal from Savrinor; more even than he knew. In the small hours of last night she had conquered yet another obstacle, and so the sickness that once had been an innate reaction no longer rose in her as she reached out to touch his hair, his cheek, his lips, with the tips of her fingers.

"Need I say it?" Her voice was soft, silky. "Do you think me so foolish still that I don't know and love my *true* lord, who has given me everything I could desire?" And slowly, with languor and seeming ardor, she kissed him, her tongue probing teasingly but with an implied intent to lick and pleasure and arouse.

Savrinor's hands tightened convulsively on her body. She welcomed the response; it was the key, the sign that the dangerous moment was past and her secret safe from his scrutiny for a while yet. She knew what he would want of her now, but there was a cold, immutable spike at the core of her heart that told her it didn't matter, it was unimportant, and she could endure it. For Kaldar's sake; for Aeoris's sake. Neither would expect any less of her. And Savrinor, who thought himself her master and she too ingenuous to deceive him, was falling into a trap which she hadn't intended to devise but which, now, she would use and manipulate to her own advantage.

His teeth sank fiercely into her lower lip. She made a sound that might have been pain or pleasure, knowing Savrinor she doubted if he would trouble to differentiate. "My lord . . . ," she whispered. "*My lord . . .*"

Savrinor thought no more of Andraia — or the name of Iselia's husband — that night.

CHAPTER XVII

So, my esteemed colleagues, that is the outline of my objective. We have allowed matters to slide for far too long, and a remedy is overdue. I intend to apply that remedy swiftly and efficiently, and I anticipate that you will not only give the undertaking your sanction but will also devote your unstinting energies to its execution."

There was silence as the First Magus finished speaking and looked coolly at the gathering of senior magi who had answered his summons to the council chamber. A few seemed reluctant to meet his gaze, as though they feared that by doing so they would betray their private thoughts to his scrutiny. Vordegh smiled.

"Am I to take it that none of you wishes to raise a caveat?" His tone was gentle and deceived no one. "Good. Then the council's decision is unanimous."

Pirane, who was reclining on a plush-covered couch next to Croin, the senior healer, focused her strange eyes meditatively on the far wall and wondered what her colleagues were thinking. The whole concept of the council had become a farce under Vordegh's rule, of course; in theory it was intended as a forum for the senior magi to air their views and debate them in a coherent way, but in practice it was now nothing more than a convenient conduit by which the First Magus could issue his orders and decrees. Oh, she *could* have spoken up. They could all have spoken up. But not one among them had been foolhardy enough to do so, and thus Vordegh's proposal, which in her view had more of the ring of a personal obsession than anything else, was agreed without a word of dissent being uttered. In principle Pirane didn't care a whit about this new development; groups of troublemakers with one grievance or another were always arising here and there and were easily put down, and to dignify them with the term *heretics* struck her as faintly absurd. But, then, it was typical of Vordegh to exaggerate the importance of his own concerns under the banner of the broader good. Ascetic he might be — she glanced with distaste around the chamber, which had been stripped, at his order, of most of its hangings and adornments — but he was also a very vain man. Vain, perhaps, to the point of unbalance. Yes, that was the nub of it, the reason why, for all her indifference to the topic at hand, she felt an uneasy stirring on a deep level of her psyche. If it were simply a matter of the new First Magus wishing to prove his authority to the world, make his mark in some spectacular way, that would have been well and good, and no one was going to cavil at the arrest and execution of a few dozen commoners who might or might not have taken it into their heads to flout the law. But Vordegh had made it clear that it would take a a good deal more than that to satisfy his thirst. She recalled the whispers that had circulated in the castle before his election; rumors the perpetrators had tried to hide but which had reached her ears nonetheless. Vordegh the unpredictable. Vordegh the sadist. Vordegh the madman. By rights a few ears, tongues, and eyes should have been forfeited as punishment for repeating such sedition, but Pirane could have named several of her fellow magi who, in private, had shared the whisperers' misgivings.

Steps should have been taken earlier, she thought. Throughout his career Vordegh had made no friends and more than a few enemies; he should never have been permitted to maneuver himself into a position where the council had had no choice but to elect him to the highest office. But he had done just that, by dint of his sorcerous skills and his overpoweringly dominant personality, and now he had what he had always wanted: absolute power and his erstwhile peers living in fear of him. Only Yandros could have prevented his elevation, and Yandros had not chosen to do so — indeed, Vordegh claimed to rule with the gods' supreme sanction, as though he himself were almost one of their number. And now this. An outright and single-minded campaign against an enemy whose very existence had yet to be proved beyond doubt. Pirane had heard all the tales of this latest rebel group and was aware that, unlike their predecessors, they had so far evaded all efforts to identify and capture them. But she was also well aware of the tendency for tales to be exaggerated in the telling and for fact to become fiction, and she considered Vordegh's resolve to be a gross overreaction. What possible threat could be posed by a peasant rabble, however well organized they might be, to the powers of the magi? Yet the First Magus behaved as though the demon lords of Order themselves were baying at the castle gates, and all else must be set aside until the "heretics" were found and destroyed. It was ridiculous. And no one dared speak a public word against it.

A hand touched her arm suddenly and Pirane realized that while she had been lost in her musings the meeting had come to an end. Croin was on his feet beside her, and quietly he drew her attention.

"Pirane. If you have a few minutes to spare, I would appreciate—"

"Croin, a word with you." Vordegh was approaching. He reached them, glanced at Pirane, and nodded aloof acknowledgment.

"First Magus." Pirane made a bow, then met his dark gaze. She was taller than Vordegh by half a head; a fact which she knew he disliked intensely. "With your permission, I shall withdraw."

"Certainly. Oh, one matter — who among the secular officers is best acquainted with overlords' demesnes, and won't need to waste time sifting through the records for their names and numbers?"

She was surprised by the question. "I think that would be Qenever, First Magus."

"Qenever . . . ah yes, your protégée's sire, as I recall. Let him know that I wish to see him at second moonrise."

"As you wish, First Magus." Pirane waited until Vordegh had nodded again, then she left the room without a backward glance. Intuition told her that Croin wouldn't be long in following, so she walked through the broad corridor that led to the dining hall, ordered wine, and took a seat near the fire to wait for him. No other magi were present and diners of lower rank kept a respectful distance, so when the healer arrived they were safe from any casual eavesdropper. Nonetheless Pirane chose to be circumspect.

"Well, Croin, I thought you'd come to bear me company before long." She poured wine for him. "A very . . . interesting meeting."

"Yes. Yes, indeed." Gems glinted on Croin's seven fingers as he raised his cup, but he didn't drink, only stared into the cup's bowl with a remote look in his eyes.

"A child was born in one of the upper rooms today," he said after a few moments' silence.

"Oh?" Despite her preoccupations Pirane was interested, for while the servant classes produced offspring with tedious regularity, births among the castle-bred echelons were growing rarer with each decade and so were an event to be celebrated. "Whose child? Not Ornath's surely?"

"Yes. Ornath and Revian's young cousin; I can never recall his name but they've had a liaison between them this past year or so."

"I hadn't realized her time was so close. Is the child healthy?"

Croin made an equivocal gesture. "It's undersized, and sickly into the bargain. But with care it should live."

"Well, it's pleasing news. And if the brat inherits its progenitors' talents, as it likely shall, it will be a valuable addition to our ranks. As to its health, with your skills — "

"Quite so. However, the First Magus wishes me to employ my skills in another direction." Croin saw her expression change and gave her a small, wintry smile. "The child is to be used for a high oracular communion."

"*What?*" Heads turned across the hall; hastily Pirane recovered her composure and lowered her voice. "Croin, is this some joke?"

"I wish it were, my dear Pirane. But no. Vordegh will perform the ritual tonight and I am to assist him."

"Yandros!" Suddenly the fire seemed suffocatingly hot and Pirane fanned ineffectually at her own face.

"Of course, it's possible that the child would have died in any case," Croin said. "The First Magus, however, is not prepared to wait for the gods to make that decision; or to wait for another birth among the servants to provide him with a candidate." He hunched his shoulders ominously. "Time, it seems, is of the essence, and the conjuration must take precedence over all other considerations."

"But the *waste!* New blood, a potential high sorcerer — is Vordegh quite — "

She had been about to utter it, about to speak the unspeakable, but before the word could spill from her, Croin reached out and clamped a hand around her wrist. "No, my dear," he said quickly, urgently. "Not aloud. Not even from your lips. There are too many changes taking place, and we must guard both our tongues and our thoughts."

Pirane understood his meaning and it confirmed her suspicion that, in the matter of Vordegh if in little else, she and Croin were of one mind. She nodded and, a little fastidiously, withdrew her arm from his reach.

"Has Ornath been told?" she asked. Her tone was rigidly controlled.

"I have that unpleasant duty still to come. I would have preferred simply to take the child away and tell her later that it had died a natural death; but the First Magus insists that Ornath should be made aware of the honor she has been granted, and will welcome it."

Yes, Pirane thought, yes; that, too, was in character. She looked at her cup, decided that she wanted no more wine, and stood up.

"Well, I, too, have my duty to perform. I must find Qenever and pass on the First Magus's summons."

"I imagine," Croin said, "that the Chaos riders will have a new commission before long."

Of course . . . Qenever's lists of demesnes, now a high oracular communion . . . Vordegh's first move in this new war suddenly became obvious to Pirane. She nodded. Then:

"Will the gods sanction this, Croin?" Her mouth grew hard as she looked at him. "*Will* they?"

The healer stared steadily back. "He passed the test, Pirane. I think you'll find that our lord Yandros has given him all the sanction he needs."

He poured himself another cup of wine as she walked slowly out of the hall.

Under normal circumstances Vordegh eschewed the trappings of ceremony in his magical work, but there were times when a certain level of formality had to be observed, if only for safety's sake. So, breaking with his usual custom, he had decided to perform tonight's ritual not in his own apartments but in the Marble Hall.

Shortly after the First Magus's brief but fruitful interview with

Qenever, as the second moon climbed in its long arc across the sky, three figures emerged from the castle's main entrance and crossed the deserted courtyard to the door that led down to the library. Vordegh led the way, behind him came Croin, with a leather bag of medical implements in his hand, and at Croin's heels Verdice walked, carrying a bundle that moved slightly but made no sound.

The library was also deserted, dark and empty. As the trio crossed the vaulted chamber toward the low door at the far side, a snuffling whimper came from the bundle in Verdice's arms. Croin looked sharply over his shoulder in time to see Verdice thrust a hand into the bundle's wrappings; immediately the whimpering faded to silence.

They walked in single file down the long, sloping passage to the Marble Hall, through the softly glowing door, and the Hall's mists enfolded them, drafts of cool air stirring and touching their faces like phantom fingers. Pale witch lights danced high among the pillars, reflecting spectrally in the mosaic of the floor, and there was a sense of vibration, of sounds pitched beyond the range of the human ear, pervading the atmosphere.

The black circle of the Chaos Gate lay ahead of them, but Vordegh turned aside, moving toward another part of the Hall. Through the mist huge dark shapes suddenly loomed and resolved into seven black stalagmites towering up from the floor. Seven colossal statues of the gods, staring silently and eternally over the Hall's peculiar dimensions. The name of the sculptor was long lost from the records, but the great age of his work was clear from the stylized nature of the carving, a crude and unrealistic fashion supplanted centuries ago by greater refinement. Before the statues, and dwarfed by them, stood a block of dark wood roughly the length and breadth of a man. The block's surface was rough and pitted and the wood's grain marked in places with brown-tinted stains. It had something of the look of an altar; but that was not its purpose.

Vordegh approached the block and laid a hand on its surface. Some of the stains were relatively new, and he smiled at Croin.

"Your experiments are as regular and meticulous as ever, I see."

Croin's shoulders lifted a fraction as though to dismiss the comment. "As always there were some useless candidates left over from the riders' last gleaning. I see no virtue in waste."

If Vordegh noted the slight emphasis on the word *waste*, and inferred any meaning from it, he gave no sign but only said, "Quite so. Well, then, if you are ready, bring the child and we'll not waste time, either."

Verdice stepped forward. She laid her burden on the wooden block and unfolded the wrappings. Ornath's son, less than ten hours old, small and wrinkled and helpless, screwed up his unfocused eyes and waved clumsy, uncoordinated limbs. Verdice stared down at the baby with detached curiosity, and suddenly Croin had to speak.

"First Magus — "

Vordegh looked mildly at him. "Yes?"

"Is it absolutely necessary that *this* child should be used?" With an effort the healer met his superior's eyes. "It seems a little profligate when births among our own kind are at such a low ebb. Good new blood is at a premium, and there are at least four girls among the lower ranks close to a confinement. A few more days — "

"I do not wish to wait a few more days." Vordegh continued to smile, but the smile had transmuted into something a little less moderate. "I informed you of my decision at the council gathering, Croin. If you wished to dispute it, you should have done so then."

Croin's throat worked. "I did not feel — "

"You did not feel it necessary?" Smoothly Vordegh turned what Croin had been about to say against him before he could finish the sentence. "No, of course you did not, for you're aware, as any wise man is, that the energies available from a newborn child of high blood are far greater than those of more lowly children. Now, my good friend, I'm sure you've not forgotten that this work must be completed before the child sees its first dawn, so *if* you are ready" — there was an implicit warning in the stress of his words now — "we shall begin."

Croin made no further protest. It wasn't the ritual itself he objected to, for he'd had occasion to use many newborn infants in his own experiments over the years, and squeamishness was a sentiment quite unknown to him. As Pirane had been the first to point out, it was the *waste* that gave such offense; the thought that the First Magus was ready to squander a potentially valuable asset for the sake of his own obsessive goals. But, like Pirane, when faced with a choice between capitulation and a confrontation with Vordegh, Croin knew that there was only one prudent response.

He smothered a faint sigh and bent to his bag. The child started to whimper again; again Verdice laid a hand on it and it quieted. Vordegh nodded to the woman and she drew back a few paces. Croin did the same, and the First Magus stood alone before the block.

He didn't speak. Ostentation in ritual work wasn't and never had been Vordegh's way, and he was too formidable a sorcerer to have any need of show. But one concession could not be dispensed with. Reaching to a deep pocket in his plain gray jerkin the First Magus drew out the wand that he had accepted from his predecessor's dying hand, the ultimate symbol of his authority, and weighed it in his hand. The wand was quiescent now, as if it were sentient and knew that, tonight, its presence was required but not its power. Vordegh touched it gently, stroked it as another man might have stroked a lover. Then with great delicacy and precision he laid it on the block, below the feet of the infant.

For a few moments the atmosphere was utterly still. Then a dark aura began to form about the First Magus as his will focused, and around his feet the pattern of the Hall's mosaic floor swam and distorted suddenly into new and disturbing perspectives. Croin sensed a gathering of power in the air, disturbing the pale mists and setting the witch lights shuddering in their dancing course. Not the raw, heady power that surged through the Chaos Gate at the highest ceremonies, the pure and giddying energy of the gods' realm, but something more human, contained and fearsomely controlled. This was not an exhortation to Yandros and his great brothers, nor even to the demons and chimeras that served Yandros and stalked between divine and mortal dimensions. This was a summoning, a demand. And the anticipation of what would answer the summons sent a tumultuous thrill through the marrow of Croin's bones.

He knew that the change was beginning when, gradually but emphatically, the sourceless light in the Marble Hall started to dim. Pastel colors lost their delicacy and brilliance, decaying down through the spectrum to dark and somber green, gloomy indigo, the murky tones of a titanic storm cloud. Quiet tranquility mutated into portentous silence and it was as though a vast, unseen weight were pressing down on Croin's head and shoulders, rooting his feet to the floor, petrifying his bones, and making granite of his flesh. He heard deep voices whispering, a strange, dirgelike song that echoed in his marrow. He saw through the gathering darkness veins of dull gold and bronze and quartz, threading the air like precious lodes snaking through lightless depths of bedrock. Once more the child cried; once more it was silenced. Then:

The cold tide came rushing from all directions at once, snatching at his breath, filling eyes and ears and mouth and lungs with drowning sounds and images. The pillars around him rippled and twisted, and his consciousness was lifted on a titanic wave, hurled into a sparkling cataract then, falling, falling, cast down into peaceful, shining depths.

The child wailed. And . . .

After water there was air. Whirling, buffeting air, vertigo and crosscurrents and a wild gale laughing and streaming invigoratingly through the Hall, as Vordegh drew on the powers of the third of the elemental planes. Then another infant cry, and another shift of the senses, and golden fire seared up through the Hall's floor and sprang into towering walls of crackling flame. Heat blasted the air; the light turned to an inferno of livid brilliance, and the child uttered a thin, whistling scream.

Silence crashed down. Earth, water, air, and fire were gone; deep darkness flickered beyond a small sphere that encompassed the First Magus and his companions, and within the sphere glowed a chilly silver nacre.

Vordegh touched the wand where it lay. It responded — for a moment Croin thought it cried out in an alien tongue, though it was hard to be certain — and silver glimmered briefly along its metallic shaft. Then Vordegh withdrew his hand. Something was laughing softly on the edge of consciousness, a voice with the quality of molten ore, and faces moved in the mist only to shiver and dissolve before their images could be impressed upon the memory.

The First Magus looked back over his shoulder to where Croin stood waiting. He inclined his head briefly, once, and Croin crouched in a swift, economical movement to the bag at his feet. He drew out a thin knife, the hilt cut from a single piece of amethyst and a blood channel running the length of the blade, and he stepped forward.

"There." Vordegh indicated with a forefinger, and with the precision of the finest sculptor Croin drew the tip of the knife across the child's stomach. A high, thin wail rose quavering through the Hall, blending strangely with the soft, unhuman laughter, and a line of vivid scarlet challenged the colorless atmosphere.

And something from another plane shifted, drawing closer to the mortal dimension.

The seven fingers of Croin's free hand flexed instinctively, anticipating the delicacy of the work they would do and evoking a feeling of familiar pride in the magus. Already he could sense the hungry response from the consciousness that stirred on this fifth astral plane, the domain of oracles, beyond the limitations of time and space. Not a hunger for blood, or anything of the flesh, but for the energy that the spilling of blood released. New energy, too new to be formed or tainted, the priceless nutriment of fresh, undiluted power that only the youngest of living creatures could offer. Now Croin could hear the sounds of breathing. Soft, yet eager, something waiting only for the door between dimensions to be eased open a little further before it came to bargain and to exchange sustenance for knowledge. Vordegh smiled the smile of a man well contented with his accomplishment and picked up the wand, holding it before him and over the child's crying, writhing body.

"By the power invested in me, I grant you leave to make yourself known in this place. Enter now, and be visible to my eyes. Enter now, and be audible to my ears."

The great oracles of the fifth plane were at best extremely dangerous beings. Like the elementals of earth, water, air, and fire, they owed no allegiance to any power, and as such existed outside the direct jurisdiction of the gods' realm. Their senses were infallible, but without the greatest precautions they could not be trusted. One mistake on the part of a sorcerer, one moment's lapse of concentration, and a rite such as this could be hurled into mayhem, with devastating consequences for anyone involved. Yet Vordegh spoke calmly and without drama, supremely assured of his own strength and his ability to prevail. As Croin watched, the air beyond the wooden block began to stir and then to agitate. An image — it couldn't rightly have been called a face, though there were unsettling parallels — formed on a level with Vordegh's gaze, its outlines suggesting dimensions far beyond human perception. At the same instant the child fell silent.

"*Come!*" Vordegh's voice dropped to a sibilant hiss, redolent with menace. "*Come!* Know that I have the sanction of the great lords of Chaos; I am master and advocate, conqueror and ruler. I command you now to speak without deception or subterfuge, not in hope of reward but only in obedience to my will, for this is my rightful domain and I permit no contender within its bounds. Speak, then, and make yourself known to me."

The atmosphere was intensely potent now. Specters moved in the mist, and the Marble Hall's dimensions stretched and twisted into eerie illusion. Croin felt himself touched by shapeless, invisible hands, and the floor beneath his feet seemed to sway and ripple and become as insubstantial as water. Then in the face that was not a face the shadow of a mouth took form, and a sound filled the Hall, forming words that seemed to reach Croin's ears through the pores of his skin.

KNOW THAT THERE MUST BE STRENGTH. WITHOUT STRENGTH I HAVE NO TONGUE TO SPEAK.

Vordegh fingered the wand lightly; it turned to a foreboding bronze hue at his touch. "I will give you strength," he said, and moved the wand lightly over the infant's body, touching here and there. At each touch a cold light glowed briefly across the child's skin; then, his gaze still steady on the image hanging in the air before him, the First Magus signaled to Croin. The physician's knife followed the pattern the wand had made, and Croin felt the release of energy from the body beneath his hands, the energy that would feed the oracle and strengthen its presence on the mortal plane.

Something which might have been a sigh rustled through the Hall. *AHH . . . I FEED AND I AM NOURISHED. GIVE ME MORE. GIVE ME MORE, THAT I MAY GROW AND SERVE YOU IN THE GROWING.*

"No more, until the first has run its course," Vordegh countered sternly. "Now I bind you and demand of you: answer what I will ask, and do not dare to withhold."

The oracle hissed, and Croin sensed anger. Its alien consciousness was testing the First Magus's strength and had found that his power was greater than its own. At last words formed again, setting up an aching vibration in the inner bones of the physician's ear.

I WILL ANSWER. STATE YOUR QUESTION. Though the being's voice had no tone, an accompanying psychic shock through the

Hall's atmosphere conveyed its savage resentment. Vordegh's lips pursed austerely.

"I have not one question but two." Instantly the air turned black and the oracle's shape began to swell into monstrous proportions, the color of the wand in Vordegh's hand changed to a livid green and his voice rang out ferociously. *"You are not great enough to resist me!"* The wand glowed dangerously as the First Magus pointed it at his adversary, and the being shrank back to its former size. Vordegh stared steadily at it.

"I repeat: not one question but two." His tone was serene again and the silver and black image before him shivered.

ASK, THEN. It had capitulated and they both knew it. Satisfaction showed in Vordegh's eyes.

"My first question: the true identity of the man who leads the heretics. My second question: the exact location in which this man may be found. And I warn you now: I will not be satisfied until I have the answers!"

Ornath's infant son took four hours to die. At Vordegh's urging Croin had brought all his considerable skill to bear in an effort to prolong the baby's life further, but in the end even he was forced to admit defeat. Too many wounds had been inflicted and too much blood spilled; the oracle had devoured all the energy the child could offer and there was simply nothing left.

And the First Magus did not have his answers.

Croin took great care to avoid meeting his superior's gaze as they finally left the Marble Hall. In all the years of their acquaintance he had never once known Vordegh to lose his temper in any overt sense, and even now he seemed icily calm, only the dead whiteness of fury about his lips giving any clue to his emotions. But Croin knew what lay beneath the surface. One misplaced word, one inadvertant look, and what would follow would be far worse than any frenzy. The physician valued his skin — and even if fear hadn't been motive enough for discreet silence, there was anyway nothing he might have said that could have made sense of what he had witnessed.

Verdice had made a move to gather up the child's remains from the block and carry them back into the castle, but Vordegh had stopped her with one searing glance. In a perfectly composed voice he said, "Leave that. The lower servants will dispose of it," and as Verdice bowed her acquiescence, he stalked from the Hall. Verdice followed, with Croin a little way behind. Croin's hands were slick and his robes stained, but he was barely aware of that small unpleasantness, for his mind was turning over the extraordinary — not to say disturbing — ramifications of the night's work.

Vordegh had received no answers to his questions because the oracle had been unable to provide them. It was as simple, as inarguable, and as impossible as that. A being of the fifth plane from whose senses nothing, in theory, could be hidden. Yet its senses had failed. To begin with, the First Magus had refused to believe that the oracle was not deceiving him, and had subjected it to a series of increasingly rigorous and pitiless ordeals to force the truth from it. Only when every test had proved useless and the child was all but breathing its last had he finally and bitterly acknowledged that the being had done all within the bounds of its power, to no avail. *I CANNOT SEE THE ONE YOU SEEK*, the oracle had said. *I CANNOT FIND THE ONE YOU SEEK. THE NAME AND PLACE OF THE ONE YOU SEEK ARE UNKNOWN TO ME*. And though the realization was like poison working in his veins, Vordegh was ultimately forced to accept that it spoke nothing less than the truth.

But the greatest conundrum of all, more baffling even than the fact of the oracle's failure, was the *reason* for its failure. Croin had not dared and would not dare to venture his opinion within Vordegh's hearing, but he was certain that there were only two possible answers. Either the heretic leader didn't exist but was a figure only of legend and rumor, or he had power of his own, great enough to shield him from the oracles' scrutiny. In theory it was inconceivable that a child born with a such a prodigious gift — and it must be innate, there could be no doubt of that — could have evaded the magi's attention throughout his early life. By rights the maverick talent should have been discovered and either nurtured at the castle or, if the child had proved recalcitrant, eradicated. Somehow, though, this heretic had slipped through the net.

If he existed, Croin reminded himself firmly. *If*. There was still room for doubt. But as he climbed the last few steps of the library staircase and emerged into the brittle chill of the night, he felt his skin contract with a rippling shiver that had nothing to do with the cold. Clear augury or mere intuition he didn't know, but in his own mind he was certain. And, reading the grim aura of the First Magus as he swept up the steps on the far side of the courtyard and vanished through the double doors without one backward glance for his companions, Croin knew that Vordegh's certainty was greater even than his own.

CHAPTER XVIII

I still find something distasteful in it." Tarod of Chaos was watching a shape that hovered in the flickering green sky far overhead; not quite a bird and not quite a reptile yet with a peculiar grace reminiscent of both, it was enacting a slow and skilled acrobatic dance on the buffeting air currents, performing quite alone and simply for the sheer delight of it.

Yandros narrowed his eyes, which at this moment were the color of molten gold, against the slanting light so that he might see the aerial dance all the better. He couldn't remember when or why the dancer had been created or even what level of being it was, but he was pleased by it, and one hand made a small gesture that materialized a shower of stars high in the atmosphere for the creature to play with.

"Your scruples," he said at last in reply to Tarod's remark, "are very admirable, but also a little misplaced. You know perfectly well that the magi set small value on human life; they always have, and there's no logical reason why they should suddenly take it into their heads to change." The color of his eyes abruptly altered to light purple and he flicked a curious glance in his brother's direction. "Or for that matter, why you should should suddenly start to trouble yourself over such a trivial matter."

"It isn't that." Tarod shook his head, and flames licked briefly in the flying black smoke of his hair. "You misconstrue my meaning. It isn't the facts of what's afoot in the castle that I find distasteful, but what those facts imply."

Yandros had returned his attention to the airborne dancer again, but these last words caught at his curiosity and he looked at Tarod with renewed interest. Of all the seven Chaos lords these two were perhaps the closest; for reasons which he'd never troubled to unravel Yandros had always felt that he shared an affinity with Tarod that in a subtle way transcended his affection, great though that was, for his other five brothers. Tarod was also gifted with a peculiar insight into the workings of the mortal mind which had proved valuable on more than one occasion in the past, and so when he had something to say on the subject, Yandros was inclined to listen.

He and Tarod were standing on a bridge of pulsating light, slung between two colossally towering silver cliffs. Yandros gazed down at the checkered, shifting landscape of Chaos, many miles below them, and his thin lips twitched in a smile.

"You have an irritating habit of distracting me from minor pleasures for the sake of equally minor concerns. Very well, then. What, precisely, do the facts imply, and what, equally precisely, is the nature of your distaste?"

Tarod raised a hand to gently wave away a cluster of tiny, jewel-colored motes, living things but barely sentient, that flittered around him, attracted as they always were to the presence of Chaos's masters. "Firstly, the fact that Vordegh was willing—I might even say eager—to sanction the sacrifice of the first healthy child born into the magi's ranks in the past decade."

"I don't doubt he had his reasons," Yandros said, in a tone that suggested he neither knew nor cared what those reasons might be.

"I agree; but what in the Seven Hells is wrong with the man's sense of judgment? That child would have been far more valuable to the magi alive and growing up among them than wasted in a rite that didn't even produce the desired result. This won't endear Vordegh to his peers, Yandros."

"That's hardly likely to concern him."

"No. But I think it should concern us."

"Do you?" Yandros looked surprised and puzzled. "Why? If the magi fall out over their own choice of leader, that's their affair, not ours. They elected him; they must now cope with him as they will." Gold lights flickered suddenly in his eyes, rivaling the molten shade of his hair. "Though I'll confess that if they were to repeal their choice and pragmatically drop Vordegh from one of the castle spires, I wouldn't shed a tear. For all his undoubted skills as a magus he's an objectionable man, and quite mad even by their standards."

Tarod's green eyes grew thoughtful. "Yes," he said. "And that's the crux of it."

"Now you're being cryptic," Yandros admonished. "Explain yourself, or I'll tire of this discussion and leave you alone here to mutter to your heart's content. *What* is the crux of it?"

"Vordegh's obsessed."

"With this business of the heretic leader? Yes, I know that, but at least while he's preoccupied with this wild-goose chase of his, it deters him from making mischief in other areas."

"Are you so sure that it *is* a wild-goose chase?"

Yandros turned his head and gave him a long, shrewd look. "My dear brother," he said at last, "I know as well as you do that we're not infallible, but if our old friend Aeoris and his forces of entropy had found a way to exert their influence on the mortal world again, d'you think for one moment that we wouldn't know of it? A powerful human sorcerer working for their cause, yet undetectable? The idea's preposterous! We defeated Aeoris and his brothers and we banished them; their power is broken, they're prisoners in their own realm and they will remain so. Oh, I know that the mortal race has long atavistic memories, and there are pockets of rebels here and there who like to think they're followers of Order; there always have been and there always will be. But this supposed heretic leader is nothing more than a mirage conjured by a mixture of imagination and wishful thinking. He doesn't exist."

Tarod, however, shook his head a second time. "That wasn't quite what I meant, Yandros. Of course I agree with you; no mortal sorcerer, however skilled, could evade detection by a fifth-plane oracle, let alone by us. That's only reasonable. But the First Magus isn't a reasonable man, which is why I foresee trouble. The heretic leader may not exist, but if Vordegh refuses to accept that and persists in his mania to find and destroy him, he may well turn myth into reality."

"Myth into reality . . . You mean that his persecutions might drive some individual to don the legend's mantle and start to amass a serious following?"

"I mean exactly that. We know the nature of the campaign Vordegh plans to wage. He's determined to balk at nothing, and spare no lives, until he's run his quarry to ground. But if the quarry is only a figment of his imagination —"

"Then the campaign won't end but will escalate to greater and greater heights, and the population will begin to rebel against such abuse . . . ah, yes." Suddenly Yandros's bony, patrician face was serious. "I begin to understand you."

"We made a mistake." Dark clouds were starting to roll across the flickering sky above them as the volatile fabric of the Chaos realm reacted to the mood of its greatest lord. The aerial dancer was no longer visible. Tarod glanced at the clouds, reading Yandros's attitude from their tumbling mass. "I don't like to say this. I know our principles and I have no quarrel with them. But I wonder if, for once, we should have stepped in and vetoed the magi's choice of leader."

The gargantuan vista was suddenly and momentarily hurled into searing brilliance as a spear of white lightning exploded from the clouds. The bolt sheared through the spectral bridge less than five paces from where the two gods stood, and they watched its blazing descent to the ground miles below. Ice blue flame shattered upward at the impact, and moments later an abysmal howl of thunder shook the bridge and its supporting cliffs. As the din subsided, Yandros spoke quietly.

"No, Tarod. No. I understand your concerns; I share them. But it has never been our practice to interfere in the lives of our mortal servants or exert any control over their actions. To do that would be to negate the entire philosophy of Chaos and make us no better than Aeoris and his despotic brothers." His eyes flickered first black, then crimson. "We both recall Aeoris's attitudes and methods very well; his demands for unquestioning obedience, unquestioning fealty —"

"We demand fealty," Tarod pointed out.

"Yes, but it's *all* we demand, and we don't expect our mortal followers to express it by blind groveling, literally or metaphorically. That was Aeoris's greatest mistake. His worshipers were *so* blinded by his dominance that they assumed he was omnipotent. Naturally, with time and his innate arrogance to help him he began to assume the same thing himself, and thus sowed the seeds of his own downfall.

No," as Tarod seemed about to speak again, "I won't consider any form of intervention. I won't risk making the same mistake as Aeoris did, not even to rid the world of Vordegh."

Tarod gazed steadily back at him. "And if our fears are realized? If Vordegh's actions provoke the very insurrection he's so determined to stamp out?"

"Then the magi must look to their own salvation. They must choose between Vordegh and the wrath of their subjects, and they must do it without instruction from us." Yandros looked away from Tarod, down once more to the shuddering landscape of Chaos, and his shoulders hunched in the characteristic, ominous way he had that gave him the air of some strange bird of prey. "If they make the wrong choice and the populace rises up against them as a result, so be it. I'm not interested in having fools for my avatars."

He turned then, walked away along the bridge's shimmering arch; after a few moments his tall figure seemed to distort suddenly and briefly, and he was gone.

Tarod sighed, and the sigh took the form of a tiny, silver cat which grew wings and drifted away, purring and treading air with minuscule claws. Idly he watched it go but didn't trouble to amend his lapse of concentration and flick it out of existence. He had a particular affection for felines; of all the creatures in the mortal world, he felt, they were the wisest, the most beautiful, and — baffling though the idea might be to a lesser mind — the kindest. Honest, too, in ways quite beyond the comprehension of the human race. He continued to gaze after his small, involuntary creation, realizing that it was perhaps more significant than seemed apparent on the surface. Many diverse things took life from the stuff of Chaos in unguarded moments, and more often than not they provided clues to deeper thoughts which might otherwise have remained buried. This, Tarod realized, was such a case. Cats, humans, and invidious comparisons. Yandros was right, of course; to intervene directly in the matter of Vordegh would go against everything that Chaos stood for. Yet how could the magi have been so foolish as to allow him to rise to power? Awe? Fear? Well, both had had a hand in it; for all their skills the magi were as susceptible to a domineering character as any of the lowly peasants they so despised, and Vordegh's talents as both sorcerer and leader were not in question. Or was there another reason for the magi's complaisance? Was it possible that he and his brother gods had misjudged the First Magus's fellows, and that they believed in their hearts that Vordegh's way and Vordegh's methods were right?

Abruptly the shining bridge and silver cliffs around Tarod shimmered out of existence, to be replaced by a stone arch overlooking a quiet, green river. Bizarre shapes moved and darted beneath the current, and dapples of light patterned the river's surface, but as he leaned over the water, elbows resting on the white parapet, Tarod gazed not at them but into another dimension.

The ancient followers of Order, Yandros had said, had believed their gods to be omnipotent, and that belief had contributed to their downfall. Now, though, ancient history was forgotten and humankind was unaware that Order had once ruled the mortal world. They believed that Chaos had always wielded sole and supreme power, and knew nothing of the titanic battle, a countless age ago in their terms, that had smashed Order's sway and ushered in a new age. Yet deep down in the psyche of every mortal, from the highest magus to the most ignorant serf, an ancestral memory remained of Aeoris and his brothers and their existence was still acknowledged. Humanity now reviled the lords of Order as demons, not knowing that they had once been gods. But there were some mortals — as there had always been — who secretly refused Chaos their fealty and yearned to call Aeoris back from exile. Theirs were small and isolated sparks . . . yet how much, or how little, kindling would it take for the sparks to become a blaze?

A misplaced belief in his own omnipotence might have been Aeoris's undoing, but at this moment Tarod wished that he and his own brothers were as all-seeing and all-knowing as mortals presumed them to be. It was widely believed that the gods could see into the minds, hearts, and souls of their human worshipers and nothing could be hidden from them. In fact that was very far from the truth, for while the lords of Chaos were able to watch and assess the general temper of the mortal realm, the thoughts and ambitions of individuals within that world were not open to their scrutiny. Still less could they even guess at what might be afoot in Aeoris's own realm, for although the dimensions of Chaos and Order had many close parallels, their fabrics were utterly inimical and each was a closed book to the other.

Aeoris and his brood might effectively be prisoners in their domain, but within that domain their activities were a closely shrouded secret. If they could find or fashion one tiny flaw in the armor, one crack in the seal of the door that barred them from the mortal world, they would use that flaw in any way they could. And if Vordegh's obsession should spiral out of control and provoke serious unrest through the land, the people who suffered at his hands might take a new allegiance and look for a champion to lead them. One crack in the seal . . . If they found their champion, and Aeoris could establish a link, however tenuous, it might be enough.

If the forces of entropy had found a way to exert their influence again, Yandros had said, *d'you think for one moment that we wouldn't know of it?* At the time Tarod had agreed with him; now, though, he would have given a different answer to his brother's confident statement. An answer of just two words, but words of warning. He would have said: *Not yet.*

The First Magus's disposition, as his peers knew all too well, was as volatile as it was unpredictable. By midmorning the great majority of the magi were aware that the oracular communion had failed, and there was a good deal of restive speculation as to what Vordegh's next move would be. But Vordegh had retired to his apartments immediately after his return from the Marble Hall, leaving instructions that he was not to be disturbed, and by late afternoon no word had come from him.

Then, as the sun was dropping sullenly behind the castle walls, turning the courtyard's black stones to an unhealthy blood red, the First Magus sent for Savrinor.

As usual Vordegh made no greeting and no preamble, but took a single sheet of parchment from his desk and held it out to the historian.

"This edict is to be distributed to all overlords with a demesne of five settlements or more," he said. "Qenever keeps the tithe lists; he or one of his servants will be able to tell you how many such demesnes exist. I shall require all the necessary copies by first light tomorrow."

Savrinor was appalled. All the overlords with a demesne of five settlements . . . That, he realized, could run into hundreds. In consternation he glanced at the document, not taking in its content — that didn't interest him now — and was thankful to see that it was, at least, brief. But the work involved . . .

. Careful to keep the dismay he felt from his voice and his expression, he bowed formally.

"As you say, my lord. I . . . ah . . ."

Vordegh stared at him. "Yes, Master Savrinor? Something troubles you?"

"No, my lord. I merely wonder whether or not the document is a confidential matter. If it is not, then perhaps you might permit me to use some assistants. . . ."

The First Magus gave him a sour, humorless smile. "Your talents are undisputed, Master Savrinor, but I doubt that even you are superhuman. By all means make use of as many assistants as you please; only ensure that they're capable of writing as neatly and clearly as that girl you've recently taken under your wing. Iselia, isn't that the creature's name?"

Savrinor blanched. "Yes, my lord."

"Mmm. Her work is quite competent. But, then, I don't doubt you've schooled her well in that." A chilly light glinted in the depths of his eyes and the smile grew a shade more sardonic. "As in other subjects dear to your heart."

Savrinor ignored the aspersion, knowing that the First Magus expected no less of him. "I'll begin immediately, my lord. The copies will be delivered to you by sunrise as you stipulate."

Verdice, glacially distant as always, ushered him out of the apartments, and Savrinor walked away in the direction of Secretary Qenever's office in the north wing. He didn't entirely like the fact that Vordegh knew Iselia's name and the nature of their relationship, though he wasn't surprised; where intimate knowledge of the castle's petty affairs was concerned, the First Magus could even teach him a lesson or two. But what concerned him more was Vordegh's manner. Savrinor knew as well as anyone else, save perhaps for Verdice and Magus Croin, what had transpired in the Marble Hall during the night. Yet Vordegh had been calm, businesslike, almost *satisfied*. Savrinor felt as though his bones were itching as his intuition worked overtime. Something was afoot. And the document he carried, Vordegh's edict to the overlords, wouldn't explain the half of it.

He waited until he had put a good distance between himself and the First Magus's rooms, then he stepped into a side corridor, where the wall torches hadn't yet been lit for the night and the light was less intrusive though still good enough to read by. Then, quickly, he scanned the parchment he carried.

He was right; the First Magus's message to the overlords didn't tell the half of the whole story. But the little it did tell, and the order it gave, was enough to send a sensation like clutching, deathly hands moving through the marrow of Savrinor's spine.

"Here." With a thin jade stick that he kept for the purpose Savrinor stirred the contents of the cup and held it out to Iselia. She didn't move to take it, and his pale eyes hardened. "My dear, I'd strongly advise you to forget your scruples and drink the damned stuff, if you've half the sense our lord Yandros gave you. The alternative doesn't bear consideration, because if you fall asleep over your work, or smudge one single copy, we'll both answer to the First Magus in person." Then suddenly, surprising her, he shrugged and the combative look fled. "For what little consolation it may be to you, I'm as unwilling as you are to drug myself into another plane of existence at this moment for the sake of duty. But it has to be done."

Iselia's fear that this was some new game Savrinor had devised was allayed, not so much by his words but by his demeanor. She was learning to judge when he was telling the truth and when he wasn't — a valuable new skill — and she had to acknowledge that there was hard sense in his reasoning. She had seen the brown bottle from which he'd mixed this concoction, and knew it was a strong stimulant though not precisely what its effects would be. That made her apprehensive; but if the task was to be completed, as it must be, then she would surely need its help before the night was out.

Slowly, cautiously, Iselia reached out and took the cup. She grimaced at the taste of the potion, which even the best and strongest red wine from the heartlands couldn't disguise, and made herself swallow steadily until the cup was drained. Expecting an immediate effect, she was faintly disappointed to find herself feeling much as usual. Savrinor, understanding, laughed.

"Don't worry. You'll notice the difference soon enough, I assure you. Now: do we have all we need?"

Parchments, pens, ink, sand. She scanned the table quickly and it seemed that her brain made the inventory almost before her eyes could take in what she saw. "Yes, Savrinor."

"And five more diligent scribes only waiting in the next room for our first copy to be taken to them so they, too, may begin." With some judicious use of his "slate" Savrinor had called in a favor or two, and the apartments next to his own had been relinquished for the night, tables set up, and a number of reliable junior clerks coopted into his temporary service. They didn't have the benefit of the historian's drugs, but when the first contingent flagged, there would be a second group ready to take their place. Savrinor wanted to keep himself separate, not to be forced to listen endlessly to the multifold scritch-scratching of nibs and rattle of ink pots, yet with only two doors between them he could make frequent inspections to ensure that all went smoothly. With a flourishing gesture which seemed to imply as much deprecation of the First Magus as of himself, the historian dropped Vordegh's document on the single table that he and Iselia would share. "Well, my dear, there is our commission: make of it what you will. I suggest we begin."

He took his seat on the opposite side of the table and selected a quill from the carved stand set between them. Savrinor was gifted with an eidetic mind and had already committed Vordegh's words accurately to memory, but this was Iselia's first sight of the document. She had brought a scripting book back from the library the previous day and had studied the style of lettering favored by the magi; she wasn't yet fully competent, but she had learned enough to decipher the First Magus's hand. As Savrinor began to write, she looked carefully at the parchment, and her mouth and throat turned arid.

The message read:

Vordegh, supreme magus at the Star Peninsula, commands that the following instructions be carried out forthwith: Twenty-one commoners are to be selected, at random or by lottery, and held in secure captivity. It shall be made widely known that these commoners are hostage against information concerning the identity of any whose loyalty to Chaos and its servants is in doubt, and who may secretly adhere to the demonic heresies of Order. After forty-nine days an emissary of the Chaos riders will collect all reports. If at that time no such information has been received, the captives are to be publicly burned. Any overlord failing to meet this obligation will be instantly dismissed from office.

"Something wrong, my dear?"

Iselia's head came up quickly and sharply. Savrinor was watching her and had seen the expression of horror on her face. His narrow mouth smiled, though the smile wasn't in his eyes.

"Child, if you're shocked by it, then you clearly know little about our First Magus."

"But it's . . ." Her tongue could barely encompass the words. "It's *barbarous.* . . ."

Savrinor reached across the table and laid a forefinger on her lips. "Hush." Though his tone was lazy, it had a deadly serious undercurrent. "You do not, and I repeat do *not,* utter such sentiments within these walls. Not to me, not to yourself, not under any circumstances whatsoever. Do you understand?"

"But — "

"*No.*" His fingernail flicked her lip, hurting her. "Don't dare to argue with me, Iselia! You heard what I said; obey it, or you'll find yourself in dire trouble and I'll be neither able nor willing to help you out of it." He lowered his hand and pointed to the blank sheets before her. "Get on with your work. For both our sakes."

Iselia could taste blood on her lip where he'd scratched her, and she hated him for the petty cruelty of it, but all the same his words, and what lay unspoken beneath them, had gone home. He, too, was disgusted by the edict. She could see it in his eyes and in the angry tightness around his mouth, and she gambled on her judgment.

"But *why* is he doing this, Savrinor?" She took great care to make her voice meek, a little bewildered and helpless. "I don't understand."

He lifted his pale gaze from the table again and regarded her sharply. "Why should you understand? You're not educated to the standards of the magi." But Savrinor's heart wasn't in the barb. In truth he knew perfectly well what Vordegh intended to achieve. The First Magus had no illusions that this stratagem would deliver the sect's elusive leader to the castle trussed and ready for his pleasure; were capture as easy as that, the heretic would have been found and executed long ago. No; Vordegh expected his bluff to be called. Doubtless the overlords would have a stream of reports for the Chaos riders when they arrived, but they'd all be worthless; the product of overeager imaginations or private spites or, most likely of all, the desperate efforts of a hostage's kin to save their relative from the pyre. The First Magus would simply discard the lists unread, knowing that his real objective had been achieved. The heretic leader would remain free, but eddies would be created in the tide of the populace's compliance to their masters' will. Some would be stirred to bitterness against the magi; perhaps even against the gods. But others would direct their hatred toward the man who, however indirectly, was responsible for the pointless deaths of a great many innocent and uninvolved victims. And that, more surely than anything else, would sow the seeds of his betrayal.

Savrinor had views of his own on the wisdom of the First Magus's actions. He was in little doubt that the ploy would work well enough — unless, of course, the magi had grossly underestimated the heretic leader, and that was unlikely. But he had neither the time nor the inclination to explain his thoughts to Iselia. She hadn't the experience or the background to comprehend the workings of the First Magus's mind, and besides, he found the subject distasteful. Savrinor abhorred violence in any form — unless it was directly connected with pleasure, but that was another matter entirely — and this wanton squandering of human lives, even peasant lives, made his stomach curdle.

"The First Magus's actions are none of our concern," he said. "Nor will they be, unless we fail to deliver this commission by dawn."

She lowered her head, taking his meaning, yet still she had to make one more protest. "But the overlords . . . will they obey? Will they *all* obey?"

Savrinor smiled acidly at her naivety. "You mean that some might find their consciences sticking at such an assignment? Well, maybe there are a few. But reread the last sentence of the document, my dear, and ask yourself how the phrase 'dismissed from office' might be interpreted in its broadest sense."

Iselia's face paled, flushed, paled again. "Oh . . . ," she said.

"Quite. Scruples notwithstanding, I don't somehow think that there'll be an overlord willing to invite dismissal, do you?"

She said no more; there was nothing more she could say. They both bent their heads to the work before them, and silence fell but for the sound of their pens and the lethargic crackling of the fire on the far side of the room. But as she wrote, copying the words, adding her own guilty compliance to the evil that was about to be perpetrated, Iselia's mind ran like a millrace on a flooded river. Perhaps it was the drug that brought a hard and terrible clarity to her thoughts, or perhaps her fear was sufficient stimulation in itself, but she knew that the embryonic plans she had made in her brief hours of solitude must now be put into sharper focus. There was no more time for mere thought; she must begin to work in earnest. She'd hoped at first that she might find a way, somehow, to get a message out of the castle, to warn Kaldar and their friends of what was afoot. Now, though, with the lucidity granted her by the drug, she realized that that was irrelevant. Her friends would need no warning; they'd learn of this all too soon and nothing she could say or do would make any difference to them. She had other work to do, and it must be done here in the castle. And, though he didn't know it, Savrinor had opened a new door to her tonight, which might prove to be invaluable. . . .

CHAPTER XIX

Savrinor personally delivered the completed copies of the edict to Vordegh an hour before dawn. Returning to the apartments, where Iselia still sat at the table, he said only, "He's satisfied," before stalking into the inner room and slamming the door behind him.

Iselia watched the door warily, unsure whether he would re-emerge and demand her presence. There were muffled sounds on the far side, as though Savrinor were venting an ill mood on inanimate objects, but after a few minutes all was silent. Iselia made herself count to a hundred and then, satisfied that he'd want nothing of her until he had had a few hours' sleep, she rose and crossed to the cupboard. He had left the key on the table; she unlocked the door, wincing at the click, tiny though it was, as the lock turned, then swung the door open and looked at the array of phials and bottles and jars. The cupboard's contents were meticulously labeled; she found the brown bottle after only a few moments and measured what she hoped was the correct dose into a cup. Her mind and body ached for sleep, but sleep was out of the question. She had work to do.

With only a splash of wine in the cup, the drug tasted vile and she gagged, only just stopping herself from spitting out the mouthful. But at last it went down, and she moved back to the table, stifling a yawn and not permitting herself to so much as look at the couch on the far side of the room, which in the early days had been her own bed. The stimulant would soon begin to revive her and then all would be well.

While Savrinor was out she had fetched a shawl from the bedchamber and now wrapped it around herself, pulling a fold over her fair hair. Then she picked up flint, tinder, and a candle, quietly left the room, and started along the corridor, thankful that she was at last beginning to learn her way about the castle. There was a shortcut to the courtyard by a back staircase; she skimmed down the steps and let herself out through a small door. An involuntary shiver made her skin creep as she stepped outside, partly because of the chilly night air but prompted more by the courtyard itself, stark and black and empty under thin starlight. She could hear the sea, a faint but constant murmur with a faintly sinister undertone, but nothing moved in the gloom, and the great building's myriad windows were unlit, only the occasional glimmer of a corridor witch light reflecting here and there from within. Iselia thrust down an irrational desire to light her candle and, shivering again and pulling the shawl more closely about herself as though it could protect her, hurried across the black flagstones toward the library door.

She did light the candle when she reached the spiral stairs winding down into the castle's bowels. Teeth clenched and shadow eddying and darting before her, she made the descent and entered the deserted vault. Here, her one shadow suddenly became fifty as tables, benches, pillars, and shelves all took on new and disturbing forms in the unsteady candlelight. With the second dose of the stimulant beginning to take effect, Iselia's heart was pounding suffocatingly under her ribs, and her imagination threatened to run amok in this eerie atmosphere. She took a mental grip on herself, whispered a soft litany to give her courage, and closed the door behind her, shutting herself in with the formless, silent dark. Holding the candle high she moved to the nearest bank of shelves and began to search. There — a herbalers' compendium which she had seen Savrinor consulting on another occasion. Iselia took it from its place and carried it to the nearest table. She didn't want to remove it from the library; what she sought should take no more than an hour or so to find. But she had slipped some scraps of paper and a small stick of charcoal into her reticule earlier; if need be she could make notes for further study later. . . .

She drew the candle nearer, opened the book, and began to read.

***

She was absorbed in her reading and had no idea how much time had passed when the click of the door latch brought her head up with a startled jolt. The light of a lantern scuttered across the floor, and the seamed face of an elderly man looked at her in surprise and consternation.

"Oh . . . I beg pardon." He peered at her myopically, clearly uncertain of her rank. "I'm to dust the shelves. . . ."

Iselia stood up, shutting the book with a snap and pushing her notes out of sight beneath it. "Yes," she said, her voice not quite steady. "I'd just finished; I shall leave you to do your work uninterrupted."

Perhaps it was her accent or perhaps the haste with which she'd risen alerted him, but she realized that the man had suddenly placed her as someone of little importance. His mouth pursed and he said, though still not quite certain and thus still carefully, "Beg pardon again, but . . . do you have sanction to be here?"

Briefly, unbidden, the memory of Verdice came into Iselia's mind and she almost wished she could dismiss the man with that same cold hauteur. But she was not Verdice and she only smiled.

"I am Iselia, amanuensis to Historian Savrinor, and I have his sanction."

"Ah." The servant made a compliant gesture. "I did not realize . . . of course, of course." He watched her as she returned the compendium to the shelves, noting how beneath the apparent poise her face had an unhealthy pallor and her eyes seemed overbright, the pupils dilated, yet with dark shadows like bruises in the skin beneath. She came back, passing him on her way to the door. As her hand touched the latch he cleared his throat.

"I would . . . ah . . . advise care crossing the courtyard."

"Care?" She looked at him, not comprehending.

"The . . . ah . . ." He waved a hand vaguely toward the ceiling. "The magi are above. An edict to be dispatched, I believe; the Maze is being opened." A delicate cough. "At such times it doesn't please them to be troubled by . . . well, by . . ."

Abruptly Iselia felt a sharp twinge of fellow feeling for the elderly servant. How long had he lived here, she wondered, serving under the magi's yoke? Was he another like her, snatched from home and family without right of protest, probably more years ago now than he could remember?

She smiled at him. "By underlings like you and me? I understand your meaning. Thank you. You're very kind to have warned me."

He blinked, then returned the smile. "I merely thought you might not be aware of the protocols. You're very young. . . ."

She felt old, weary and old, but she didn't say so, only nodded. "I'll take care. Thank you again."

Her candle was all but burned away now and flickering its last, but as she started to climb the stairs she realized that day had dawned and there was enough light filtering down from the outside world to show her way. Twice she glanced back; then, when she was certain she must be out of earshot of the old man below, she gathered up her skirts and started to run up the steps three at a time.

Iselia emerged into the bloodred light of early morning. The sky was cloudless and the upper edge of the sun's crimson disk was just showing above the high eastward wall. On the castle's south side the great gates in the barbican arch stood open, and a number of people were grouped nearby. She knew several of the magi by sight now, and recognized Croin, Pirane, and a tall, hawk-faced and reputedly violent sorcerer named Menniam among the group, while a servant stood at a deferential distance, holding a stack of parchments. The edict . . . The First Magus had wasted no time, it seemed.

She was about to make her way as unobtrusively as possible along the stoa, hoping to slip into the castle undetected, when movement by the main doors made her freeze where she stood and she saw Vordegh himself emerge onto the steps. Sparely elegant and modestly dressed, in sharp contrast to most of his peers, he stood watching the gathering, a faint smile on his face. Croin saw him and touched Menniam's arm; the tall sorcerer turned and bowed.

"All is ready, First Magus. The Maze is open and we await only your choice of messengers."

Vordegh nodded acknowledgment, then without any show or flourish raised his arm and spoke five words in a strange and ugly language. Instantly the courtyard flashed into utter darkness. Iselia bit her tongue, reeling back in shock as blackness seemed to crash down on her like a wall falling — then it was gone and the daylight stabbed back with renewed brilliance.

And she heard something grunting.

It was a hideous sound, deep and malevolent and menacing, and growing louder with every moment. It seemed to have no one source but to be echoing from the air all about her. Or if not from the air, then —

Iselia clamped a hand over her mouth to stop herself from gagging as suddenly she saw them. They were coming out of the walls, forming from the stonework and taking on repulsive form as they flowed groundward. They had the look of black pigs but were too horrible to be mortal animals; their fleshy bodies quivered with an unnatural and brutish power, their black hides glowed evilly; and from the snouts in their great, misshapen heads they foamed and slavered, showing mouthfuls of decayed yellow fangs like daggers. One erupted from the wall close by where Iselia was huddling, and she had a moment's appalling glimpse of tiny, glittering white eyes beneath pulsing membranes as the monstrosity went snorting and drooling past her. A stench of corruption erupted across the courtyard as the first of the gruesome herd reached the ground; then in their dozens, in their hundreds, they were streaming toward the castle gates. The hapless servant cringed away in terror; with a swift movement Magus Menniam snatched his bundle of documents and stood ready to meet the oncoming horrors. As they passed him, each snatched a parchment and swallowed it. Then, like a foul, dark tide, they raced under the arch and out into the gory sunlight, where the Maze stood ready to receive them and transport them to their destinations.

Iselia heard the grumble and creak of the huge mechanism inside the barbican tower as the gates ground slowly shut once more, but she couldn't look. She had dropped to her knees, her face pressed against one of the stoa pillars and her hands clutching at its smooth surface as though it were her only link with sanity. Her stomach heaved and heaved, but somehow by a miracle of self-control she forced herself not to vomit. The stench was passing, that dire grunting noise had faded. They were gone, she told herself. They were *gone*.

She had never before witnessed the magi's sorcery. Oh, she had *imagined* it. But the reality . . . She couldn't stop shivering. It had been so effortless, so *careless*. Five words, to conjure such horrors out of nowhere. . . . For the first time she found herself beginning to comprehend just what order of power she and her fellow disciples of Aeoris were setting themselves against.

Voices carried across the courtyard as the magi walked back toward the main doors. They sounded so nonchalant; she heard laughter, and a woman's voice made a comment about the pleasant weather. A shiver of green light passed across her and from high above came a brief snap of energy as a last burst of the power the First Magus had employed was dissipated between two of the spires. Slowly and shakily Iselia raised her head and pulled herself upright, then drew further back behind the pillar to wait until the magi had gone. Her pulse was running perilously fast and her mind, goaded perhaps by the second dose of the drug, couldn't banish the memory of the hideous black pigs and the manner in which they had materialized. But she was calmer now, her resolve beginning to return at last. Very well, she told herself; very *well*. She had seen something of Vordegh's skills now, and though what she had witnessed was frightening, and doubtless a petty show by the magi's standards, it was *information*, another piece of fuel for her fire. She must be positive, not allow herself to be daunted. And she must waste no more time but begin her private studies and work at them hard, harder than she had ever thought to do in her life before.

The last of the magi had disappeared through the double doors. Iselia raised both hands to her face, pressing the tips of her fingers together and touching them to her lips. Silently she mouthed a fervent prayer: *"Lord Aeoris, lend me strength if you can!"* Then she left the shelter of the stoa and started at a run across the courtyard, toward the small entrance and the back stairs and the security of Savrinor's rooms.

Alerted by the sudden quick movement below, a pair of green eyes watched Iselia hurry across the courtyard and vanish through the side door, and Andraia raised her elegant eyebrows in a mixture of surprise and curiosity. Little Lady Purity . . . Now, what business might *she* have alone in the library at this hour of the morning? Not Savrinor's business if Andraia was any judge, for Savrinor must by now be soundly asleep after his night's exertions. As Iselia should have been, too. Unless she had some more personal concern to attend to? . . .

Andraia filed the small piece of intelligence away in her mind for later consideration, and turned back into the room behind her.

"Pigs," she said equably.

"What?" Puzzled gray eyes looked back at her from the disordered bed, and Benetan sat up.

"I said, pigs." She glided back to him and sprawled full length on the coverlet, reaching out to tug at a strand of his loosened hair. "Or as near to pigs as anyone could judge from this distance. That's what he chose as his couriers. He conjured them out of the walls, and they each swallowed a message before they all went streaking out through the Maze. They're a very original form of messenger — they'll put the fear of Yandros into the overlords when they materialize in their strongholds and spit out their parchments. I'm impressed by the First Magus's imagination."

Benetan hadn't wanted to watch the couriers going out. Perhaps it was yet another legacy of his lowly birth, but he found occult matters disquieting, in spite of the fact that, as a Chaos rider, he used them himself; and many of the magi's practices made him downright queasy. He had resisted all Andraia's attempts to persuade him to the window, but all the same he gave private thanks that she was in an ebullient mood this morning after the tentative and difficult evening which had led to their cautious reconciliation. Notwithstanding their hot-blooded and impassioned lovemaking last night he still felt that he wasn't entirely forgiven, and in all honesty he couldn't blame Andria for still harboring mistrust. But although it had taken days of planning on his part and three sharp rejections on hers, at least the first hurdle was overcome; and, being Andraia, even if she didn't feel inclined to forgive his transgressions she was likely as not to forget them before too long.

He slid a hand beneath the flimsy robe which was her only garment, and caressed her while she nibbled at the muscle of his upper arm. "I'd be more interested to know the nature of the message than the nature of the messengers."

"Doubtless you'll find out soon enough, if it concerns your riders in any way."

"I know. In a sense that's what worries me. Life has almost been *too* quiet for us these last few days. I can't help wondering why, or wondering what might lie in store when the hiatus is over."

Andraia nipped him, hard, then sat up with a sigh, pushing impatient hands through the mass of her hair. "Oh, Benet, you're so *tiresome* sometimes. You worry about things that have happened, then you worry about things that haven't happened, and when you can find nothing to worry about at all, you invent something! I don't know why I tolerate you."

He rubbed at his arm, which bore her teeth marks in twin red crescents. Her tone along with the severity of the bite had warned him that her temper still wasn't entirely settled, and he said hastily, "I'm sorry, my love, I'm sorry. But . . ."

She looked at him over her shoulder, a little hostile. "But what?"

"Oh . . . it isn't of any consequence. Just something Savrinor said the other day."

"Savrinor?"

"Mmm. I encountered him on his way to the First Magus's apartments with a report he'd been preparing, and he made a comment about the riders and Lord Vordegh's future plans."

"Well, what of it? It would be more of a surprise if a good number of Lord Vordegh's plans *didn't* include you. Besides, if I know Savrinor, he was probably under the influence of a cauldron's worth of drugs and couldn't even have been trusted to tell you what time of day it was."

Benetan opened his mouth to protest at that, but had the wisdom to stop himself in time. Andraia knew Savrinor only slightly and, like many others in the castle, her view of him was subjective and largely inaccurate. No, Savrinor's mind had been working as shrewdly as ever on that wet, dismal morning, but Benetan couldn't explain the nature of their conversation to Andraia or make her understand the fear, unspoken since that one brief encounter, that he and the historian shared. Besides, he recalled suddenly, he had made Savrinor a promise that not a word of what had passed between them would ever be repeated to another living soul.

But then he'd broken that promise once already. . . .

Andraia's mood was softening again and she stretched out once more and began idly to tickle his feet under the bedclothes. With an effort Benetan hauled his mind out of its dark vault. He was trying to think of a happier topic to turn to when she said,

"If you're really so set on finding out what was in the message, I could always ask Father."

That took Benetan completely by surprise, and his astonishment was reflected in his voice. "Your father knows?" he said.

"I imagine so. After all, Savrinor went to him for a list of the over-lords and their demesnes yesterday, and there must be a connection." She released his toes and slid under the blankets beside him. "I'll be your spy and ask him for you. But later." Her hands began to explore. "*Much* later."

Secretary Qenever was, as always, delighted to see his daughter, and was easily persuaded to leave his office and take lunch with her in the dining hall. But he also her knew well enough to be aware that she was motivated by more than the desire for his company, and when she casually mentioned the First Magus's edict his suspicions were confirmed. It was the unlikeliest topic for Andraia to take an interest in, but by the time she had phrased an oblique question or two, Qenever understood. The Chaos riders. Of course, her concern was for that young captain she was so inexplicably enamored with, Bene-tan Liss. Qenever didn't approve of her long-running liaison with an inferior who wasn't even castle bred, but he knew better than to voice his disapproval in Andraia's presence. Besides, she was old enough to make her own mistakes. All the same her inquiries, and what lay be-hind them, gave Qenever the embryo of an idea. He had been sum-moned to a brief interview with the First Magus two days previously, and Vordegh had let drop an enlightening hint about the next stage of his plans. Nothing concrete as yet, of course; that wasn't Vordegh's way. But enough, perhaps, to be useful.

"Oh, indeed," he said in answer to his daughter's apparently care-less interest. "There'll be work in plenty for your young paramour and his men." He paused. "One commission in particular might have . . . well, let us say it might have interesting ramifications for whoever is deployed to carry it out."

Andraia was instantly alert. "Ramifications?"

Qenever shrugged. "It's a matter of pure speculation at the mo-ment. And naturally it isn't for the ears of anyone who won't be in-volved — "

"Of course," she said, her eyes avid. "But you know you can trust *me*, Father. Do tell me. I'm greatly interested."

He disguised a faint smile by pretending to clear his throat. "Well,

I think — and only *think*, mark you — that if the First Magus's strategy goes according to plan, he may soon have a special assignment for one reliable man. It goes without saying that whoever is chosen will earn Lord Vordegh's favor, not to mention a considerable rise in status, if he is successful."

He saw immediately that the ruse had worked. Andraia was perfectly well aware of his attitude toward her lover and had striven, though unsuccessfully so far, to change it. Now, with two key phrases, he had offered her the perfect opportunity to win him round. "Lord Vordegh's favor" and "a considerable rise in status" would, as Andraia saw it, elevate Benetan to a position which her father considered worthy of her. The bait was irresistible, and she snapped it up.

"Father." She leaned forward, one hand clasping his arm. "If Lord Vordegh needs a skilled man, a man who can be trusted to carry out this commission and not fail . . ." Then her voice trailed off as her pride suddenly rebelled. She couldn't importune him. It was undignified and shameful; he'd despise her for trying and her purpose would be wrecked before it could even take form.

But it seemed she had stopped herself in time, for Qenever was gazing across the hall, his brows knitting meditatively.

"You're suggesting that Benetan Liss might be an appropriate choice?" He spoke as though the idea hadn't previously occurred to him.

"No — or at least, I — " Andraia licked her lips uneasily. "I'm not *suggesting* it, no. But if the First Magus wants the best . . ."

"Then you believe Benetan Liss is the best. Yes, I suppose that's only natural, though I think you know that I don't entirely agree with you."

"You might agree with me," Andraia said with marked delicacy, "if Benetan had the chance to prove himself."

Qenever smiled fondly at her. "I can't deny that, my dear, and I do understand your desire to have my sanction. Indeed, I'm flattered by it — so few young people seem to care at all for their parents' opinions that I take your concern as a great personal compliment. And perhaps you have a point; perhaps the young man hasn't yet been given the chance to show his full mettle. You obviously see qualities in him which escape me, but my judgment isn't infallible and I'm willing to be persuaded by the evidence. Even a peasant is entitled to that courtesy."

Andraia bristled. "Benet is no longer a peasant!"

"Of course not, my sweet. If you say so." Qenever made an apologetic, peaceable gesture, aware that the calculated slur had only strengthened her determination, which was exactly what he had desired.

She subsided. "Then you'll — "

"Ah, no." He cut off her question before she could utter it. "If you want someone to help you influence the First Magus, then I'm afraid you must look elsewhere. Not because I don't want to help you," he added, seeing her about to flare up, "but simply because I'm unlikely to have any involvement with the endeavor; it's not within my sphere. Besides, Lord Vordegh may change his mind; as I said, the idea's barely been mooted, and you must say nothing to anyone about it, least of all to Benetan Liss." He paused. "But if, and I say only *if*, such a commission is to be awarded, the man likely to know the details will of course be Savrinor."

"Savrinor . . ." Yes, of course, that made sense in more ways than one. As the castle's chief archivist Savrinor would have an official role — and unofficially, his ear for information was legendary.

Andraia stood up, leaned across the table, and planted a kiss fully and firmly on Qenever's lips. "Thank you, Father," she said. "You've given me just the help I needed." Her eyes glinted warmly but with a combative edge. "I'll speak to Savrinor. And as for Benet — well, we'll soon see whose judgment is right, won't we?"

There was satisfaction in Qenever's eyes as he watched her stride ebulliently from the hall. He thought it unlikely that Savrinor would refuse to help her, for when she set her mind to it Andria could charm birds from the trees and the historian's susceptibility to beautiful women was well known. And Savrinor might well be the ideal medium for a solution to his own long-standing dilemma. There was no doubt that Benetan Liss would be an excellent and able candidate for the proposed mission, and with Qenever's and Savrinor's endorsement to add weight it was quite likely that the First Magus would choose him. Benetan would then be absent from the castle for a good length of time. Long enough, Qenever judged, for Andraia to grow tired of waiting for him to return and to begin to look elsewhere for her diversions. Then, with a little luck, this infatuation would become a thing of the past and she would find a new paramour, better suited to her station and breeding. It might take a little subtle manipulation on his own part, but that was a small matter, and no more than any devoted father would do for his only child.

All in all, Qenever thought, this had been a very productive hour's work.

Though patience didn't come naturally to her, Andraia was subtle enough to bide her time and wait until she could judge the ideal moment to speak to Savrinor. Before she could find such a moment, though, one event created ugly ripples in the castle's quiet hiatus, like a stone cast into a still pool.

Ornath, mother of the ill-fated baby, had been placed in the care of Physician Revian, partly because Magus Croin was discomfited by the prospect of continuing to attend her in the circumstances and partly because it was thought that Revian, as cousin to the dead child's father, might be better placed to offer her comfort. Four days after the dispatch of Vordegh's edict to the overlords, Revian made his regular morning visit and pronounced Ornath fit to leave her bed. She nodded, thanked him with quiet courtesy, then when he had gone asked her servant to lay out her best day gown and leave her to dress in private. The servant returned after an hour to find the apartments empty, the gown gone, and the bed neatly made, with Ornath's night robe folded tidily on the pillow. Relieved that her mistress seemed to be taking the bereavement so well, she turned her attention to other business and thought no more of it until, some two further hours later, word began to circulate that Ornath was missing from the castle.

Then the servant remembered that she had found the bedchamber window wide open, and that her mistress's apartments were on the north side of the castle, directly overlooking the stack's edge and the huge, vertiginous drop to the sea.

A search party led by Revian found Ornath just before the incoming tide could claim her. At first sight she looked as though she had merely fainted on the shingle at the foot of the stack, falling forward to lie between two small rock outcrops. Revian, though, knew better, and when he steeled himself to turn her over even his training and experience couldn't stop him recoiling in revulsion from the mad, dead stare of the eyes in the smashed crimson mask which had been her face, or from the coiling, bloody wetness spilling onto the stones where her body had burst on impact.

Revian refused to have her carried back up the stack's internal stairway. Instead, he sent one of his party to break the news in the castle and fetch a magus to conduct the proper funeral rite. Pirane came, and with her, looking haggard and sick, was Savrinor, obliged by his archivist's duty to witness and record the tragedy. Her eyes hard as gemstones and her voice peculiarly gentle, Pirane spoke the Elegy of Passing and commended the dead woman's soul into the peace of oblivion and absorption with Chaos, while Savrinor stood a little way apart, one hand covering his face and his lips moving in profound prayer. The corpse was wrapped in linen and given to the sea, and all stood watching in silence until the swell of the tide carried the bundle from their view. No one uttered a word on the long climb back to the castle.

In his rooms, Savrinor wrote his account of the episode in a flat and prosaic tone quite unlike his customary style, then opened his cupboard and mixed himself a fearsome concoction of drugs that would guarantee his brain several hours of oblivion. Iselia was missing from the apartments but he felt no curiosity at her absence, only relief that she wouldn't see him in this sorry condition. A lesser servant was sent to file the new document in the archives, then Savrinor went to his inner chamber and fell to his knees beside the bed, hiding his face in crossed arms on the coverlet. He had said it once, he'd found the words and made the plea, but he had to give voice to it again; it was boiling and raging in him like a fire burning in his stomach and he couldn't quench it.

"Lord Yandros, sweet Lord Yandros!" His voice was no louder than a whisper, but the mind behind the voice was screaming. *"I know this isn't what you want of us! Not pointless sacrifice, not needless death — this isn't your way! Help me, my lord; help me to understand! I truly believe that our First Magus is committing an outrage against your will; but without your word, how can I be sure? I implore you, great Yandros, if I'm worthy to be Chaos's servant, show me the truth!"*

Even as he uttered the last words, Savrinor felt a surge of self-denigrating despair. Of course Yandros wouldn't answer him. Why should he? What was Savrinor in Chaos's great scheme? Just one life, one spark in a vast bonfire. The fact that the great god had deigned to speak to him at the inauguration revels was indicative of nothing, and if he believed otherwise, then he was a deluded and arrogant fool.

Clumsily, coordination failing him, Savrinor got to his feet. His mind was already fogging from the effects of the drugs and he couldn't continue to pray to the gods and trust his prayers to make any sense. *Damn the First Magus,* he thought savagely. *Damn Croin, damn Revian, damn them all. . . .*

The small, ornate table beside the bed held a tray, and on the tray was a flagon of something — wine, mead, he didn't know and didn't care. It made a comforting liquid sound when he shook it, and unsteadily Savrinor filled the unwashed cup beside the flagon before tipping the cup to his mouth. He drained it, and went on refilling and draining until he'd finished the flagon's contents to the last drop. Though he was an expert at holding his liquor, his head spun as he lay down on the bed. Sleep came quickly, dreamless and blissful sleep, and Savrinor slid into it with tears glinting on the drawn skin of his face.

And in another place, another dimension, apart from and incomprehensible to any human mind, eyes like animate emeralds gazed from a fine-etched face, not seeing Savrinor's especial anguish but aware on some subliminal level of a faint disturbance in the warp and weft of the physical world. In his Chaotic homeland Tarod watched as a scene took form, water sliding by under the parapet of a stone bridge, and recalled his most recent conversation with Yandros. His great brother believed that matters on the mortal plane would resolve themselves to Chaos's satisfaction without need for the gods' intervention. Tarod couldn't gainsay that, couldn't claim a deeper insight than Yandros possessed. That wasn't the way of Chaos. But whatever knowledge and experience might dictate, he couldn't entirely banish the shifting maggot of disquiet that moved within his psyche.

And he knew that a maggot, if left alone to do its work, was as likely as not to destroy the host that had given it life.

CHAPTER XX

It was not the custom to observe an official period of mourning for the departed, but Ornath's death stirred profound grief among all the castle-dwellers . . . or almost all. Only the First Magus was unmoved. Though he knew all there was to know of the tragedy, he was clearly indifferent to it and showed not the smallest sign of sorrow or regret. His attitude cast a further blight on the castle; people were subdued, unwilling to show their own sadness too publicly and less willing still to discuss the matter in any detail. And if many were privately angered by their ruler's indifference, they took care to keep their feelings well hidden.

No one was surprised when Physician Revian's young cousin, Ornath's lover and the father of the child, sent a stilted, formal request to the council of magi for permission to leave the castle. The matter was not brought to the First Magus's attention; Croin and another elder sent word that permission was granted, and the young man departed, accompanied by one servant, on the following day. What he intended to do and whether he would ever return to the Star Peninsula were questions about which many speculated but no one spoke. He'd said nothing of his intentions, and — beyond the obvious protocols of sympathy proffered — it would not have been in good taste for even his close friends to probe further unless invited. And the bereaved man's face and demeanor made it clear that no such invitation would be forthcoming.

But some days after his departure the shock and sorrow inevitably began to fade. Life returned to normal, and Vordegh, uninterested in and possibly even unaware of the scars that remained, waited calmly for the arrival of the overlords' responses to his edict. He had calculated the likely interval precisely, and, as always, his calculation was accurate. So when the first messages reached the castle the next stage of his strategy was prepared and ready, save for one detail, to be brought into play. And when he received word that the First Magus wished to consult him concerning the selection of a secular agent, Secretary Qenever remembered his promise and spoke, briefly and discreetly, to Andraia.

Benetan was away from the castle, having taken a detachment of his younger recruits to the mainland for a day's schooling in horsemanship, and so Andraia was able to call on Savrinor without any need to resort to subterfuge. The historian was taken aback when he opened the door of his apartments and saw his visitor, and he smiled, making no attempt to hide his curiosity.

"Lady Andraia. This is a *very* unexpected pleasure."

Andraia returned the smile with caution. "Master Savrinor. I hope this is not an inconvenient time to call on you, but I would greatly appreciate your advice on a . . . well, a business matter."

Savrinor made a moue of disappointment. "Ah, and I thought for a moment that perhaps you wanted the pleasure of my company. A pity, but I must be stoical." Another smile seemed to imply that he was teasing, but she couldn't be entirely sure. "The time's perfectly convenient. Please, come in."

She entered and looked curiously about the room, which she had never seen before. There was a woman's touch in evidence, she thought, small things, but unmistakable. As Savrinor closed the door she said, "Your protégée is not here?"

"Iselia? She's in the library, I believe." He indicated a chair and waited until she sat down before crossing to his cabinet. "She spends a great deal of time there, studying to improve herself." A pause. "Her absence, I presume, is an advantage?"

"It is."

"Mmm. You'll take some wine?" He didn't wait for her to reply but poured a cup and gave it to her. Andraia sipped for a few moments, then, telling herself that there was nothing to be gained from equivocation, said:

"Savrinor, this matter does concern the girl — Iselia — after a fashion." She met his gaze with something of an effort. "You'll recall, I don't doubt, our last meeting, in the library, and the advice you gave me then."

"Certainly." Savrinor smiled. "And I'm glad to hear that you and Benetan have been reconciled. If you'll forgive the presumption, I like to think I had some small hand in it."

"You did, and I'm grateful." Andraia was glad to find that he wasn't mocking her as she'd half expected. "However, the — cure, so to speak, isn't entirely complete yet. Or if it is, I think it might be prudent to make absolutely certain of it. So . . . I hope you'll not think me importunate or audacious, but I have a favor to ask of you. A great favor."

Savrinor sat down and regarded her keenly. "Ask it. If it's within my power, I'm at your service."

A little haltingly and more than a little defensively she told him of the hint her father had dropped, and of her scheme to secure the commission for Benetan. "I think you must agree that he would be an admirable choice," she finished. "And with your own and my father's recommendations to support him, the First Magus would be far more likely to look favorably on the idea."

Savrinor raised his eyebrows. "I think you overestimate my influence."

"No," Andraia countered. "I don't think I do — if you should choose to use it."

"Ah. And there we come to the nub, don't we? What motivation is there for a self-seeker like me to make this recommendation?" Suddenly, softly, he laughed. "Andraia, you are extremely cunning, and I hope you'll take that as a high compliment, because it's intended as one. You have very neatly turned my own self-righteous lecture back on me, and put me in a position where I can't possibly refuse your request without damning myself as an unrepentant hypocrite!" Mischief glinted in his eyes then. "If, of course, the commission actually exists and is more than just a rumor."

Andraia returned his look coquettishly. "I think you know the answer to that better than I do."

He didn't rise to the bait. "Let's agree for the time being to say *if*, shall we? Very well. I'll be delighted to put Benetan's name forward to the First Magus. As you say, he'll be an excellent choice on his own merits anyway, and a little time spent away from the castle will blow away any lingering cobwebs and fully restore his sense of perspective." He set his cup down. "I presume you haven't yet mentioned this to him?"

"To Benetan? Oh, no."

"Good. I'd strongly advise you not to give him even the smallest hint. After all, we don't want him to form the impression that his two most affectionate friends are manipulating him, do we? Even if it is for his own good."

"And for ours."

"Quite. Well, then, dear Andraia, you may leave the matter safely in my hands."

She rose. "Thank you, Savrinor." She smiled. "I'm in your debt twice over."

Savrinor laughed. "The debt is mutual — though if you graciously insist, I'll mark it on my tally slate and call in a favor or two from you at some time in the future." He gave her a long, assessing look, making no attempt to hide his appreciation of what he saw. "The gods must be exceedingly fond of Benetan; he doesn't deserve you. One of these days I must learn the secret of his success. . . . Good-bye, Andraia."

Andraia was surprised to find herself blushing, but not altogether displeased. She reveled in compliments, the more so if they came from charming and handsome men. This meeting, brief though it had been, had altered her view of Savrinor.

She said, "I'll remember you in my prayers."

For a moment Savrinor thought she was being flippant; then suddenly he realized the promise was quite serious. And he, in his turn, began to further revise his view of Andraia. . . .

He was at his desk when Iselia returned. She came in weighed down by several large volumes from the library, and stopped, surprised to see him.

"Savrinor . . . I thought you would be in the dining hall."

Savrinor had in fact intended to go to the hall, to enjoy a leisurely meal and catch up on any new gossip, but Andraia's visit had altered his plans.

"Did you, now?" He set his pen aside, leaning back in his chair and smiling at her. "I'm so sorry to disappoint you, my dear."

"Disappoint me?" She was puzzled.

"What? You mean you *weren't* planning a secret revel while my back was turned? Well, well. Clearly my tutelary efforts have been remiss. I must do better!"

Iselia looked at him warily. His moods had been more unpredictable than usual since the unhappy affair of the suicide some days ago, his temper often on a dangerous knife edge, but she had the distinct impression that there was no dark twist underlying this mood. He was simply cheerful, and it disconcerted her.

Savrinor beckoned lazily. "Come here. I see you've been borrowing books from the archives again. Come and show me what you've brought to enlighten your mind with this time."

Iselia was dismayed; since she'd plucked up the courage to begin taking books to the apartments to read in greater detail, he'd never once showed an interest in her choice. Anxious that he shouldn't see her unease, she said nothing, only approached and set the books down on the desk. Savrinor looked at them in turn. "A lexicon . . . very diligent, though this isn't one of the best. A herbal . . . Mmm." Then his expression changed. "Fador's *Compendium of the Stimulant Properties*? What in the Seven Hells do you want with that?"

Iselia swallowed as though something were caught in her throat. "I . . . ah . . . I thought . . ."

"Look at me. Closer." Suddenly he was on his feet, hands gripping her shoulders as he stared hard into her eyes. "Ah yes. Ah yes, I begin to *see*." Abruptly he released her. "So you've been experimenting, have you? I thought the stocks in my cupboard were getting inexplicably low."

"Please, Savrinor," Iselia said in a small voice, "don't be angry with me. I only wanted . . ." She swallowed again, then, as though with a great and brave effort, met his gaze. "I wanted to please you. I wanted not only to do my work well, but to learn and better myself so that you wouldn't find me lacking." A hint of tears glittered on her lashes. "There simply weren't enough hours in the day for everything, and I was becoming so *tired*. . . ."

Her timid confession took Savrinor completely by surprise, but suddenly he saw logic to the pattern. Hours of work, further hours of study . . . yes, she *was* diligent. Too diligent for her stamina to stand the strain without help. He'd told her that himself, on more than one occasion. And, he recalled, it was entirely his doing that had started her on this road. . . .

Iselia put out a tentative hand and touched his breast, her fingers moving gently. Her gaze was cast down now as she said, "And there were my other duties . . . the other ways in which I hoped to please you. . . ."

There was no trace of suggestiveness in her voice but Savrinor knew exactly what she meant. Emotions moved sharply in him and he half turned away.

"Don't cry, damn it! I can't abide weeping women!"

"I'm sorry," she whispered.

His teeth clenched. "And stop apologizing. You're not at fault; I am. Here." He took a kerchief from a neat and newly laundered selection on the desk and pushed it at her. "Dry your eyes, or you'll make yourself ugly and that *won't* please me." He waited until she finished dabbing her face, then turned to look at her again. His composure was restored. "Now. What have you been taking? Is it the stimulant I gave you to see you through the First Magus's commission, the one from the brown bottle?"

She nodded.

"Anything else?"

"No. Not . . . not yet." She glanced nervously at the *Compendium* and he sighed.

"Have you read that?"

Iselia shook her head.

"Well, perhaps you should have done, because it would have told you something which the lesser tracts don't mention; that the potion you've been taking is highly addictive. It's distilled from a seaweed called the Moonwrack — a very interesting process in fact, though that's hardly relevant now — and it doesn't take long to become dependent on it." His mouth curled cynically. "I speak from experience."

"It's only been a few days," Iselia said uneasily. "Perhaps five doses, or six."

Savrinor regarded her thoughtfully. "When did you take the most recent?"

"Early this morning."

He calculated the time that had elapsed. "And do you feel in need of more?"

The quick flush of her cheeks told him the answer without the need for words. Savrinor shrugged. "Well, it seems my warning has come a little late." He hesitated. "You probably still have time to reject the habit. There'll be discomfort for a while but it'll pass, provided you don't give way to temptation again."

"Is that what you want me to do?"

His gaze held hers. "The choice is entirely yours, Iselia. I may have possession of your body, but I don't claim to own your soul. That, as with all of us, is our lord Yandros's privilege."

She saw something in his eyes before he turned away from her then, something he was unwilling to express more overtly. Again, and with more confidence now, she reached out and touched him lightly.

"But if I were to ask you . . . not as my master, but as my friend . . ."

"Oh, gods . . . I'd still say the choice is yours to make. But I might add that there are times when life's little trials" — an image, unbidden and unwanted, of Ornath's corpse flashed across his inner vision, and with it the memory of the First Magus's edict — "can be greatly alleviated by some outside help."

Iselia didn't answer that. He felt her walk away, heard the key of the cupboard door click, but didn't look round. Silence then for perhaps a minute, before the sound of wine splashing into cups broke the quiet.

She came back and slid one of the cups into his hand, keeping the other for herself. They didn't speak as they drank, and Savrinor tasted the sharp edge of the Moonwrack she had added to the wine. Strong, very strong. If this was the dosage she had been taking, little wonder that she'd made the decision she had, and though he didn't like himself for thinking it, that gave Savrinor a sense of obscure pleasure. If one was to be damned, it was better to be damned in company than alone.

Iselia sipped steadily from her own cup. She'd suspected the truth about the drug's effects long before Savrinor had confirmed it, for the cravings as each dose wore off were already beginning to increase. No matter; no matter. Whatever damage it might do and however dependent she might become on it, the price was worth paying for the solitary and private hours it granted her; time to be spent in study and planning. And, unlike Savrinor, she allowed herself no other serious indulgence. There were other herbs, she'd lied to him about that; in particular those she'd discovered that numbed her mind and sometimes her body to the demands he made on her; but they were only simples with no lasting effects. Savrinor, on the other hand, had needs far beyond mere stimulants. She had watched him, noted names and dosages, read books and documents, and memorized vital details. His back had been turned to her as she measured out the potion they were sharing, so he was unaware of the other drugs — tasteless; she'd taken great care that he wouldn't suspect anything untoward — that she had added to his cup. Later, she knew, there would be a penalty, for other appetites would be aroused. But before that, his mind and attitude would be open to her gentle probing. . . .

Savrinor drained his cup and returned to the chair before the desk. Iselia waited a few moments before moving to stand behind him, her fingers lightly massaging his shoulders in the way she knew pleased and relaxed him.

"That," he said, "is not a seemly activity for this hour of the day."

"It's seemly enough when it distracts you from overworking." She bent forward so that her unbound hair fell across the nape of his neck, and her blue gaze lit again on the uncompleted parchment before him. Yes, that earlier glimpse had been true. A name had caught her eye. Benetan Liss's name . . .

"What is this document?" she asked. "Surely not another commission from the First Magus?"

Savrinor chuckled and gave himself up once more to her gentle massage. "No." Gods, he felt light-headed. It was a delicious sensation. "Although it concerns a commission. Or it might." He made a sudden serpentine twist and caught hold of her hair, tugging lightly on it. "Why? Of what interest is it to you, pretty one?"

She laughed, taking care to make the sound conspiratorial. "Simple curiosity. I saw the name of an old friend."

"Benetan Liss? He's no friend to you, not now."

"Oh, but he is." Iselia's mind was working quickly and sharply. "After all, it's thanks to him that you took me under your wing." She nuzzled the crown of his head. "What has Benetan done now?"

Her words allayed the flicker of suspicion that had been forming in Savrinor's mind, and he chuckled. "Done? Nothing. At least, not yet."

"I'm intrigued." Another Iselia, the Iselia who had been dragged a bitter and unwilling captive to the castle, the Iselia who loathed Savrinor and all he stood for, the Iselia who had loved and married Kaldar, cried out inside her. But the cry was short-lived. There was a greater cause to be served.

"Tell me." Her hands slipped down his back, over his spine, lower. "Tell me what mischief that fool Benetan has been in, and we'll laugh about it together. Just the two of us. . . ."

Lotro, the young Chaos rider from the southwest, was as susceptible as any of his peers to the lure of a pretty face and an alluring smile. So when the blond girl, whom he had never spoken to before but who said she was servant to the archivist Master Savrinor, approached him next morning and asked him to carry a private letter to his captain, Lotro was only too happy to oblige her.

Andraia had arranged to meet some of her friends in the dining hall for the midday meal, and Benetan, a little reluctantly, was on his way to join them when Lotro intercepted him in the courtyard.

"Beg pardon, Capun." The young rider saluted briskly. "Might I have a word, private, like?"

Benetan glanced toward the hall windows. "I'm in a hurry, Lotro. Can't it wait?"

"Well, yes, sir, I reckon, but . . . 'tis just that a lady asked of me to give you this." From a pocket he produced a carefully folded slip of paper, and added in a conspiratorial whisper, "A young lady, sir. Not the lady Andraia, but another."

From his gangling frame and pleasant, moonlike face people often gained the impression that Lotro was slow-witted, but in truth he was nothing of the kind and Benetan knew it. His look sharpened. "Young lady?" Irrationally his mind jumped to a conclusion. "What was her name?"

"She di'n't say, Capun. But she had yellow hair and blue eyes, and she said as 'twas urgent."

Iselia . . . it had to be. Aware of Lotro's curious scrutiny, Benetan schooled his expression to impassive stone. "Oh, yes; I think I know what this is about. Thank you, Lotro." He took the paper, then paused. "There's — ah — no need to mention this to anyone else."

"The lady already told me same, sir. I'll say nothing, certain sure." He saluted again and strode off across the courtyard, back erect and with a hint of satisfied pride at a task correctly done.

The courtyard was busy enough at this hour for one individual to melt into the general traffic without attracting attention, and Benetan withdrew to the pillared walkway to read Iselia's message. It was brief and to the point:

> *Benet: Please meet me on the beach below the stack at first moonrise tonight. It is a matter of grave importance to us both. Tell no one. I shall wait. Please come. Please.*

There was no signature, just her initial, and as he crumpled the note in his hand Benetan felt all the ground he'd gained over the past few days crumbling beneath him. He'd tried not to think about Iselia. He'd worked to mend his relationship with Andraia, to win her back and return to the happiness they'd enjoyed before Iselia had come between them. And it had been working, he was certain of it. But now . . .

His fists clenched involuntarily at his sides and he pressed his back against the nearest pillar, shutting his eyes as he felt something akin to despair flood through him. One message, one brief note, and in the space of a moment all his good resolutions were ashes. Gods, it was days now since he'd last *glimpsed* her, let alone spoken to her; and last time they met she'd made it painfully clear that her only feeling toward him was bitter resentment. He had been learning to ignore his own feelings for her, pretend they were nothing more than the last flicker of an old and long-burnt-out fire, and learning to ignore the jealous, queasy revulsion that assailed him each time he thought of her with Savrinor and wondered what her life with him had become.

But he couldn't ignore this. He *couldn't*.

His palm was sweating, Iselia's note now a damp, crushed tatter between his fingers. First moonrise . . . that would be about the time when the main evening meal was served. It wouldn't be difficult to invent an excuse to convince Andraia; and the assignation surely wouldn't take more than an hour at best. . . . With a bitter surge of self-reproach Benetan faced the knowledge that he didn't have the strength to stop himself from keeping the rendezvous, and that the goad was far greater than simply the fond concern of one friend for another. He wouldn't give it a name; he dared not. But the old wound had opened again, and this time he wasn't sure if he could stanch the bleeding.

Although darkness had gathered, he saw her the moment he stepped out from the cave at the foot of the stack. She was standing in the lee of the towering cliff, where a tumble of boulders half buried by sand and shingle formed a finger reaching out into the sea. The water, reflecting the first moon's light, cast an unearthly phosphorescence on the scene and for a brief moment her figure seemed to be one with the rocks, gray and indistinct and strange. Then the wind lifted the edge of the shawl covering her hair, and she moved toward him.

"Benet." Her voice was clear in the night air; she reached out, then thought better of it and withdrew her hand. "Thank you for coming."

The moon hadn't yet cleared the eastern horizon, and a blade of light cut a glittering silver swath across the sea's surface to the beach. In the eldritch glow, and half shadowed by the shawl, Iselia's face looked haggard and Benetan felt his heart constrict painfully.

"Your message," he said. "When I read it, I thought — " He couldn't say what he'd thought, and finished lamely, "I was concerned."

"Were you?" She asked the question so quickly that it took him aback. He might have imagined it, but there seemed to be a hint of eagerness, even hope, in her voice. Then before he could form a reply she continued.

"Benet, I'm sorry that I had to ask you to come here." A shiver and a swift glance over her shoulder expressed something deeper than mere distaste for the beach. "But there was nowhere else where I could be sure of our being safe. If Savrinor were to find out — "

"Savrinor?" Benetan pounced on the name. "What has he to do with this? What has he *done* to you?"

"Nothing!" She might or might not have remembered, as he was remembering, the miserable night of the inauguration festivities, but she was suddenly unwilling to look directly at him. "He's done nothing, Benet; nothing that I can't . . . cope with well enough. This is something else, something he told to me in confidence. That's why he mustn't find out. And it concerns you."

The turbulent impulse to run back up the twisting stairs to the castle, break into Savrinor's apartments, and put the blade of his knife through the historian's heart sagged into confusion, and Benetan said bewilderedly, "Me?"

"Yes." Iselia shivered suddenly. "It's so *cold* here. . . ."

He pulled off his coat and wrapped it round her. As his hands touched her every nerve ending in his body seemed to quiver, fire followed by ice.

She huddled gratefully into the coat, moving closer to him as she did so. "Benet, the First Magus is looking for a spy. One man, a trusted and skilled man, whose task will be to infiltrate the innermost circle of the — the heretics, he calls them . . . calls us . . . and discover the identity of their . . . our . . . leader." She paused, watching the mix of emotions on his face as this news went home. Then, very softly, she added, "Savrinor intends to recommend you for the commission."

Benetan stared at her. "*What?*"

His voice rang harshly in the quiet, and seagulls sleeping on the slack tide rose protesting into the air, water shattering behind them in the moonlight. Iselia clutched at his arm. "Benet, hush! If someone should hear — "

"There's no one to hear; no one between us and the castle!" He pulled roughly away from her and took three strides across the shingle before the tide's edge brought him up short. In a single, sharp movement he turned to face her again. "I don't believe this! Savrinor, recommending me — why, in all the gods' names? *Why?*"

"Because," Iselia said, "he believes you are the best man for the task. And because your lady, Andraia, asked him to."

Then, as Benetan stood rigid and incredulous, she told him all she had learned from Savrinor on the previous day. The potion with which she'd plied the historian had worked well, mellowing him to a state of languid indulgence, and he had revealed the entire story to her. Iselia had pretended to be amused by Andraia's subterfuges on Benetan's behalf, expressing pity for her foolish and unfounded jealousy and flattering away any suspicions Savrinor might still have harbored. But she said nothing of this to Benetan, confining her account only to the bare facts.

The bare facts were more than enough. As he listened, Benetan's reactions ranged from rage at Andraia's presumption and Savrinor's deviousness to fury at himself for having given them both ample grounds for their attitudes. Yet a clear, cold streak of honesty, struggling to be heard amid the turmoil in his mind, told him that in truth he had brought this on himself. How could he blame Andraia, who loved him, for wanting to remove him from Iselia's sphere of influence for a while — especially if in doing so she would also give him the chance to earn advancement and the approval of the magi? And Savrinor: he had every right to resent Benetan's old links with Iselia and to wish to see them broken. Perhaps he should even take the historian's maneuver as a compliment, for Savrinor wouldn't jeopardize his own reputation by making a false recommendation, least of all to Lord Vordegh.

But all the reasoning in the world did not change the harsh facts.

Iselia was a shadow against the towering backdrop of the stack. She was silent now, watching him. She looked very vulnerable.

"I . . . I don't know what I can say." He was shivering, with more than cold. "If the First Magus should choose me . . . gods, what possible reason can I find for refusing?"

"Refusing?" Iselia's eyes opened very wide, moonlight reflected in them suddenly. "Oh, Benet — you don't understand!" Suddenly she ran to him, her voice urgent, almost pleading. "Benet, I don't *want* you to refuse! Don't you see? That's why I sent my message, why I so desperately needed to tell you — because I was afraid you *would* refuse!"

"I don't understand you!"

"Listen. Listen to me, listen." She drew him back from the sea's edge, into the lee of the cliff. Her breathing was quick and nervous. "Benet. I have to trust you; I've no choice. You may betray me, but—"

"No. I won't. You know that."

"Yes, I do know it, because I know that when you give your word, you don't break it. You never did." She found his right hand in the darkness and gripped it. "You alone, of all the living souls at the castle, know my two secrets. One, that I am Kaldar's wife, and two, that he and I are . . ." She faltered, and Benetan supplied softly,

"Heretics?"

Pain flared in her look. "If you think — "

"No." He raised his free hand and touched a finger to her lips, silencing her. "I have two kinds of devotion, Iselia. Devotion to my gods, and devotion to my . . . friends." He had to use that word, he didn't dare utter the other and truer one. "At this moment I'm not a Chaos rider. I'm only Benet, and that's where my human loyalty lies. Speak freely. I won't give you away."

She knew with a sure instinct that he was telling her the truth, and her body relaxed as though suddenly released from imprisonment. "Oh, Benet . . ." Her voice caught. "I wish — "

"What? What do you wish?"

"No. It doesn't matter, and it's far too late now. Listen. Kaldar told you that he is traveling south, to meet our . . . the leader of . . ."

"Yes." He saved her the need to find a word with which they would both be comfortable.

She nodded. "The First Magus doesn't yet know where to begin his search. But I fear that may change. The edict he sent to the over-lords — I know what he has ordered them to do, you see; I was one of those who helped Savrinor to write out the copies of the document." Her words came quickly; she was almost babbling now. "There's to be a campaign, a purge, to seek out anyone and everyone who opposes Chaos. The First Magus has commanded the overlords to take hos-tages. After forty-nine days, if others have not come forward with information to expose the guilty, the hostages are to be burned alive."

Benetan hadn't seen the edict. He felt his stomach turn over.

"Some will break," Iselia said. "They *must*. People won't stand by and see their friends and kin slaughtered, and who could ask such a monstrous thing of them?" She swallowed convulsively. "Someone will confess; someone who knows where our leader can be found. Armed with that knowledge, the First Magus's spy will be able to in-filtrate his stronghold. And . . ."

"And your friends will die. *Kaldar* will die."

"Yes." She hung her head. "I have no right to plead for him. You and Kaldar were never friends, and now that . . . now that he and I . . . oh, but it's not just Kaldar. Not only him."

He suspected she was crying, and it all but broke him. "What, then?" he asked desperately. "Tell me, *please*."

Her voice dropped until it was barely audible. "I feel so ashamed. . . . But if our leader is found and taken, and our circle broken, then the power that has protected all of us from discovery will be gone. I won't be able to hold out. I'll be named; my secret will be known. It's inevitable. And although I'd die for our cause, I . . . oh, Benet, I'm so afraid of the death the magi would give me!"

Benetan felt as though an earthquake were shaking the ground under his feet. Tears were streaming down Iselia's face now and she whispered, "I'm a coward; I should be thinking of Kaldar, of all of them, but — I don't know if I have the strength left, not anymore."

He didn't pause to think. His reaction was pure, reckless instinct, and the consequences were too far in the future to bear an instant's consideration.

"Iselia." He caught hold of her, drawing her close to him. "Whoever is chosen for this commission will either succeed in his task, and break your circle, or fail."

"I think," Iselia said, "that he will succeed. I think it's inevitable."

"Not if he should *decide* to fail."

"Decide . . . You mean . . . ?"

"I mean that he might find himself pursuing a false trail, until finally he is obliged to admit defeat and inform his masters that the quarry has eluded him. And if on his travels he should find some way to take news of you to Kaldar . . ."

She looked up at him, her eyes intense. "I can't ask it of you!"

"You can. I want to help you and I *will* help you, and I'll ask nothing from you in return. Don't you believe me?"

"Yes," she said unsteadily, "I think I do."

"Well, then. If the commission is offered to me I'll take it, and I'll buy what time I can for Kaldar and your friends before I return to report failure." He paused. "I can't condone your cause — you know I can't, and never could — but neither can I condone the methods Lord Vordegh is using to stamp it out." And on the heels of those words, silently, came the desperate thought: *And I don't believe the gods will condone them, either. Pray Yandros I'm right, and that the lords of Chaos will put a stop to this madness. . . .*

Iselia was silent for what seemed a long time. Then at last she said, very quietly,

"I don't know how to thank you, Benet."

"You don't need to." He smiled at her. "Whatever you may think of me, I still have a conscience."

"More than that, I think. Much more. . . ." Gently she disengaged his hands, which were still holding hers, and began to move slowly toward the cave and the staircase beyond. It was a tacit acknowledgment that there was nothing more to be said, and Benetan followed her. At the cave mouth she stopped.

"A little earlier I began to say something to you, then changed my mind. But perhaps it should be said after all. It's just that . . . I'm sorry."

"Sorry?"

She looked at the shingle beneath her feet. "Sorry that our lives couldn't have been different. But when I agreed to marry Kaldar you had been gone for twelve years, and I had good reason to believe I'd never see you again."

Benetan's heart seemed to turn over under his ribs. "Iselia, are you saying . . ." But he didn't have the courage to ask.

She looked at him at last, but obliquely. "Did you think I could change so much? Or that Kaldar could ever truly take the place that you once held? I can't let myself regret my choice, Benet. That would be cruel, and — and pointless, now. Kaldar is my husband, and I do love him. But sometimes . . . sometimes I'm sad for what might have been."

She turned away then, moved into the darkness of the cave. Behind her Benetan stood staring blindly, unable to speak, unable to think, utterly lost.

And two days later, when the First Magus completed his deliberations and consultations and summoned the captain of the Chaos riders before him, Benetan accepted the commission with a heart dazed by terror and joy in equal measure.

CHAPTER XXI

Kaldar woke shouting from a nightmare in which he'd been bleeding to death from a hundred bite wounds whilst pursuing an eight-legged monstrosity that was carrying Iselia away. As his body came jolting out of sleep his flailing arms were caught and held and, shuddering, he opened his eyes to see Shammana leaning over him.

"Kaldar!" She shook him, but gently. "Kaldar, it was a dream, a dream, nothing more! You're awake now, it's all right. You're safe awake with us."

He stared back at her for a moment, uncomprehending. Then he burst into tears.

Shammana didn't speak again, but held him as though he were a small child while he cried out his pain and fear and misery in her arms. This wasn't the first time it had happened since their journey had begun and she knew now how best to comfort him until the storm was over. Nanithe woke and started to move toward them across the floor of the wagon, in which they'd all slept, but Shammana shook her head and the girl sat back, watching the scenario with wide, troubled eyes.

At last Kaldar's weeping subsided. Still without a word Shammana gave him a scrap of cloth with which to wipe his eyes and blow his nose, then she wrapped one of their two spare blankets about his shoulders as he began to shiver with reaction. As always he felt too ashamed to meet her gaze, but he closed a hand over her fingers and squeezed hard, silently conveying gratitude and an apology.

"There's no call to be sorry," Shammana told him a little gruffly. "It's nothing more than we've all done before now, and you'll be the better for not keeping it crushed down inside yourself." She rose, steadying herself on the wagon's side, and climbed stiffly down to the ground. "Well, dawn's come, for what little it's worth; time we were on the move. I'll go and see for the horse."

Kaldar's mind was beginning to function properly again, the last tatters of the dream and its aftermath fading. For the first time he took in his surroundings fully. They had camped for the night well off the road in an overgrown and uncoppiced wood, now shot through with the light of a gray and dreary morning. Water was dripping onto his face from somewhere overhead; he could hear the dull, monotonous patter of rain on leaves, and the wagon floor was wet where the hide covers had proved inadequate. This was nothing unusual, for since they'd left Chaun seven days ago the weather had been unremittingly foul, contradicting all Kaldar had ever heard about the supposedly warm and kindly southern climate. But if the calculations over which he and Shammana had pored two evenings ago were right, then they were now no more than a day's journey from the coast and their goal.

Abruptly Kaldar slipped the blanket off his shoulders and scrambled to his feet, determined to put his nightmares behind him. There was work to be done before they could take to the road again. Horse and humans must be fed, water bottles refilled, and they would need some fresh branches to decorate the wagon and maintain their pretense of being a family party traveling to a cousin's marriage feast. It had been Shammana's idea to embroider on Kaldar's original guise, and now the three were masquerading as mother, daughter, and daughter's husband, with Kaldar given the new and more suitably southern name of Wilm. Kaldar had felt deeply uncomfortable at the idea of pretending to be married to Nanithe, for it seemed to him a betrayal of Iselia, even if only in name. Also, in his most cynical moments, he wondered if Shammana had decided that Iselia must now be considered lost forever and was misguidedly trying to steer him toward a new intimacy with the mute girl. But Shammana had pointed out quite reasonably that despoiling virgins was a popular game among many overlords' militiamen, and Nanithe would be safer posing as Kaldar's wife than as his sister. Nanithe seemed to hold no opinion either way, but when Kaldar finally if reluctantly agreed she had given him a shy little smile and reached out to hold his hand, indicating her pleasure in a way that made Kaldar feel more uncomfortable than ever.

As matters turned out, the precaution had been unnecessary, for they had had no trouble on the road. The vile weather made traveling unpleasant, but it also deterred all but the hardiest or most purposeful from venturing out. They'd met only the usual trains of toiling produce wagons whose masters couldn't afford to delay their journeys, and a few farm carts on short forays, but of militia, brigands, or any other potential dangers there was no sign. Now, with Aeoris's continued blessing, they had almost reached their final rendezvous.

Shammana came back as Kaldar was mopping water from the wagon floor.

"There's little point our trying to start a fire in this," she said. "There's not a dry stick to be had anywhere and even our own kindling must be damp by now. We'll have to make do with a cold breakfast. A pity, because there are some fine gold-eye mushrooms growing down by the stream. They make very good eating, but only if they're cooked."

"I'll pick some anyway, when I cut the fresh branches," Kaldar suggested. "We can carry them with us. Who knows — the rain might stop."

Shammana raised her eyes skeptically heavenward. "Praise the day! Well, do, then; there's no harm hoping, I suppose. Now, Nanithe — no, child, we'll not want the cooking pot this morning. Is there any of the bread we bought two days ago still left? It'll be stale, but our dear lord Aeoris knows our bellies will be thankful enough for it by noon."

They sat under the scant shelter of the wagon covers to eat what breakfast they could, then the two women harnessed the horse while Kaldar collected the branches and mushrooms, and soon they were on their way, emerging from the rough woodland path onto the southward road. Even this was little better than a rutted trail, although some local farmers had tried in a haphazard way to improve the surface with cartloads of stones and broken brick, and as the wagon lumbered along, the clop of hooves and creak of wheels was accompanied by the gurgle of water running freely to either side of the track.

"Another day of this and the whole road will be awash," Shammana observed, peering through the veils of rain. "Let's pray it does abate soon, or we may well have to abandon the wagon and walk."

But the rain didn't abate. If anything it grew heavier, with no sign of a break in the murky cloud that stretched solidly from horizon to horizon. Then, at what Kaldar judged to be an hour or two after noon, the temperature began to drop and the wind rose, driving the rain in their faces and threatening to turn it to sleet. Even with all the blankets wrapped around them and the hide covers — save one with which Shammana covered the dejected horse — pulled up over their heads, they were soon soaked and chilled through. To make matters worse the landscape, or what they could see of it, was becoming bleaker and more inhospitable with every mile. The road had almost petered out entirely and the wood where they'd spent the night appeared to have been on the last margin of the great forests, for now there wasn't a tree to be glimpsed anywhere. The surrounding land was uncultivated, bleak moor without one solitary building to break the monotony. No crops, no steadings, no other travelers; not even a bird in the sky. They might have been the only living souls in this entire tract of country.

Kaldar was driving, gallantly taking the brunt of the sleeting downpour and giving Shammana and Nanithe what shelter he could behind him. He'd dropped into an almost mesmeric state, numb with cold and hypnotized by the view of the horse's swaying hindquarters and the sound of its plodding hooves, and had to keep shaking himself awake for fear that he'd fall off the wagon. Then suddenly his nostrils flared and he raised his head, sniffing at the air. Nanithe, who was huddled against his back, felt his body tense and grasped at his arm, silently communicating alarm, and Shammana said sharply, "What? What is it? Something amiss?"

Kaldar shook water from his eyes and peered through the rain's blur into the distance. "I'm not sure," he said, trying to quell the excitement he felt, "but I think I can smell the sea."

"Smell the sea?" The wagon rocked as Shammana crawled out from under the hide to see for herself. She sniffed. "Ugh! All I can smell is salt fish that's been kept too long in the barrel!"

Kaldar hid a smile. "Have you ever seen the sea before, Shammana?"

"Indeed I've not. Chaun is well inland, as you should know."

"I've seen it." Memories crowded into Kaldar's mind of his mining days and of one sojourn in particular, at a productive but dangerous working on the hostile north coast. He'd volunteered for that turn, he remembered, because it offered the chance to earn a good bonus. A bonus which he'd hoped to put toward a home for Iselia, to make him feel worthy of her . . . but that had been in the days before the magi's servants had put a price on his head. . . .

He realized abruptly that there were tears on his face again, mingling with the rain, and he shook his head, forcing himself back to present reality. "I've seen the sea," he repeated. "And I've smelled it. Fish and weed and brine. Shammana, we've reached our goal."

The settlement that clung to the coast at the moorland's edge barely deserved the term. It was no more than a ramshackle collection of huts, put together with whatever sparse materials the surrounding land could provide and littering the flat, wind-scoured acres where a small river estuary met the sea. Some fifteen or twenty small boats that looked as dilapidated as the huts were drawn up on the shingle bank, clear of the high tide line, their sails flapping soddenly like shabby gulls' wings. And dominating everything was the sea itself, a vast, foreboding gray waste stretching away into limitless distance. The tide looked restless and dangerous, powerful breakers assaulting the long beach in unbroken lines while currents clashed and swirled at the estuary mouth. The horse tossed its head and stamped uneasily, afraid of the unfamiliar smells and the sea's roaring, and Kaldar heard Shammana mutter under her breath. He turned on the wagon seat and saw that Nanithe had hidden her face against the older woman's shoulder and was shivering violently, while Shammana herself stared at the scene with wide, horrified eyes.

"It's so — so *vast* . . . ," she whispered, her voice barely audible over the racket of wind and waves. "I'd never thought, never *dreamed* it would be like this!"

Nanithe was too frightened even to look, and though Kaldar did his best to reassure them that they were in no danger, they were unconvinced and huddled fearfully back in the wagon as he urged the reluctant horse toward the settlement. The sole trades hereabouts were fishing and salting, and as they approached the first of the huts, Kaldar saw not only that the settlement was larger than it had seemed at first sight but also that there was a fair amount of activity going on, particularly in the area of three larger buildings set a little way apart from the rest. The smell of fish had grown to a stench, and as the track gave way to a rough shingle road on the settlement's outskirts, a barking clamor started up at the sudden sound of hooves and wheels on the stones. Several mangy dogs came bounding toward them through the rain; a voice yelled out a furious order and the animals slunk back toward the huts, though still growling. A group of men by the largest building had also seen them, and two detached themselves from the group and walked toward the wagon. A thought occurred suddenly to Kaldar and he looked over his shoulder.

"Shammana, the branches — we still look like a wedding party. Quickly, cover them!"

Shammana rallied from her fear to swiftly pull the wet greenery down onto the wagon floor and throw a hide over it, and Kaldar turned to meet the two men.

They were both stockily built, their skins brown and seamed with constant exposure to salt winds and their hands rough and gnarled like tree roots. They wore peculiar hide caps with wide, drooping brims from which the rain streamed over their caped shoulders.

"Good day." The taller of the two smiled grimly at the irony of his own greeting. "Don't mind the dogs; they only attack anyone who do make trouble. Are you here to buy, or to sell?"

"To buy." Kaldar and Shammana had rehearsed their story carefully. "We're from a village northward; looking for a barrel or two of salt fish."

"Just a barrel or two?" He raised an eyebrow. "That seem you've gone to a lot of effort for so little."

"With our new overlord doubling the prices we've to pay for everything, it's that or go without," Kaldar said, then grinned. "We'll buy three if we can afford it."

The second man, who was a generation older than the first, uttered a hacking bark of laughter. "New overlord, eh? Well, that's not something we do need to worry about here. Come you down, then, and your women, too, and get into the dry. And I've no doubt some food will be welcome."

The apparent hospitality of the fisherfolk did much to allay Shammana's and Nanithe's fear of their alien surroundings, but it soon became clear that the kindness was based on hard pragmatism. With their horse housed in the village's rough but weatherproof stables, they themselves were taken to a large hut where communal meals were prepared and eaten and where a driftwood cooking fire warmed their bones. A squat, fierce-looking woman served them with bowls of fish stew and then demanded three coppers in payment. A little wryly Kaldar handed over the coins. He should have known better than to expect anything for nothing, he thought, and at least the price was fair. Other inhabitants of the settlement came and went as they ate, paying them little heed other than a casual glance or dour nod of acknowledgment; although the weather prevented the fishing boats from putting out, there was clearly work enough to keep everyone busy, and food was snatched hastily between tasks. Kaldar was puzzled by the people's lack of curiosity toward them, for he presumed that they saw few outsiders here other than the regular merchants who came to buy salted fish in bulk. A little later, however, he learned he was mistaken.

The elder of the two men who had originally met them had returned to the hut and suggested that Kaldar should go with him to the salting houses, where he could look over the barrels and choose what he wanted to buy. Kaldar was lent one of the wide-brimmed hide caps to keep the worst of the rain from him and, leaving Shammana and Nanithe in the care of the squat woman, he followed his companion — whose name was Heryea — out into the driving squall. As they hurried, heads down and leaning into the wind, toward the three large buildings which dominated the settlement, Heryea suddenly said, raising his voice to be heard above the sea's roar,

"That seem there's been a fair spate of new overlords these last few months, then."

Kaldar looked sidelong at him. "New overlords? I don't understand."

"Well, now, if you do have a new one as you say, then that's the fourth we've heard about since last Quarter Day, and you the fifth band of strangers to come buying for theirselves." Heryea grinned, showing two missing front teeth. "And the story always the same, new overlord demanding higher prices and no one can't afford them. I do never recall when our catches have been so popular with outcomers before."

The *fifth* bands of strangers? Kaldar was momentarily taken aback—then he felt a quick pang of excitement. His party was not the only one heading for the rendezvous with Simbrian Tarkran. . . .

Keeping his voice casual he said, "There have been upheavals in some districts, or so I've heard."

"That have," Heryea agreed, in a tone which suggested he would have liked to know a good deal more about it than he intended to ask. "But we do take little notice just so long as that doesn't make trouble for us, and so far it haven't."

"Quite the opposite, I should think. Good for trade."

The old man nodded. "Can't say that isn't. Though we could do with a letup to this weather, or there'll be nothing left to sell." He eyed Kaldar speculatively. "Prices have already had to rise a notch or two. Demand and supply, that is."

"Well, I hope there'll be sufficient for our needs — and our purse. If four other parties have been here before us — "

"Oh, we won't send you away disappointed," Heryea assured him. "Anyways, one of the outcomers is a merchant in a big way, or so he say, buying all up and down the coast. He won't miss a barrel or two from his load if that's all you're needing."

They reached the lee of the salting house, and the sudden drop in the wind's force made Kaldar shake his head, momentarily disoriented by the change. Heryea took off his hat, banging it against the wall to shake out the worst of the water, then led the way through the open door into smoky, fish-reeking gloom.

"That's the salted catch to the right and the smoked to the left," he said, pointing.

Kaldar peered, his eyes not yet adjusted to the dimness — then stopped, standing motionless. There were some half dozen other people in the salting house, two women and a boy tending the smoke kilns while three older men stood a little apart, apparently deep in discussion. One of the men towered above his companions; he had a shock of thick, dark hair and a full beard, and his bulk was huge, giving him the look of a bear in human guise. And intuition sent a violent stab through Kaldar's mind. . . .

The man turned his head, and their gazes met. Heryea nudged Kaldar in the ribs, startling him out of his paralysis.

"There, then. That's the merchant, so you can speak to him yourself."

The stranger was approaching them, one hand raised in greeting. Now Kaldar could see that he was wearing a heavy fur coat, although even without this his frame was still enormous.

"Afternoon to you, Heryea." Memories of past psychic communications filled Kaldar's mind and he thought, *Gods, I know his voice! And his face.* . . .

The big man looked down at him and smiled broadly. His brown eyes glinted, but as well as expressing warmth they also urged caution. "And to you, young man. I don't believe I have your acquaintance."

"Another new private party in," Heryea said. It wasn't in his nature to be deferential even to his wealthiest customers, but his tone was respectful nonetheless. "He only want one or two barrels."

"Well, that shouldn't be a problem to anyone. Perhaps I can help him to make the right choice. Allow me to introduce myself." The man held out a hand to touch palms with Kaldar in the universal gesture of friendship, and as he did so his thumb and finger curled, briefly but emphatically, to form the sign of Aeoris. "I am Simbrian Tarkran."

"I'm sorry that I startled you so greatly," Simbrian said, "but as the magi and their agents know me by three different names, and none of them the right one, it's safe enough to use my own in my dealings here. Shammana, the kettle's still hot and your cup is empty. Let me refill it."

They were gathered around a fire of gorse and turf and driftwood, in a hut which by a combination of charm and exorbitant payment Simbrian had rented for his personal use during his stay in the fishing community. It was on the outskirts of the settlement, which gave it the advantage of privacy, but all the same he had set a subtle shield about it that would deter idle priers without alerting anyone with a faint psychic sense.

"There are few if any with a latent psychic talent in this place," he'd told them. "But don't make the mistake of believing that they're not curious about us. They are very curious indeed, and it's only in the past few days that they've started to conceal it, which warns me that curiosity is turning into suspicion."

Shammana looked over her shoulder to the hut door, unable to suppress a shiver. Dusk had fallen, and the wail of the wind and the deeper growl of the sea sounded to her overwrought senses like the voices of an attacking horde from the depths of Chaos. Her voice not quite steady, she said, "Then we're in danger?"

Simbrian smiled a little sadly. "We are always in danger, Shammana, and will be so until our lord Aeoris has the strength to protect us as he wishes to do. But if you mean in danger from the fisherfolk, then I think not, or at least not immediately. They suspect something is afoot, but they don't know what it could be. Word of the magi's actions hasn't yet reached this far south, and even when it does, there's no overlord hereabouts to disseminate the news."

"No overlord?" Kaldar was astonished.

"Oh, they have one, but in name alone and hardly worthy of the title. He's an old man, I gather, he keeps no militia and never stirs from his stronghold. Provided the quarterly tithes are paid, the people here are left to be a law unto themselves, which suits them — and us — well enough. But even with this factor on our side, news of the search for us will reach here eventually. When it does they'll have the wit to see a connection, and there are sure to be some who, if they think there's financial gain to be had from their knowledge, will have no scruples about betraying us." He refilled Shammana's cup and set the kettle of hot herb broth back on its trivet beside the fire.

Kaldar stared into the flames, his face somber. Simbrian had told them all he knew about the magi's newest gambit, and although the information he had was scant enough, and doubtless outdated by now, it had made very unpleasant hearing. Simbrian was well acquainted with First Magus Vordegh's reputation, and believed that these first maneuvers were only the beginning of a savage and unremitting campaign. An edict had gone out to the overlords, ordering them to use any method, however brutal, to flush out anyone suspected of being a secret devotee of Order, and there were rumors of reprisals to be taken against any who failed in their duty, though Simbrian didn't know what form such reprisals might take. All Kaldar could think of was Iselia. Was she in greater danger now? It would be madness to underestimate the magi's arcane powers; what would happen if they should turn their attention on her and she was unable to shield her thoughts and her allegiances from their scrutiny? Benetan Liss had promised to protect her, and Kaldar knew that Benetan's guilty conscience, together with his muddled and half-realized infatuation, would ensure that he kept that promise if he could. But if he could not . . .

"Kaldar." He started as a hand came lightly to rest on his sleeve, then looked up, blinking, to meet Simbrian's gaze.

"Kaldar, my dear friend, I know what you're thinking, and I wish with all my heart that I could find some way to ensure her safety. But I daren't try to use my powers to shield her, not while she's in the castle. The risk of exposing us all to the magi would be too great."

Kaldar nodded, then bit down hard on his lip as to his shame he felt hot tears welling in his eyes. "I know." His voice caught and he cleared his throat. "I know. I could have tried to use my own skills to protect her, but I didn't dare, and for the same reason." For a moment, and with a surge of emotion, he asked himself silently whether even their great cause could mean as much to him as Iselia did; then he crushed the question out of existence. Iselia would have her own fierce answer to that, and he knew what it would be. He rubbed his eyes, wiping the tears away before they could fall. "We can only help her by helping our lord Aeoris. I know that, Simbrian."

"Yet knowing it doesn't make your loss and your fears any easier to bear. I understand, Kaldar — and I admire your strength and your dedication. You're truly worthy of our gods."

He was smiling kindly, sympathetically, and Kaldar was greatly comforted. Strange though the feeling was, it seemed to him that a great bond had already formed between the four of them. Simbrian's warmth, his humanity, his — Kaldar had no other word for it: his *goodness* — was like a balm, spreading out to encompass them all and enfold them in a powerful embrace. And Simbrian had tremendous power, of that Kaldar was certain now. How he had gained it, what personal trials he had undergone, and above all how he had kept his secret from the searching eyes of the magi and their Chaotic agents was impossible to imagine, but Kaldar believed it could have only one source. Simbrian must draw his strength from the wellspring that was Aeoris, and that knowledge was enough to keep the fire of Kaldar's hopes and dreams ablaze.

Shammana sipped at her broth. Nanithe had fallen asleep, exhausted by her earlier terrors, and her head was cradled in the older woman's lap. Setting the cup aside and stroking the girl's tumbled hair, Shammana said, "What are we to do, then, Simbrian? We can go no further south. Where will we be safe?"

For a moment Simbrian closed his eyes, and Kaldar's senses caught the quick flicker of power that emanated from him as he probed beyond the hut to ensure that no other ears were listening. Then he relaxed.

"Thanks be to Aeoris, there's no need for us to delay here any longer. You're the last of those who arranged to gather here; the others arrived before you and are waiting for us a little further eastward along the coast. We *can* go further south, Shammana. In fact we can, and will, leave the mainland altogether."

Her eyes widened in horror. "Across the sea?"

"Yes. It's not as fearsome a prospect as you think, though I'll admit that better weather would make it more pleasant. But the weather gives us an advantage, for it will enable us to lay a false trail behind us. Or rather I should say, a trail that even the magi won't consider worthwhile pursuing.

"A day's sailing from this coast lies an island. It's uninhabited, but it's a kindly place and has everything we need for survival — fresh water, game and fish and good vegetation, and wood for building. That's where our people are gathering; most are already there and only waiting for me to bring the last of our followers across. As soon as our numbers are complete . . . Well, I think you and Kaldar both know what then lies ahead of us."

Shammana nodded, and Kaldar's fingers flexed and clenched with excitement. "To make contact with our lord Aeoris . . . ," he whispered.

"Yes. More than two hundred friends await us on the island, and they are only the tip of a long, bright sword in the hands of our gods.

But most important of all is that our arrival will complete the number of magically talented souls we need to perform our great ritual. The sacred number — seven times seven."

"And the number of Chaos, too," Kaldar said with soft bitterness.

"Indeed, for there have always been seven demons of Chaos, just as there are seven lords of Order," Simbrian reminded him. "But that will change, Kaldar." He reached out again and gripped Kaldar's hand in a strong clasp. "We will change it!"

He sat back. "Now, my friends, this is what we must do. Tonight you will stay here in my lodging; I'll be away until dawn, making the final arrangements for our departure. In the morning I shall tell our hosts that I've agreed to sell you three barrels from my own purchase of fish, and I'll give the wink and a few extra coppers to old Heryea, to let him think that he and I between us have extracted more of your coin than you intended to part with. The barrels will be loaded onto your wagon and you will depart on the road by which you came. As soon as you're clear of the village, turn eastward across the moor — the going's safe enough, if rough — and keep the coast in sight until you see a rock spur jutting out to sea where the land begins to rise. The place can't be mistaken, for there's a narrow arch in the rock where the sea has eroded a softer stratum. Halt there, and our other friends will come to you."

"And you?" Kaldar asked.

Simbrian chuckled. "I will spend a convivial morning settling my account and drinking a health to all these good people and their ancestors and descendants alike, then I too will depart, against all their seamanly advice, in the ship in which I arrived and into the teeth of a storm."

"A storm?" Shammana's voice rose anxiously.

"Oh yes, there'll be a storm tomorrow. The grandfathers have been predicting it and I have been publicly and noisily scoffing at the idea." He smiled. "The grandfathers will be proved right, of course, and I'll be proved wrong. Doubtless they'll shake their heads in righteous sorrow when they hear of my failure to to reach my supposed destination, and say, 'Fool that was, but no one can say we didn't warn him.' And if anyone should ever come looking for Simbrian Tarkran, they'll say, 'Simbrian Tarkran is drowned and feeding fishes, fool that was and fool that stay.' "

Shammana gazed into the fire, her shoulders hunching. She said no more, but Kaldar knew what was rampaging through her mind. Not only to venture onto the terrifying sea but to do it in the teeth of a storm . . . On a sudden impulse he leaned toward her.

"Shammana . . . there'll be no danger."

She looked up quickly. "No *danger* . . . ?"

"No." He glanced at Simbrian but didn't need the reassuring nod the sorcerer gave him in return. In his own mind he was certain. "Our lord Aeoris will protect us, Shammana. And what he can't do, Simbrian will do in his name. Trust him, Shammana, as I trust."

Her brow furrowed and she put a hand up to her mouth. "I . . ." Then her expression cleared. "Yes, Kaldar, yes; you're right." She managed a pallid smile which she offered to them both in turn. "I'll not be afraid." The smile quivered but then became a small, nervous but heartfelt laugh. "I'll have enough to occupy me soothing Nanithe's terrors without worrying about my own!"

Simbrian left them an hour later, when he could be sure that all the fisherfolk were asleep and wouldn't see him depart. Nanithe was curled now on a pile of hide rugs by the fire, and Kaldar had nodded off with his back against the hut wall and his head cushioned on his own folded coat. Shammana, though, was still awake and moved quietly to the door with the sorcerer. As he set his hand on the latch she said softly, "Thank you, Simbrian."

He smiled down at her. "For what, my dear? I've done little enough."

She shook her head. "That isn't so. You're the cornerstone of all our hopes. Without you, we —" She struggled to find the right words, failed. "We'd have nothing."

"Without the cause to give us hope, we'd all have nothing." He raised her hand to his lips and kissed it, not intimately but in a way that expressed deep respect. Shammana blinked and sniffed.

"You put me in mind of my husband," she said. "In other days, when we were both younger . . . he would have been proud to know you."

"Thank you. I take that as a great compliment." His gaze slid past her, then to the two sleeping figures near the fire, and he sighed. "You lost one family, Shammana, but it seems now that you've unwittingly gained another."

"Yes." She cast her own gaze down. "Poor creatures. For Kaldar I think it must be worse, in some ways, to know that his wife still lives, even though she's beyond his reach and in peril. And Nanithe . . ." She didn't finish the sentence but only shook her head.

Simbrian was looking at Nanithe. "I wish I could help her. I have some healing powers, but they're not enough to break down the barriers in her mind." There was a strange, sad look in his dark eyes. "Perhaps . . ."

"Perhaps?" Shammana prompted gently when he didn't continue.

"No. No; forgive me, but I think I should keep my own counsel for now. Kiss her when she wakes, and tell her the kiss is from her friend and servant Simbrian." He opened the door, blocking it with his body so that the wind and rain couldn't come swirling in. "Good night, Shammana."

"Good night."

The settlement dogs didn't stir or make a sound as he walked away from the hut. Shammana smiled at that small but telling display of his powers, and watched until his figure was swallowed by the howling darkness.

CHAPTER XXII

Midway through the afternoon of the following day the ship that was to carry Kaldar and his companions to their island hideaway rounded the rock spur and dropped anchor off the cove where her passengers waited. The weather was peculiarly calm; the rain had ceased and the wind had dropped almost to nothing, but the restless growl of the sea was enough to warn any weather-wise coast dweller that the respite wouldn't last for long. Even now a new and formidably dark cloud bank was forming threateningly in the west, and the occasional brief but emphatic breath from that quarter gave hints of the trouble to come. Taking advantage of the lull, Simbrian had used both his sailing expertise and his sorcery to pilot the vessel single-handed along the coast, and as soon as the anchor was secure he lowered the ship's dinghy and rowed shoreward to collect his friends.

Shammana had given Nanithe a strong sleeping draft, aware that the girl would otherwise be too terrified to make the crossing. But as she waited for the dinghy and watched the steady darkening of the western sky, her own courage all but failed, and on the short but nerve-racking passage to the ship she crouched in the dinghy's stern, hands covering her face, and lips moving in desperate prayer.

It took two ferrying trips to carry everyone across to the ship. There were nine in the party apart from Simbrian himself, a mixed group consisting of Kaldar and his companions, two brothers from the east, with the wife of one, a serene, sad-eyed woman and her niece, and a reticent widower whose few remarks were unfailingly accompanied by a vague, gentle smile. This man, it seemed, was also a skilled seaman, and when the women were settled as comfortably as possible in the ship's cramped cabin belowdecks, he joined Simbrian in directing the less experienced men to make ready to sail. The sails rattled up the masts again, filling with a sudden snap as another westerly gust sprang up, and Kaldar, hauling up the anchor with the two brothers, felt a purposeful tremor run through the ship from stem to stern as she began to go about. The anchor was heaved over the rail, and Kaldar raised his head to look back at the shore. Already they were moving, water churning under the ship's keel, and the shingle beach with its sheltering cliff, and the tall, jutting landmark of the rock point, began to slip away and recede. A pang of mixed fear and anguish went through Kaldar as he realized that in leaving the mainland behind he was severing his one link, however tenuous, with Iselia. For a moment it felt like a betrayal, a desertion, and it took all his willpower not to turn to Simbrian and shout, *"No, no, I'm going back, I won't leave!"* Then with a great effort he pulled himself together, forcing his mind to think rationally. He wasn't deserting her. The distance between them was already far greater, far more unbridgeable, than any physical separation, and by crossing the sea to Simbrian's island he was offering her the only hope within his grasp. Iselia would understand, he told himself fervently. She would understand, and she would want him to go.

"Kaldar!" Simbrian's voice hailed him from further along the deck. "Secure the anchor and help us — we'll need all hands to keep us on course and see us through what's coming to meet us!"

Blinking like one coming abruptly out of a dream Kaldar saw that the sorcerer was gesturing emphatically toward the starboard beam, and turning his head in that direction he also saw that the dark storm cloud now filled a third of the sky. It was fanning out as it came, swallowing the lighter cloud above it, and it had taken on the evil purplish black hues of a vast bruise. Even as he watched, lightning flickered silently seaward from the cloud's heart, and moments later a distant rumble of thunder was audible above the sounds of sails and wind and water.

"I'm coming!" He was suddenly thankful for activity, however strenuous and however alarming, and almost welcomed the storm's approach that would keep him too busy to brood. He bent to lash the anchor to its stanchion, and as his hands secured the knots he made a silent promise to Iselia.

I'll come for you soon, my love. I swear it!

He ran to join the other men.

The voyage which in calm conditions should have taken no more than six or seven hours became instead a fourteen-hour nightmare. The storm overtook them as dusk fell two hours out from the coast, heralded by a violent upsurging of the sea and a raging wind which quickly became a full-force gale. Colossal waves smashed against the ship's sides and over her deck, and when the rain came it was a near-horizontal onslaught, beating against the struggling figures of the men who fought to keep the vessel from turning broadside into the wind where she would surely capsize. All but one of the sails were furled, the remaining sail streaming wildly as the gale tore into it, and the stays groaned and strained against the elements' onslaught, threatening every moment to crack free from their moorings and smash lethally across the width of the ship, cutting down anyone in their path. Amid the roar of sea and wind and the almost continual din of thunder, one crash following so closely on the heels of another that it was impossible to distinguish between them, Kaldar heard Simbrian's voice yelling words that were spell and exhortation combined. He strove to add what little psychic energy he could to the sorcerer's frantic efforts, but in howling darkness and on a pitching deck awash with surging water it was all but impossible to think of anything but immediate physical survival. The world about them was all black insanity now, their only illumination the incessant shudder of blue lightning and the brave but frail glow of a single witch light on the bowsprit, a sphere of protective power created by Simbrian's sorcery to lend them what little help it could.

No one on deck knew how the women were faring below, and no one could be spared to find out. The two easterner brothers began to shout prayers to Aeoris, and soon Kaldar and the widower joined in, their voices falling into grim rhythm like a hellish chantey. Once Kaldar was almost washed overboard when a titanic wave broke across the bows and swept him off his feet in a battering wall of water; by a miracle one flailing hand caught at a fluke of the anchor, which providentially was still in its place, and he clung to it until someone came to his aid. After that, Simbrian ordered every man to secure himself by a line to the mainmast, and the battle to preserve their ship and their lives went on.

Kaldar realized much later that he would never know just when it was, before dawn or long after, that the storm finally blew itself out. For ten hours which had seemed to him like as many lifetimes he had existed in a pummeling maelstrom of lightning and thunder, shrieking wind and boiling ocean, stunned beyond any semblance of lucidity by the elements' ceaseless battering of his body and mind. Soaked to the skin, frozen to the marrow, his legs like lead, and his hands almost too numb to grip a rope, he at last found his senses crawling back from the black pit in which the storm had buried them, and he realized that, though the sea was still heaving and turbulent, the thunder had ceased and the clouds had cleared, and the water flying in his face was not rain but salt spray from the waves crashing against the ship. Simbrian and the widower were running up full sail, day had broken, and though the storm clouds, eastward now, blotted out the rising sun, the sky overhead was washed clear. Kaldar felt the ship go about, and then the newly hoisted sails filled and bellied and the ship seemed to leap forward like an eager cat, cleaving the huge swell as she set to her new course.

Simbrian came down the deck a few minutes later, walking easily with the roll and pitch of the ship to where Kaldar clung dizzily to the mizzenmast.

"We're on our way." The sorcerer looked exhausted and bedraggled, his hair sodden and flattened to his scalp and his beard dripping, but there was an exuberant light in his eyes. "If I've calculated our position rightly — and I think I have — then we should be in sight of the island within an hour." He expelled a deep breath. "It was worse than I expected it to be — but by Aeoris, Kaldar, we came through! We triumphed!"

Kaldar nodded. He tried to smile and tried to speak, but managed neither, for suddenly his stomach was churning. Before they had left the mainland — days ago now, it felt — he'd wondered fleetingly whether he would be seasick on what was his first-ever passage to sea. The storm had driven all such thoughts from his mind, eclipsing them behind the more immediate danger. But now . . .

He made it to the rail just in time, and as he retched miserably over the side he felt Simbrian's hand clamp sympathetically on his shoulder and heard the sorcerer say,

"Don't worry, Kaldar. The sickness will pass in a few minutes — and it's a true saying that the world's best sailors are always ill on their first voyage!"

They were all on deck when the ship put in to shore. For an hour they had watched the island grow from a green haze on the horizon ahead to a distinct landmass contoured by low cliffs and the crescents of sandy coves, until at last they sailed into a wide bay that formed a natural harbor. Kaldar, who stood with Shammana and the three easterners at the rail, was astonished to see that a rough but sturdy stone pier had already been built, stretching out some three or four ship lengths from the beach, and a further jetty was under construction. He wondered how long it was since Simbrian and his followers had first come to occupy the isle. Not more than a matter of months, surely; yet they'd clearly accomplished a great deal in that short time.

There were people waiting on the shore to greet them. Kaldar counted thirty or more waving, smiling figures, including a number of children, and as the ship drew slowly alongside the pier and the sails came rattling down, men ran forward to catch the ropes thrown from the deck and made them fast to great mooring rings set into the stonework. A gangplank was flung across the short, swaying gap between vessel and shore, and as the first of the voyagers crossed it and set foot on the island, a cheer went up.

Simbrian came last of all, gently holding the arm of Nanithe, who was still dazed and frightened in the wake of the storm. As he stepped down he was surrounded — almost mobbed, Kaldar thought — by a press of people, all talking eagerly, congratulating him on his sailing skills, exclaiming over the new arrivals, and giving thanks to the gods, their own gods of Order, for bringing the ship and its passengers safe home. Within minutes Nanithe's expression began to change; her tense posture relaxed and the first ghost of a smile caught at her mouth below wide, awestruck eyes. Seeing it, Simbrian relinquished her back into Shammana's care, and at once all the women in the party were engulfed in a tide of friendly warmth and hurried away to where a horse and wagon waited to convey them inland. Shammana felt a pang of regret for her own faithful horse, unharnessed when they reached the mainland cove and left to wander away. She had no doubts that it would be found, taken in, and well tended, for horses were too valuable to suffer mistreatment; but she wished all the same that it had been possible to bring it with them.

Gradually, amid a clamor of eager talk that showed no sign of subsiding, the new arrivals' meager possessions were unloaded from the ship and the rest of the party set off on foot, following the wagon which had gone ahead. Kaldar's senses were spinning as he strove to take in so many new impressions. He felt as though he had been transported into another dimension; even the weather here was warm and kindly, the sun brilliant overhead, the air warmer, colors brighter, everything more *alive* than in the world he had left. As the harbor fell behind them and they began to climb a gentle green hill, he gazed around, mute with wonder yet feeling out of his depth, almost an intruder in this strange new land.

"It affects everyone in this way to begin with," a voice behind him said. "Don't worry — it'll pass soon enough, and you'll start to feel at home."

Kaldar turned to see Simbrian coming up with him. The sorcerer fell into step at his side and pointed toward the crest of the hill they were ascending. "From the top you'll be able to see our village. It's by no means complete as yet, not even halfway to completion in fact, but we're quite proud of it."

"You've built a village?" Kaldar was freshly awed. "I was greatly impressed by the harbor alone!"

"We've nearly two hundred pairs of willing hands, remember." Simbrian grinned. "And no greedy overlord to sap the will to work."

Kaldar nodded, understanding that only too well. "But don't you fear that the activity here—even the fact that the island is inhabited—will attract the attention of the magi before too long?" he asked. "They've enough agents, and by no means all of them human. If they were to scry, or if some harbinger were to fly over — "

"No." Simbrian shook his head, his voice emphatic. Then he smiled again. "Don't forget that we can fight fire with fire. We may not have the might of Chaos behind us — "

"Nor would we want any dealings with that kind of evil!"

"Quite. But even without such powerful allies, we have strengths and skills of our own. Don't underestimate what we're capable of, Kaldar. I know my own talents and I'm not going to be falsely modest about them; as a sorcerer I'm a match for any magus, and there are a good few here who have the potential to equal me, you included."

Kaldar stared at him, silenced and a little shocked by the compliment. Simbrian continued.

"We've cast a protective shield around the entire isle," he said. "Any exploration by the magi or their acolytes will reveal only an empty land. And on a more physical level, the southern fishermen never venture this far from the mainland, for these waters, like those in the far north, are largely uncharted."

"I'm relieved to know it. But," Kaldar frowned, "what I don't understand is why this island has been left uninhabited for so long." A gesture took in the lush grass to either side of the path. "It's fertile ground, and from what you've told us it's rich in animal life, too. And the climate . . . The yield, and the tithes, would surely be enormous. How have the magi overlooked it?"

"I truly don't know. Perhaps the fact that it lies such a great distance from the Star Peninsula means that the magi simply aren't interested in it. I think you've already seen for yourself that the further south one travels, the less their direct influence is felt."

"That's true. But the overlords' influence doesn't change."

Simbrian laughed. "You're forgetting our intractable friends in the fishing settlement, who have no respect for their masters! No; if the fishermen don't venture this far, then the overlords aren't likely to mount an expedition just for the sake of seeing what might or might not lie beyond their demesnes. They don't even know that the isle exists — and to be honest, Kaldar, I doubt if the magi know it, either, because they've never taken the trouble to find out."

They reached the top of the rise then, and Kaldar stopped, staring in astonishment. Before them, like a great green bowl, lay a shallow natural valley, a patchwork of pastures and deciduous woods bisected by the silver ribbons of two streams. In the far distance were great tracts of fine open land, reminding Kaldar — though the comparison was invidious — of a well-tended park, private hunting reserve of a wealthy overlord, which he had skirted on his southward journey. A company of deer grazing in the valley raised their heads to gaze curiously at the intruders, and on the light wind came the calls of herd beasts. And at the valley's heart, half hidden by a grove of trees, the village of Simbrian and his followers glittered.

Glittered . . . Kaldar blinked, staring and wondering if his senses, or the sun, were deceiving him. Now that his eyes had focused on the village, he could see that it was, as Simbrian had said, far from completed, its finished buildings simple and roughly thatched, while the walls of others stood half built, in some cases barely more than a few handspans high. But the stone from which the village was built — if, indeed, it was stone and not some fabulous metal — sparkled with thousands upon thousands of tiny, brilliant pinpoints, as though an uncountable host of fireflies had alighted on the walls. And the *colors* — a clear pinkish crimson predominated, but Kaldar also saw orange, amber, gold, carmine —

Beside him the other newcomers were also gazing at the scene in astonishment, and he turned to Simbrian, his eyes wide. Simbrian was smiling broadly.

"It's beautiful, isn't it? Crystal quartz. It's the most abundant mineral on the island, in a form of sandstone which is ideal for building. It's more impressive still at dawn and dusk, when the sun strikes it at a low angle, or at night when both moons are up."

Once, in the northern mines, Kaldar had worked in a gallery where deposits of luminous ore cast a strange, nacreous glow on a network of gemstone veins, creating shimmering rainbow fantasies in the cavern. Until now he had thought it the loveliest sight he had ever seen. But this . . .

Their companions were urging the newcomers on now, amused by their reaction but more concerned with the prosaic matters of offering food and comfort. They set off down the valley slope, and as they neared the village the sights and sounds of activity became clearer; smoke rising from several chimneys, voices calling out, the noise of hammers and chisels on stone as building work continued. Two children were herding a flock of white birds toward an enclosure; they were the first to see the approaching party and one ran shouting toward a long, low building at the village's heart. The wagon and its passengers had already arrived and the horse was being unharnessed; Kaldar looked for Shammana and saw her with Nanithe and two island women. Then, as at the harbor, they were surrounded by smiling faces, welcoming hands, eager voices, and Kaldar's eyes filled suddenly with tears as he thought how happy he would have been at this moment, had Iselia only been by his side.

Simbrian saw the tears, saw Kaldar hang back as the others went forward to meet their new friends, and the sorcerer smiled sadly. He reached out a hand and took Kaldar's arm, squeezing it to convey both sympathy and understanding.

"In the name of our exiled gods, Kaldar," he said softly, "welcome home."

That first evening on the island was an occasion that Kaldar and his companions would remember fondly for the rest of their lives. Life here was still rough and simple, for the rebels had been settled only a bare few months; no crops had yet been grown and most people still slept in the open or under makeshift hide shelters. Yet despite this, a welcoming feast was produced for the new arrivals which would have graced the table of any overlord. Sea fish, game birds, and a whole deer cooked over a smoldering roasting pit; roots, sweet grasses, and fruit from the vast wild acreage of woodland. There was even a small supply of mead, made with honey collected — at some personal cost, Simbrian said with wry humor — from bees' nests. It was too new to be truly palatable, but as this was a unique occasion it seemed only right to broach a jar or two.

Talking with this individual and that as the isle's inhabitants sat around the roasting pits, Kaldar heard many of his new friends' personal histories. The recitations were both illuminating and sobering, for it would have been hard to imagine a greater diversity of backgrounds, or a broader spectrum of cruelties, outrages, and injustices under which the great majority had suffered at some time in their lives. One thing, however, was common to them all — hatred for the powers of Chaos, be they overlords, magi, or the gods themselves.

Kaldar also learned more of Simbrian's own past, which until now had been a enigma. Simbrian had been born into a wealthy household, his father a cousin to the overlord of a profitable western demesne. His upbringing was privileged but orthodox; he was highly educated, had learned his catechisms, and had been taught to honor the gods of Chaos and the magi who represented them among mortals. When his tutors had taught him all they could, there was some talk of his being sent to the Star Peninsula, firstly to further his studies and then after a year or two, if all went well, to join the privileged class of secular officials in the magi's service. But the young Simbrian had been horrified by the prospect, for he knew that if he once set foot in the castle, the magi would instantly divine the secret which he had been nurturing for the past ten years — his extraordinary natural talent for sorcery.

"Once within those black gates," he said, "my choice would have been simple. I could have become a magus. Oh, yes," he smiled as Shammana, who sat listening beside Kaldar, drew in a sharp, shocked breath. "It's quite true; the magi have no strictures against initiating outsiders into their ranks. In fact outsiders with a magical talent have been actively sought for the past two hundred years, for the Old Ones' blood has run so thin and become so intermingled that they rarely produce healthy progeny to inherit their skills more directly."

"The Old Ones . . . ?" Kaldar hadn't heard that term before.

"It's our particular name for them; more accurately, it means the older race. Those among the magi who aren't entirely human." Simbrian frowned. "There are still a good many left, but no one can be sure now precisely what they are or where they originally came from. One story has it that they were specifically created by Chaos's rulers to serve them on the mortal plane; another says their ancestors were mortal men and women who mated with demons and thus produced a hybrid with the power and knowledge of both. The truth is lost in prehistory and I doubt if even the magi themselves know it now. But the Old Ones — or some of them — still live on. And they were the ones I feared, the ones who I knew would recognize my ability. The magi don't tolerate the existence of any magical talent that isn't under their control, and as soon as they divined my secret they would have given me the simple but stark option of either becoming one of them, or being killed." He glanced from Shammana to Kaldar and his dark eyes were suddenly intense. "For most mortals in such a position that would be a simple decision to make, for to become a magus is an honor beyond price even in this corrupt world. But for me it was different, for by that time I had come to detest not only the magi but the gods they serve."

Simbrian had had no personal reason to hate Chaos, for under the magi's rule he had been granted a richly contented life and an assured future. But the mantle conferred on him by his birth had never sat easily on his shoulders. He saw injustice and iniquity all about him; he saw the many exploited by the few, he saw greed, cruelty, brutality; and in his mind the only power that could bring change and put right all that was wrong lay in the hands of the magi — and, through the magi, in the hands of the gods who demanded mortal fealty.

Yandros could have acted, he said. The magi were fallible, but gods by their very nature should transcend mortal failings. Yet the lords of Chaos were content to ignore the evils of their human — or half-human — servants. They gave the magi unfettered freedom to commit any wrong, any atrocity, without so much as a word of censure. And for that, Simbrian had come to reject, despise, and finally loathe them.

"Yet," he said, "in truth, what would I have done? I was twenty-two years old, and I was not courageous. Given the choice between death and the utter betrayal of my conscience, I think I would have chosen betrayal."

Kaldar looked at his own hands clasped in his lap. He felt embarrassed by Simbrian's confession of his shortcomings, yet he also admired the older man's ability to be brutally honest about himself. When he recalled his own displays of reckless bravado, and how often they had consisted of nothing more than empty words, he felt shamed. And he also remembered Benetan Liss, and what he himself might have done had he been faced with such a choice. . . .

Someone else, too, was moved by Simbrian's admission. Nanithe sat close to the sorcerer's side as she had done since the feast began, eating very little but watching and listening to the proceedings with wide, uncertain eyes. Now abruptly her expression changed; she reached out and laid one small hand on Simbrian's arm. Startled, he looked at her, and she smiled a sweet smile of sympathy and understanding. She couldn't give voice to her thoughts, but her face said far more than any words could have expressed.

Simbrian's fingers closed gently over hers. "Nanithe, you are too kind to me," he said. "You offer sympathy where I deserve only condemnation."

Nanithe shook her head emphatically and Shammana, who knew the girl better than anyone else did, chuckled softly. "Nanithe thinks you are wrong, Simbrian, and I agree with her. Who else among us can truthfully say that they wouldn't have made the same decision?"

Simbrian held Nanithe's gaze for a few moments more. Then, as though shaking off some old, psychic wound, he hunched his shoulders briefly.

"Well. Perhaps that's neither here nor there now. For our purposes, what matters is that I did *not* go to the Star Peninsula." The cloud began to fade from his face. "My father was a wealthy man but he was also simple and straightforward in his attitudes, and he hoped I would follow in his footsteps, continue his mercantile business and with it our family's wealth and prestige. So I set out to play on his desires and ambitions for me. I evaded my tutors, and turned from a young scholar into a young merchant. I learned how to buy and sell, how to use and exploit, even — and I'll give him his due, my father was a fair man in his way — how to manipulate my servants and my masters alike to the greater profit and benefit of all concerned. I made myself indispensable, and so the prospect of my being sent to the Star Peninsula became more and more remote until at last it was abandoned altogether. And I was thankful for that. So thankful. Because I knew, by then, where my true loyalty lay."

Simbrian's tone changed suddenly, becoming very soft, and his eyes focused on something far away, beyond his companions' perceptions. "In my twenty-third year," he said, "I learned to travel on the astral planes. I made many journeys, explored many dimensions . . . and then on one such journey I discovered a pathway the like of which I'd never encountered before. The studies I had made, the experiments I'd conducted, told me nothing; I was perplexed. So I followed the pathway — reckless, I know, but I couldn't contain my curiosity; something seemed to draw me, and my instinct told me that this was *right*.

"The pathway led me to a door of pure golden light, so brilliant that I could hardly bear to look at it. I laid my hand on the door; instantly the light softened, then the door seemed to melt away and I looked through. What I saw . . ." He laughed ruefully. "I'll never find the words to describe it, for they simply don't exist. More than beautiful. Far more — it was a place of transcendent wonder; of utter serenity, kindness, loveliness, justice. A place where the soul could flower and bloom; a place of *hope*." He shifted his position, his eyes seeming to stare hard into the depths of his own memory. "I'd been idly exploring the planes — you know the exercises, Kaldar, you know how they're done and how the mind can reach out beyond the physical world into unimaginable realms. I was attuned, that's the only way I have of explaining it. The specter of the Star Peninsula and discovery by the magi was haunting me, and there was disgust and hatred for them in my heart. Such *hatred* . . . I wanted no part of their evil regime, no part of Chaos's ethic. I asked myself, I remember asking the question: *How can I pretend to love these demons? How can I continue to live such a lie under their rule?* There must be more, I told myself. There must be something better, something kinder. I was in turmoil and trying to escape from my own turbulent thoughts in the disciplines of astral venturing, but I lost both my concentration and my control, and it was as though something else, something outside my own mind, directed me to that golden portal.

"I tried to cross the threshold, but no matter how hard I strove, my power and skill weren't enough. I could see, but I could not enter. At last, in desperation, I called out — and an answer came. Not in words, but suddenly I knew . . ." He hesitated, and a strange flush came into his cheeks, a hectic look as though he'd been suddenly overtaken by a violent fever. "I knew what I had stumbled on, and the nature of the barrier I had breached. I was gazing into the realm of Order."

His listeners were silent. Even Kaldar said nothing, though a hundred questions were crowding to his tongue. After a few moments Simbrian continued once more.

"What it was that communicated with me then I don't truly know. I think — I believe — it was a fraction of the spirit which is the essence of Order's realm, though that's only a poor metaphor, and again words are too inadequate to describe it. But whatever it was and whatever power moved within it, it opened my eyes and granted me knowledge. And that was when I understood the true evil of Chaos, which cares not one whit for the mortal realm yet which rules and uses it as a child might rule and use a toy. That was when I understood the hope that Order offers to our world, the hope of peace and justice, where a man can be more than a plaything to be exploited by greater powers than he can muster. The hope of . . . of *sanity*."

The story of the downfall of the seven lords of Order was enshrined in the catechisms taught to every child. But from the power that communicated with him across the threshold of Order's realm Simbrian had learned that the catechisms distorted the truth. Order's forces had not attempted to rise up against the rightful rule of Yandros and his six brothers, as the ancient legends claimed. Instead centuries ago, before that cataclysmic battle for supremacy took place, it was the lords of Order and not of Chaos who were worshiped by mortals as the only true gods.

Kaldar could keep silent no longer at this, and his eyes lit feverishly. "Then what so many of us have always believed is true — Yandros and his evil kin are nothing more than demons!"

"No." Simbrian's head came up sharply. "Don't make that mistake, Kaldar; don't *ever* make that mistake. The powers of Order and Chaos are two faces of the same coin. They may be utterly opposed, anathema to each other, but they are very closely matched. We call Yandros and his brothers demons, but a demon is a low thing, easily controlled, as I don't doubt you've discovered during your own studies and experiments." His brown eyes focused briefly but keenly on Kaldar's face. "Try those tactics against one of the great lords of Chaos, and you won't live long enough to rue your stupidity. They are not demons, any more than our lord Aeoris is a demon. Yandros is night to Aeoris's day, darkness to his light; his absolute inversion, but also his absolute equal."

Kaldar frowned. "If that's so, how did the monstrosities of Chaos turn the world on its head and usurp Order's rule?"

"They caught the gods unawares. The lords of Order had thought them safely banished, but they found a weak link in the armor, gained a foothold in the world, and used it to mount a challenge." Simbrian's mouth twitched into an ironic smile. "Very much as we are resolved to do in our turn. As the old adage puts it, the rising sun sees nothing unfamiliar in a new day. So, our lord Aeoris and his brothers were defeated, and Yandros exiled them from the mortal world. 'To a place of illimitable emptiness, beyond the borders of time and space' is what we are told. But we've been misled. Aeoris's realm — the true realm of Order — is within our reach. Not in this dimension, nor on any of the seven astral planes known to us; but it is there, and we can touch it."

Kaldar ran his tongue over dry lips. "And . . . what of Lord Aeoris?

Have you . . . ?" He couldn't finish the question.

"Have I glimpsed our gods? No, Kaldar, I have not. As yet the link between our realm and theirs is weak and tenuous and the seven lords themselves are still confined by Yandros's interdiction. But they're not entirely helpless. They may be unable to communicate directly with us, but through the powers their realm still possesses they have been able to shield us and offer us what help they can. And we in our turn can give them our strength. It's not enough yet to allow the greater barriers to be broken, but it *is* enough to begin the weakening of Chaos's defenses. Thus the circle of energy is created and the power starts to build. That is what we have achieved thus far, though it's a small-enough beginning."

Shammana reached out to touch him, so lightly that he could barely have felt the contact.

"It is a great beginning, Simbrian. No one else could have accomplished it."

Simbrian glanced warmly at her, then shook his head. "I don't know, Shammana. I'm nothing but an instrument, a conduit. Perhaps our gods chose me because they had a reason, or perhaps I broke through by accident and merely provided them with a means to establish contact with mortals once more. I don't know, and I never shall. But that's of no consequence. All that matters is that, for the first time since Chaos overthrew Order and cast justice to the four winds, there is hope for change. And with Aeoris's blessing, we shall *make* that change!"

CHAPTER XXIII

There seemed to be little more to say in the wake of Simbrian's revelations, and a strange but pleasant sense of peace settled on the company as the celebration slowly meandered to a natural end. People began to drift away to their shelters or new-built homes; the second moon had risen and the village clearing was filled with the eldritch light of both satellites near the full. The fires in the roasting pits were damped down, wafting scented smoke through the quiet night air. Nanithe fell asleep on Simbrian's shoulder and stirred only long enough for Shammana to shepherd her away. Then at last, perhaps by accident or, as Kaldar believed, by design, only seven were left in the moonshot darkness around the pits' dying embers.

Kaldar was surprised and more than a little awed to find himself included among this last coterie. The widower was also present but the remaining four, two men and two women, were strangers. By some instinctive but unspoken agreement they maintained their silence until the last bright sparks of candles or lanterns had gone out in houses and shelters and the village was still. Then Simbrian spoke.

"My friends, I don't think I need to tell you that I have a reason for manipulating this small group into staying behind while our companions seek their beds. You know, I think, that with the arrival of our ship today the numbers we have been waiting to amass are finally complete. We now have among us forty-nine men and women with a strong and proven psychic ability. And of those forty-nine, seven — the seven gathered here — are skilled and experienced sorcerers."

Six faces watched him intently; no one said a word, but their eyes were alight.

"Lord Aeoris and his brothers have been unable to reach us directly," Simbrian continued. "Yandros of Chaos controls the portal that once allowed our gods to step between their realm and ours, and that way — the old way — is sealed off. But there is a means of breaking Chaos's stranglehold. A ritual which, if it is successful, will crack the dam that Yandros has built against the powers of Order. We can muster seven times seven souls whose minds, linked and in unison, can invoke and command immense psychic power. With that power to draw on, we of the inner seven will attempt to perform that ritual.

"In truth, I can't estimate our chances of success. There are dangers in any sorcerous rite, as you all know; and the more powerful the rite, the greater the risks become. We may attract unwanted attention despite our precautions, and be annihilated by the servants of Chaos. We may encounter something on our journey through the planes that devours our minds and bodies before we can rally our defenses. Or we may, simply, fail. But if we do *not* fail" — Simbrian paused to draw breath, and in that moment the atmosphere around the dying fires seemed charged with the energy of a Warp — "If we do *not* fail . . . then the flame of Order's power will ignite and shine once again in our world. And our lord Aeoris, the great god himself, will return to us from his long exile!"

After only a brief period of rest and recuperation Kaldar was surprised and a little dismayed to learn that they were to embark on a second sea voyage. But Simbrian had good reason for not wanting to conduct the great ritual on the rebels' island. The ceremony had attendant risks, he said; not least the danger that the energies summoned and unleashed by their sorcery might draw the attention of Chaos's followers either on the physical or the occult planes. Although they would be magically shielded, and in theory the shield should hide them, in practice nothing could be guaranteed, and Simbrian was unwilling to risk the lives of more people than was absolutely necessary. So they were to sail to another and far smaller island some five hours to the west. It was uninhabited and, like their own isle, uncharted and unknown, but there the resemblance ended, for the White Isle, as the rebels had dubbed it, was nothing more than a bare and barren cone of rock. Simbrian believed it to be the remnants of an ancient volcano; there were a number in the south, he said, all long-extinct and their origins largely unrecognizable now. He had discovered it while traveling in his astral form, and with several companions had made a physical sortie by sea to explore further. The isle's interior could be reached by a narrow inlet, and though it would mean an arduous climb, there was a perfect natural amphitheater at the cone's heart which would be the ideal site for their work.

The ship was made ready within two days, for there were willing hands in plenty to repair the storm damage to sails and rigging, and on a bright, calm morning forty-nine men and women crossed the gangplank to her decks. Of Kaldar's companions on his first voyage, Shammana, the widower, one of the easterner brothers, and — surprisingly — the young niece of the sad-eyed woman were included in the party, and every island dweller came down to the shore to wave them out of harbor and wish them godspeed. Shammana fretted about Nanithe, who was left behind, but Simbrian assured her that the girl would be well cared for by the island women, and the warmth and certainty in his tone, which hinted at something more than a tenuous personal concern, reassured her.

The contrast between this voyage and the first could not have been greater. The weather was perfect and the sea calm; even the wind, it seemed, had set out to favor them today. To his relief Kaldar wasn't seasick this time, and when the cone of the White Isle rose slowly into view on the horizon a little after noon, he was at the rail with the others, peering eagerly ahead across the glittering sea.

The island grew until it was a towering mass above them, blotting out half the sky and giving the unnerving impression that it was toppling toward the ship. The single, massive crag of the ancient volcanic cone dominated the view, and clustered around it was a tangle of lesser crags, sheer cliffs, and broken ledges falling to the sea in an apparently impenetrable wall. Here the tide surged and foamed, creating treacherous races and eddies between the teeth of rocks hidden just below the swell. Simbrian called all skilled hands to the sheets and the ship tacked about, standing well off from the rocks as she skirted the island. Then Simbrian shouted, "There! Just beyond that spur — can you make it out?" and shielding his eyes against the glare of the water Kaldar saw a narrow fissure in the towering wall. They sailed toward it, and after three heart-stopping attempts in which it seemed their vessel would run shatteringly onto the waiting rocks, the prow nosed into the fissure's mouth. The tide race caught them and bore them into the narrow strait, then gradually the current's turbulence slackened until they were sailing in calm water between sheer cliffs, with the sky no more than a vivid ribbon far above them. Shadow enclosed them, the temperature dropped, and the reek of salt and dank weed made Kaldar's nostrils curl; he shivered in his thin shirt and trousers and glanced covertly at Shammana, who gave him a wan but determined smile in return.

They reached the end of the fissure at last, and emerged into the relatively open waters of a huge, still pool. Rock walls rose on three sides, blotting out the sun and turning the water to a murky and brackish gray green, but directly ahead the cliffs were broken by a broad ledge abutting the water almost on a level with the ship's deck, beyond which a steep but scalable slope led into the isle's interior and the great central cone.

Kaldar swallowed, attempting to induce saliva as his mouth grew unpleasantly dry. Though he was mountain born and bred, there was something about this island that struck dread into him. Perhaps it was the silence and the stillness engendered by the absence of any living thing or perhaps it was something far more arcane, but this place had a brooding and terrible atmosphere. It was almost a physical aura, he thought; a sense that colossal energies lay just beneath the visible surface, dormant but by no means dead.

He shook the disquieting feelings off with a quick shiver as Simbrian's voice started to call out orders. On their first sortie here the sorcerer and his party had hammered several iron spars into the ledge near the water's brink; now the ship was maneuvered against the ledge wall, touching with a gentle bump, and three men scrambled ashore with ropes to secure her to these makeshift moorings. The anchor went down, the gangplank rattled across the short, swaying divide, and within three more minutes everyone was ashore. They stood gazing at the slope ahead of them, voices silent, faces thoughtful. Simbrian checked that the moorings were all secure, then turned to face them.

"Well, my friends." Though he spoke softly, the cliffs reflected his words back, creating eerie echoes. "The climb ahead of us is arduous, but our goal is closer now than it has ever been before. The power of Order has guided us here — it is for us now to find the strength and the skill to do justice to our lord Aeoris's inspiration; to carry out the task we have set ourselves — and to succeed!"

They toiled up the slope of the crater in a long, silent procession. Simbrian led them, picking the easiest route he could find over terrain that was one moment painfully rough and the next as smooth as glass. The cone was formed from a variety of rocks which had fused an uncountable age ago into a bizarre mosaic; in some places the going was treacherously slippery while in others the surface was a mass of tiny, knife-sharp ridges that cut through shoe soles and drew blood from tender feet. No one had breath to spare for speaking, but as they trudged on and up and the crater's broken summit began to seem less remote, a new mood began to impel them, an air of eager anticipation — almost exultation — that spread and strengthened the higher they climbed. Aching calf and thigh muscles seemed suddenly regenerated, energy flowed back into tired bodies, and even Kaldar's qualms were swept away as the new feeling took hold of him. If this was Order's doing, then he was fervently grateful.

They were less than five hundred feet from the volcano's summit when Simbrian veered toward what at first sight appeared to be a darker, triangular scar on the rock face ahead and a little to the left of their path. The others followed but Kaldar hung back, waiting to help Shammana over a hazardous patch as slick as untrammeled ice. When it was safely negotiated and he was able to look up once more, he was startled to see that the head of the procession had reached the scar and appeared to be vanishing through it. Then he realized his mistake. The scar wasn't simply a patch of discoloration but a crack in the crater wall — the entrance to a cave or passage.

They reached the triangular mouth with the last half dozen climbers, and peered in. Tiny pinpoints of light bobbed in the crevasse like will-o'-the-wisps, forming a line, and their thin glow was just strong enough to reveal a narrow and claustrophobic tunnel beyond the entrance.

Kaldar felt in his pouch for one of the beeswax tapers that Simbrian had asked them all to carry. Others followed suit, and with the feeble illumination to guide them they entered the tunnel in their companions' wake. Darkness closed in; the shuffle of cautious footsteps echoed softly in the confined space and once someone up ahead uttered a nervous laugh, quickly stifled. The passage twisted and turned, and before long Kaldar lost all sense of direction and distance. They might have covered ten yards or ten miles for all he knew, and the bobbing tapers were mesmeric, drawing his eyes and playing havoc with perspective. But at last there was a perceptible lightening in the tunnel. Silhouettes at the head of the line began to emerge from the surrounding gloom, color slowly bled back . . . and, quite suddenly, they emerged into full daylight once more.

Kaldar stood staring and blinking, stunned both by the light and by the scene confronting him. The tunnel had led them through the cone and into the heart of the ancient volcano. From their vantage point — a broad ledge some two hundred feet or more above the floor — the crater bowl was a shimmering expanse of white pumice and black basalt, once molten but now petrified into fantastic patterns through which streaks of vivid color ran like arteries. Above them the cone itself towered dizzyingly, its colossal walls pitted with the scars of violent prehistoric eruptions. And higher still, framed vertiginously by the near-perfect circle of the cone's summit, was the cloudless sky of the outside world.

Shammana and several others who had no head for heights were clutching at the rock behind them and staring determinedly at their own feet. Kaldar had never suffered in that way, but even he felt like a fly clinging to a cliff. It wasn't the scale of the crater that dwarfed and overpowered him, but its simple yet relentless *dominance*. From this vantage point the bowl and the towering volcano were an enclosed world, complete in itself and inescapable, and the sensation that produced in him was awesome.

Simbrian's voice brought him back to earth. The sorcerer had moved to one end of the ledge and was beckoning them to join him.

"There's a way down here," he said. "It's awkward in places but negotiable enough even for the unfit sluggards among us." A smile accompanied the last words and there was a ripple of nervous laughter in response, which the crater walls transmuted into a carillon of echoes. *Everything echoes on this island,* Kaldar thought, remembering the inlet, the harbor, the tunnel. *Echoes and is amplified. . . . Perhaps that's why Simbrian chose it. Perhaps it will also amplify our power. . . .*

"Kaldar?" Shammana was beside him and took firm hold of his arm, still refusing to look about her. "I must have your help again, I think, if I'm to reach the floor in one piece." And under her breath she added, "Unfit sluggards indeed. . . ."

The ghost of a grin made Kaldar's mouth twitch as he led her toward the downward path.

Preparations for the ritual were to begin at sunset. Though the astral rite itself was startlingly simple, a great deal of preliminary work needed to be done before the seven sorcerers could safely embark on their journey. Firstly, they must conduct the ceremonies that would hide and protect them from Chaos's prying. Then the circle of power must be created and fed with psychic energy. Only when that energy had reached its peak could the final and most perilous stage of the rite begin.

The patch of sky overhead was changing from pale, hard blue toward a warm indigo as they sat down on the crater floor to eat a ceremonial meal of bread and fruit. A bronze chalice filled with water, over which Simbrian had intoned a solemn prayer, was passed sunwise from hand to hand until each person present had taken a sip, then the sorcerer set the chalice, still half full, at what he judged to be the exact center of the uneven bowl surface. It glinted in the fading light, reflecting the colors of the surrounding rock, and from the bag he carried Simbrian brought four more objects which he set carefully around the chalice; a white bird's feather, an unlit candle, a small cup, and a single stone. The silence was acute; even the sea couldn't be heard through the rock ramparts surrounding them. Then, at a signal from the sorcerer, four women rose from the group and stepped into the center of the circle. Each took one of the four artifacts; then they turned about and formed up, two by two. The rest of the party got to their feet; Simbrian held out a hand to the man on his left, he in turn took the hand of the woman beside him, and they formed a human chain. When Shammana grasped his hand in hers Kaldar felt a tingling thrill as the current of energy which Simbrian had generated and the others now magnified flowed through him; then the final link was made and, with the four women leading them, the long line began to walk across the bowl in an easterly direction. The vast crater wall loomed before them; the procession halted and the woman who held the white feather stepped forward, then turned to face the others. She raised the feather high, and a shudder of power flickered through the human chain as Simbrian reached out to touch its tip. The feather seemed to flare with light; then suddenly in its place a spectral silver bird balanced delicately on the woman's hand, its body translucent and its wings beating slowly and gracefully.

Simbrian's voice echoed richly through the crater. "So by the guardian of air is the east protected. In great Aeoris's name, let no cold abomination descend from the sky to break this chain of power!"

The woman stepped forward to join their line leaving the ghostly bird hovering at the crater rim. Its image was vividly imprinted on Kaldar's mind as the chain moved onward, sunwise, to the southern quarter. Here the woman who held the candle stepped out, turned, raised the candle high. Again there was the shiver of energy as Simbrian reached out, and a bright, scarlet flame leaped into life where the candle had been, casting a roseate glow over the woman's face as she held it fearlessly in her hands.

"So by the guardian of fire is the south protected," Simbrian declared. "In great Aeoris's name, let no burning abomination devour the flame of this chain of power!"

The flame hung unsupported, burning brighter as they moved on to the western rim. Here, the small cup became a rippling reflection in the crater wall, as Simbrian summoned the guardian of water and sealed them from all engulfing abominations of the sea. And lastly they stood in the north quarter, where the stone became a shining, phantasmic tree, guardian of earth, protector against all evils from the land. The four symbols shimmered at their cardinal stations, illuminating the dusk-filled bowl, and finally Simbrian led his chain of followers to the east once more, completing and sealing the circle in the name of Aeoris and his six brothers of Order. As the last words were uttered, a huge, silent flash of white light erupted through the crater. When vision cleared, the four symbols were gone . . . but a sense of peace, of strength, and of enormous yet gentle power filled the bowl.

Slowly the forty-nine participants relaxed, releasing hands and letting arms fall loosely to their sides. The soft sound of expelled breaths resonated in the crater like the rustling of leaves in a light breeze; Kaldar shook his head, dispelling lingering mental images. Then Simbrian said:

"We can do no more to protect ourselves. Now the real work can commence."

No one else spoke as they moved back to the center of the bowl. The bronze chalice still stood where Simbrian had placed it, and now they gathered in two concentric circles around the cup. Simbrian's seven chosen sorcerers formed the inner circle, while the rest spread in a ring about them. As they seated themselves cross-legged on the rock floor, Simbrian looked up. The sky had dimmed to the deep and infinitely translucent blue purple that heralded the coming of night. No stars were visible yet, nor the thin silver filigree of the first moon's light, but out beyond the island and over the western sea the sun had set below the horizon. Simbrian smiled, then from his bag drew a soft and pliable bundle that, to Kaldar's eyes, seemed to shine faintly as though with an inner radiance of its own. As the sorcerer unraveled it they all saw that it was a single cord of finely spun flax. Wordlessly, Simbrian held one end of the cord out to Kaldar; as he took it Kaldar sensed instantly that it was charged with power and knew what its purpose must be. This was the physical link that would bind the seven sorcerers to their companions in the outer circle, and the medium through which the combined psychic wills of that outer circle would flow to energize the great ritual. A shudder of mingled eagerness and dread shot through him and he began to pay the cord out, watching intently as it passed from hand to hand until the inner circle was complete.

Very quietly, Simbrian said, "Wrap the cord once round your right hands. Whatever happens, the contact between us must not be broken."

They obeyed him, and when he was satisfied he turned to the nearest of the forty-two silent watchers beyond their tight group.

"Take hold, and keep hold. This is our lifeline — if you love our cause, I beg you not to forget that for a single instant!"

Silently the remainder of the cord was taken and paid out until the twin circles were linked and completed. Kaldar had one glimpse of Shammana's face, taut but eager in the gathering darkness, and beyond her the sharp little features of the girl who had accompanied them from the mainland, calm now with a wisdom that belied her years. For a few moments longer Simbrian stood motionless; then suddenly and quickly he exhaled the breath that had been pent in his lungs.

"Very well." Though he did his best to disguise it the tension in his tone was palpable. "We are ready. No more words, now. Let us begin."

CHAPTER XXIV

Kaldar knew that the change was taking place when the steady, harmonious humming sound that rose and fell in his ears began to alter by subtle yet unmistakable degrees. His rational self, the self which sat between two of his fellow sorcerers, eyes closed and breathing steady as he held the charged cord, knew that the sound came from the throats and lips of their forty-two companions in the outer circle, a focus for the power and energy they summoned from within themselves as they reached out toward the astral planes. But rationality was starting to fall away, and as his senses slowly grew attuned to higher and more ephemeral levels the new harmonies became stronger. They were not quite discordant, yet they were strange enough to send a psychic shiver through him. Sounds from another dimension, a fractional but crucial shade out of kilter with their own, as two worlds touched and the door between them began to open. . . .

There was a sudden sensation in the pit of his stomach, a lurch as though part of his being had been wrenched out of place without warning. Dizziness swept over him; instinctively his right hand clenched, gripping the cord that was wrapped around his palm. To his left he heard a hiss of indrawn breath, and the cord pulsed with energy as the lurching sensation assailed him again, more emphatically this time. Kaldar knew what would follow and he prepared himself, readying his mind for the giddying swing and jolt as his physical and astral bodies separated. When it came it was vastly stronger than he'd anticipated, fueled by the psychic energies of the outer circle; a great, giddy rush that seemed to tear him in two. He thought he cried out, thought he heard other voices echoing his, and for an instant he seemed to be spinning amid blazing rainbows of color that flashed through his closed lids and burned his eyes. Then, like a swimmer thrown inshore by a huge breaker, he felt the undertow of power sweep back and away from him. Confusion metamorphosed into stillness, and Kaldar's astral senses awoke.

He hung — or that was the closest approximation he could find, for he was no longer aware of his physical self — some twenty feet above the crater floor. Darkness had fallen by this time, and the twin circles of human figures below him were mere shadows, featureless and indistinct. But the cord that linked them glowed strongly, almost fiercely, a ring of golden light pulsing to the rhythm of a heartbeat. At their stations by the crater walls Kaldar could now see the four symbolic guardians clearly. The silver bird, the scarlet flame, the rippling fall of water, and the spectral tree, each one shining and pulsing as the cord pulsed, drawing power from the human circle.

Another mind touched his, and he sensed the presence of Simbrian and his fellow sorcerers beside him. They had no visible form, and Kaldar realized that the initial surge of power had achieved far more than a simple transference onto the astral. In one step they had passed beyond the four lower planes of earth, water, air, and fire and had reached a dimension of pure potential, in which the doors to many hidden worlds waited only to be opened by anyone with the skill to find and use the key. He waited — below, the body he'd left behind held in a tense breath — and after a few moments a faint grid of silver gray light began to form in the air before him. It stretched and spread like a giant spiderweb, firstly in two dimensions, then in three, and then into other and stranger depths beyond the reach of any physical human senses. Kaldar, his mind attuned, saw every spiraling anomaly of time and space within the web and he gazed at it, rapt, until again he felt Simbrian's mental contact and understood the sorcerer's urgent, wordless message. The crossroads had been reached, its many paths had been revealed. Now they must seek out the one that would lead them to their goal.

On the crater floor, the seven central figures drew closer together and their hands, still linked by the glowing cord, reached out to the middle of the ring. Their minds, freed from the body's constraints, had no awareness of their movements, but in the outer circle there was a shifting and a tautening and a sudden intent concentration as their comrades saw what was taking place. The sorcerers' fingertips met above the chalice, touched, and the cord that bound them together seemed to catch fire. Pale flames that did not sear or burn sprang upward and outward, and the contours of seven faces sprang into stark relief, light and shadow creating eldritch patterns across mouth and cheek and jaw. The sorcerers' eyes were open now but their earthly selves saw nothing, and in the outer circle the soft, low humming that had continued without a pause since the ritual's opening began to change. An urgent note crept into the sound; slowly it rose both in pitch and in intensity, and to a keen ear it might have seemed that words were taking shape, though in no language known to a conscious mind. With the new intensity came rhythm, the bones of a steady chant, fueling the supernatural flames and urging the power to *come, grow, come, rise*. At the heart of the inner circle, where fingers now entwined and gripped, a column of cool fire sprang to life from the chalice and streamed through their hands and skyward like a river of light as power from the chanting men and women flowed along the cord and into the bodies and psyches of Simbrian and his companions. The single flame grew taller, stronger, fanning and opening high above their heads into a burning, brilliant flower. . . .

In another dimension, an infinite distance from the crater yet melding and merging with it, seven minds took hold of the power, absorbing it, becoming one with it and drinking in its strength. The silver gray network that was all possibilities quivered and swam before their vision, and together they reached out toward its shining heart, where one path, one way, seemed to call to them and draw them and open before them. They projected themselves forward, entering the web; immediately it began to twine and spiral around them, moving faster and faster until it seemed they were enclosed in a spinning cocoon. Kaldar's senses were dazed by it; he felt as though he, too, were starting to spin, merging with the web and becoming a part of it —

"Don't be distracted! Watch our path — concentrate only on our path!"

Simbrian's mental warning shattered the enchantment, and a jolt went through Kaldar as he realized how close he had come to falling under the web's spell. As he dragged his senses back under his command the sorcerer communicated again.

"Whatever happens, don't let the web ensnare you! That is this plane's greatest danger — if it takes you unawares, you may be led into dimensions over which you can exert no control and from which your mind might never return. Our path lies directly ahead. Focus on it, and on nothing else!"

Kaldar concentrated his will, opening himself to the current feeding from the human circle in the crater, and felt a thrill of exultation as one strand of the web began to glow more brightly. As it brightened it seemed to become more substantial, and its color changed from silver gray to gold, until to his astral eyes it was a broad, golden ribbon, an unwavering road running perfectly straight and true through the confusion of planes.

A new wave of energy shuddered through the seven travelers, and Simbrian's communication came in an eager surge.

"Together — now!"

As one they surged forward, and the power of the golden road took hold of them. It was, Kaldar thought later, like being caught up in a vast, singing embrace of light that carried him as easily as though he were a leaf in a gale. Exhilaration filled him; the golden road grew wider, stronger, more brilliant; his senses expanded in the giddy race of their progress, and suddenly ahead he saw something rushing to meet them. It resolved into the shape of a shimmering golden arch, dazzling him, calling to him; in his astral form he stretched out welcoming arms, and his physical self, far away in a world that no longer had any meaning to him, gave a shout of joy that echoed through the crater.

Then, so suddenly and so shockingly that it almost hurled Kaldar back to that physical body, Simbrian roared out,

"No! Wait! SHIELD YOURSELVES!"

An enormous, buffeting shock hit the travelers as, at the same instant, their leader snatched control of the power that sustained them and twisted it in on itself. Kaldar felt a colossal weight crashing down on him, felt himself spin and fall, and suddenly the seven were encased in a suffocating cage of gray nothingness. Panic rose, but before it could overwhelm them they all felt Simbrian's fierce mental grip and heard his urgent words in their minds.

"Block all thoughts. Be calm, and be utterly still. If we're detected it will be the end for us all."

With a sense of terrible foreboding Kaldar looked beyond the nothingness even as he reflexively obeyed the order. For a moment his perception failed, but then he sensed it. A vast wing of darkness, moving slowly through the multiple dimensions of the web like a thundercloud sweeping across a sunlit sky. He glimpsed the savage spectral flicker of pent energy at its heart, heard an unearthly howling that vibrated through all of his being, and as it passed above them he strove to crush his mind into submission and *think of nothing, of nothing, of nothing.* . . .

The dark horror glided past and onward, leaving them behind. Gradually, cautiously, Simbrian released his hold on the psychic shield he had flung around them. The gray nothingness faded, the suffocating sensation eased, and the golden road appeared once more.

The same question formed in all their minds, and Simbrian answered it.

"Chaos's sentinels patrol the planes," he told them. *"There is no pattern to their vigilance, but they keep a constant watch. This time we were fortunate, and perhaps, too, the powers of Order were able to give us additional protection. But we dare not risk a second encounter, or it will drain the energy we need to open the final door. Focus your minds, draw on all your strength. We must work fast!"*

The glorious exhilaration of their earlier progress was swamped now by a sharp sense of dread as they began to move again. Faster, faster; ahead now the shining arch towered and seemed to pulse, and then came the final whirling rush and they hovered before the golden door that was the gateway to Order's realm.

They couldn't bear to look at it. Its light blinded them, burning their vision, and they were forced to turn aside. Only Simbrian held his ground. With an astral hand he reached out and touched the door, as he had done once before . . . and, as before, the light dimmed and the glittering door melted away, leaving only the arch shining softly and framing the scene beyond.

Before them, through the arch, was a garden of living light. Incredible shades flowed and blended together, forming lustrous rainbow banks; colors that no mortal mind could imagine merged into a perfect harmony of sheer loveliness. Tiny, jewel-hued sparks danced among the rainbows like fireflies and, though it was so faint as to be barely audible to the seven travelers, a cascade of sublime musical notes shimmered in the air.

Like captivated children, the six who had never before been privileged to witness the beauties of Order's realm gazed at the wonder before them in silent awe. Simbrian, though, remembered the harbinger of Chaos which had so nearly brought disaster on them and his words cut into their rapture and broke its mesmeric hold.

"Quickly," he urged them, *"we must waste no time. Remember the ritual — summon the power, and pray that our friends on the physical plane have enough resources left!"*

In the volcano's cone a shudder ran through the outer circle as everyone within it sensed his intentions through the link of the glowing cord. The pillar of flame streaming from the chalice burned more vividly, sending long shadows darting across the crater, and the rhythmic chant took on renewed vigor. The circle began to chant a name, repeating it over and over again, their massed voices growing stronger, louder, more emphatic as they called upon their exiled god.

"Aeoris . . . Aeoris . . . great Lord Aeoris! Aeoris . . . Aeoris . . . great Lord Aeoris!" Their minds were becoming one mind, their wills uniting into one will as they drew on their deepest reserves of purpose and resolution and stamina. Clenched hands sweated and grew slick as they gripped the cord, inspiriting it with their energy, feeding the power through its pulsing length to the seven sorcerers of the inner circle. The cord crackled, jerking and twitching in their hands; the sorcerers' bodies were glowing now, radiating a cold, blue white light that robbed their flesh and hair and clothing of all color and gave them the ghastly semblance of marble statues.

On the astral plane, before the golden arch, Simbrian's consciousness merged with those of his companions. As one entity they drank in the power and drew on its potency; as one entity, heart and mind and soul, they reached out to challenge and defy the barrier that stood between them and their gods.

As contact was made, the arch was shaken by a searing jolt and the scene beyond wavered violently. The seven felt the shock reverberate through them; they stood fast, tightening and intensifying their focus, then again their minds coalesced and, as Aeoris's name rang out again in the human realm, they projected a second surge of power toward the barrier.

There was a small, brief, and muffled noise, like the sound of a glass pane cracking cleanly across. A thin sliver of intolerable brightness stabbed down from the apex of the arch, cutting the image of the peaceful garden in two. As the livid rent appeared, the sweet, faint music swelled to a deafening pitch and became one shrill, high, and breathtakingly pure note. The sound beat against their senses, wave upon wave, growing louder and higher, until with his last floundering scrap of individual awareness Kaldar was certain he couldn't bear the pressure of it for an instant longer. He would break, he *must* break, he couldn't maintain control —

Then through the flood of sound that swamped him he heard Simbrian's commanding voice, and at the same moment felt the rise of power, vast and overwhelming and orgasmic, as their comrades on the mortal plane gave all they had in one final supreme effort.

"Now! NOW!!"

The power filled their souls and erupted from them in a huge, united surge of will. The deafening note became a shriek, losing its purity, climbing the scale until it seemed to tear the air apart. The golden arch shook as though in an earthquake — then from the realm of Order a titanic blast of light exploded outward through the gateway. In the crater Kaldar's physical body screamed; on the golden road his astral body echoed the scream as he felt himself plunging into the heart of a sun, its radiance blinding him, its fire searing him, its colossal, triumphant voice roaring and dinning in his ears. He fell, flailing, twisting, his mind a mayhem of terror and ecstasy. And at the core of the sun was a white-hot eye, and the eye began to open, and twin tongues of silver fire flowed out from it, reaching toward him to catch him and embrace him and absorb his soul in one last instant of blissful agony —

A terrific concussion imploded in on him, and he hit a solid surface with jarring force that knocked the breath from his lungs in a staccato *whoof* of expelled air. *Breath . . . his lungs . . . oh gods, he felt sick . . .* and everything was still. No blazing sun, no roaring sound, no all-consuming heat and power and glory but only darkness and the feel of something cold and hard underneath him, pressing against his aching ribs. His legs were awkwardly contorted and his eyelids screwed tightly shut; he felt his hands flex and the sensation, unused as he was to having a body to control, sent a wave of disorientation through him.

Then other hands were closing on his arms and a familiar voice reached his ears as though from far, far away.

"Kaldar . . . Kaldar, it's Shammana. You're back, you're back with us on the White Isle. Careful, now. . . . You collapsed, you all collapsed and we couldn't catch you as you fell. Can you sit up?"

He could, he thought. Nothing was broken, though the impact onto hard rock would have given him a few bruises. Tears were squeezing themselves past his eyelids; he disentangled a hand from Shammana's solicitous grasp and rubbed at his face, then, blinking, cautiously allowed his eyes to open.

The first moon had risen and a scatter of reflected light from the sky was enough to make shapes and shadows visible in the crater. In that faint glow the first thing Kaldar saw was the cord. It lay abandoned on the ground, not shining now but only a dull length of woven flax, its charge and its energy spent. Beyond it the men and women of the outer circle were stirring. Some sat on the rock floor like rag dolls, limp and weary, but others had recovered enough to help the seven sorcerers. A short way off, the widower was sitting up, supported by a burly man and gratefully accepting sips of water from a leather flask, and somewhere behind him Kaldar could hear the soft, unsteady voice of one of the women, thanking her helpers between alternate bouts of laughing and sobbing. He felt suddenly bewildered. They were all safe back, they had come through — but had the ritual succeeded? The crater looked no different. He *felt* no different. Yet he remembered it all; the contact, the surge of power, the gargantuan blast that had rocked the golden arch —

"Shammana!" An urgent voice cut through the disarray of his thoughts, and Shammana's head jerked up sharply. "Shammana, come quickly! It's Simbrian — "

They both turned in time to see a woman's thin figure rising from the confusion of shadows a few paces away. Behind her there was a scraping of flint and tinder; someone swore and then the spark caught and a small hand lantern flared into life. By its glow Kaldar recognized the thin woman's face, though he couldn't recall her name. She looked haggard and terrified.

"Hurry!" A hand clamped on Shammana's arm. "You know something of herbs and healing, don't you?"

Shammana started to protest that she had no more skill than any other farmer's wife, but she was already being towed across the uneven rocks to where several others were grouped round a supine figure. The lamplight flickered across a burly torso, a dead-white face framed by a lush beard, and Kaldar's voice cracked from his throat.

"Gods, Simbrian! *Simbrian!*"

His legs were weak but he stumbled after them and dropped to his knees amid the group, staring in horror at their leader.

"He won't stir," the thin woman said distractedly. "And we can't see him breathing, we think he isn't breathing!"

Shammana, horrified as Kaldar and completely out of her depth, looked wildly about for help or inspiration or both. Then suddenly the widower was among them, pushing his way through the gathering crowd around Simbrian's still form.

"I trained as a herbaler." His voice was clipped, anxious. "Let me look at him."

They moved back, allowing him room to crouch down at Simbrian's side. For several tense minutes no one uttered a sound while the widower touched Simbrian's eyes, his lips, his hands, and, lastly, bent to rest his ear to the sorcerer's motionless chest. He stayed still, listening, for what seemed an agony of time. Then at last he raised his head.

Kaldar saw his eyes in the moment before he spoke. All animation had gone from them; they were hollow, empty wells, drained of light and drained of hope. Then the widower said starkly:

"He is dead."

At his side, Kaldar felt Shammana's body freeze. She couldn't move, couldn't react, and neither could he: all they could do was stare helplessly at the ring of stunned faces around them, silently and desperately searching for someone who would tell them the widower was wrong, who would say, *"No, look, Simbrian is breathing, his eyes are opening, he is alive!"* But in every face they saw only their own disbelieving misery reflected back at them. No one could deny the truth. The great ritual had failed — and Simbrian, their leader and their inspiration, had paid the price of failure with his life.

Very softly, a woman began to keen. It was a dreadful, desolate sound, lonely in the night's silence and made more terrible by the doleful echoes that rang back from the crater walls. Gradually, as though they couldn't bear to hear that one solitary voice raised in grief, others joined in. Men and women alike were weeping; the widower knelt with his face hidden in his hands, unable to express the misery he felt. And as Shammana began to sob and Kaldar held her close to him, his mind reeled and raced with tortured thoughts. *It was too much for him, too much for any one mortal! Sweet gods, why did we let him take so great a burden on his own shoulders? We could have done more! We should have been stronger! We failed him, and now he is gone, for he was ready to sacrifice everything and we did not match his courage!*

"Aeoris!" Suddenly he couldn't control his emotions, and his cry went up to the indifferent sky, clashing with the voices of Simbrian's mourners. "Lord Aeoris, we have failed him, and we have failed you!"

As he cried out he turned, Shammana turning with him and her hands clenching convulsively against his body as she sobbed. Kaldar's eyes stared blindly at the heavens and hopeless anguish swept over him like a riptide. He couldn't even weep, couldn't even find that release, for he was beyond tears. It had all been in vain and there was nothing left, nothing, *nothing* —

NO.

It was as though a giant sword had descended and pinned him rigid to the rock. Not a voice, not a word; not even a sound that the physical ear could detect. But the denial was *there*, around him, within him, a huge and all-embracing certainty that transfixed him and seemed to stop the flow of blood in his veins. On a subliminal level he knew that Shammana, too, had felt it. And others; for there was suddenly an awesome stillness in the crater. The keening dirge ceased and its echoes died away. For the space of two, perhaps three heartbeats, time seemed to be suspended —

Then a bolt of lightning seared down from the clear sky, and struck the chalice on the floor of the bowl.

For a moment it seemed that pandemonium would break out. But in the afterimage of the colossal flash, every man and woman stood motionless, eyes wide and faces turned to the spot where the bolt had struck.

A long, dark scar now furrowed the rock of the crater floor, the chalice at its center. Incredibly, the cup was undamaged . . . and then a thin, vertical bar of light sprang up from within it. Briefly Kaldar's mind and memory were hurled back to the astral plane, to the searing rent that had split the vision of the glorious garden. But this light was softer, kinder. . . . So slowly that at first Kaldar thought his senses were deceiving him, it spread and resolved into a perfect oval of golden brilliance. A soft sound, almost like a sigh, rustled through the crater. And within the oval, a figure took form.

He was taller than any mortal, his frame powerful yet slender and with an innate grace that no earthly being could command. Shimmering white hair cascaded over his broad shoulders, and the long cloak that shrouded his body was also white, though golden flecks sparkled and danced within it, forming strange yet regular patterns. His face, pale-skinned, was a serene and magnificent sculpture of pure symmetry, the mouth set in a perfect line that blended strength with compassion and an infinite depth of knowledge. And his eyes . . . his eyes were twin golden orbs, without iris or pupil, that radiated utter tranquility.

As the gathering stared, stunned, at him he turned his head and regarded Kaldar.

"My good friend." His voice was rich, mellifluous. "You did not fail."

Kaldar's face, already pale, had turned ashen as the being addressed him. He couldn't convince himself that this was not some eerie, impossible dream, and this second shock, in the wake of the events of the last few dreadful minutes, had frozen his mind.

"M . . . my . . ." he tried helplessly, desperately, to form the words, though they seemed hideously inadequate. "My l-l-lord . . ."

"Peace, Kaldar." The tall figure stepped forward, out of the oval of light, and Aeoris, greatest lord and master of the realm of Order, smiled a smile that all but broke Kaldar's heart. "This is no dream. Your raising of power succeeded. You have cracked the seal in the fortifications our enemies raised against us, and allowed us to reach out to you again."

Kaldar began to shake uncontrollably. In wild and secret flights of imagination he had envisioned what he might say and do if this moment should ever come to pass. But now it *had* come . . . and he was bereft. He had no words of welcome or veneration for his god, for no words could even begin do justice to the shattering emotion moving within him. And underlying the emotion was a suffocating ache of misery at the thought that this longed-for triumph had been achieved at the cost of Simbrian's life.

"Oh, my lord . . ." he whispered. "If only I could . . . if only he . . ." But still the words wouldn't come, and in powerless grief he could only gesture towards the still, lifeless form of the sorcerer with the group of mourners gathered around him.

Aeoris turned his head, and a shadow seemed to pass briefly across his magnificent face. "Ah," he said, and the rocks echoed the sound back in a gentle sigh. "I understand you." Then, startling Kaldar, the serene smile returned. "But you have much to learn about your gods, Kaldar, and about the powers that I in particular once wielded in this dimension. Many centuries have passed since that time, but with the breaking of the seal I can command those powers again. And my faithful servants are as dear to me as cherished sons and daughters."

He walked slowly to where Simbrian's body lay. Mutely the gathered humans drew back, and abruptly the silence in the crater seemed to close in like a solid wall. Aeoris paused meditatively for a few moments, then one hand made a slight, graceful movement. Kaldar felt a resonance in his bones, a small shock; then from Aeoris's fingers a shaft of light flowed in a flawless stream to illuminate Simbrian.

"Good friend and servant," Aeoris said, "once, in your world, I was lord of life and death. By your courage and your sacrifice you have invested me with that ancient power again, and now it is my privilege to invoke it. Wake, Simbrian Tarkran. Wake, and live."

An eldritch, flickering aura came into being around the body. Kaldar felt the charge of power, and even as his companions abased themselves he, too, dropped to his knees on the hard rock floor of the crater, his heart pounding as an incredible, giddying hope filled him.

"Wake, Simbrian," Aeoris said again, his voice a sibilant whisper. "Wake."

A tremor ran through the sorcerer's corpse. His eyelids fluttered, his chest heaved. Against the acute backdrop of silence every man and woman in the bowl heard the first hiss of his breathing as his soul returned to his body. Then his eyes opened, focused, and a look of wonder spread across his face.

"M . . . my . . ." His first attempt at speech wavered, as though words were a strange and new concept to him. Aeoris smiled again, with great compassion.

"Don't fear, my friend. All's well with us now."

Eager hands reached out to help as Simbrian sat up. Slowly but surely color returned to the sorcerer's face and he gazed at Aeoris as at last he found his voice.

"My lord. . . . *oh, my lord!!*"

The gold oval in which Aeoris had stood burned more brightly and light spilled out from it across the crater. Like a gentle sunrise it illuminated the great bowl of the volcano, softening the shadows, lifting the faces and forms of the entranced watchers from darkness into light. Dimly, within the light's halo, other figures began to materialize: shining forms, each one a perfect twin to Aeoris, as the six remaining lords of Order ranged behind their great brother and looked out from their own realm into the world of humanity.

Aeoris turned his head and his golden gaze swept across the figures kneeling on the rock floor. His followers, his worshipers, the sons and daughters of Order.

"You have breached the barrier that Chaos set up against us so long ago," he said softly, and as he spoke it seemed that his six brothers spoke with him, their voices blending in harmony. "The first breach is small, but it shall prove to be of immense significance to us and to the world of mortals." Yet again he smiled, but this time the smile was one of fierce joy, pride, triumph. He raised his hands as though in blessing, and his voice rang through the crater bowl.

"Beloved and devoted friends, your promise to me has been fulfilled and now I make you a promise in my turn. You have called your gods back from exile — I vow to you that from this moment on the lords of Order will walk beside you, will inspire and sustain and protect you." His eyes blazed suddenly, like twin suns, and their gaze seemed to focus beyond the crater, beyond the island, looking across sea and land into the far north, and a new ferocity crept into his voice that sent a shiver through them all. "We shall not rest until our victory over the powers of darkness is complete, until the taint of Chaos has been purged and banished — and until Order reigns supreme as it did long ago. We will work together for that end, my friends. We will bring peace and justice back to this world." And, unknowingly echoing the words that First Magus Vordegh had uttered in the stark silence of his own sanctum in the days following his inauguration, Aeoris added with soft intensity, *"We will prevail!"*

And, as though the words had carried across the great distance that divided her from all that had meaning in her life, Iselia woke suddenly from sleep and sat upright, staring into the claustrophobic dark of Savrinor's bedchamber. She did not know what had snatched her from her dreams, but her heart was pounding as though from shock, and a feeling of tense excitement crawled and tingled in her marrow. And in the strange, almost narcotic atmosphere of torpor that steeped the castle in the small hours before the coming of dawn she knew that something, *something* was in the air. . . .

Moving with the cautious, deer-like silence that she had learned so well in her time with Savrinor, Iselia slid from the bed and, leaving the historian soundly sleeping, padded like a ghost to the door and the outer room beyond. The window was ajar and the curtain stirred sluggishly; she closed the casement and drew the curtain close again, ensuring that not even the tiniest chink could betray her. Then she turned to face the south, lit a candle, and knelt before the tiny, fragile flame, her body quivering as her lips began to form and whisper a prayer. No one and nothing could hear her, no power, mortal or otherwise, could eavesdrop on her devotions. But in another part of the castle Benetan Liss stirred restlessly at Andraia's side and a small, uncertain sound, half sigh and half groan, escaped him. For a moment a shadow imbued his dreams and gave them a new and chill dimension, but then the uneasy flicker passed on and away like a zephyr. Andraia lay untroubled, her fingers interlaced with his, and the small movement he had made to try to free himself from her hold relaxed once more into surrender. They slept on; Savrinor slept on; the castle slept on. In all the darkness and the silence of the deep night there was nothing to observe Iselia, and nothing to discern her small invocation of dedication, of veneration, and of hope.

END OF BOOK I

TOR
BOOKS The Best in Fantasy

ELVENBANE • Andre Norton and Mercedes Lackey
"A richly detailed, complex fantasy collaboration."—Marion Zimmer Bradley

SUMMER KING, WINTER FOOL • Lisa Goldstein
"Possesses all of Goldstein's virtues to the highest degree."—*Chicago Sun-Times*

JACK OF KINROWAN • Charles de Lint
Jack the Giant Killer and *Drink Down the Moon* reprinted in one volume.

THE MAGIC ENGINEER • L.E. Modesitt, Jr.
The tale of Dorrin the blacksmith in the enormously popular continuing saga of Recluce.

SISTER LIGHT, SISTER DARK • Jane Yolen
"The Hans Christian Andersen of America."—*Newsweek*

THE GIRL WHO HEARD DRAGONS • Anne McCaffrey
"A treat for McCaffrey fans."—*Locus*

GEIS OF THE GARGOYLE • Piers Anthony
Join Gary Gar, a guileless young gargoyle disguised as a human, on a perilous pilgrimage in pursuit of a philter to rescue the magical land of Xanth from an ancient evil.

TOR
BOOKS The Best in Fantasy

TOR
fantasy

LORD OF CHAOS • Robert Jordan

Book Six of *The Wheel of Time*. "For those who like to keep themselves in a fantasy world, it's hard to beat the complex, detailed world created here....A great read."—*Locus*

WIZARD'S FIRST RULE • Terry Goodkind

"A wonderfully creative, seamless, and stirring epic fantasy debut."—*Kirkus Reviews*

SPEAR OF HEAVEN • Judith Tarr

"The kind of accomplished fantasy—featuring sound characterization, superior world-building, and more than competent prose—that has won Tarr a large audience."—*Booklist*

MEMORY AND DREAM • Charles de Lint

A major novel of art, magic, and transformation, by the modern master of urban fantasy.

NEVERNEVER • Will Shetterly

The sequel to *Elsewhere*. "With a single book, Will Shetterly has redrawn the boundaries of young adult fantasy. This is a remarkable work."—Bruce Coville

TALES FROM THE GREAT TURTLE • Edited by Piers Anthony and Richard Gilliam

"A tribute to the wealth of pre-Columbian history and lore."—*Library Journal*